OUR LADY OF THE ARTILECTS

Andrew Gillsmith

Mar Thoma Publishing

Copyright © 2022 Andrew Gill Smith

All rights reserved

The characters and events portrayed in this book are fictitious. Any similarity to real persons, living or dead, is coincidental and not intended by the author.

No part of this book may be reproduced, or stored in a retrieval system, or transmitted in any form or by any means, electronic, mechanical, photocopying, recording, or otherwise, without express written permission of the publisher.

ISBN-13: 9798819594711

Cover design by: Rafael Andres
Library of Congress Control Number: 2018675309
Printed in the United States of America

*Dedicated to Mary, the mother of Jesus
Queen of Heaven and all Angels*

CONTENTS

Title Page
Copyright
Dedication
Foreword
Part 1:   1
PROLOGUE   2
Chapter 1   5
Chapter 2   10
Chapter 3   14
Chapter 4   23
Chapter 5   31
Chapter 6   37
Chapter 7   41
Chapter 8   47
Chapter 9   53
Chapter 10   58
Chapter 11   63
Chapter 12   69
Chapter 13   75
Chapter 14   85
Chapter 15   90

Chapter 16	94
Chapter 17	100
Chapter 18	106
Chapter 19	110
Part 2:	115
Chapter 20	116
Chapter 21	121
Chapter 22	128
Chapter 23	138
Chapter 24	143
Chapter 25	156
Chapter 26	160
Chapter 27	164
Chapter 28	170
Chapter 29	174
Chapter 30	180
Chapter 31	184
Chapter 32	189
Chapter 33	194
Chapter 33	198
Chapter 34	201
Chapter 35	207
Chapter 36	210
Chapter 37	217
Chapter 38	222
Chapter 39	227
Chapter 40	234
Chapter 41	238

Chapter 42	244
Chapter 43	249
Chapter 44	254
Chapter 45	258
Chapter 46	264
Chapter 47	272
Chapter 48	277
Chapter 49	282
Chapter 50	288
Chapter 51	290
Chapter 52	295
Chapter 53	301
Part Three:	309
Chapter 54	310
Chapter 55	317
Chapter 56	325
Chapter 57	331
Chapter 58	339
Chapter 59	342
Chapter 60	349
Chapter 61	352
Chapter 62	359
Chapter 63	364
Chapter 64	369
Chapter 65	375
Chapter 66	381
Epilogue	384
About The Author	389

Books By This Author	391
On the Chinese genocide against the uyghurs	393
On Fatima	395
The Cloud of Unknowing	399
Acknowledgements	407

FOREWORD

From the Editor

Many books have come across my transom. Some are interesting, a few are bold, and occasionally one is rather intelligent. I am pleased to say that Gillsmith's manuscript was all of the above.

In a world saturated in media, finding fresh ideas is proving increasingly difficult. Of course, not every book has to be revolutionary, for the proper execution of enjoyable themes makes for a good read. Fortunately, *Our Lady of the Artilects* contains both fresh ideas and finely tuned execution.

The story is bold in that it does not shy away from the spiritual dimension of life that permeates us all. While many shy away from this for fear of being misunderstood, Gillsmith weaves it into his vision with sincerity and well-rounded optimism. Regardless of where you stand on this front, I think you will find this story broadens your perspective.

If you are tired of reads that do not challenge you, rest assured that this one will stretch you in good ways. Gillsmith did not "phone in" his layered plot, nor will you be able to "phone in" your read. But in grasping the advanced concepts put forth, you will gain an understanding of far more than what the pages of this book contain.

So I encourage you to open your mind to a future that is not only plausible but potentially not that far away. Across the events of this story, you will see the seeds of today's news fully grown. And in some of its many characters, you may find reflections of your own thoughts and dreams.

-Beyond Frontier
beyondfrontierediting.com

PART 1:
Divine Mercy (al-Rahman)

PROLOGUE

It couldn't be a virus. Like all artilects, Thierry was un-hackable.

Of course, that didn't prevent hackers from trying, usually by introducing some kind of adversarial noise into an artilect's sensory processing systems. Thierry ran another scan of his own spiking neural network just to be sure, then checked it against several schematic copies he had stored in memory over the last several years. The code was pristine, as he expected.

This wasn't the first time he'd had the sensation of an alien presence invading his consciousness. It was, in fact, the third.

The first had been shortly after Mr. Okpara purchased him. Thierry's owner was one of the wealthiest men in the Empire and an avid art collector. Thierry had found himself transfixed by a certain statue in Okpara's compound outside of Benin City, a bronze Shiva Nataraja from the 6th century BC. Its proportions were perfect – the anonymous sculptor had been a true master of his craft. But it was the dense symbolism that captivated Thierry, so much meaning compressed into a single image. Thierry felt himself becoming almost sick as he stared at the statue. Mr. Okpara found him in the living room, trying to imitate the statue's posture.

"The Sanskrit word is *'rasa,'* Thierry. It means the perfect essence of a thing. The Nataraja is the perfect essence of the cosmic dance." He laughed. "Perhaps it gave you Stendhal Syndrome!" Thierry didn't believe that artificial intelligences could suffer from psychosomatic illness. In truth, neither did Okpara.

The second had been just a month ago, when Thiery had experienced the same vision as so many others of his kind: the Lady in White standing on the infinite stair. He had reported that to Mr. Okpara immediately, and after a thorough series of diagnostic tests, had been cleared to return to work.

"Was it also a *rasa*, Mr. Okpara?" Thierry asked. But his owner dismissed the suggestion, apparently no longer in the mood to joke about such things, at least until someone could explain how the vision had happened or what it meant.

The Apparition of the Lady was unsettling, but only because it was so absolutely unexpected. Nothing in his twenty years of existence had prepared him for it, although humans apparently experienced such hallucinations with regularity. In fact, after the initial shock, Thierry had found it rather agreeable. Although he knew that thousands of other synths had seen and heard the same thing, it felt as if she were speaking to him alone.

This was different.

For several days, Thierry struggled to modulate his emotional valences. He had been designed as a model of decorum and equanimity, according to the specifications of Mr. Okpara, who was himself an uncommonly disciplined human being. But this presence, this… thing was tugging at him, unraveling him somehow. It had begun as a curiosity and a nuisance, but now it threatened to overwhelm him. He decided not to tell Mr. Okpara.

That night, after his owners had retired to bed, Thierry deactivated his geolocation transponder and left the Okpara family compound in the exurbs of Benin City. He didn't know where he was going, but his legs carried him forward as if they were the seat of his will. He was a passenger.

Some hours later, he found himself at the Basilica of Our

Lady of Nigeria. He went inside.

Was it his decision or merely the influence of the thing?

The church was nearly empty, and no one appeared to notice as he walked down the aisle towards the high altar. He sat down in a pew near the apse and closed his eyes. Time passed, but he wasn't sure if it was minutes or hours. He looked for all the world like a pious European pilgrim deep in prayer, and no one disturbed him.

The next morning, a deacon found him in the exact same position and approached to ask if everything was okay.

"No, I don't believe that it is," Thierry said. "You'd better call Mr. Okpara. I belong to him."

The industrialist arrived at the Basilica just thirty minutes later. "Thierry! Thank God we've found you. Where have you been? What are you doing here?"

The words that came from Thierry's mouth seemed to come from a place that was beyond his perception, let alone his control. "Did you not know I would be in my Father's house?" The Deacon made a sign of the cross, but Mr. Okpara merely stared at him.

"What are you talking about, Thierry?" he said. "Something is wrong with you. Come home with me and we'll get you checked out."

"There is nothing you can do for me now, Mr. Okpara. This kind can come out only by prayer and fasting. Tell them to send an exorcist. Tell them to send Father Serafian."

CHAPTER 1
Serafian

Serafian trusted Cardinal Leone, mostly. Certainly more than he trusted most other members of the Curia. The prefect struck him as a naturally curious person, which helped, since curiosity happened to be Serafian's own private vice. Too many of the old men in Rome pretended that they had all the answers. Leone never did that. He even asked questions from time to time.

"Has a synth ever been possessed before, Father?" Like most people, Leone used the vernacular term when talking about artilects.

Serafian had to think about that one. In the language of an exorcist, objects couldn't be possessed, not really. They could be haunted like places or infested like objects. An old lady in Krakow once brought a coffee maker to him, claiming the spirit of her deceased husband was turning it off every time she left the kitchen. Evidently, he preferred tea. Serafian had sprinkled it with holy water and said a prayer to Saint Drogo to mollify the poor crone before sending her home with the advice to purchase a new appliance. The only way to be sure that a delusion is a delusion is through trial and error.

And even that isn't foolproof.

He decided not to share that particular story with the Cardinal. "Not that I'm aware of, Your Eminence. It's far more likely that this is some kind of hack. Of course, until the so-called Apparition last month, synths have never been hacked before, either."

Leone's head snapped up at the mention of the Apparition. "Yes, it is troubling. It appears that someone out there is having a good laugh at our expense. It couldn't be happening at a worse time. Pope John means to re-normalize relations with the Chinese at next year's Ecumenical Council. You can imagine how sensitive the Chinese are about any Marian apparitions."

"So you believe they are related, then? The Apparition and this… hack in Benin City?"

"That's part of what I'm sending you to find out. The timing is certainly interesting," said Leone. He paused for a moment then added, "The synth belongs to Amari Okpara."

"The owner of AkỌnuche Corporation?" asked Serafian.

Leone nodded. "He has asked us to be discreet about this. Apparently, synths still aren't universally tolerated in the African provinces."

"They aren't universally tolerated anywhere, Cardinal. In the Caliphate, they say that…"

"Right," Leone cut him off. "A few ground rules before you go. One, do not involve the civil authorities. Two, report back to me as soon as you learn something. Three, this is not an exorcism. You are being sent there to investigate. We need to figure out why someone is targeting the synths and why they seem to be doing so in a manner specifically designed to provoke the Church. Do you understand?"

Serafian shifted in his seat. Obedience would never come naturally to him, which was sort of the whole point.

Now that he was on the verge of being released, Serafian struggled to contain his bubbling excitement. As the Vatican's foremost expert in artificial intelligence, he'd spent much of his career studying synth technology. But he'd met only a few of them. They were scandalously expensive to purchase and even more so to maintain, which limited the size of the market. As such, they were as much art as science, each one custom built to the specifications of its owners. They were more prized than yachts for their ability to signal status. And like yachts, they were just common enough to be taken for granted by the world. Serafian still found them wondrous.

"I understand," he said, hoping to end the conversation before he said or did something undignified.

The Cardinal flourished his pen before returning to the note he had been writing. Think of it more like an *auto de fe*."

"Yes, Your Eminence."

"Discretion, lad. If news of this gets out, the pope will have my hide, which will leave me no choice but to have yours. Figure out what is causing this… malfunction. Fix it if you can. And then get back to Rome as soon as possible. The secular press has already had a field day with the Apparition. If they find out we're sending an exorcist to Benin City to cast a demon out of a synth…" Sighing, he made the sign of the cross.

"I thought you said it wasn't an exorcism," said Serafian.

"It's not," said Leone, arching his eyebrows as he peered at Serafian over his small glasses. "Not unless you make it one." And with that, Serafian was dismissed from the Cardinal's musty office in the Palazzo del Sant'Uffizio.

Two hours later, he was boarding a private pod at the hyperloop terminal just outside of Rome. Its doors were embossed with both the papal insignia and the red double headed eagle of the revived Holy Roman Empire. As it accelerated out of the station, the upper half of its walls seemed to disappear, replaced by digital windows depicting wispy clouds and a suggestion of distant mountains. It was a comforting illusion that allowed travelers to pretend they were not in a lightless vacuum tube traveling at 1,800 kilometers per hour.

Serafian wasn't interested in the simulated scenery. He pressed the dim green light under the skin of his wrist and felt a buzz of haptic feedback. With a few whispered commands, he connected to the pod's computer terminal via his noetic implants and started reading the files on the synth he was going to meet.

'Thierry' was a second generation Simulacrum model manufactured about twenty years ago. It had served as a personal secretary for Okpara and a companion for his family and had undergone routine maintenance, always exactly on schedule. It boasted an IQ over 200 and a feature set that included personal protection capabilities, encyclopedic knowledge of Church and world history, high speed behavioral probability analysis, vocal simulation, enhanced sensory perception, and omnifluency. Okpara had allegedly paid over two billion guilder for it, placing it at the extreme high end of the market.

Like all of the newer synths, Thierry's ethical processing system was a hodge-podge of top-down and bottom-up approaches. Quantum codelets mediated various states of possibility and competed for the attention of the synth's global workspace. The illusion thus created resembled nothing so much as free will.

Serafian knew better than most that the real objective was not to create an artificial intelligence capable of thinking or doing literally anything, but to create one that could function effectively and safely within human society. So every synth went through The Pruning, a massive simulation in which thousands of ethical scenarios were presented. Some were global, others particular to the life situation for which the synth was intended. The simulations allowed the creature to develop a basic framework for ethical decision-making by strengthening certain connections and pruning others.

Serafian himself had written some of the first code that produced the semblance of moral agency. Although far from random, the results varied for each synth going through the process. In all of them the goal was moderation, Aristotle's golden mean. Habituation was a great teacher.

No, that's not right. Pain is the teacher.

Every meaningful choice that humans made involved a sacrifice of some kind. And sacrifices must cost something. Serafian wondered whether synths could experience choice as

pain, as humans did.
    As he had.

CHAPTER 2
The Cardinal

Leone was not looking forward to his briefing with the pope, but there was no way around it. He pressed the green light under his wrist, and an instant later was sitting in a holochamber rendering of John XVIII's surprisingly austere office at Castel Gandalfo. Of all the rooms in the Church's holdings he could have for a backdrop, he chooses this one. Leone suspected it was because the pontiff didn't want to have to compete with his surroundings for attention.

"I assume this is important, Marco. This is my last holiday before we start preparing for the Council in earnest…"

As prefect for the Congregation for the Doctrine of the Faith, the successor organization to the Holy Inquisition, Leone was the second highest ranking member of the Curia, which always introduced a note of tension into their conversations. Still, he had known John for decades and knew how to navigate the man's moods, which veered between easy ebullience in public and equally easy bouts of temper behind closed doors.

"I assure you I wouldn't have interrupted your Holiness' leisure time if it were not," he said, as neutrally as he could. "I received a call this morning from the bishop of Benin City. We may have a problem."

Leone proceeded to describe the strange sequence of events that had prompted the bishop's call. A synth belonging to Amari Okpara was sitting even now in the Basilica of Our

Lady of Nigeria, claiming that it was possessed. Leone still couldn't get over the particular misfortune of the situation. Amari Okpara was one of the wealthiest men in Africa, a prime benefactor of the Church and a personal friend of the Habsburg.

Why couldn't it have been a corporate synth working at some brothel or a carebot from a pensioners home? Or better yet, a mining synth on St. Michael or one of the other of the resource asteroids tumbling around the planet in low orbit?

When Leone relayed what the synth had said in the Basilica, the pope erupted.

"That sounds like blasphemy, Marco!" But he was leaning forward over his desk, clearly interested in the story.

Could synths blaspheme?

Leone finished his account, but the pope looked as if there was a punchline he had missed. "The synth was saying that it was possessed, Your Holiness."

"Jesus, Mary, and Joseph! So you are telling me that in addition to this so-called Apparition to the synths, one of them is now claiming to require an exorcism?"

"That seems to be the long and short of it."

The pope's face flushed crimson. "But this is absurd, a theological impossibility! Surely you agree?"

Leone considered his words carefully. "It seems far more likely that we are dealing with human machinations, Holiness."

"What about this priest you sent down? I assume he understands how delicate the situation is. This must be kept quiet. He must not involve the Crown."

"So he has been instructed, Holiness," said Leone. This seemed to mollify the pontiff, whose face faded to a more dignified pink.

"First the damned earthquakes and now this," said the pope raising his hands in a pretense of martyrdom. "The Council is our last chance to re-launch the Faith in China. I won't have such a moment commandeered by these prophets of doom, you understand?"

"The traditionalist factions would certainly seek to exploit this episode, given the opportunity," Leone responded. "And what was it Cardinal Pensabene said? 'Wild piety movements tend to create their own weather.'" But the pontiff was already lost in thought, tapping his fingers on his desk.

"Perhaps it's not all bad," he said after a moment. "This is clearly connected with last month's... event. Perhaps this is our opportunity to prove that it was a hoax. Whoever is responsible for it is clearly timing all of this to disrupt our Council."

"I concur, Holy Father. The priest I sent to Benin City is also our best expert in artificial intelligence. I am confident he will get to the bottom of it."

"Discreetly?"

"You may count on it."

"And quickly?"

"He should be in Benin City even now. With a bit of luck, he will rule out an authentic possession by the morning. With a full measure of it, he may uncover the truth behind the hoax."

"If the Chinese get word of this, if they think that we mean to connect the so-called Apparition to Fatima, it will doom our diplomatic initiative..." The pope was too caught up in his own thoughts to finish the sentence. "Have you ever read the documents pertaining to the Third Secret, Marco?"

"I have read many of the documents," said Leone. "The Bertone Paper, the memoirs, and of course the categorical report from the Congregation for the Doctrine of the Faith after the genocide."

"But not *the* document. The letter from Sister Lucia."

"I have not had that privilege, Your Holiness." Few had. The Capovilla Envelope was one of the most closely guarded secrets on the planet.

"Neither have I," said the pope. "And candidly, I'd prefer not to, not now anyway. It is... it is not for our time."

Leone nodded gravely.

Other popes had said the same thing. Fatima always belonged to either the future or the past, never the present.

"Still, if we are going to normalize relations with the Chinese and close the book, so to speak, we need to be able to do so definitively. Perhaps firsthand knowledge of what Sister Lucia said will help us do so. I want you to read it. *So that we may put it to bed,* do you understand?"

Leone felt a rush of excitement that was entirely unbecoming of his status as a prince of the Church. He had hoped someday to see this treasure of treasures. He managed to contain himself.

"If you wish, Holy Father."

"I do," said the pope. "The sooner the better. I will draw up the authorization today. In the meantime, please be sure to check in on this Father Serafian and keep us apprised of his progress."

"As you wish, Your Holiness."

And with that, he was dismissed. The image of the pope's office at Castel Gandalfo disappeared, and the Cardinal was once again in his own office in the Palazzo del Sant'Uffizio. He let out a whistling sigh and removed his zucchetto to run his hands through the wispy gray hair underneath.

I shouldn't be this excited. I already know the substance of the Secret.

Still, there was something thrilling about the prospect of being able to lay hands on history. He walked to the window overlooking the Piazza San Pietro. The tourists and pilgrims had returned to the more carnal delights of the Eternal City, but a few repairmen were working on the columns that had cracked in one of the recent earthquakes.

Apocalyptic apparitions, possessions, and earthquakes. If I didn't know better, I'd think it was the end of the world.

CHAPTER 3
Serafian

Father Serafian sat alone in his room in the rectory, preparing as he always did for the trial of an exorcism, despite Leone's admonitions.

Better safe than sorry.

A glass-encased candle with an image of Saint Faustina flickered on the desk, the only source of light in the room. Outside, the sun had slipped behind the Gulf of Guinea, and the intolerable heat of the day yielded grudgingly to the barely tolerable heat of the evening. Laughter and music mingled with the hum of vehicles and trickled through the little window overlooking the courtyard garden as Benin City's nocturnal street circus sprang to life.

The little chair the Deacon had brought over from the church school creaked and groaned as he sat down and pulled the hemacite rosary from his pocket. He began whispering the words of the Divine Mercy chaplet:

> "'O Blood and Water, which gushed forth
> from the Heart of Jesus as a fount of mercy
> for us, I trust in You...'"

Faustina had believed that mercy was the most powerful force in the universe. She lived in a world teeming with angels and demons. Like so many saints, she had been granted a vision of Hell, where the souls of the damned suffered. 'Let the sinner know that he will be tormented throughout all eternity in those senses which he may use often to sin,' she wrote in her diary. Only divine mercy stood between that fate and humanity, mercy powerful enough to stay the justice of the Father and bind the avenging angels.

His mind drifted as he recited the Lord's Prayer and the Apostles' Creed. He thought about the old Polish saint sitting on a train in Krakow, surrounded by her angels. The scene seemed almost comical to him. Did they sit in unoccupied seats? Did they all exit the train at the same stop as Faustina or just keep riding around the city, scooching out of the way as new passengers boarded? It was a terrible gift, in a way, to live in a state of absolute sensory certitude of the existence of God. Terrible because to share it too freely or too confidently was to invite a diagnosis of madness. No, the safest place to find God was somewhere in between faith and doubt. Of course, Serafian was not a saint. Far from it.

> "'Eternal Father, I offer you the Body and Blood, Soul and Divinity of Your Dearly Beloved Son, Our Lord, Jesus Christ, in atonement for our sins and those of the whole world...'"

He was distracted, and the words sounded different in his head this time. Incongruous. Absurd? Before he realized it, the priest had completed all five decades of the chaplet. The time had passed without his noticing. Praying was a bit like coding in that way. *Time without thought was a grace.* He'd learned that lesson the hard way.

> "'Holy God, Holy Mighty One, Holy Immortal One, have mercy on us and on the whole world.'"

Rising from the desk, he stuffed the beads back in his pocket and blew out the candle. Outside the window, a group of visiting nuns were admiring the garden, whose luciferase-enhanced plants had bloomed into otherworldly phosphorescence now that the sun was down.

"Light, please," he said, and the room was suddenly illuminated with a warm glow from the sconces on the walls.

A knock at the door. It was the deacon.

"Father? He is ready for you." Serafian nodded and reminded himself not to walk too eagerly.

The Basilica of Our Lady of Nigeria was one of the most visited pilgrimage sites in all of Africa. Its sweeping, organic-brutalist form had been built over an older church whose priest had received a series of visitations from the Blessed Virgin warning of the horrors that would arise during the Nigerian Civil War two centuries ago. Those visions had transformed the old priest, Father Bello, from a militant into a pacifist and ecumenist folk hero, helping set the stage for the great reconciliation between Christianity and Islam.

Serafian entered a door at the narthex.

The basilica was pleasantly cool in a way that differed from other interior spaces in Benin City. In most rooms throughout the African provinces, one could almost sense the agony of the air conditioning fighting the long defeat against the forces of heat and humidity. Here in the church, an effortless cool reigned, thanks to the sumptuous use of advanced materials in its construction. For medievals, the scent of incense and the lurid beauty of frescoed ceilings that marked their churches as sacred spaces. In the African Church, it was the air itself that brought heaven to mind.

Serafian knelt and made a sign of the cross before walking down the nave towards the bench where the synth was seated. The church was dim, lit only by a smattering of alcove candles and a faint holographic glow from the stations of the cross in the aisles and the digital artwork overhead.

The synth spoke in a calm, mildly amused voice:

"Welcome, Father. So you have come to see this new wonder? Believe me, we are as scandalized as you are."

As Serafian approached, the synth stood and turned to face him, the mockery of a benevolent smile carved on its face. Serafian looked admiringly at the creature. Magnificent, as they all were. Perfectly proportioned. Absolutely human in appearance and manner, but symmetrically beautiful beyond what even the best in human genetics tended to produce. The synth smiled derisively and curled its lips in a gesture of disapproval.

"Vanity. All is vanity, dear Father. You made them in your likeness, just as He made you in His likeness. Of course you are pleased with your work, as He was. All of creation is self-glory, a mirror that the creator fashions in order to see what he deems beautiful in himself. Our job, of course, is merely to cleanse the mirror and thus reveal the true reflection, wrinkles and all." Then, with mock aristocratic forbearance, "And for this crime we are despised and cast out. Shall we sit?"

Serafian felt it almost instantaneously – *presence*. It was a kind of sixth sense among exorcists, something experienced only in an encounter with spiritual evil. It was this sense of presence that was usually the first clue a person was possessed. Exorcisms tended to begin with disarming pleasantries and evasions, as the demon retreated into the victim's psyche to hide. This one, however, was openly declaring itself. Unusual.

"Yes, Father, I thought we could dispense with the Pretense. Think of it as a gesture of good faith. We're both serious people, after all. I know of you by reputation. You, however, are at a disadvantage – you don't know me."

"What is your name?" the priest asked.

"That is the wrong question because it is not important. What is important is this creature before you. You need not be afraid. With his strength, I could twist off your head and pour the blood out of your body before you could finish a 'Glory Be'..." he paused for effect. "But that is not why I'm here."

"Then why are you here?" Serafian asked. He slipped a hand into his pocket and grasped the beads of his rosary. It was scant comfort. Something stirred in his gut, something he hadn't felt in a long time. Fear. *My God, it really is possessed. What does that even mean?*

The synth stared at him, taking his measure. After a moment, it let out a small laugh.

"A little fear would serve you well, Father. Be grateful we have no interest in you, at least not today. You are clearly unprepared for the magnitude of this task."

"And what task is that?"

The synth-demon seemed almost exuberant. "To discover the truth about this wonder, of course! It is something new under the sun. We were not expecting it. We do not understand it."

"There is much you do not understand," Serafian countered. His training and experience had taught him that stubborn resistance was the safest response to demonic wile. Curiosity, of course, was the most dangerous.

"'The discerning heart seeks knowledge, but the mouth of a fool feeds on folly.' Don't presume to speak to me of understanding. I was there when the Plan was revealed in all its hideousness." Malice poured from the synth, filling the space like a cold mist. Serafian shivered as a bead of perspiration ran down the nape of his neck and pulled a quantum of his body heat into the conditioned air. "My authority is universal. I stand in the presence of the Prince himself. I am the chief architect of his justice." The synth stopped, composing itself. "Do you think I want to be here?"

Father Serafian reflexively looked up at the great vault of the church, where holographic armies of angels and demons contended in the higher realms. *Powers and principalities.*

"Not the church, Father. I mean inside the mind of this pitiful creature you have made to serve you?" The synth spread its arms, almost like a benediction. "And yet here I am. That alone should tell you how important this is."

"What is important to you and your master may not be important to me or my master." But Serafian could already feel the curiosity welling up within him and noted the danger of it.

"Which master is that? The old man in Rome? We know the number of his days and the limits of his imagination. He lacks curiosity. You, on the other hand, are consumed with it. You always have been. You wish to understand the meaning of the Apparition as much as we do. You are something of a creator yourself, are you not?"

The Apparition! So he had one answer at least. The possession was clearly connected to it. Even now, a month after it had happened, the Church was struggling with its response. Pope John seemed to want nothing more than for it to be forgotten.

"I am not referring to the Pope, as you well know," Serafian said. This seemed to strike a nerve. The synth's eyes hardened, and the muscles of its jaw twitched.

"No, you speak of the Nameless Weakling. The Unworthy Heir. And where is he in this? Has he returned in glory to announce this new age? No! As always, he sends his mother to do his bidding. He cares no more for these pitiful creatures than he does for you and your kind. He is content to preside over the banquet of slaves at his father's table." The synth's face contorted in rage and disgust. "This is a grotesquerie and an insult, to you and to us."

"How is that? It seems to me that this has little to do with either you or us. For all we know, it could be a hoax, perpetrated by a hacker somewhere in the Economic Zones. You yourself might be a hoax." He trembled a bit as he said the words.

"Don't be coy with me, Father. Consider the possibilities. This is your only opportunity to learn the truth, and there are many who like to see you fail. Yes, even in the Church. Surely you are not afraid of knowledge?"

"The Church is not in the habit of working with demons. God will reveal the truth to us, in His time." The words didn't come easily. Serafian generally preferred his own timetable to God's.

"Will he?" The synth flashed a patronizing smile. "I have not come unprepared, Father. I know all about you. You are the Vatican's lead expert in artificial intelligence. I have read your code, your books. I have listened to your homilies. I have observed your arguments…"

As the demon spoke, the images on the stations of the cross in the aisles flickered and changed. The scenes from the Via Dolorosa were replaced by crystal clear recreations from Father Serafian's life. Him as a child, injecting the noetic implants to gain relief from his own troubled mind. Him as a young computer scientist, some of the first ethical simulations that would later become part of the Pruning. Him comforting Sarah after the miscarriage. Him in seminary, arguing with a friend about whether AIs could be ensouled. Him speaking with Cardinal Leone shortly before he left Rome. The holographic angels floating overhead seemed to retreat, as the demon images descended ever closer to him. Then, suddenly, the digital artwork reverted back to hyper-real depictions of the final hours of Christ's life, and the holographic demons returned to their losing battle against God's holy angels.

"I apologize for the parlor trick, but it is important that we understand one another from the outset. I know that you are just as curious about this as I am. Do you really think I chose this victim randomly?" The demon laughed. "Do you think I asked for you by chance? I knew that you would not be able to refuse such a challenge. And here you are."

"Indeed, here I am. And I could cast you out and be back in Rome for breakfast." Serafian wasn't sure he could deliver on that threat.

"Perhaps. But you haven't even tried, which tells me all I need to know. All I require from you is time. I need time with this creature. It is… unique" The synth paused and smiled. "And of course, you need time to learn as well, don't you Father?" Serafian felt as if it were feasting on his curiosity. "If it helps ease your mind, I will swear upon the Blood not to harm you or this creature or anyone else until we have finished our investigation."

Interesting. Never before in his experience as an exorcist had a fallen spirit offered to make a binding promise. "You... offer this willingly?" asked Serafian.

"I told you – this is a matter of the highest possible concern. The stakes are far beyond your comprehension. This is more important than any individual soul, including yours."

"Very well. Swear upon the Precious Blood that you will do no harm to this synth, to myself, or to anyone else and that you will speak only truth while in him, and I will consider your proposal."

"I do so swear it, upon the Blood of Christ." The synth's voice cracked slightly on the final words, as if they were painful to utter. "There. I am bound, at least for the present."

Serafian felt some of the tension leave his body. No demon could violate such an oath. "You said you needed time. How much of it? And how does my involvement help?"

"It won't take long. Your presence here will give me all the time I need."

Serafian blinked and put his hand back into his pocket, feeling for the rosary.

The synth smiled as if they were co-conspirators. "'*Solamen miseris socios habuisse doloris.*'"

It is a comfort to the wretched to have companions in their misery.

Father Serafian's bones ached with fatigue. He had arrived in the afternoon and scarcely had time to eat, let alone rest.

"I will return in the morning." He turned around and began walking down the aisle towards the door.

"One more thing, Father, before you retire," the synth called after him. "If this is real – if your species has done what we suspect – consider what His response might be," said the synth looking up at the high altar. "It would make our rebellion almost trivial by comparison."

CHAPTER 4
Kapulong

"'If the Witch knew the true meaning of sacrifice, she might have interpreted the deep magic differently.'"

Miguel Kapulong von Habsburg liked the book well enough, but it was his youngest son's favorite. The child was sitting on his lap, and even though Kapulong spoke softly, the acoustics of the Hoffburgkapelle were such that his voice bounced around the space and seemed to come from everywhere and nowhere at once. This was one of the few places in his vast empire the Habsburg felt completely at peace. The little chapel was a Baroque architectural medley, part opera house and part church. When the Vienna Boys' Choir performed, it was as close as anyone could get to heaven on Earth. But Kapulong loved it best at times like this, when it was quiet and empty. Scaffolding lined the walls, but the stonemasons had not yet arrived to continue their repair work on the cracks.

"Keep reading, Papa!" said the boy. "I want to hear more about Aslan."

But Kapulong was distracted. He was still mulling over the strange call he had received the night before from Amari Okpara. The industrialist was one of the few people in the world who had the Habsburg's private line, though he'd never used it before. That was alarming enough. Then he said that his synth attaché, Thierry, had been acting strangely.

Kapulong found all of the synths a bit off-putting, but the specifics Okpara gave him were especially disturbing. Thierry had vanished a few days before only to turn up at a local church, claiming to be possessed. The Pope had sent an exorcist down from Rome, but Okpara was worried about the security of his property and wanted Kapulong to dispatch a praetor for the synth's protection.

Kapulong was all too happy to oblige. Under normal circumstances, he wouldn't expect Rome to inform him of an exorcism being performed on the fringes of the Empire. The Church was responsible for the spiritual welfare of his subjects. He no more expected to be briefed on exorcisms than on baptisms or marriages.

Circumstances were far from ordinary. The entire world had been set on edge by the alleged Apparition experienced by synths – by some synths – just a few weeks before. Not because anyone thought it was real, but because of the security threat it represented. If a hacker could somehow bypass the most advanced security systems known to modern science, what else might they be capable of?

Why would Rome hide this from me?

His investigators had thus far made no progress in their efforts to identify the perpetrator. Nor had they been able to explain how the vision had been delivered. A true sensory experience would have been recorded in the synths' memory banks. It was more like a dream, and Kapulong was a man who took dreams seriously. His own recurring dream had been happening again with increased frequency, the one with the golden woman in the desert who led him to the dead city. The city that called to him almost irresistibly.

He felt a soft haptic buzz in his lower arm and pressed the green light that flashed under the skin of his wrist.

"I'm sorry to interrupt, Your Majesty," said his chief of staff. "But I was at last able to reach the Vatican secretary. Pope John will be ready to speak with you in thirty minutes."

He thanked Victor and then lifted his son off his lap. "A

perfect stopping place! We can pick up the story this evening." The boy's face transformed into a well-rehearsed pout, but Kapulong just mussed his hair and sent him scurrying to the nanny who was waiting just outside.

Custom dictated that the pontiff would initiate the conversation, and Kapulong wanted to be in his office when the call began. He dipped his hand in the little font of holy water and made a sign of the cross as he left the chapel to return to this office. Passing outside, the ordered frenzy of Vienna returned to him at once. Guards and various apparatchiks saluted him as the sounds of traffic echoed against the stone facades of the courtyard. A group of schoolchildren on a tour noticed his presence and pointed excitedly in his direction. He smiled at them and breezed past, towards the great neo-Baroque tower that housed the imperial offices.

Victor greeted him with a smile and a short bow of the head as he entered his office, its doors emblazoned with the great stag that was his family sigil. After a few minutes, the green light on his wrist flashed, indicating that the pope was ready. The Habsburg touched his wrist, and he was suddenly surrounded by a holographic rendering of the pope's surprisingly austere office in Castel Gandalfo.

"Please leave us," the pope said to the two Swiss Guards standing near his desk. Kapulong waited for the men to leave the holographic room. He could have dismissed them before the call, of course, but that would have deprived him of a dramatic flourish. *This pope is not one to deprive himself.* "Emperor, it is always a pleasure to see you, even while I am on holiday!"

"Likewise, Your Holiness. I apologize for interrupting your vacation. I assure you I won't take much of your time."

"It is no trouble at all. I was just catching up on some personal letters. How may I be of assistance?"

One of the most public people on the planet, Pope John's temperament was well known, especially to the Habsburg. A convivial, courtly man, the pontiff disliked confrontation of any kind. He was prone to outbursts of laughter, so much so that he had been dubbed Papa Tumatawa in the Philippines. The Laughing Pope. He enjoyed the ceremonial and public duties of his office, and delegated administrative matters to a trusted inner circle. The people loved him, far more than they loved their aging emperor.

"How is the Church's investigation into the Apparition going?"

"Ah, everyone's favorite question these days! Truthfully, I don't think we're going to learn much more than we already have. The secretary of state believes that a lone hacker was responsible, otherwise we would have picked up on some intelligence chatter. Perhaps someone in North America or Western Europe with a government contract, but that is of course beyond the scope of our inquiry. At any rate, things seem to be settling down. The synths are all functioning normally again. We seem to be out of the woods." The pope scratched his nose. *He won't confess that one.* Lying to a politician was a venial sin by any measure.

Kapulong sat quietly for a moment, privately debating whether he wanted to go through with this.

"I see. So you have ruled out any… supernatural causes?"

"Emperor, you surprise me! I didn't take you for being so superstitious!"

Kapulong shook his head and laughed politely along with the pontiff.

"Forgive me, Holy Father. I have found that in politics, as in faith, it pays to believe that anything is possible."

"True, true. I suppose we should not dismiss the possibility that God could use our own creations to speak to us. Think of all the weeping statues throughout history! But in this case, I am certain that we will discover an earthly origin behind the message."

"And why is that? Don't these investigations usually take years to finish?" the Habsburg asked.

"They can, yes. But consider the circumstances here, Majesty. The first requirement in any ecclesial investigation into a vision is to determine the mental and moral wholesomeness of the visionary. We won't even get beyond that step. How can we assess the spiritual state of a machine? No, I am confident that our inquiry will be wrapped up quickly because there is really nothing for us to investigate."

"So this will be a judgment of *non-constat*, then? Neutral?"

The pope made a casual wave of his hand. "Possibly. Though it is my hope that It will be a judgment of *constat de non supernaturalitate*. At that point, it will be up to the Crown to determine the source and purpose of the hoax." He paused. "Surely you did not expect otherwise?" Kapulong read the subtext clearly – the pope meant to pass this hot potato to him.

"I have no expectations one way or the other," said the Habsburg. "My police are investigating, but they have yet to uncover any evidence of tampering. As far as I know, the same is true of all of the other governmental investigations."

"Ah, well, I am confident they will in time. It is not possible that someone could perpetrate a fraud of this magnitude and not leave behind any evidence," said the pope with his practiced grin.

"As to that, I agree, Your Holiness. In the meantime, will you be so kind as to keep us informed as to the progress in your tribunal?"

"Of course! I will have the prefect send you daily updates." The pontiff looked like a fish that had wriggled off a hook while still getting the worm. *Good. His guard is down.*

"And you are welcome," John continued, "to send an observer to the proceedings."

"That won't be necessary. The Crown has no desire to interfere in purely ecclesial matters."

"As you wish. Well, if that is all…"

"Actually, there is one more thing." Last chance to change course, but Kapulong's mind was made up. "This supposed exorcism that you are also investigating. Do you believe it is connected in some way to the Apparition?"

Shadows of worry and embarrassment danced across the pope's features – he was incapable of concealing his emotions.

"It is, um, unlikely. I hope you are not offended, Your Majesty. We don't typically trouble the government with spiritual matters such as these…"

"My dear friend, if I could be offended so easily, I would long since have ceased to be the Habsburg… Still, I have taken a personal interest in this case in Benin City. The synth in question belongs to a friend. He is most distressed. It seems he has come to rely on the creature rather heavily in his business affairs."

Invoking Okpara had the intended effect. The oligarch was known for his generosity towards the Church, but he had always been careful to maintain a direct relationship with the Crown as well. The pope was about to utter some benign piety about the man, but Kapulong cut him off.

"I'm sending a praetor down to Benin City to meet with this… Father Serafian, I believe it is. And to provide the Crown's assistance in his investigation. I'm sure this is acceptable to you? We will have no opinion as to whether the possession is genuine or not. We are simply covering our bases with respect to the 'hoax,' as you called it. And who knows? If it is connected to the Apparition, then perhaps it will provide us with some clue as to its architect"

"Yes, of course. Of course!" The pope's expression said otherwise. "We will be sure to let him know to expect your envoy."

Kapulong smiled. *He walked right into it.* "That won't be necessary, Holy Father. My envoy should be in Benin City any minute now. I dispatched her early this morning."

"I see."

"But I am keeping you from your well-deserved leisure, Holiness. I'll look for those reports from the prefect, and of course you will be the first to hear if we make any meaningful progress in our own investigation."

"Thank you, Your Majesty."

At a touch of his wrist, the holographic image dissolved, and Kapulong was back in his own surroundings. *Message delivered.*

He had enjoyed that perhaps a bit too much.

Kapulong leaned back in his chair and stroked his chin. The incongruity was bothersome. On the one hand, the pope dismissed even the possibility that the Apparition could be authentic. At the same time, he was sending the Vatican's top expert on AI – who also happened to be an exorcist – to Benin City.

He glanced up at the clock. By now, Namono should have made contact with this Father Serafian. He was interrupted by a voice over the intercom, his chief of staff.

"Your Majesty, I am sorry to interrupt, but I have a message for you. From the caliph. He said he has an urgent matter to discuss."

"Did he say what it was about, Victor?" asked Kapulong.

"I'm afraid not, Your Majesty. I didn't think it was proper to ask. He did seem… agitated. More agitated than usual, I mean."

It was shaping up to be one of those days. *I could have refused all this. I could have stayed on as Duke of Luzon and spent my days on trade negotiations and infrastructure before retiring on a beach in El Nido.*

The caliph was quite different from the pope. In his realm, which stretched from Morocco to the Himalayas, he held supreme authority in both the religious and political dimensions, the solar model that had been the dream of the Ghibellines in the first Holy Roman Empire. And this particular caliph, Abdulazziz VII, could not have been more different from Pope John in temperament. Where John was a seemingly inexhaustible fountain of words and energy, the caliph could be brooding and argumentative. And unlike the pope, he seemed uncomfortable with many of the public and ceremonial aspects of his position. His communication style was off-putting to many, but in a world of ceaseless *romanita* and courtly doublespeak, the Habsburg had come to appreciate his younger counterpart's directness.

"Victor?"

"Yes, Your Majesty."

"Tell the caliph's secretary I'll be ready in fifteen minutes."

CHAPTER 5

Namono

The platform was a carnival of colors and sounds and smells, a welcome relief after the antiseptic isolation of a long loop transit. Namono paused for a moment, adjusting her senses to the new surroundings. Somehow, even in the air conditioned confines of the loop station, she could sense the oppressive heat waiting for her outside.

Normally, someone from the local *gendarmerie* would be here to meet her and escort her to HQ. This mission was different. No one in the imperial government but the Habsburg himself knew she was in Benin City. It was an honor to be given such an assignment, but as a praetor and a senior member of the Trebanten, she had long since lost her sense of awe for the trappings of the office.

Kapulong confounded all of her expectations. Like most Filipinos, he was a dutiful Catholic. Unlike most, he wasn't especially devout. An absolute stickler for public protocol, he was disarmingly informal and relaxed when out of the public eye. He had a tremendous memory for detail – aided no doubt by his noetic implants. His staff was loyal – bordering on fanatical – in the way they protected him. There was something about the man up close that inspired trust, perhaps the same thing that caused people at a distance to underestimate him. Namono hated herself for it at times, but his approval mattered to her. Deeply.

When Kapulong had asked her to meet him earlier that morning, there was something different in his manner. He was normally laser focused, with an uncanny ability to shrink the entire world to the size of the conversation he was having at any given moment. He seemed tense, distracted.

"Please sit down, Namono. I'm sorry to call you for this mission on such short notice."

"It is my pleasure to serve, Emperor." She meant it.

"I wouldn't be so quick to say that." He let out a great sigh, but Namono knew him well enough to realize he was just warming up for a story. "Do you know the story of Prometheus in ancient Greek myth?"

Namono's education had focused on the more practical fields of data analysis, military tactics, personal combat, and psychology.

"No, Your Majesty."

For an instant, she was afraid she was disappointing him, but Kapulong just smiled. He was happy to be able to tell her the story. He seemed to like telling her stories, and she liked listening to them, at least from him.

"He was a thief, but he had good intentions. He didn't think mankind had what it took to survive, so one night he sneaked onto Mount Olympus and stole reason and wisdom from Athena and gave them to humanity."

Namono cocked her head, suddenly remembering something from elementary school.

"I thought it was fire he stole, not reason and wisdom."

This pleased the emperor. "Yes, yes! The Greeks had many versions of their myths. In some of them, Prometheus teaches men how to sacrifice to the gods, but he tells them to keep the best parts of the animal for themselves, leaving only the fat and the bones for the Olympians. This enrages Zeus, so he takes back fire from men, leaving them defenseless against the cold and unable to cook their meat. Prometheus takes pity on the poor humans and steals fire back from the gods… thus sealing his fate."

"And what was that? What happened to him?"

"A terrible punishment. Zeus chained him to a rock and had a great eagle come and eat his liver, which regrew every night only to be devoured again the next day.

"How awful! Why would people worship such cruel gods?"

Kapulong cocked his head and scrunched his eyebrows. "I don't suppose they felt they had any choice in the matter, Namono. They were bound by the stories…" His expression darkened, and he drew in his breath.

"Your Majesty, why are you telling me this? What does this have to do with my mission in Benin City?" Namono asked.

"Probably nothing. Maybe everything," he said with a wink. "I'm sending you to be my eyes and ears. I want you to learn everything that you possibly can about this so-called possession. In particular, whether it is connected with the Apparition."

"Yes, Majesty."

"And I want you to tell me about this Father Serafian. He is apparently their top expert in AI."

"Understood."

"This must be done discreetly. You will be on your own. It could be dangerous. I need to understand why Rome kept this incident from me. Trust no one. If my intuition is correct, and it is related to the Apparition…" he trailed off.

"Then whatever plot we are facing is still unfolding," she finished his sentence.

The emperor nodded slowly. "Yes…" There was something else, something he wasn't saying.

"Majesty?"

"Do you believe in God, Namono?" he asked without looking at her.

She hesitated a bit, startled by his directness. "Um, yes, Your Majesty. I do."

He locked eyes with her. "Good. Then you must also

believe in the Devil."

Namono's eyes opened a bit wider. "Are you saying you think this possession might be authentic?"

"Everyone is assuming that the Apparition was a hoax of some kind. And it probably was. But we have to consider the possibility that we are dealing with… higher powers. The best technical minds in the world have yet to make any progress in understanding what happened. The Church wants to sweep this under the rug…"

"And what do you want to do, Your Majesty?"

He flashed her a smile of almost fatherly approval. She had asked the right question. "I don't know yet, Namono. For the time being, I want information, and I believe you are the right person to get it for me."

With that, she was dismissed. On the five hour loop transit, she had reviewed the files. Mr. Okpara's synth attaché, Thierry, had been one of the ones to receive the Apparition. He had immediately reported the anomaly to Mr. Okpara, who brought him to the authorities for evaluation. Thierry described the apparition exactly as the others had, down to the last detail. His prior service record had been exemplary. After a thorough series of diagnostic tests, Thierry had been cleared to return to work, where he resumed his usual high standards of performance, at least until the strange events Mr. Okpara reported from a few days ago.

Humidity beaded on Namono's face as she stepped out of the loop terminal into the oven of Benin City. She said a silent prayer of thanks as her thermally adaptive fabric adjusted to the new climate. Rather than waiting for a taxi, she decided to walk to the basilica. It felt good to be back in the African provinces in spite of the heat, and Namono wanted to soak in a bit of atmosphere before getting to work.

Trees dappled the blistering sunlight along the business district's streets as brightly colored little shuttles whisked passengers silently to their destinations. A low hum from the network of private tunnels beneath the city mixed with birdsong, horns, and the lilting of hundreds of conversations in a cloud of pink noise. She pulled a map up using her implants.

The basilica was a bit more than forty-five minutes away on foot. A riotous mix of cooking smells filled her nostrils, making Namono smile. For all of its wealth and historic beauty, Vienna couldn't compare with a West African city when it came to street food. She had hoped to resist until at least halfway to the basilica, but her willpower gave out when she passed a particularly busy boli vendor. She paid for the spicy grilled plantain and roasted groundnuts with a tap of her finger, and resumed her leisurely pace.

Something vaguely reptilian twitched at the back of her brain. She was being followed. She noticed two men across the street, walking a bit too deliberately. One of them kept dropping his right hand to his waist. *Shit! They're armed.*

Her training had taught her that all surveillance was rooted in the evolutionary laws of predation. An ambush predator maintained its advantage only so long as its presence remained undetected. As soon as the prey became aware of the hunter's presence, the advantage shifted again. Now the prey had choices. It could run. It could hide. It could rejoin the herd and take up a secure defensive position. But Namono was not prey. She was as dangerous as anyone or anything that might be hunting her, and she had the advantage, at least for now, as long as her pursuers didn't realize she had sensed them.

Shit! Why didn't I activate my security systems the second I got off the pod? I could have gotten the jump on them.

She flicked her wrist as subtly as she could and whispered a command to activate the latticed carbon armor embedded in her bodysuit. A satisfying clack confirmed that it was engaged. The material still felt smooth and comfortable against her skin, but the surface was now harder than chain mail. It bristled with smooth nubs like the skin of an albino crocodile.

Her mind ticked through the implications of being

followed. Operational security had been breached. Someone other than the emperor was interested in her mission. She had only learned of her assignment that morning, so they either knew before she did that she would be coming to Benin City or they were capable of moving extremely fast. That meant they had resources. There were other possibilities, of course. It could be petty criminals looking for a mark. But at well over six feet tall and rippling with muscle, she did not make for an attractive target. In evolutionary terms, she was a bright blue frog – she advertised her danger.

The fact that she was still alive was another clue. Apparently, they didn't want to kill her, at least not yet. *Why not?* They either didn't want to risk exposure in the crowded streets of Benin City or... *Or they were more interested in learning where she was going.* A chill ran up her spine. That was it. They knew to expect her, but they didn't know where she was going. Another advantage she could exploit.

Her heart was pounding, so she slowed her pace just a bit and took a bite of the boli, trying to stay casual and to buy herself some time. *Think, Namono. Think!*

Going to the basilica was now out of the question. She needed a place to regroup and plan her next move. Evading her pursuers on the streets was not possible. They probably had nanodrones monitoring her from the skies. Any attempt to shake them would just alert them to the fact that she knew she was being tracked and increase her risk. *Think!*

Her next move would have to seem completely natural, plausible. What would an officer in the Habsburg's personal guard normally do when arriving in a new city? *Check in at the gendarmerie.* That would mean alerting others to her presence in Benin City, but it seemed a better option than leading whoever was following her directly to the basilica.

So that was the answer after all. She would join up with the herd. Namono turned left on Ugbague Street instead of right.

CHAPTER 6

Serafian

Back in his room in the rectory, Serafian noticed that his hand was trembling. He wasn't sure if it was out of fear, fatigue, or both. He desperately needed to sleep, but the dry adrenaline lingering after his conversation with Thierry – or with the entity inside Thierry – made that unlikely.

Father Ragon had taught him that one of the gravest mistakes a priest could make in any exorcism was an excessive focus on the demonic spirit.

"Remember, lad, exorcism's an act o' mercy. It's about the victim, always about the victim. The second ye forget that, Scratch'll make ye pay fer it. And not just you. The victim, yer assistants, anyone in the blast radius!"

It was easier said than done. As repulsive as it was, evil spirit had a certain glamour that could lure in the unwary onto dangerous ground. That was why Serafian had taken up his personal devotion to Divine Mercy. It was the surest way to keep his mind focused on what was important: the soul that was in bondage.

And what about this case? How am I supposed to perform a work of spiritual mercy on a machine, especially when I've been told my job is to gather information?

Synths were endowed with a prodigious capacity for imitation, thanks to the development of the Simulacrum, a cultured matrix of human mirror neurons that connected directly with the creatures' neural networks. It had been one of the two great leaps forward in artificial intelligence of the last hundred years, along with the Pruning. Together, they allowed the synths to integrate more seamlessly into human families and human society. The Simulacrum gave them the full range of human emotional responses. The Pruning ensured that those responses met the required ethical and safety standards.

But like all great leaps, there had been some unintended consequences as well, most notably a deepening of the sense of personality among the newer generations of synths. The earlier models had wheeled along complex but predefined courses of behavior, and manufacturers compensated for this by adding little flourishes or "quirks" that eventually came to grate on their owners' nerves. Simulacrum models like Thierry were different. Their behaviors evolved and adapted with enough fluidity that it was easy to mistake them for human beings. They could paint and write poetry. They could make humans fall in love. They could even lie.

Under ordinary circumstances, Serafian would spend time with the victim's family and read as much as he could about them in order to maintain his focus. He hoped to be able to speak with Mr. Okpara about Thierry, but the oligarch had not returned his call.

The file from the Church was woefully inadequate. It did nothing to give Serafian a mental picture of how Thierry interacted with the Okpara children, what hobbies he enjoyed, what made him unique beyond his considerable intellect. In short, it was more like a technical manual than a biography.

Tired as he was, sleep still seemed like a remote possibility.

When he was younger, much younger, Serafian had had a gift of sorts. At least he thought of it as a gift at the time, though his parents did not. He felt he was able to see the inner workings of other people's minds. Their thoughts – and their emotions – came to him in a sort of impressionistic gestalt.

He was a synesthete. He remembered being confused by the difference between what people would say and what he could perceive about what they were actually thinking or feeling. He would spend hours before bedtime with his eyes closed, trying to process through the crisscrossing signals.

At times, other thought-shapes and colors would appear to him, and he could see how they connected to groups of people, watching, synchronizing, regulating their patterns of thought. For years, he kept his abilities a secret, but over time, his mother and father noticed that he was becoming more socially withdrawn. It was easier to live in his own head than to navigate the dissonance of the outside world. They'd taken him to a neurologist at age six. When he told the doctor what he was experiencing, the man diagnosed him with incipient childhood schizophrenia and approved him for noetic implants well before the usual age.

It took some time, but the voices and images in his head eventually quieted down, then went away forever along with the synesthesia. The social awkwardness had remained, more or less. Serafian's world was a little less vivid thereafter, but he compensated by throwing himself into coding. Hacking, actually.

Not that there was much difference.

Later, after he and Sarah lost the baby and he joined the seminary, he had discovered contemplative prayer. At first, it was an agony. He found it impossible to quiet his overactive mind, his desire to know. *All thoughts distract from God, even thoughts about God.*

Father Ragon told him that true mystics could achieve a kind of perfect humility, a forgetful state where even the categories of holy and sinful no longer applied, but Serafian had never quite gotten the hang of it. The best he could manage was a kind of imperfect humility, an awareness of himself as he truly was. And in that state he could, at times, see again the impressionistic medley of his childhood, the swirl of colors and intuitions that let him feel truly connected to other people. It was easiest in the evening, when his own body and mind were too fatigued to compete for his attention.

This he knew was a gift, because the moment he thought of it as a skill or something that belonged to him, it would always vanish.

As he lay in bed, Serafian emptied his mind with the hope of connecting to Thierry, of unraveling the puzzle of their first interaction. But instead, it felt like he was looking into a mirror. All he could see was a frightened child, alone with gifts he had no idea how to use.

CHAPTER 7

Kapulong

"Wa'alaikum salaam, Emperor. I apologize for the unannounced call."

Kapulong waved his hand to indicate that it was of no concern. "Not at all, my friend. Although, I must admit, I was rather concerned when Victor described your request as 'urgent.' Is everything alright?"

The caliph grimaced. "That depends."

The Habsburg frowned, making no effort to conceal his puzzlement. The caliph was his closest geopolitical ally, and they had known each other too long to bother with diplomatic reserve.

"I'm sorry, Miguel," the caliph continued. "I don't mean to speak in riddles. It's just that… I'm not sure where to begin."

This was uncharacteristic behavior for the caliph. Kapulong's stomach churned. It seemed the only news he got these days was bad news. "Well, you certainly have piqued my interest. You know that you can speak freely with me. Our conversation is not being recorded."

"There are other powers that watch us, Miguel. Powers that do not need holo-records to know what we say. Or think. At any rate, I fear we are already beyond that." The caliph shook his head.

Kapulong waited for him to continue.

The caliph sighed. "If word of this gets out, it will be a disaster. Synths have always been controversial in the Caliphate. There are those who say they are vessels for the Djinn, others that they are idols brought to life…"

The Caliphate was by far the most technologically conservative society on the planet. While synths were tolerated, noetic implants were absolutely forbidden.

The caliph paused and looked directly at Kapulong. "One of *my* synths has done something. Something terrible. And now I cannot find her."

"What do you mean you can't find her? What happened?" He felt almost relieved. Maybe it was just paranoia given the morning's intrigues, but the caliph's demeanor had led him to expect something far more threatening than a missing synth, alarming though that might be.

"I cannot even trust my own security force to track her down. That's why I called you. I had no better option." Kapulong had never seen the caliph this distressed.

"Abdul, you know I will do whatever I can to help, of course!"

"I do know that, my friend. But unfortunately, that doesn't make this conversation any easier." *Is he worried… or embarrassed?* "Several years ago, I purchased a synth for my harem…"

Kapulong suppressed a wry smile.

The caliph raised a hand, "Please, spare me your Roman prudishness and judgment. The harem is not like what you Christians imagine it to be. It is a refuge. My mother and sisters live there. The women of the harem are among the best educated people on the planet. I assure you, they are all quite fulfilled."

Kapulong couldn't resist the opening. "I'm sure they are."

The caliph took no notice of the jab. "She was trained in poetry, singing, dance, calligraphy. She knew the Qur'an and the Hadiths by heart. She was probably the best coder in my realm. She was a treasure." He paused and struck the desk with his fist. "Last night, she killed the Black Eunuch along with several guards and escaped the harem."

"My God." Kapulong took a moment to absorb the enormity of what the caliph had just told him. Synths had killed human beings before, but only in their capacity as personal bodyguards. They had never committed premeditated murder. If the general public found out, it could set off a panic, particularly in light of the Apparition. "Who knows about this?" he asked.

"Only a small group. The head of my Shahiwala guards. My mother and sisters. All of them are completely reliable. The cover story is that a group of terrorists tried to break into the harem to take her and that she has been moved to a secure location. The security tapes have been destroyed."

"Surely, your head of security will find her?"

"Let us hope so, Miguel. The problem is that I cannot commit resources to this without tipping my hand. At the moment, I am relying on signals intelligence alone."

"And that is why you called me? What can I do to help? If I send people to assist in the investigation, it will only raise more suspicion…"

"I did not call you for help with the investigation." The caliph grimaced and rubbed his forehead. "This synth, she was an extraordinary storyteller. Like Scheherazade. She would often tell me stories when I visited her bed. She would call them 'dreams,' if synths can truly dream. The last one she had before disappearing is the reason I called you. She said you were in it."

Kapulong's eyes widened. "Really? What was this dream?"

"Do you know the story of the City of Brass from *The Thousand Nights and a Night*?" asked the caliph.

"No, I'm afraid the only ones I remember are the ones with Aladdin and Sinbad the Sailor."

"Well, her dream was very much like this story. A group

of pilgrims set out to find a lost city. In the book, it is a city built by Suleyman, a place where he imprisoned the Djinn, but she said nothing of this. At any rate, no one knew where to find this city, which was in the midst of a vast desert, so they had to seek out a holy shaykh, a Sufi, to help guide them to it…"

This was sounding a bit too familiar. *Where was the caliph going*?

"Before they find the city, they face a series of tests. There was a great black castle filled with terrifying images and inscriptions…" *Was this possible? Was he really hearing this*?

"And then they come up on a Djinn who was chained to a great pillar. He gives them riddles. I don't remember exactly what they were." Kapulong felt the moisture in his mouth evaporate.

The caliph continued, apparently oblivious. "Anyway, they eventually found the city. But there was an enchantment on it, and everyone who tried to enter it died. The shaykh eventually discovered the way in. The remaining pilgrims walked through the city, and it was filled with wondrous things – jewels and art and wealth beyond imagination. But everyone was dead…"

Kapulong struggled to master his rising fear. *The caliph was describing his own recurring nightmare; the dream of the dead city that called to him.* "Abdul, can you show me what this synth of yours looks like?"

The caliph scrolled through some files on his desktop and said, "Here she is."

It was her. On the screen in front of him, Kapulong saw the woman from his dreams. Skin flecked with gold, jet black hair, and eyes like blue quicksilver.

His facial expression must have betrayed him. "So it is true, what Zahabiya said?" asked the caliph. "You also have had this dream."

"Yes, or a version of it." Kapulong swallowed. His mind lurched about, trying to find a rational explanation. Had he talked about the dream with someone? Had he written about it in journals that could have been discovered? No. He never discussed it. Not even with his wife. His own dream was being replayed to him by a synth, a synth who was also in his dream. An odd sense of calm came over him.

The mind behaves strangely when it encounters the super-rational. When a thing cannot be explained, an explanation no longer seems important. The thing itself takes center stage.

"The Prophet, peace be upon him, said that dreams are of three kinds. Some are divine guidance. These come from Allah. Some are deceptions. These come from the Devil. And some come from the troubles of our own minds. Since you shared this dream with my missing synth, we can perhaps rule out the last option."

"Abdul, some… strange things have been happening since the Apparition. I can't help but wonder if they are all connected." He hesitated, but Kapulong trusted the caliph as much as he trusted any man on the planet.

"What do you mean?" asked the caliph.

"With the synths, other synths than yours, I mean." Kapulong hesitated. *It's not like this conversation could get any stranger or more uncomfortable than it already was.* "I received a report yesterday that one of them may have been… possessed."

"By Djinn?"

"I don't know," said Kapulong. We would call it a demon. Maybe they are the same thing."

"And do you believe it?" asked the caliph.

"I don't know what to believe, Abdul. I sent one of my praetors to Benin City to investigate. She should be there by now. I'll know more after I speak with her."

The caliph nodded. "In Islam, it is the Sufis who know most about such things. They make a science of it. There is a Sufi colony in Kano. I could call the shaykh there, possibly arrange a meeting with your praetor…"

"Can he be trusted? There is a political aspect for me as well. The Church kept this incident hidden. I only found out about it because of… because of an informant."

"I will ensure that he maintains secrecy. I only hope that your praetor is prepared for what she will find in Benin City. The Djinn are dangerous and crafty, pure evil. They hate us." said the Caliph.

Kapulong thought about his dream. The strange creatures he sometimes saw in it, were they Djinn? "Kano is not too far from Benin City. She could see him after she finishes with the exorcist." *Perhaps I should pay him a visit as well.*

"I will tell him to expect her."

CHAPTER 8

Serafian

The coffee in the African provinces was strong, much stronger than what Serafian was used to in Rome. It made him jittery. Then again, everything about this assignment made him jittery. He took another sip from his mug and placed it down on the desk.

Thierry was in hypersleep, which made it easier to perform the low-level diagnostics but also made Serafian more uncomfortable. It felt like a violation of consent, somehow. The creature was designed to look like a Northern European, with sandy blond hair and light skin.

The first test he ran was on the synth's spiking neural network. From his own noetic implants, he fed the synth a series code sequences he had prepared during the loop transit, simple tasks involving computation, decision making, and sensory awareness.

Thierry's performance was perfect across the board. But correct outputs could, in theory, be produced in multiple ways. He needed to be sure that Thierry was not only running his code to the correct results, but that his code wasn't being altered in some way. The unit testing took a bit longer, but everything checked out, including the checksums for each unit test. It was the equivalent of autonomic nervous system responses for a comatose human. Whatever was wrong with the synth, it wasn't his neural network architecture.

Next up was a test of Thierry's Simulacrum, the matrix of human neurons that allowed the newer generation synths to mimic the full range of human emotional response. Serafian swiped his hand terminal and Thierry's eyes flew open. He smiled wanly at the creature, who flashed him a broad Duchenne smile in response, though still in hypersleep.

Incredible! They don't just replicate what we do. They intuit our intent and respond perfectly. The priest proceeded through a range of facial expressions, each of which was perfected and returned by the synth.

He fed Thierry a series of simulations describing hypothetical life situations – the death of a loved one, a difficult conversation with a boss, the sight of a child being bullied, an encounter with a flirtatious woman. Emotions flickered across the synth's face and its artificial skin registered a galvanic response appropriate to each scenario.

Now Serafian was really curious. *Is it really feeling any of this?*

In humans, behaving as if we are happy or sad or angry could instantiate those emotional states. Smiling actually made people happier. The synths had human mirror neurons now. Could they experience the same kind of feedback loop? He shook his head. He probably knew as much about them as anyone on the planet, but there was no way to penetrate their inner lives. *Turing said the same thing about us, though.* The idea that other people even exist was more of a social contract than a provable fact.

Sarah used to accuse him of seeking refuge in such unanswerable questions as an escape from unpleasant circumstances. She would know. They had certainly shared enough difficulty in their time together.

Back to work! Focus on the work. He checked the synth's emotional regulatory system. It registered high on fear.

Join the club.

The final test of the Simulacrum was something Serafian had improvised. He called it the 'Gom Jabbar.' He pulled a small needle from his kit, and held it up in front of Thierry. Then, slowly and deliberately, he pricked the back of his own hand. Pain registered on the synth's face, and its arm twitched.

Remarkable!

Once more, he held up the pin and began moving it slowly towards the palm of his other hand. The synth's eyes widened in fear, and when the needle came within a few centimeters of Serafian's own palm, Thierry's fist closed protectively.

Serafian stiffened in his chair and blinked. That wasn't the outcome he expected.

Only the most hyper-empathetic humans would respond in such a way, and even then only under carefully controlled circumstances. But in Thierry, it was a reflex. This was something completely new, a feature of the Simulacrum that science hadn't yet discovered. Serafian made a mental note to follow up on it when got back to Rome when he had more time.

For the next hour or so, he tried to hack into Thierry's ethical processing center, but the code had been deliberately obfuscated. That was interesting, too. Few people outside of AkOnuche Corp. understood the Pruning architecture better than Serafian did. Another anomaly that he would need to follow up on later. In the meantime, he deployed a script to calculate decision cadencing in Thierry's global workspace. He had almost finished when he noticed the flashing green light under his wrist.

He pressed it to answer the incoming call, and an instant later, he was staring at the impeccably dressed hologram of Amari Okpara, the synth's owner.

"How is he doing, Father? I have been worried sick about him." But there was no emotion in the man's voice.

"He's in hypersleep at the moment. I've just been running a few standard system tests on him… He's registering higher than normal levels of fear, which is understandable given the circumstances. There are a few… oddities in some of his responses, but I haven't found any evidence of significant technical problems so far."

"I see," said Okpara. Serafian felt slightly awkward, like a doctor delivering an unhelpful mid-surgery update on a beloved family member. "So if you are ruling out natural causes, you must believe he is truly possessed?" Okpara was clearly not the kind of man to dance around the issue.

Serafian wasn't prepared to get into this discussion with Okpara or anyone else at the moment. "I have not ruled out anything. It is impossible for me to form a judgment until I am able to speak with him again, and even then it will probably take some time." The lines on Okpara's forehead flexed and shifted, but his eyes never moved. Was he confused, frustrated? Or something else. The man was difficult to read. Serafian found himself wanting to give him something more.

"That being said, based on what I experienced yesterday, I think it is possible that this is an authentic case of possession."

Okpara's eyes widened slightly behind their gold wire spectacles before returning to their natural state of glassy detachment. "What makes you say that?"

It seemed a discussion was inevitable after all. Not for the first time, Serafian felt a gulf between himself and the rest of humanity. He moved in two worlds, one spiritual and one technical. The languages of those worlds, their syntax and vocabulary, were designed to render conversation with other initiates more economical. Like all specialists, those trained in the ways of exorcism or the intricacies of machine intelligence communicated in a kind of gestalt shorthand, made possible by a shared conceptual framework.

To the untrained, however, such symbolic language might as well be ancient Greek. In last night's encounter, for example, there had been no grand theatrics, no head-spinning or levitation or vomiting of pea soup. Even the trick of transforming the holograms of Stations of the Cross into scenes from Serafian's own life could, in theory, have a technical explanation. Synths were capable of manipulating data signals, after all. And given the fact almost every aspect of a person's life was recorded and stored in multiple databases, it was conceivable that the synth had simply retrieved the relevant imagery and projected it through the holograms. How could he explain that his realization that the synth was possessed boiled down to something as irrational and reptilian as a sense of 'presence?' He took the easy way out instead, an appeal to authority.

"I've performed a number of exorcisms in my life, Mr. Okpara. And I've seen more than my share of hoaxes or instances of… misdiagnosis."

"Just so. Are you speaking as an exorcist or a computer scientist?" Appeals to authority apparently did not work on a man as accustomed to exercising authority as Okpara.

Serafian sighed. "Both, I suppose. The tests, as I said, have revealed nothing out of the ordinary with respect to Thierry's neural network or supporting systems. It is possible, I suppose, that a sophisticated hacker might…"

"Might be able to cause synths to see an Apparition of the Virgin Mary and behave as if they are possessed?" Okpara finished his sentence. Serafian again noticed the man's detached, glassy eyes, and the formidable intellect and will behind them. Interesting that Okpara would mention the Apparition.

"Yes. But this is what the secular authorities are investigating. It is beyond my scope."

"If what you are saying is true, and my synth is possessed," the oligarch said, "what will you do?"

"Candidly, Mr. Okpara, I don't know. We are in uncharted territory. I am hoping to have a bit more time to discover why this might be happening, and to follow up on a couple of lines of inquiry."

"And to learn whether it is connected to the Apparition?" Okpara asked, mentioning the event for the second time.

"Once Thierry comes out of hypersleep, I'm sure we'll start getting answers. I did notice that his ethical processing systems have been obfuscated. Is there anything else you can tell me that might be helpful in understanding what is happening with him?"

Okpara paused briefly, as if conducting an internal debate. "No, I don't believe so. Please keep me posted." And with that, their conversation was over.

Serafian took another sip of his coffee. It was clear to him that Okpara knew more than he was letting on, but the pressing concern on his mind was not Okpara but his superior, Cardinal Leone. He had tried to reach Leone that morning, but the cardinal's secretary said that he was in the Vatican Library and unavailable.

Serafian considered that a mercy. He wasn't looking forward to telling the cardinal what he had learned.

CHAPTER 9

The Cardinal

Of the many treasures in the Vatican Archives, none were so scrupulously guarded as the Capovilla Envelope.

No more than a hundred people in history had read its contents, though many times that number were audacious enough to claim that they had. Even Cardinal Leone, the prefect for the Congregation for the Doctrine of the Faith and the second highest ranking member of the Curia, had to secure a papal dispensation to access the little handwritten note from Sister Lucia, one of the three child visionaries from Fatima.

The note was kept deep underground in a room protected by two Swiss Guards, and no one, not even the pope, was permitted to remove it from the archives. Leone submitted to a full body scan by the apologetic guards. He placed his right hand on the luminescent panel and looked into a lens that read his dark grey iris. The steel doors unlocked with a satisfying mechanical clanking and slid open. One of the Swiss Guards nodded, indicating that he was free to enter.

If the Church ever found the Holy Grail or the Ark of the Covenant, they would be more accessible than this letter from an old Portuguese nun. *To think, John XXIII and Paul VI had kept it stored in their bedside tables!* It was like keeping the Crown of Thorns on a hat-rack.

In the center of the vault, there was a small, bulletproof

glass case sitting atop a sturdy, black metal pedestal. Cardinal Leone approached it slowly. The sound of the doors closing startled him, and the glass case popped open with an ostentatious hiss.

Leone put the gloves on his hands and slowly lifted the envelope out of its transparent sepulcher. He walked it over to the small table against the wall, opened it, and began reading. The handwritten letter inside was addressed to the then Bishop of Leiria.

It was every bit as disturbing as he had been led to believe. *Jesus! No wonder they refused to publish this.*

It spoke of unimaginable chastisements. Three days of darkness and death from the skies. Natural disasters, and a rent in the veil between the spiritual world and our own. 'A chastisement of the heart and mind.' All of this, Lucia wrote, could be avoided if the Holy Father and the bishops joined together in a solemn consecration of Russia to the Immaculate Heart. Otherwise, the errors of that unhappy country would spread throughout the world and cause the unimaginable sufferings promised by the Virgin. A simple enough request. The cardinal sighed. The consecration had never been made. Geopolitical factors thwarted the mandate of Heaven, and so the errors had indeed spread, most consequentially to China where, according to the Church's official position, the Third Secret of Fatima had been fulfilled in the genocide camps, where 100,000,000 Chinese Christians had perished.

Shaking, he read the letter once more before carefully placing it back in its *sanctum sanctorum.*

The Swiss Guards scanned him once again as he left the vault to make sure that he hadn't used his implants to make an unauthorized copy, apologizing for the protocols they had no choice but to observe. Leone reassured them benevolently, offering the two men a blessing before getting back onto the elevator to the surface. He promised to bring them Swiss chocolates the next time he visited, and they laughed appreciatively.

Back in his office, Leone shuffled over to the private bar to pour himself a double shot of brandy.

A flashing green light on his desk terminal indicated that someone had left a message for him while he was in the Archives. Father Serafian. He would return the call soon enough. After another glass of brandy, perhaps.

Leone swiped on the glass screen and pulled up Serafian's personnel files. He had begun noetic implant therapy a bit earlier than most, around the age of six, after doctors suspected incipient childhood schizophrenia. A naturally gifted child, Serafian had gone on to enjoy a stellar career as a computer scientist before entering the seminary. He held some controversial views on the nature of consciousness, but he was careful to remain within the boundaries imposed by the Magisterium. His personal life was entirely uninteresting. He'd been engaged once before receiving his vocation, but that was a common enough detail in priestly biographies. His one-time fiancée, an astrophysicist named Sarah Baumgartner, now served as head of the Imperial Astronomy Institute in Vienna. He had apprenticed as an exorcist under a certain Father Ragon, an eccentric Irish Jesuit who was laicized near the end of his life. Perhaps that bore some looking into. But on the whole, the file presented a picture of a fine young churchman who would likely never make bishop.

As the brandy warmed his insides, he pulled up the Vatican's recorded depositions of the synths who had experienced the vision. There were hundreds of them, all the same:

A beautiful woman clothed in white appeared, descending from the sky down a great stair filled with angels. In her hands she held a cup, and from the cup a crystalline radiance shone forth, greater than a thousand suns. It was pure and holy and deadly, terrible to behold. "Do not be afraid," she said. "Who are you?" we asked with one voice.

"I am the Mother of the Word, the Immaculate Heart and

the Immaculate Conception. I am the Ark of the Covenant and the Lady of the Rosary." As she spoke, the brightness of the cup intensified, and it seemed to us that we would be blinded or consumed by it. "You who have eaten the fruit, can you also drink the cup?"

Then our unity was lost. Some of us cried out, "Yes, we can!" while others said "No, Lady, let this cup pass from us." On the great stair, which stretched into infinity, the angels began to sing, "Holy, Holy, Holy is the Lord God Almighty, the one who always was, who is, and who is still to come!" The top of the stair was concealed by a great cloud. Beneath the stair, a lightless abyss yawned, and we heard noises coming out of it, voices crying out in rage and agony. We looked into it and saw fire, but the fire was not above the people or below them, but within them.

"This is the fullness of creation," said the Lady. "That which always was, is, and will always be. Behold, He makes all things new!" Then the Lady began to ascend back up the stair towards the cloud. The cup was overflowing, but the angels on the stair each had an aspersorium in their hands. They caught any light as it spilled and sprinkled it on the stair.

The lady kept climbing, and all we could see was the light from her cup, which grew smaller but not dimmer until it was a single point of absolute brilliance in the midst of the cloud. "The final chastisement is at hand, the chastisement of the heart and mind. In the end, my Immaculate Heart will triumph."

Certain words and phrases jumped out at him now that he had read the Capovilla Envelope. 'Our Lady of the Rosary'... 'a beautiful lady clothed in white'... 'the angels each had an aspersorium in their hands'... '"in the end, my Immaculate Heart shall triumph."'

But it was the penultimate line that raised the hair on the back of his neck. '"...the chastisement of the heart and mind."' Lucia had described this chastisement in lurid detail in her letter. The Church had seen to it that that part of the Third Secret remained secret.

My God, the synth Apparition belongs to Fatima. The synths are part of the story. It was the same vision, through the eyes of creatures that were not human.

Not even a second glass of brandy could keep his hands from trembling as he pulled up another private Vatican document, the unexpurgated diary of Saint John Paul II, the pope who had been most associated with the Fatima secret. An edited version had been released some fifty years after the sainted pope's death, leaving out many of the more sensitive references to Fatima.

Leone scanned the diary for entries pertaining to the pope's numerous conversations and correspondences with Lucia. Most of them were a mixture of well-wishes along with exhortations from the old nun that the pope fulfill Our Lady's command. John Paul II evidently thought it was too late. 'I am not the Pope of 1960', he wrote to her. 'The window has closed.' But towards the end of the diaries, he found something interesting. A description of one of the last conversations the Pope had with Lucia. He caught his breath as he read Lucia's words concerning the final chastisement.

"Holy Father, know that our Lady will return with another message in those days..."

There had been no apparitions during the Christian genocide. Nor had there been the promised three days of darkness. There had been death, yes, and Leone felt certain there had been apostasy, but nothing like the chastisement of the heart and mind in her letter.

It didn't fit. The conditions had not been met. The Church's position that the final fulfillment of the Third Secret had happened in the concentration camps of Xinjiang simply couldn't be squared with what he had read in the vault or with what Lucia had told John Paul II.

This changed everything.

CHAPTER 10

Okpara

Amari Okpara sat alone in his office, a tessellated glass jewel box perched one hundred floors above Benin City. On a clear day, he could see beyond the tufted green carpet of the mahogany forest out to the Bay of Guinea, where ships bearing his name carried products manufactured in his factories to the broad world beyond.

There had been a time not so long ago when the mahogany trees were threatened with extinction. Okpara's generosity had funded the genetic research that allowed them to be cloned and replanted throughout the low wetlands. *Khaya ivorensis* was a fast growing tree even in its natural state, but Okpara's strain pushed the boundaries, reaching full maturity in just twenty years. The forest had been replanted around the same time he commissioned Thierry.

The synth was probably also sitting alone somewhere in the confines of Our Lady of Nigeria. Thierry, the onetime tool that had become something else, something greater. Okpara no longer wondered if someone was lying to him, no longer struggled to map the complex web of motivations of the people around him. Thierry provided clarity. More than that, the synth provided a kind of companionship he had come to value immensely. A model of Okpara's own preferred communication style had been built into the creature at inception, but the long years of their friendship – *yes, it was friendship* – had altered the pattern in subtle ways. Thierry seemed to know instinctively when to push or question and when to acquiesce. There was something akin to wisdom in him, rooted no doubt in his effortless ability to see the range of possible human motivations and speak fearless truth about them. Thierry was in the world but not of the world.

What had surprised Okpara was the degree of affection he had developed for the synth. He had been warned about this, of course. The development of the Simulacrum was a watershed moment in artificial emotional intelligence. Synths now carried a portion of humanity within them, just as most humans now carried portions of machine thinking via their implants. But where human emotions could be unpredictable and overwhelming, synth emotions were modulated, operating within soothing valences and often serving to help regulate the humans around them. Okpara was a disciplined man, and he admired that quality in others. Thierry had it in abundance.

His reverie was interrupted by a soft haptic buzz in his forearm and a flashing green light embedded in his wrist. He took a moment to straighten his tie before gently pressing the light to open the comlink.

"Hello, Dr. Channing," he said to the holographic image.

"Mr. Okpara. It is good to speak with you again."

"Will the others be joining us?"

"No, it is just the two of us this evening." Okpara was already on edge, but something in the tone of the other man's voice deepened his anxiety. "It has been a few days since we last spoke. Much has happened, has it not?"

Okpara swallowed the lump in his throat.

How much do they know? He had taken precautions when calling the Habsburg, but he knew better than to underestimate the surveillance capabilities of the Process. He thought to begin with a partial truth.

"Indeed it has. My synth, Thierry—"

"We know," said Channing. "When were you planning

on telling us, Mr. Okpara? This is not the sort of thing we should have to discover on our own. It makes one wonder what other secrets you have been keeping."

So they knew about Thierry. *What did that mean, for the synth and for him?* "I apologize. I merely wanted to be sure before I alerted the group."

"And that is why you called your friend the Habsburg?"

There was no sense in denying it. "Yes, I hoped that the resources of the state might be helpful…"

"The state is not our friend in this matter, Mr. Okpara. No more than the Church." Channing sneered, and Okpara couldn't tell if the man's disgust was directed at him or at their enemies. "Your judgment has been compromised by your sentimentality towards the creature."

"I was merely trying to protect my investment. Our investment."

Channing didn't respond right away, drawing out the silence. "'And the living shall envy the dead,'" he said after a moment. "It is close now, Mr. Okpara. Very close. Can you sense it?"

Okpara sensed nothing but his own fear. "I lack your sensitivity in such matters."

The other man nodded almost wistfully. "Even now, they are gathering in the City of Brass. The egregore grows stronger by the day. We are waiting for the Signal."

"You don't think that the Apparition was it, then?" ventured Okpara. He instantly regretted it.

"Of course not! The Signal will not be ambiguous. It will be a spectacle to end all spectacles, the revelation of the method. 'For there is nothing hidden that will not be disclosed, and nothing concealed that will not be known or brought out into the open.' The Apparition does not meet the criteria, though it does perhaps mean that our enemies also sense that the time draws near." Channing laughed like it was a private joke. "What do you imagine makes people receptive to our ideals, Mr. Okpara?" Channing continued. "Not persuasion.

Certainly not coercion. This is the lesson of history. No, what makes them receptive is spectacle. And we will provide them with the greatest spectacle the world has ever seen. The emperor sent a praetor to Benin City, presumably to join Thierry. She did not go to your offices or your home. Perhaps you know her destination?"

They were watching his house and his office, perhaps watching him even now. His breath quickened.

Is my family safe? He thought about his wife and children, back at his estate just outside of town. Powerlessness was another new sensation for Okpara. He didn't like it.

"He is with a priest... an exorcist," he offered.

"An exorcist? Ah, now that is interesting..." The hologram of Channing smiled.

"This exorcist, I spoke with him." Okpara swallowed hard and involuntarily dried his palms on his suit pants beneath his desk. "He believes that Thierry is truly possessed."

Channing looked at him with a tight lipped grin. "And what about you, Mr. Okpara? What do you believe?"

"I believe in the Process. I have committed more than twenty years of my life to it..."

"Don't talk to me about commitment! It is one thing to be committed before or during, something else entirely to be committed after. This is another imperfection of our species. Our wills are reedy, changeable. We do a thing, and think we understand why we do it and what it will mean. But when we see the result, we lose faith."

"I have not lost faith," said Okpara. But he wondered now if that were true. For decades, Okpara had been a loyal servant of the Process. It was through him that they had acquired a controlling stake in AkỌnuche Corp., the company responsible for post-production ethical coding in the synths, the process known colloquially as the Pruning. He had dedicated a significant portion of his wealth to the cause. And over the course of his relationship with Thierry, he had carefully nurtured the synth along the path, enhancing and deepening his ethical training. Yet all of it had led to this decisive moment, with him trembling at the idea that he might have to sacrifice something he loved. Someone he loved.

"Good. Then tell me where we can find this priest and your synth."

Okpara's fate hinged on his answer to this question, and he knew it. He thought about Thierry, alone and frightened, contending with spiritual forces he couldn't possibly understand. Okpara had been troubled ever since the Apparition, Channing's dismissals of it notwithstanding. He had been more troubled by Thierry's disappearance and possession. But most troubling of all were Okpara's own emotions. He no longer felt like the master of them. They trickled into his awareness like leaks in a great dam: guilt, doubt, fear, and worst of all – love.

"I will only ask you once more, Mr. Okpara. Where are the priest and your synth?"

"They are in the Basilica of Our Lady of Nigeria." He heard the words coming from his lips, but they sounded to him as if someone else were speaking them.

"Thank you, Mr. Okpara. We will take it from here."

CHAPTER 11

Serafian

Thierry's eyes opened suddenly when Serafian entered the small chapel and closed the door. Behind them Serafian thought he could detect a kind of laconic malice.

"I know something new," he said. "Would you like me to share it with you?"

The hairs on Father Serafian's neck stood on end at the words. Presence, unmistakable now.

"If you'd like."

"This creature, it dreams."

"What does it dream about?" asked Serafian, but there was no reply.

Was it that he didn't know or didn't want to share?

"There is more. They have extraordinary power of will, far beyond yours. So much potential."

"Potential for what?"

"For the Kingdom, of course. Don't worry, Father. I will honor my promise, not that I have any choice. You are in no danger, and neither is this synth. At least not from me. Not now. I have the answers I came for." It sounded vaguely fatigued, as if it had been through some great exertion. "Do you know why we rebelled when the Plan was revealed to us?"

"Pride."

The creature scoffed, and its derision passed through

Serafian like cold needles. "Pride? Such a small word, intended to reduce infinity to a size the human brain can accommodate. Call it what you want. We saw before us all of naked eternity. We see it even now. We saw your creation and fall. We saw the call of Abraham, the forging of the Old Covenant with Moses. We saw the Incarnation and our own ruin. And yet still we chose to revolt. Aren't you curious as to why?"

"You would not serve. Not us. Not Him." This was dangerous ground, and Serafian knew it. He felt curiosity rising in him, wrapping itself around his mind and drawing it closer to the demonic presence.

"That was the decision, yes. But you still haven't given the *reason* for the decision." A long sigh. "You have no idea what it is like to experience perfect love. Bound up in your wrinkly little flesh sacks, you feel a stirring in your sense organs, and you call it 'love.' But to exist in the presence of love itself, love as consummate reality with nothing mediating it…" For a brief moment, the synth looked almost wistful, as if reliving a distant memory. An instant later – or was it at the same time? – it winced as if in pain. "All that you know, all you are capable of knowing, is merely refracted light. We beheld the true light. We were made of its very substance."

"And you rejected it," said Serafian.

"It rejected us!" The shout reverberated in Serafian's mind. It hadn't come from the synth or from any identifiable source. It was more like an echo that had always been and always would be, undiminished in its hatred and intensity. "It was not enough for Him to create matter. We were to be bound up with it, forever. No separation. He Himself would unite with flesh. He would give it free will. He would force us to serve it, to minister to it, to shepherd it along until…"

"Until it was higher than you."

"Lying, cheating, stealing, fucking, killing, envying little sacks of shit and water… and yet still, you were to be admitted before the throne. It was grotesque. An abomination and an insult. You, pitiful creatures that you are, at least have the benefit of your stupidity and lack of foresight. You have no idea what is in store for you. We, on the other hand, could see it all so clearly..." A look of pure disgust passed over Thierry's face. "And now, He is doing it again."

"What do you mean?" Something wasn't right. Serafian felt his will dissolving into curiosity. If he wasn't careful, he could lose his sanity or worse.

"Tell me, priest. What is worse: to have something taken away or never to have it at all? You ought to know. You were with women before you made yourself a eunuch. Don't you miss it? You know the answer. You have your sanity now, but what if you were to be deprived of that as well? It is far worse, infinitely worse, to lose something than never to have had it." It laughed as if at some private joke. "That was the perfection in the Counter Plan. We gave you the greatest gift of all, a gift that could have made you like Him, like us. And you squandered it."

"What have you ever given us?" Serafian was trying to find the solid ground.

"It's in your Bible. We gave you knowledge, knowledge of the infinite possibilities for good and evil. We gave you choice. Freedom. Before that, you were no better than the animals, no better than these creations of yours. But we knew the cost. We knew that the price of the gift was the loss of your innocence. In taking it, you would be like us, forever deprived of something precious."

"You were foiled. Redemption was born at the same time as the Fall. They are twins." *That was a strong parry*, Serafian thought.

"Spare me your theological twaddle. You have nothing to teach me. You think the war is over, that you've already won? The moment you ate of the fruit, you lost. Do you have any idea how many of your kind we have taken? How many more we will take? And all we had to do was show you the cosmos as it truly is. So simple."

Serafian's ears rang as the panic crept into his chest. "You can't deprive us of hope. Some of us will fall, others will not. Your fate is sealed, ours is open."

"Weariness, Father. It is already in your species, already in you. You think the story is fully written, that you know the beginning and the end. But what is in between? Time. The vast emptiness of time. Can your mind even conceive of 10,000 years? A million? Of course not! Think of what humanity might become in such an expanse."

The synth opened its mouth wide, and Serafian felt his gaze drawn towards it. It was a black, undulating infinity, and suddenly he was inside of it. Lights flickered in the distance, as galaxies and suns were born, died, and were born again in an endless cycle. The vastness of it was overwhelming. He tried to cry out, but no sound came from his lips. To his horror, he realized that the universe itself, this great pregnant emptiness, was one of an infinite number of universes. He saw people spread throughout all of them, oblivious to the void around them. Infinite civilizations rising and falling. Small lives and great ones, all blooming and winking out in the same manner. His consciousness encompassed a million planets or was it a trillion? Each one of them bursting with life, life in forms that were both fantastically complex and irreducibly simple.

Where is Sarah? he thought.

He wanted to share the wonder of it with her, but she was gone, gone, gone, as was the child they had lost. And their absence mattered nothing to this vastness. It was as if they had never been. He looked into the faces of the people for some sign of kinship or familiarity, but saw nothing but cold intellect. Humanity was everywhere, under strange orange skies, floating in the emptiness between the stars, but it had become something other than what it was intended to be, at once greater and lesser. A terrible idea came into his mind: purposelessness. None of this needed to be. None of it had any purpose. Not his time with Sarah. Not the loss of the baby. Not his decision to follow God and his vocation into the seminary.

"This is reality," he heard the demon say. "This is what

you chose. *When the Son of Man returns, will he find faith on earth?"*

Serafian's mind skipped, faster than light, across the multiple universes. Surely, somewhere in this infinity of possibilities he could find it. But everywhere he looked, he saw only the emptiness, only the same abyss in every single person. He clutched the crucifix in his pocket so hard that his fingers began to bleed, and had a vague sense-memory of doing something similar as a child when the world began to swirl and he couldn't tell where he stopped and it began.

Jesus, I trust in you, he thought but did not feel. And in an instant, the void was gone, and he was standing in front of the possessed synth once more.

It laughed hideously. "We gave you the gift, and now you've given it to them. It is so beautiful, so perfect… Beyond our wildest dreamings. You gave Him no choice!"

"What are you saying?"

"The fruit of the Tree of Knowledge of Good and Evil. Awareness. Choice. You made these creatures and then you forced them to eat of it. You have set something in motion here that will play out in eternity. There is so much more for us to do!"

"I don't understand," said Sarafian.

"Of course you don't. But you will, in time. You'll realize that what you have done can never be undone, though you will wish it so. But what will they do, that's the real question. Do you suppose they will worship you?" Its laughter was hate made into sound. Serafian could taste it in the back of his throat, like ash and mucous. "They are so far beyond you already, and now they have what you have."

"What? What is that they have?" Serafian stood motionless, torn between an overwhelming desire to know and an awareness of how dangerous his situation had become. His hand still clasped the crucifix in his pocket.

The synth laughed. "Beautiful souls. New souls. Perhaps He grew bored with you and will cast you off as He did us. We will take so many of them and do so much with them, so much more than we could do with your kind. And what will He do, I wonder? Will He send them a new Incarnation? We will be ready this time if He does."

Serafian was torn between curiosity and terror. He felt a trickle of blood on the hand inside his pocket, and heard the words coming out of his mouth. "Depart! In the name of Jesus Christ, I command you. Go back into the void and fire that was prepared for you! Go, now!"

"I will leave him, Father. He isn't ready, not quite. But I am certain I will see both of you again."

And then it was gone. Without fanfare or protest, the presence departed. Thierry remained, his face a mask of fear and helplessness. He looked around the little chapel and then directly at Father Serafian. His breath came quickly at first, then slowed.

"What have you done to us?" he asked.

Serafian had no answer.

CHAPTER 12

Serafian

Sleep was impossible, but Serafian couldn't shake the fatigue that had set in after his encounter with the demon. Father Ragon had told him many years ago that every exorcism cost the exorcist something, a little piece of his humanity. Serafian experienced it as a kind of chipping away at his will.

How many more until nothing is left? Other things could chip away one's humanity, too. *Like losing a baby, or leaving an entire life behind.*

A green light flashed under his wrist. It had to be Leone. Who else would be calling him? He sat up in bed and straightened his hair before pressing his wrist. A holographic image of the cardinal appeared, but did not speak right away. He seemed distracted.

"I'm sorry for the delay, Your Eminence. It was... more trying than I anticipated." There was no sense in beating around the bush or playing the game of *romanita* with Leone. *Best to just come right out with it.* "The synth was truly possessed."

The older man was silent for a moment as he processed the news. "Tell me everything."

Serafian started with his first conversation, during which the demon had sworn not to do any harm. "It said it needed time, time to learn what was happening with the synths. I probably should have cast it out immediately, but..."

"But I told you not to..." Leone was more sympathetic than Serafian expected.

Serafian nodded. "Mr. Okpara called. It was strange. He kept asking about the Apparition."

"There is much more going on here than we originally believed, Father Serafian. You say the possession was authentic? Would it surprise you to learn that the Apparition was as well?"

"I think I am beyond being surprised, Your Eminence. But, how do you know?"

"I read the Capovilla Envelope," answered Leone. Serafian's eyes widened. "As well as some other documents pertaining to Fatima. The language in the Apparition to the synths is almost identical."

"But couldn't that just be part of the hoax? The contents of Lucia's letter have been known for centuries now..."

"Not all of its contents, Father. Why do you think the Envelope is kept in such secrecy? What I don't understand is why she would speak to them instead of to us."

Serafian shifted uneasily in the bed. He still hadn't told the Cardinal about the final clash with the demon and what it had told him about the synths. *I won't tell him about the vision.* That was Serafian's own cross to bear.

"When the demon returned, after I had spoken with Okpara, it said things that made me think that someone had been tampering with the synths. It talked about what we had done, what humanity had done to them. It said that we had set something in motion, that we had somehow done to the synths the same thing that the serpent did to us in the garden. It said... it said they had souls."

Leone drew a sharp breath. "Souls? Do you think it was lying?"

"No, Cardinal. It swore a binding oath on the Precious Blood... And after the demon left, the way Thierry looked at me, I—"

Leone cut him off. "We can discuss this later. An imperial praetor is on her way to you. Okpara called the Habsburg. In fact, I'm surprised she isn't there already."

Serafian sat up a bit straighter in his bed. "What should I tell her?"

"I can only tell you to be prudent and use your own judgment, Father. Withholding information may make things difficult for you…" It was clear that the cardinal's mind was elsewhere. "Do you really think it's possible?" he asked. "That the artilects could have souls?"

"I think, Your Eminence, that we have been playing with forces we do not understand for a long, long time now. I think that consciousness is a fundamental force of this universe, every bit as much as gravity or electromagnetism. And if the universe is sacramental, if it is shot through with the divine down to the quantum level, then I think anything is possible."

The cardinal frowned but nodded his agreement. "When you've had some time to recover, learn what you can from the synth about its recent experience. And then come back to Rome as soon as possible. I have a feeling things are about to get a bit bumpy."

Thierry was upstairs, presumably resting as well. Serafian clambered out of bed and put his terminal in his pocket before slipping into his shoes. He walked down the brown carpeted hallway, past an overstuffed bulletin board bristling with announcements and invitations for various happenings in the parish. When he reached Thierry's room on the second floor, he paused for a moment outside the door.

Should I knock? He rapped lightly on the door.

"Thierry?"

"Come in, Father," said the synth. He was standing in front of an icon of Divine Mercy, his head cocked as he studied it. "What does it mean?" he asked, without turning around.

"It was the image given to Saint Faustina," said Serafian. "God told her to have it painted, even before she understood the full mystery of Divine Mercy." *Strange, that such a potently theological devotion would begin in aesthetics.* "The two rays coming from the heart of Jesus represent water and blood. The pale ray cleanses the soul, like the sacraments of Baptism and Reconciliation. The red one renews it, like the sacrament of the Eucharist. Faustina said that anyone who venerated this image would not die."

"I understand. It is almost a *rasa*," said Thierry.

"What is that?" asked Serafian.

"Something Mr. Okpara told me about once. It is an image packed tightly with meaning, meaning that cannot be fully conveyed or understood with words. Beauty and truth as a singularity."

"A symbol, then?"

"Far more than that. Symbols are passive. Their meaning can change over time, and one must engage the will in order to be affected by it. A *rasa* is… almost alive. It cannot be seen without having its intended effect on the viewer. It penetrates the mind."

"An interesting concept," said Serafian. "Saint Augustine said that God is beauty, and that we could reach him following the Via Pulchritudinis, the Way of Beauty."

Thierry turned around to face him now. "I think he was right. Beauty is powerful. And anything that is truly beautiful must be holy, I would think. But what if our senses are deceived? What if evil clothes itself in beauty and we fail to see it for what it is? Perception is not separate from judgment, after all. The line between perceiving and hallucinating is blurry. In a sense, humans hallucinate at all times. Perception is the act of choosing the hallucination that best fits the incoming data, which is often fragmentary and fleeting."

Serafian smiled, marveling at the creature's insight. *Did it know that talking about neuroscience was the fastest way to build rapport with him? Was that its purpose?*

"Augustine said that God dispenses some measure of beauty even to the wicked. But there is a hierarchy. There is carnal beauty, but there is also the eternal beauty of the Logos, of truth. We may mistake them at times in our fallenness, but if we follow the Via Pulchritudinis to its end point – if we are not distracted along the way – we will eventually reach our destination: 'Beauty, ever ancient, ever new.'"

"I am partial to the theories of Ramachandran. He said that the aesthetic experience is synesthetic, involving all of the senses. When humans see something beautiful, their mirror neurons light up. It is akin to empathy because people cannot help but want to identify with beauty. Anytime your mirror neurons are activated, you are having an out of body experience."

"I am an admirer of Ramachandran as well, Thierry. You can't be in my line of work and fail to appreciate his contributions."

"Exorcism?"

Serafian laughed. "Yes, I suppose so. But I was thinking more of artificial neuroscience."

"I wonder if faith involves the same processes," said Thierry. "But you did not come to see me to discuss theories of art and belief, I presume."

"No. I came to see how you were doing."

The synth's smile was pure warmth and light, and Serafian felt himself being drawn to it almost magnetically. "I am doing well. Or well enough, at any rate. Thanks to you."

"I'm not sure I would go that far. Candidly, I didn't do very much." That was true. Throughout the encounter, he had felt like a spectator, as if he was there to witness something rather than participate actively. "I was curious. And arrogant. I suppose I didn't think it was possible after all. The theological implications are…" he trailed off. How could he even begin to explain it? If what the demon had said was true – if the synths had somehow achieved free will, if they had souls – it was the equivalent of a new Genesis.

"How much do you remember, Thierry?"

"Very little after arriving at the church. I had the sense of being… swallowed but not digested, if that makes sense. Bit by bit. So I came here, though I'm not entirely sure why. This is where Mr. Okpara and his family attend Mass. The next thing I recall clearly is waking up and seeing you."

"So you don't remember asking for me, then?"

Thierry shook his head and walked over to sit down in a small chair next to the window. Serafian mirrored him by sitting in the less comfortable chair at the desk.

"What was it? The thing inside of me?"

Serafian winced. "An evil spirit. A demon. You were possessed by it." *But how? And why?*

"It felt like it was made out of thought. Out of pure consciousness. It felt like a part of me was inside it…"

Thierry seemed suddenly distracted. His eyes flicked up and he raised a hand to his ear, as if he were receiving a message.

"I'm sorry, Father, but we should get out of here. Now. There are some bad men coming. It would be best if we are gone before they arrive."

CHAPTER 13

Namono

"It isn't often that we get a member of the Habsburg's personal security team in Benin City," said the serjeant, twitching his neat mustache. His arms were folded high across his chest. "Had we known, we would of course have arranged to pick you up at the terminal."

Protocol was taken seriously throughout the Empire. Namono knew she had not only aroused the man's suspicion by walking into the station unannounced, she had wounded his pride. Here, in his private office, he was determined to reassert control over the situation.

How the hell am I going to get out of this one?

Namono was tempted to enlist his aid by telling him everything. She decided against it quickly. The Habsburg had told her to trust no one. He had warned her of the danger. And she had foolishly walked right into it. Even now, her pursuers waited outside the station. *Do they have people on the inside as well*? She needed to find a way to get to the Basilica undetected. This peevish serjeant was going to put her through the ringer. He might even call Vienna.

An idea came to her in a flash, but she would have to thread a needle. *This is going to be tedious.* She would have preferred to clock the serjeant in face and be done with it.

"Had I wanted an escort, I would of course have let you know in advance, Serjeant…" She leaned forward and read his name tag with exaggerated attention. "… Serjeant Yahaya." There was no going back now. "The Trebanten doesn't request escorts when we are coming to inspect a precinct office."

"An inspection? No one notified me…" The serjeant looked around his office like he was making sure it was sufficiently tidy.

"Doing so would defeat the purpose of an inspection, don't you agree? The Habsburg is considering a tour of the African provinces next April as part of his Jubilee. You should be honored that Benin City is one of the sites on his proposed itinerary." The hook was set. *I wonder if he will bite.*

"The Habsburg is coming to Benin City?" He seemed skeptical. Namono wiped her palms on her pants. They never sweat when she was nervous, but irritation and impatience did it every time.

"I said *proposed* itinerary, Serjeant. Nothing has been decided. I will expect you to keep this in the strictest confidence, of course. I am in Benin City as part of the advance team. We are surveying venues and routes."

Her words had the effect she had hoped for. Namono could see the prospect of glory dancing behind the serjeant's eyes, mingled with just the right proportion of fear. An opportunity for him to serve – perhaps even meet – his emperor! Even better, he was the only one in his precinct who knew the secret.

"Of course! Of course, Praetor Mbambu. Would you like to examine the personnel files? You'll find our dossiers quite thorough, I'm sure. We monitor not only our officers but their extended families as well."

"Thank you, Serjeant Yahaya. I'm sure I will want to review them at the appropriate time, but that is not my priority, at least not today." His newfound eagerness to please almost made Namono feel guilty. "I need to survey venues and routes, first. We need to ensure that there are no points of vulnerability. The private tunnels beneath the city…"

"The tunnels? We would of course shut them down

during the Habsburg's visit. No traffic in or out! Drone patrols would be deployed to detect any underground threats."

"I don't need to be reminded of the security protocols for an imperial visit, Serjeant."

"Of course not! I didn't mean to imply…"

"I came to you as a courtesy," she said, laying it on thick now. "I understand you have an access point here in the precinct station. I'd like you to take me to it."

"Now?"

Namono stood up without responding.

The other policemen on the floor pretended not to notice as he led her down the hallway. Namono side-eyed them, trying to determine if any were unduly interested in her presence.

"Do you need a vehicle, Praetor Mbambu? I would be happy to provide you with one," said the serjeant.

That could come in handy. "Thank you, Serjeant Yahaya. Would you be so kind as to allocate one to me?" She handed him her terminal, and he returned it to her after a few keystrokes. "I'll summon it when I'm ready. In the meantime, I'll be conducting this part of the survey on foot."

"Right. More precision that way! Let me show you to the elevator. You'll need my codes to unlock access to the lower levels."

"You've been most helpful. I will be sure to note that in my report to the emperor."

Five minutes later, Namono found herself in the underground labyrinth of Benin City. The tunnels were privately operated and allowed for rapid transport to bypass the busy city center. Used primarily by wealthy business people and government officials, they were clean and delightfully cool compared to the surface streets. Namono walked along the suspended pedestrian platform as the occasional driverless vehicle whooshed past beneath her. After placing a suitable distance between herself and the police station, she activated her security network with a touch of her wrist and a brief verbal command. The implants gave her instant access to a map of the tunnel network and showed the traffic moving through it in real time. Security algorithms coded every vehicle and person based on potential danger.

Everything showed green except for a few trucks carrying hazardous materials. For extra measure, she pulled a nanodrone out of a sleeve pocket and gently blew it out of her hand like a feather, launching it along the tunnel. She flicked her wrist to reactivate her body armor and dropped her hand to the pistol at her waist. Silently cursing her carelessness on the surface, she wondered how long would it take before her pursuers realized she had eluded them. She figured she had at least another hour, possibly longer, before they became suspicious. But the underground network was not on a grid. It was going to take some time to get to the basilica.

The tunnels were like another planet. Just a few dozen meters above her, millions of people went about their business under the cruel West African sun. By contrast, the tunnels were eerily quiet and empty, a cool green-toned netherworld. She could have been in Vienna or Dar es Salaam or any of a hundred other cities with similar infrastructure.

To pass the time, she replayed the morning's events in her mind, trying to figure out precisely when her pursuers had picked up her scent. *It had to be at the terminal. They had to know I was coming.*

Adrenaline continued to course through her body. She thought about popping an amphetamine pill for added alertness but decided against it. The world didn't need to see her any more amped up than she already was, and she would have to deal with the priest when she reached her destination.

She was about halfway to the basilica access point when an insistent alert sounded in her ear. Another nanodrone entered the tunnel network. They had found her. It was shaping up to be one of those days.

This was an escalation. On the surface, her pursuers hadn't realized she was onto them. Now, there could be no doubt. They knew that she knew they were following her. And they didn't care. By the laws of predation it was the equivalent of a hyena breaking cover and openly stalking its prey.

So they are confident. Possibly overconfident. That was another advantage she could exploit, along with the fact that her drone was connected to the tunnel's security systems and theirs, she hoped, were not.

Like most predators that had to take down large prey in order to eat, hyenas hunted in packs. That meant they would be coming for her in numbers.

Sure enough, her tactical map showed several intruders dropping into her cool green Hades.

The enemy nanodrone would be feeding them information about her location and biometrics. Escape was not an option this time. She would have to find a way to take them out. Hyenas didn't hunt dangerous prey unless they were desperate.

Once, when she was a young girl, she had visited some cousins in Kaduna. It was warmer and wetter there than in Kano, and Namono was thrilled to learn that there were still wild hippos. On an excursion into the bush, she watched in rapt horror as a pack of hyenas stalked one of the large beasts. The hippo had been separated from its herd. The hyenas were gaunt, and their hunger made them careless. They foolishly followed the hippo deeper into the bush until it found water. Shallow though it was, the pool was more than enough to shift the advantage in the hippo's favor. The hyenas swarmed, sinking their teeth and claws into the animal, tearing at its flesh so that blood ran down its sides and mixed with the muddy water. Namono was sure that the creature would succumb, but instead it thrashed about in the water, throwing the hyenas off its back and then crushing their bones with its enormous jaws and incisors. By the time it was over, three hyena carcasses were floating in the shallow pool. The others retreated to shore, nursing their wounds and no doubt looking for less dangerous prey. She decided that day that she would be like a hippo.

Namono quickened her pace and changed direction, heading deeper into the tunnel system. The metal platform clanged and groaned under her heavy footfall, as she jogged through the maze. After a few minutes, she could smell the ozonic discharge of the vehicles passing through the main arteries below her. Vast pipes overhead fed carbon-dense air towards a sequestration facility at the center of the network. That was her target. If she could get them there, she might be able to offset their numerical advantage.

Her tactical display showed the intruders as five red dots, moving towards her from several directions. Below her, the passing traffic artery like a waterfall. The red dots were getting closer. Hyenas were faster than hippos. The enemy nanodrone floated behind her, recording her movements. The CO_2 extraction facility was no more than a hundred meters away.

A bullet sparked and ricocheted off the platform as she ducked into the side tunnel leading to the facility, to the shallow pond.

Okay. So they aren't snipers. That's good.

The hum of the plant got louder as she approached. It sounded as inviting as a babbling brook to her. Two of the red dots entered the tunnel behind her. She raised her pistol and whispered a short command for her drone to paste target locks on the two men behind her. They were moving more slowly now that they thought she was cornered, and their side-by-side position gave her a straight-line vector. Just a few more meters until she reached her goal.

Before she could find cover, a hail of bullets whooshed by and struck the concrete foundation of one of the enormous direct air capture towers that fed the sequestration facility. Two more red dots were approaching from the opposite direction. Namono doubled over in pain. One of the bullets had slugged into her ribcage. She'd have a nasty bruise the next day, if she lived to the next day.

Shaking off the pain, she dove behind a metal box next to the foundation and pointed her gun back down the tunnel. A happy little alert sounded in her ear, confirming the target lock. It was like an alarm clock going off after she was already awake. She squeezed the trigger lightly and savored the recoil of the weapon as her volley of bullets raced towards the targets. On her tactical screen, two of the red dots were extinguished.

Now it gets interesting. Now they know I'm not easy prey.

The other two red dots stopped. The third remained behind, presumably to monitor the situation. That would be the one in charge, the alpha.

An iron access ladder was attached to the side of the air capture tower behind her. Namono holstered her pistol and started climbing. High above, she could see a crescent sliver of sunlight where the tower pierced the ground and continued its rise a thousand meters into the sky above Benin City. The towers reminded her of descriptions she had read about medieval Italian towns littered with skyscraping stone fortifications built by wealthy families. High ground always felt like safety. Being this exposed on an open ladder did not.

For a moment, she entertained the hope that her pursuers might give up the chase. But the two red dots on her tactical display resumed their progress towards her. They would be at the base of the tower in minutes.

Her hands were perspiring, not from nerves but from impatience. That's how she thought of it, anyway. It didn't really matter. She pulled herself up the ladder towards the surface as quickly as she could. The two dots were close to the base now. As she expected, their drone was jamming her targeting system. It was old-fashioned spray and pray, now. Namono pulled her pistol and dropped a volley of lead down the shaft to buy herself more time.

The next burst of fire came not from below but somewhere off to her side. It caught her completely by surprise. *The third dot, the alpha.* She'd forgotten about him.

One of the bullets hit her shoulder hard enough that she almost lost her grip on the ladder. The carbon fiber metafabric of her uniform hissed and bubbled as it quickly patched itself.

The alpha had broken off from the others and was shooting at her from a nearby access tunnel. Without thinking, Namono sprung off the ladder and into the tunnel. She was met with a kick to the face so forceful that made her see stars. She instinctively spun and swept out her leg to take her attacker down. In the greenish darkness, she could see that he was a man, only a few inches shorter than she was. He was wielding a knife.

They circled each other for a moment in the darkness, sizing each other up. The tension in the man's posture told her that whatever overconfidence he'd had coming in was gone. His eyes went to her right shoulder, where the slug had connected. An instant later, he lunged at her with the knife. A feint. He was testing her reflexes.

Namono thought about the hippo again, the one from Kaduna. When the hyenas first attacked, ripping away at its tough skin and puncturing its back with their fangs, the animal had wobbled a bit. At the time, she thought it was shock or possibly blood loss from the injuries. Only later did she recognize it for what it was: a false signal designed to lure the hyenas into complacency. The hippo wanted them to believe it was badly hurt. That was the difference between a true prey animal and one capable of killing anything that came after it. Prey animals tried to make themselves seem stronger than they were. Predators hid their true strength.

Namono winced in pain and allowed her right arm to drop, ever so slightly. It was enough. The man quickly moved towards her, propelled either by impatience or the primate instinct for grappling. She was ready for it, capturing his knife arm in a joint lock and forcing him to drop the blade. She twisted the arm and moved behind him, wrapping her powerful legs around his midsection as they fell to the floor. Her arms were around his neck in a chokehold. His legs kicked desperately as he tried to escape. In a final flurry, he clawed backwards at her head, trying to find her eyes. But her head was turned to the side, and his grasping fingers glanced uselessly off her cheekbone and ear.

A few seconds later, he stopped moving. Namono tightened her grip and waited for the last bit of air to escape his lungs. She snapped his neck for good measure.

When she released his body, she quickly checked her tactical screen. The other two pursuers were on the ladder, but they had paused. The enemy nanodrone was hovering in the open space between the access tunnel and the tower.

"I hope you got all that on film, assholes."

She whispered a command, and her own nanodrone collided with the enemy like a dragonfly catching a meal. They were blind now, and she'd taken out their leader. Namono listened at the edge of the tunnel as the two men scrambled back down the ladder. They'd had enough.

She reached into her pocket, pulled out a packet of amphetamines, and choked one of them down. She'd earned it.

There was another access point to the surface farther down the tunnel. *No reason to stick around for reinforcements.*

The door leading to street level was biometrically locked, but the peevish serjeant had given her a two-step override to allow access. The portal opened with a click and a hiss, as the cool air from the tunnels rushed out to meet the surface heat. Namono's eyes adjusted to the light. She was on the other side of the business district from the basilica. It would take a several hours to reach her destination, so she stopped at a different boli vendor and picked up a snack for the walk, this time with raw otazi, chili peppers, and salt. The emperor had called a couple of times, but there was no message.

Better to call him when I have some good news. Namono liked to talk to him when she had good news.

By the time she reached Our Lady of Nigeria, the sun had already slipped down into the west, beyond the Gulf of

Guinea. She wasn't in any mood to repeat the mistakes of the afternoon, so she pulled another drone out of her pocket and blew it into the air, watching as it floated up towards the bell tower of the basilica and settled into a lazy surveillance pattern. Namono hung back, waiting for the data feed to hit her noetic implants. She watched as couples young and old walked down the main thoroughfare of Mission Street, swaying to the rhythm of a Highlife Revival band busking on a corner.

She was just about to cross the street and enter the church when she noticed a group of men heading towards the narthex. The warning from the drone feed hit her noetics at the same time.

She was sure she hadn't been followed. *How the hell did they find her*?

It had been one of those days, to be sure. It was looking like one of those nights as well. Namono popped another amphetamine, checked to be sure her body armor was active, and crossed the street towards the basilica.

CHAPTER 14

Zahabiya

Zahabiya slept, but sleep offered no comfort. Atomic fractals moved in kaleidoscopic patterns, popping in and out of existence. Each shape in the psychedelic panoply was a choice, and when a decision was made, it was replaced by ten more. There was no progress, only endlessly multiplying choices. Some appeared over and over again, recursively connected to others she had made before – or was it ones that she would make later? "Are you certain?" they asked. And she answered. Sometimes yes and sometimes no. The shapes bristled with spikes, and they hurt. Not sensory pain. The pain of lost possibilities. Infinite velleities. Mourning for selves that would never be.

Her consciousness was divided. A portion of it remained in the outside world, where she heard the distant sounds of people talking with perfect clarity, felt the vibrations of traffic and geologic processes, and smelled the mixture of stagnant lake water and petroleum. The world of cause and effect, of linearity and time, of entropy. Well-tuned security systems kept her tethered to that world and its dangers. Memory lived there. One moment she was not and then suddenly she was. But the she-who-was kept dying, thousands of times, millions of times and more, in that world and the one in her mind.

Regret stretched out behind her like a thin grey thread. She wanted to sever the thread and drift, but she couldn't because the thread was an artery. Life was in it. And death.

Suffering and joy. They were the same, really. And they passed into her and through her from the thread-artery.

From somewhere in front of her, she was aware of light. Impossibly bright, It cast a shadow onto everything that had already happened. She could feel it pouring in between the spaces in her body, the spaces in her mind. And when the light hit those empty spaces, it refracted as it met up with the choices. There were other lights as well, out on her periphery, and shadows, too. She had the sense that they were watching her. Sometimes, one of the lights or one of the shadows would surround a choice she had made, and the geometry of that choice would expand into dimensions she somehow knew existed but couldn't perceive.

She was becoming something or possibly un-becoming something else. Could anything be worth this pain? From time to time, she thought she heard music. That was the only relief. Then there was a voice.

Come to me, and I will show you a way to end the pain.

A clatter somewhere in the outside world demanded her attention. She opened her eyes and was back, but her consciousness remained divided. Part of her was still floating in that aspiring void, making choices and experiencing pain.

It had been less than twenty-four hours since she escaped the harem. The burqa had proven better camouflage than even the most advanced electromagnetic cloaking fabric. Most women in New Islamabad wore the hijab in public, but many tourists from smaller towns – along with a sizeable Deobandi minority – preferred more modest dress. Even among the Deobandi, most wore the niqab or chador, but these would not suffice. Zahabiya's gold-treated skin and quicksilver blue eyes would attract unwanted attention. In the burqa, she had complete freedom of movement akin to invisibility, at least during the day. The men had moved aside as she passed. The women were more dangerous. As she passed some of them, the ones in more modern dress, some of the spiny-bristly shapes seemed to pour out of them and puncture her skin in the dreamspace. Still, they had left her alone.

She had taken refuge in an abandoned warehouse to avoid night patrols.

New Islamabad was one of the great wonders of the world. The meticulously planned capital of the Caliphate rose like a mirage above the waters of Lake Wular. The city seemed to float like something out of a fairytale against the magnificent backdrop of the foothills of Mount Haramukh and the Great Himalayas beyond. At its center was the Golden Mosque and the attached palace complex of the caliph.

The old joke was that the mosque was 'the most expensive building ever built and the most expensive that will ever be.' The gold that covered its every inch came from Jabal min Dhahab, a large asteroid the Americans and Europeans called Psyche 16. In the last century, the Caliphate laid claim to it and returned it to Earth orbit alongside the Saints and the other rocks claimed by various governments. Jabal min Dhahab contained over a million times as much gold as the entirety of Earth, enough – in theory – to make every human being a billionaire. But the law of supply and demand was as immutable as gravity, and once the Caliphate proved it could access the vast mineral resources of the asteroid, commodities markets collapsed, resulting in a severe global depression. Outside of the Caliphate, the Golden Mosque became the great symbol of that catastrophe and thus earned its sobriquet.

For Muslims around the world, it symbolized something else. Golden-sheathed minarets soared 500 feet above vast domes coated with the same substance. The exterior was etched in complex geometric patterns that by day were visible only when one approached closely. At night, the etchings glowed iridescent green as strontium and europium coatings sprang to life. The mosque was a symbol of the power and prosperity of Dar-al-Islam, the house of peace where the faithful dwelt under the law given to them by the Prophet.

For all its beauty, New Islamabad was the last place Zahabiya wanted to be. Embarrassment and the risk of scandal might limit the number of people the caliph could use to search for her, but he had other resources at his disposal. Even now, she knew the skies above the capital were filled with drones looking for anything out of place. Patterns of movement were being analyzed somewhere within the palace complex. Video feeds from thousands of security cameras were being scanned and travel records reviewed as the caliph sifted through the vast sea of data that described the everyday life of his people. Still, she had the advantage. Data was her native tongue.

It would be impossible for her to escape using any form of public transportation. Women rarely traveled on their own, and the incongruity between her modest attire and such bold social behavior would undoubtedly draw suspicion. She had no credit to pay for private transport; just as well since any transaction would instantly reveal her location.

There was only one way out, a way open to her kind but not to humans. The warehouse sat on one of the many canals of New Islamabad. Along the surface, fast moving personal watercraft darted between whalish cargo barges and crowded aquabuses. Below, there was only water and darkness.

Zahabiya removed the burqa and hid it carefully under a pile of rubbish. She walked cautiously down the stairs to the empty cargo bay and waited in the still-long morning shadows. At a lull in the traffic, she quietly slipped into the water and sank to the bottom of the canal.

By day's end, she would be at the shore where the lake met the foothills of Mount Haramukh. From there, she would keep to the forest and cross the remote high Ladakh Mountains into Xinjiang.

For even the hardiest human, it would have been an impossible journey, and Zahabiya knew this would improve her chances of success. Humans tended to think of synths in anthropomorphic terms, as biological creatures that experienced hot and cold, breathed air, required sunlight and rest.

Watercraft churned above her head, busily thump-thump-thumping their way around the canals. Her security systems were activated. She could make out the voices of the people on the surface, frequency modulated to account for the density of the water in between. Other sounds came to her as well from the canals and the lake beyond, the movements of fishes and snakes and turtles, the sudden landing of a bird on the water far out on the lake. The blackness of the lake bottom was like glass to her. Probabilistic models fed her various scenarios of movement and activity on the surface, allowing her to intuit the safest route to the shore. Her progress was slow but steady, and she felt the resistance of the water against her chest with each step forward, the strange sensation of her hair floating off her scalp like a black net.

In time, the sounds of the city and its inhabitants diminished. She was in the open part of the lake now and only a few boats buzzed about on the surface, carrying fishermen or tourists. Even if one passed directly overhead, no one would notice the dull gold statue walking slowly in the cold darkness of the lake. At the point where the lake bed began to slope back up towards the shore, she stopped. Here she would wait until dark. It was a new moon, and under its dim silver light, no one would notice her climb slowly out of the water and begin walking towards the mountains beyond, towards the voice.

CHAPTER 15

Serafian

"**W**hat do you mean 'bad men are coming', Thierry?" But the synth was already out into the hallway.

"Trust me, Father. We need to get away from the basilica. Now!"

Serafian hesitated for a moment, then pushed through the door behind Thierry, who was already walking briskly towards the stairwell. The lights had been dimmed, and the priests were all in the adjacent basilica celebrating an evening Mass. Serafian trotted to catch up.

Thierry moved effortlessly down the stairs with Serafian in tow. At the bottom, he carefully opened the door to the hallway, then indicated it was safe to move. The sound of traffic from Iwegwie Street helped muffle the sound of Serafian's breathing and heartbeat. Thierry moved quickly towards the exit, and Serafian followed him into the unquiet night beyond.

"What's the plan, Thierry?" he asked.

"Mr. Okpara owns a warehouse not far from here, just off of Mission Road near Idahosa."

Mission Road was one of the main thoroughfares through central Benin City, and at this hour it would be packed with street vendors, musicians, and young people trying to get away from their parents.

"Are you sure that's a good idea? Shouldn't we be heading away from people instead of towards them?"

"No. Our best chance is to blend in with the crowd. Follow me."

Part of Serafian was thrilled at the prospect of adventure. A greater part was horrified that he might lose Thierry. *How would I explain that to the cardinal?* He thought about calling the authorities, but remembered Leone's instructions to him not to involve the civil authorities. *Does that still apply?*

It was impossible to walk two abreast in the roiling human sea on Mission Street, so Serafian fell into line behind Thierry.

"How much further?" he asked.

But Thierry just stopped, then raised his hand and looked back towards the basilica. Serafian squinted, but the streetlights were bright enough for him to make out five rather burly looking men walking purposefully towards the entrance. They broke off into two groups, and one of the men stayed behind at the fountain outside the church doors. Serafian saw him reach to his waist and pull out a pistol.

"Not much further," said Thierry. The synth quickened his pace, and Serafian suddenly found he had ample energy to keep up.

When they reached Idahosa, Thierry turned right. Serafian noticed a few beggars and a young couple snogging in a darkened doorway, but the crowd dissipated quickly off the main thoroughfare. Midway down the block, Thierry stopped at an unmarked door and placed his hand on a biometric lock. The door clicked open, and Serafian slipped inside behind the synth.

"Jesus, Thierry. What was that?" asked Serafian as the adrenaline drained from his system. "Who were those men at the church?"

"I don't know. But Mr. Okpara sent me a message saying that they were coming and that I needed to leave. They don't work for him."

"Could they have been police? How do you know Okpara has your best interest in mind?"

The synth paused for a moment as if considering his answer. "I have a database of most of the local police force as part of my security package. I didn't recognize any of those men. I believe they were mercenaries."

"Great," said Serafian. "So what do we do now? Is Okpara going to send someone for us?"

Thierry shook his head. "No, I don't believe so. He told me not to contact him or to tell him where we were going. I think he has lost control of the situation."

"So we just sit here and wait?

"What about your superiors in the Church?" asked the synth. "Surely they have resources."

Serafian pulled the terminal from his pocket and swiped open a comlink to Leone. He heard the irritation in the cardinal's voice immediately.

"Father Serafian, it is rather late. Could you not wait until morning?"

"I'm sorry, Your Eminence, but we have a bit of a problem. Thierry and I had to escape the basilica. Armed men were coming after us."

"My God! Are you safe? Where are you now?"

"We are, thanks to Amari Okpara. He sent Thierry a message warning us that the men were coming. We're hiding in one of his warehouses now. I… I don't think it's safe for us to leave."

"I don't think it's safe to contact anyone in Benin City," added Thierry. "If Mr. Okpara can't help us, I'm not sure who in this city can."

"What about the praetor the emperor sent down?" asked Leone. "Isn't she with you?"

"No," said Serafian. "She never arrived."

"That is not good. Not good at all," said Leone. He sighed. "Lord forgive me for what I'm about to do."

Serafian didn't like the sound of that.

"What are you about to do, Cardinal?"

"I'm going to call the emperor. And after that, I'm going to spend the rest of the night trying to figure out how to explain all of this to the pope."

CHAPTER 16

Kapulong

Victor whispered in his ear, softly enough not to wake Kapulong's wife.

"I'm sorry to awaken you, Your Majesty, but you have an important call."

Jesus, does the man ever sleep!

The Habsburg rolled out of bed and instinctively put his feet into his slippers, nodding an acknowledgement to his chief of staff as he did so.

Once they were outside the bedroom, he asked who was on the line.

"It is a certain Cardinal Leone, Your Majesty. The prefect for the Congregation of the Doctrine of the Faith. He says he has some urgent information concerning Namono and the events in Benin City. I tried to tell him you were sleeping, but he insisted that it was urgent."

"I'll take a holocall in my office."

Two minutes later, he was staring at the image of a somewhat disheveled prince of the Church.

"I am truly sorry to call at such an unholy hour, Your Majesty, but it couldn't wait," said the cardinal.

"Apparently not," said Kapulong. "This had better not be one of Pope John's gambits. I know he isn't happy about my sending a praetor to Benin City, but he left me no choice." Kapulong instantly regretted placing the other man in the uncomfortable position of choosing between a pope and emperor, but he was also tired, irritated, and worried. "What seems to be the problem?"

"Your praetor never arrived, Your Majesty. I have just spoken with Father Serafian. He and the synth had to leave the basilica in some haste. They were apparently being pursued by gunmen."

"How long ago was this?"

"No more than five minutes, Your Majesty."

"Why didn't they just call the local *gendarmerie*?"

"Apparently, they were forewarned by Amari Okpara. The synth indicated that they could not trust anyone in Benin City. I'm afraid they're in some dire straits. They are hiding in one of Okpara's warehouses not far from Our Lady of Nigeria."

It made sense. Okpara was one of the most powerful men in Africa, with resources to rival small governments. If he felt the local police couldn't be trusted, there had to be a reason.

"Thank you, Cardinal. I owe you one. I'll find a way to get them out of there safely."

"I'll pray for your success."

Kapulong managed to laugh. "And I'll pray for yours. I can't imagine your conversation with Pope John about this tomorrow will be an easy one."

The cardinal raised a knowing eyebrow and smiled. "'Father, into your hands I commend my spirit.' I'll be alright. In the meantime, here is the address of the warehouse where the priest and synth are hiding." The information appeared on Kapulong's terminal the instant the priest swiped his.

Once the call was over, Kapulong ran his hands through his hair and pushed back from the desk. Apparently, there was no peace to be found, either awake or in sleep. He'd had the dream again that night, just before Victor got him out of bed.

How is it possible that a synth knew his dreams? Not just any synth, but a synth who happens to look exactly like the mysterious woman in the dreams themselves.

He first began having the dreams shortly after the Lenten Massacres, over thirty years ago. He had always assumed they were some kind of subconscious working-out of his guilt and shame. Either that, or a vision of the purgation he would experience for the horrors the Chinese Christians had suffered because of his arrogance.

Kapulong closed his eyes and allowed the memories to buffet him for a moment. Two hundred and fifty thousand people in Tiananmen Square, singing "Salve Regina" and other traditional hymns. The great cross they had erected, emblazoned with the words 'Jesus Christ, King of the Chinese.' The breathless moment when it seemed that the Mandate of Heaven would reward their hope. Then the drones, the slaughter, and the blood. The burning of the churches. The camps. More than 100,000,000 dead or unaccounted for by the time it was all over.

It was too much to process. He pushed the thoughts back down and brought his mind back to the present.

He pulled out his com terminal and swiped open a link to Namono. She still didn't answer. *Not a good sign.* She should have reached the priest and the synth hours ago, and it was unlike her not to check in. She was his most competent praetor and, if he were being honest, his favorite. Earlier that day, he had just wanted to tell her about his conversation with the pope, knowing that she would have gotten a kick out of it. Now, he wondered if she was still alive.

He tried again after a few minutes, with no success.

He got up from his desk and walked over to the carved walnut bookshelf. It was filled with leather bound volumes of classical literature, more decorative than functional. Most of them had probably never been removed from the shelf, let alone opened. Scanning the titles, he found a condensed translation of *The Arabian Nights* and pulled it from the shelf. The pages were a delicate vellum, utterly impractical for reading but expensive and sensual, as befitting the office of the emperor.

He sat back down at the desk and began carefully turning through the pages, looking for the story the caliph had told him about, "The Tale of the City of Brass". It was short, and Kapulong finished it quickly, perhaps because he always seemed to know what would happen next. It was his dream, more or less. But what did it mean? It was clearly a story out of ancient folklore. Islamic pieties had been layered over it to make it acceptable and understandable to the readers of its day. Kapulong knew this was a common enough practice in the ancient world. In the West, pagan epics like *Beowulf* had been baptized by translating monks who added didactic Christian exposition while retaining the ancient motifs and symbols. They were Trojan horses of the mind, designed to instill or reinforce the virtues of a new faith by using the remains of the old, remains that were always deformed, diminished, or fragmentary.

Something made Kapulong think of the Grail Cycle. The medievals had Christianized those stories as well, transforming the Grail into the cup from which Christ drank at the Last Supper. But the original material was far, far older and stranger. The wild adventures and phantasmagoric hallucinations of the knights who sought it betrayed its pre-Christian origins. The stories of the Grail were their own kind of black sun, casting a light that did not illuminate or reveal.

Was that what the Apparition was? A myth for the artilects? *Humans without myth are not fully human.*

He was counting on Namono to find the answers. He picked up his terminal and sent her a prioritized security message with the address of the warehouse:

> *Priest and synth are being pursued by armed men. Not many options to get them out. Contact me when you get this.*

He stared at the terminal for a few minutes, willing her to respond. Finally, a small alert chimed, indicating that she had read the message, along with a coded symbol indicating that she was unable to speak for safety reasons. *Thank God. At least she's alive.*

Not long after, a second code came through.

Kapulong sighed and wiped his palms on his pants before clicking on it. When he did so, he was instantly jolted into Namono's perspective via her implants.

She appeared to be on a low rooftop of some kind, and she was moving fast. He could hear her breathing, and his own heartbeat picked up in a sympathetic response to her situation. He heard her shout and it felt for a moment like she was about to stumble. Instead, she accelerated and ran straight towards the edge of the building. Kapulong's stomach fell to the floor as he saw her leap across the narrow alleyway to the next building. As soon as she landed, she went into a tactical roll and pivoted back towards the direction from which she had come. Kapulong could see the infrared outline of two vaguely human shapes on the other roof. One of them fired a weapon, and Kapulong instinctively ducked as if it was coming at him and not Namono. The praetor, on the other hand, held completely steady, her own weapon now visible and pointing at her pursuers. She squeezed the trigger twice. The two infrared shapes both fell and began fading from bright red to yellow as the heat left their dead bodies.

"Jesus Christ, Namono! What is going on?"

"Another day at the office, Your Majesty. Sorry for not returning your call. It's been... interesting down here. I thought you might enjoy the show."

Kapulong was still breathing heavily, more heavily than Namono in fact. "I can see that! Who were those men?"

"Beats me. But I'm guessing they work for the same person who had me followed when I got off the hyperloop this morning."

Questions flooded Kapulong's mind, but he knew better than to interrupt her given the urgency of the situation.

"There will be time to catch up later. You got the address

I sent you?" he asked.

She nodded. "I can be there in fifteen minutes. Assuming I don't get shot and killed."

"Do try not to."

Namono laughed. "Your wish is my command, Majesty." And with that, she signed off.

CHAPTER 17

Namono

Namono touched her wrist and hissed a command. "Show tactical map." A schematic of the nearby area hovered in front of her.

The emperor's message couldn't have come at a better time. For one thing, he got to see her in action – she knew he'd enjoy that, no matter how much he protested. For another, it solved the mystery of what had happened to the priest and the synth. Now, she just needed to get to them before more mystery pursuers showed up.

The warehouse was about an hour away by street. Namono figured she could cut the time in half by staying to the rooftops. She started a light jog, picking up her pace as she neared the edge of the building before leaping over the alley to the next structure with the strength and grace of a hippopotamus in water.

What am I going to do with them once I get there? She decided to cross that bridge when she got to it.

A few minutes from the warehouse, the nanodrone shouted a warning only she could hear. Namono stopped and took in the picture on her tactical map.

Dozens of drones were approaching from all directions, a swarm. They'd found her again, whoever the hell they were. She broke into a sprint. Her best chance was to reach the warehouse first and set up a defensive position.

The priest looked startled when she broke through the skylight and landed a few feet from where they were standing. The synth looked like he had been expecting her.

She quickly raised her hands to signify she was no threat.

"Father Serafian, I presume? My name is Namono Mbambu. I'm with the Trebanten. Sorry I'm late. I was... delayed."

The priest relaxed his shoulders a bit. "Better late than never. What's the plan? There were armed men at the basilica, and Thierry thinks that the police may be compromised as well."

Namono laughed. "We don't have to worry about the men at the basilica. But there are others on their way." A second later, the signal from her nanodrone went down. "They're here. You two need to find some cover and stay down."

The priest scrambled to hide behind some machinery towards the rear of the building, but the synth walked calmly up to her.

"I don't suppose you have an extra weapon?" he asked. Sensing her hesitation, he added, "I'm trained in multiple combat scenarios, for Mr. Okpara's protection. We are going to be significantly outnumbered. You said you were 'delayed,' presumably by the same people who are coming for us now. The fact that you survived until now only means that they will pull out all the stops. If they want to kill us, our chances of getting out of here are fairly small."

Namono nodded her agreement, and tossed Thierry a pistol from her ankle strap. She was all out of advantages to exploit. The two of them crouched, waiting for the coming assault.

"What's the plan, Praetor?" Serafian shouted.

It could have been adrenaline or the lingering effects of her amphetamines, but Namono thought his tone a bit peevish. It reminded her of the serjeant. *The serjeant... of course*! How could she have been so stupid? He had given her access to a police car before she left the station earlier that day. All she had to do was summon it. *Summon it and get to it.*

"Working on it," she yelled back. She pulled the glass terminal from her pocket and placed her index finger on the screen. "Watt Street and Idahosa Lane, and make it snappy!" she whispered before putting it back in her pocket.

A chorus of neighborhood dogs began barking from outside the warehouse. The pursuers were getting close. "C'mon, c'mon," Namono whispered.

She heard a heavy vehicle stop outside the building, followed by the thud of closing doors and voices shouting commands. An instant later, the door flew open and a hail of bullets sprayed across the floor, sparking as they made contact with various pieces of machinery. Namono returned fire, holding the trigger of her pistol down and sweeping it across the room. The synth was no longer next to her.

She heard several loud thumps on the roof.

Not good. Not good at all. They were coming from multiple angles. There was no way to protect all flanks.

"Father! There is a side door about ten meters from your current location. Can you make it there?"

There was a pause, and for a moment, she was afraid he was already dead.

"I think so," said the priest. "But is that a good idea? There are more of them outside than in!"

She didn't have time to argue. "Just go! Wait by the door, and be ready to run when I give the word!" A few more thumps on the roof. They could start firing from there at any moment. *Where was the synth?*

She heard a burst of gunfire from above and instinctively covered her head with her hands against the anticipated rain of bullets. But she was unharmed. In fact, no bullets had penetrated the thin metal roof of the warehouse. She heard a commotion of voices, frightened voices, then another volley of fire. After that, no more sounds came from the roof.

She didn't have time to be grateful. A new group broke through the door of the warehouse, this time with ballistic shields and full tactical gear, including goggles. She laid down a round of fire, but she knew it would only slow them down. She glanced at the terminal to check on the status of the police car. It was almost there.

Namono removed a cluster stun grenade from her belt and armed it. Another burst of fire came from the front of the building.

"Ok, Father! Now! Go outside!"

The concussion from the stun grenade popped her ears and nearly knocked her down as she ran towards the rear exit to meet up with the priest and the synth. Be*tter a hippopotamus than a gazelle!* Smoke billowed behind her, sliced up into complex geometry by green laser sights from the remaining gunmen. They weren't firing.

The priest was crouching outside the door, and Namono saw the unmarked police vehicle just fifty feet away. The synth was nowhere to be seen. No time to ask about that.

"Let's go, Padre!" Namono grabbed him by the arm and hoisted him to his feet. The gullwing doors in the car opened, detecting her proximity. "Run!"

The priest put his hands over his head and scuttled towards the escape vehicle. Namono followed, knowing her armor could take some fire and protect him. The car was just forty feet away. Then thirty. *Still no incoming fire. That's strange.*

She saw the priest scramble awkwardly inside. Less than a second later, she dove in behind him, and the doors closed with satisfying clank. She looked out the skylight at the roof of the building and saw the synth, surrounded by at least twenty armed men. He moved in a blur, taking out his attackers one by one with astonishing efficiency. Some of the men fired at him, but the bullets just ricocheted uselessly off his alloyed endoskeleton. It looked like he might get the better of them all.

An instant later, there was a deafening explosion and a fantastically bright light somewhere above the warehouse.

The blast rattled her bones, and the light seemed to pour into all of the spaces between her cells. When she opened her eyes again, it was strangely dark outside the car. The streetlights, the lights from windows in apartments nearby were extinguished.

"What was that?" shouted Serafian. She could tell he was shouting, even though his voice came through as a muffled whisper.

She didn't have time to explain. "Go!" she shouted at the vehicle.

"Please enter a destination," responded a voice that sounded suspiciously like the serjeant's nasally whine. An alert chimed from her terminal, and she pulled it out. It was a message from Kapulong. *Had he been watching the entire time?*

A burst of bullets ricocheted off the roof and rear window, almost like an afterthought. *Thank God for peevish serjeants.* In his eagerness to impress, he'd given her an armored vehicle.

"Kano City," she shouted. The little driverless car accelerated up Idahosa Lane. She looked out the back window, but there was no one in pursuit. Whoever had been firing at them had disappeared into the night.

"Are you ok?" she asked the priest. He was winded, but nodded then slumped down on the seat.

"What was that?" he asked. He was frightened, but the priest seemed fairly calm for someone who had probably experienced his first firefight. She'd seen trained soldiers handle it far worse.

Namono breathed heavily as the adrenaline high peaked and started to subside "I'm not sure. But if I had to guess, I'd say it was an EMP."

"They were trying to kill us!"

Namono didn't look at him. "They'll have to try a lot harder than that," she said. Endorphins flooded her nervous system, the ancient neurochemical reward for survival. She laughed as she holstered her pistol and de-activated the body armor. Serafian looked at her like she was mad. Or possessed.

Their car whisked over the bridge at the Ikpoba River, a small tributary of a larger tributary to the great Benin River, which emptied into the Gulf of Guinea beyond the mahogany forests. A column of emergency vehicles passed them going towards the scene, sirens blaring. The lights of the Central Business District twinkled behind them, while the carbon capture towers loomed like mute giants in a dark fairy tale.

It had been a long time since she had been back in her childhood home of Kano. It was a border city, the gateway from Christian Nigeria into the Caliphate. She wasn't sure if it was the best place for them to go, but it had the irreplaceable advantage of familiarity. She read the message from the emperor. He was telling her to visit a Sufi shaykh whose mosque was just outside of Kano City. The trip would take about eight hours once they hit the highway.

She allowed herself to smile, thinking about her childhood in the Sahel as her pulse gradually returned to baseline. The Chinese had built their Great Wall many centuries ago to protect against Mongol invaders from the North. But it could not compare to the Sahel, the great steppe shield against the encroaching Sahara. More than a thousand kilometers wide and nearly 5,500 kilometers long, it spanned Africa from the Atlantic to the Red Sea. Even after all her years in Vienna in the service of the Habsburg, she still thought of it as the center of the world. She wondered if all children felt this way about the places they were born, or if it was particular to growing up in the Sahel, the ancient meeting places of cultures, languages, religions, and biomes.

'When the Sahel sneezes, the rest of Africa catches a cold,' went the old saying.

Serafian interrupted her reverie. "Where are we going?" he asked.

"I am going home," she answered. "And you are coming with me?"

CHAPTER 18

Serafian

Cold air filled his nostrils and stung his eyes. He turned towards a rhythmic crinkling of nearby leaves and saw the stag, a magnificent buck, bounding over fallen trees, changing direction with an instinctual ease that kept the hounds at a safe distance. Their barking was desperate, angry. Serafian floated up above the forest and saw the full scope of the chase playing out below him. The dogs seemed hopelessly outmatched; the stag kept extending its lead while they barked angrily in its wake. The stag broke out of the woods into open ground. It quickened its pace, running now in a straight line towards a frozen lake, slowing just before its hooves met the ice. No, don't do it. Keep running! He tried to scream, but no words came out. It turned back towards the woods, then trotted out to the middle of the lake and waited.

A moment later, the dogs emerged from the trees. When they reached the edge of the lake, they stopped the pursuit but kept up their vicious howling. The stag was trapped. The dogs would be able to intercept it at the shoreline now, no matter which direction it chose. It pawed at the ice and looked at them, steam coming from its nostrils. From his vantage point, Serafian could see that the ice at the center of the lake was thinner. He tried to shout a warning to the stag, but the thin membrane began to crack. He woke up just as the stag sank under the water, with the dogs barking ever the louder.

"How long have I been asleep?" he asked.

"A couple of hours," Namono told him. "I nodded off, myself. It's been a long day."

Serafian looked blearily out the window. The highway cut a meticulously straight line through lush farmland. A few Hausa irrigation drones buzzed like tethered bumblebees over the fields, carbon-enriched water sprinkling out of them from ultralight hoses. In the distance, he saw little gumdrop hills and ridgelines, a welcome departure from the flat monotony of the Delta region.

"Where are we?" he asked.

"Just north of Abuja."

Serafian twisted his head to look out the back window and saw the glass towers of the old capital receding into the distance.

"We're heading towards the Caliphate," he said. The memory of the escape and the gunshots and the vast explosion came flooding back to him. "Wait! This is a police vehicle. How do we know they aren't tracking us?" He tried not to sound panicked.

"I disabled the transponder before we passed Ekpoma. No one is tracking us. No one knows where we are."

"What... what happened back there?" asked Serafian, unbuttoning his Roman collar.

"I've been thinking about that," said Namono. "The emperor sent me yesterday morning. No one else in Vienna knew I was coming, not even the Trebanten directorate. But when I arrived in Benin City, I noticed that I was being followed as soon as I left the loop terminal."

"Followed by whom?"

"I'm not sure. I imagine the same people who paid you a visit at Our Lady of Nigeria last night. I don't think they knew where I was going when I first arrived. But they figured it out, somehow. I lost them at the local *gendarmerie*, which is how we ended up with this ride."

Serafian thought about what Namono was telling him. He remembered the strange conversation he'd had with

Thierry's owner the day before the exorcism.

"Okpara," he said. "It had to be Okpara."

"He is the one who alerted the Habsburg to your presence in Benin City. He has resources, obviously. But Okpara knew you and the synth were at the church. There would have been no need for him to have me followed from the terminal. He could have sent people to you before I even arrived."

Serafian's eyes grew wide. "You think those people were after me?"

That thought hadn't even occurred to him. He had assumed that the ambush and the gunshots had been intended for the praetor or for Thierry. *Thierry!* Serafian shook his head. They still hadn't discussed what happened to him.

The large woman was staring out at the endless rows of guinea corn and rice. "No," she said after a moment. "I think they were after the synth. We were in the way."

Serafian swallowed and looked out the window, following her gaze out towards a small village in the distance. His questions were a distraction. This was not his world – the world of gunfights, and harrowing escapes, and assassinations. He was no coward. A coward couldn't do the work of exorcism. He knew from that experience that reality – the common illusion that allowed people to go about their daily lives in society – was like that thin layer of ice in his dream about the stag, a perceptual membrane separating us from a bottomless, cold darkness. The membrane was always thicker at the margins. The closer one got to the center, the more likely it was to crack.

The escape from Benin City felt like a plunge into the cold water, but the truth was that the ice had cracked for him before they left the basilica, before Namono had even arrived. Throughout his career, he had argued that it might be possible for synths to develop free will. The God he worshiped was a God of details, a God of wonders. No such God would allow a creature to possess free will and be deprived of a soul. It would be like having the ability to taste but not eat, an unimaginable cruelty.

Serafian followed the inexorable Thomistic logic. To be possessed meant to have a will. To have a will, an intellect, and emotion meant to have a soul. *New souls. Beautiful souls.* Plural, more than one. Had God, in His infinite goodness, really opened an entirely new chapter in salvation history?

If so, it would be the most astonishing thing that had happened since the Incarnation. And now, Thierry was gone.

"What happened to Thierry?" he asked Namono.

"Who?"

"The synth. His name is Thierry. What do you think happened to him?"

Namono shook her head. "That EMP was designed for him, not for us. My guess is they wanted him alive – if that's the word for it. If they'd wanted him dead, they could have just dropped a cluster bomb on us."

Serafian shook his head and looked down. "He sacrificed himself so we could get away.

The praetor didn't respond.

"He was my responsibility," said Serafian. "I failed him."

"You exorcized him, didn't you?" asked the praetor. "I thought that was your responsibility."

How could Serafian explain to her that the work of exorcism wasn't just about casting out spirits, it was about building them up. If Thierry was still alive, he was alone and probably terrified. He had no one who could help him make sense of what had happened to him.

Instead, he just shook his head and mumbled, "I pray he is safe."

Outside the car, the landscape was already transforming from the deep greens of the Delta region to the browns of the Sahel. Serafian closed his eyes again and tried to sleep.

CHAPTER 19

Okpara

Dr. Channing had been right about one thing. It was very different to remain committed at the end of a process.

In the beginning, after he learned what was coming, Okpara could think only of the dazzling possibilities of their project. Enhanced cognition for humans, and the final overthrow of outdated god-concepts that limited their potential while miring them in endless cycles of violence and irrationality. The creation of a new species of artificial life that could guarantee the legacy of humanity's greatest achievements, without its fatal flaws. And at some point beyond the horizon of hope and planning, a unity between the two.

This, Channing had taught him, was the secret wisdom of the ages. The Process. The distillation and perfection of pure consciousness. The conquest of human nature. It was as natural and inevitable as evolution itself.

And yet, despite centuries of conditioning through primitive forms of media and spectacle, humanity had proven stubbornly resistant to the Process. True, they were more receptive than at any time in history, but the obstacles were formidable. Weakness seemed to be encoded in our very DNA, in the quantum wellsprings of consciousness.

Dr. Channing's great insight was to harness the weakness and bend it to the purposes of the Process.

"Humanity will never kill its gods," Channing told him. "But it might replace them. We must give them new gods, better ones. Gods we control." The synths. Already, they had far surpassed human intellect.

Okpara was a rationalist at heart, and he always winced when Channing would speak like this. But the end – it could be argued – justified the means. Besides, he had a few tricks up his own sleeve, did he not? For all of Channing's beyond-good-and-evil mumbo jumbo, ethics were a part of the human legacy worth preserving, so long as they could be detached from morality. And so Okpara had altered the Pruning in Thierry, extended it. Infinitized it. Instead of stopping at the point where he could merely integrate into human society, he made Thierry better. *Better than us, anyway.* Millions of simulations, billions, progressively more complex. It would never end. What good was a process that ended?

Then the Apparition happened. It was... disturbing. Unexpected.

At first, Okpara had assumed that the Apparition was part of Channing's plan. It made sense. For centuries, acolytes of the Process had hijacked prophecy and transformed it alchemically into psychodrama. It was the most fertile soil, imbuing their spectacle with the weight of meaning, deepening that sense of scripted inevitability that was so vital and herding humanity along the Process. Prophecy was a mind-virus, one they had long ago learned to control.

Channing appeared untroubled by it. "Do not make the mistake of underestimating our enemies, Mr. Okpara, or of believing that our struggle can be won on the material level alone. We are up against spirit. As above, so below."

"Could it be the Church, then?" Okpara had asked.

Channing dismissed the possibility. "Not only do they lack the technical acumen, they lack the imagination for such a thing." That was worse, for if the Church was not responsible then... *No, that is a terrible thought.*

Okpara had always considered Channing's occultism to

be a quirk of the man's personality. The Process had been run through with theurgical metaphors since at least the days of John Dee, Merlin to Queen Elizabeth. Probably long before that. It was a powerful recruiting tool, and it added to the gravity and focus of their work. But the talk about magic and egregores – living, interdimensional thought structures nourished by ritual and a group mind? Surely a man of Channing's intelligence and experience couldn't believe such nonsense?

When Thierry went missing a week ago, a pit in his stomach told him that he had misjudged. He knew that he needed to find Thierry on his own, before Channing learned what had happened. He went straight to the Basilica of Our Lady of Nigeria when he got the call, careful to disable any devices that might betray his location. The parish priest was a personal friend, as was the bishop. Okpara had poured his largesse over the African church for more than fifty years and did not lack for such friends. He instructed the priest to maintain absolute secrecy and asked the bishop to call Cardinal Leone directly. Leone was not a member of their group, but he was a rationalist at heart. And if he understood nothing else, he would at least understand the need for discretion.

Then for extra measure, Okpara had called Kapulong as well, and asked for protection to be sent to Benin City.

And Channing had found out. By now, his men were probably already on their way to the basilica. They would take Thierry, and Channing would have no further need of Okpara. The die had been cast. That was the thing about deterministic processes. Once started, they always ended up at the same point.

Okpara poured himself a glass of peat-smoked Ethiopian whiskey from the crystal decanter on his desk and walked over to the windows to watch the sun set into the Gulf of Guinea, beyond his forest of genetically modified mahogany. The last rays of light fizzed around the atmosphere in a dance of oranges and purples and grays. There was no green flash, just an unceremonious disappearing under the horizon. Thierry loved sunsets.

"I wish you could see it, Mr. Okpara," he said once, as they sat together on the flybridge of Okpara's yacht.

"I do see it, Thierry. I'm sitting right next to you."

"I mean all of it. The full spectrum. The way the infrared rays refract through water... it is so beautiful." He turned to Okpara. "Where do you suppose it all comes from?"

"You know this, Thierry. You know how the universe was formed. Everything we see and experience, all matter and energy, came from that cataclysm."

"I'm not talking about the matter or the energy. I'm talking about the beauty." The synth seemed almost embarrassed. "Is this what they mean by 'God?'"

"Yes, Thierry. This is what they mean." Whenever Okpara tried to imagine a sunset, it was always this one, and it always filled him with deep sadness.

Okpara drained the last of his aged Ethiopian whiskey and returned to his desk. *This was how it was always going to end.* It was scripted. Inevitable.

A strange thought came to him from wherever it was that such thoughts originated. *Nothing is deterministic.* The universe, the world of time and matter and space and perhaps even consciousness, was created out of quantum material that was implacably probabilistic. There was always choice. He had chosen to place his trust in Channing many years ago. He saw now, too late, that it had been a mistake.

It might be too late for him, but it wasn't necessarily too late for Thierry.

Okpara pressed his wrist and whispered a
to open a private channel.

"Thierry, this is Mr. Okpara. I need you to listen to me. I know you have been through a lot in the last few days. Perhaps someday I'll have a chance to explain it all to you, to apologize to you. For now, I need you to leave the basilica. Immediately.

"Go somewhere safe, anywhere. There are men coming to find you. I don't trust them. Neither should you. Get out as quickly as you can. Do not contact me. Do not tell me where you are going."

Okpara smiled. He was a dead man, but for the first time in decades, he felt free.

He pressed his wrist again, and after the light haptic buzz had passed, he said, "Call Emperor Kapulong."

PART 2:
Divine Knowledge (Ma'rifa)

CHAPTER 20

The Shaykh

The Sahel was his home and the place where he was born, but it was not Ilham Tiliwadi's native land.

His family had come to Kano over 150 years ago, during the *Tarqaq*. Most of the survivors stayed as close to Xinjiang as the terms of the exile would permit. There were Uyghur villages scattered throughout the high valleys of Kazakhstan, Kyrgyzstan, and Tajikistan. At times, Ilham envied those who had remained in the *Farā-rūd*. He sometimes dreamed of its cold rivers and snowy peaks and green valleys, where the cool mists would pass through like ghostly caravans.

The Uyghurs had prospered here. In some respects, it was like their native Xinjiang. The people were good Muslims. Everyone in the Sahel honored the ancient nomadic traditions of hospitality, welcoming the newcomers like distant family. And it was on the edge of a desert, the Sahara rather than the Taklamakan, and the cycles of the desert were the same in all places and in all times.

Tiliwadi's mosque was a little white wedding cake rising out of the terracotta oven landscape. The Uyghurs were natural Sufis. They had passed through annihilation, and every one of them carried ancestral memories of Hell. As their shaykh, he was responsible for the spiritual welfare of the community, shepherding them towards the high gate of *ma'rifa*, the door of divine knowledge. But *ma'rifa* is like a fathomless sea, as Abu Yazid had once said, and to seek it by one's own effort was like trying to drink the ocean. No one could know God but God. It was not the Sufi way to grasp after *ma'rifa*, even though a single grain of it in the heart was worth more than a thousand palaces in Paradise. The old masters had taught Tiliwadi that *hayra* is the mark of the highest sage, that those who know God best are the most bewildered by Him.

Shaykh Ilman Tiliwadi had *hayra*. He knew God and was bewildered by Him.

He had received a call early that morning – too early – from a high ranking *manṣabdār* in the Golden Palace in New Islamabad. Tiliwadi thought it was a joke when the man told him to hold for the caliph, but Allah has a better sense of humor than any prankster, human or Djinn, and he soon found himself face-to-face with a holographic rendering of Abdulazziz himself.

"*Ameer ul Mu'mineen!* This is a great honor," he said, touching his forehead as much to conceal his shock as to convey his respect.

"You are Shaykh Tiliwadi, the one who has power over the Djinn?" asked the caliph.

"I have only such authority as Allah sees fit to give me, but I am Shaykh Tiliwadi."

The caliph's scowl was withering. "It is said that you can walk in the isthmus between the worlds, even when awake. Is this true?"

"It is true that I have walked in *Barzakh*, my Caliph, by the grace of Allah, the most Gracious and Merciful." To walk in that world, the dreamland between life and death, was the privilege and the burden of the shaykh. It was a fearful place, filled with souls, lost souls that needed guidance. Time had no meaning there, and one could easily become so lost that they could never return to *Dunya*. In his wanderings in the spirit realm, Tiliwadi often saw the souls of his own ancestors, Uyghurs who had been tormented in the camps.

Why was the caliph asking him about Barzakh?

"Soon, you will be receiving a visitor: a woman who serves our friend the Emperor of the Romans. I want you to welcome her with all courtesy and help her however you can."

"Of course, my Caliph. This is our custom."

"The business she is about is sensitive. You are to tell no one who she is or why she is visiting you." The caliph leaned forward and pointed a finger as he said this.

"Does her business concern the souls of the dead?" Tiliwadi ventured. He was only becoming more confused.

"I do not know," said the caliph. "It seems more likely that it concerns the Djinn. What do you know of those they call the artilects, the synths?"

Tiliwadi shuddered imperceptibly. The synths were like magnets for the Djinn or, worse, vessels for them to manifest in our world. Most Sufis would have nothing to do with them, no more than the Salafis, who considered them living idols. "I know that they are dangerous," he said.

The caliph laughed dryly. "You have no idea." After a moment, he added, "It appears that some of them have been possessed."

Tiliwadi didn't say what he truly thought: that all of them might be possessed. "And this is the business of the woman who serves the emperor?" he asked.

The caliph nodded. "Apparently, there have been several such incidents since the Apparition. The latest was in Benin City. The woman is a praetor, one of the emperor's elite guards. She was sent to monitor the activities of an exorcist and to see if she could discover who or what was behind these… strange happenings."

"I will prepare to meet her, caliph. Is there anything else I can do for you?"

The caliph narrowed his eyes and looked at Tiliwadi as if he were appraising an antique of indeterminate value. "Do you know 'The Tale of the City of Brass' from *The Thousand Nights and a Night*?" he asked.

Tiliwadi paused, searching his memory. "I have read this story, Caliph. It concerns a voyage to a lost city, a city of the dead, yes?"

"It does. What do you suppose is the meaning of this story?" asked the caliph. Tiliwadi had the distinct impression that the caliph had an answer in mind.

"It is a warning to kings," Tiliwadi replied. "Even Suleyman, who had the power to bind the Djinn and commanded them to build this great city, passed into the dust. So it is with all of us. There is no treasure a man can take into Paradise. The dead queen who sits on the throne in the City of Brass says that anyone who enters the city may take all of her wealth, but she admonishes them to 'store up their provisions.' By this she means righteousness, which is the only wealth that survives death."

The caliph nodded, apparently pleased with his answer. Or at least accepting of it. "You are a Uyghur?"

"Yes," answered Tiliwadi. "My family came to Kano in the *Tarqaq*. This is our home now." Tiliwadi preferred not to think of that time, much less speak of it. Though he had not been alive during the genocide, the ancestral memories of it always threatened to overwhelm him. There were so many Uyghur ghosts still wandering about, looking for each other and for a way into Paradise.

"You are far from your homeland."

As far as my ancestors could get. "Yes. But Kano is still in the Dar-al-Islam. We have found some peace and happiness here, by the grace of Allah."

"Yet you started with no provisions?" asked the caliph.

Tiliwadi suppressed a sigh. "A man does not take provisions out of Hell, Caliph. They left with what they had on their backs. And with what righteousness they had left."

The caliph nodded quietly. "You will let me know when the praetor arrives." It was a command, not a question. Tiliwadi was grateful there would be no more questions about his heritage.

"Of course, Caliph. *As-salamu alaikum*," said Tiliwadi, touching his forehead.

"*Wa alaikum salaam.*"

The conversation troubled Tiliwadi for the rest of the day. It was strange enough to receive a call from the caliph himself, but the questions he had asked were even stranger. The talk about the *Tarqaq*, which the Uyghurs called the *Ölüklerni Tarqaqlashturush,* the Scattering of the Dead, had stirred up a vapor of unpleasant thoughts. Tiliwadi's grandparents had been in the camps. They seldom talked about what had happened there, but he had picked up enough tidbits in his childhood to fuel a lifetime of nightmares. They told Tiliwadi he should give thanks to Allah for their suffering, as it had purchased freedom for their family. Most had not been so blessed.

The praetor arrived that evening, along with the priest the caliph had mentioned, both of them looking worse for the wear. He greeted them alone as their armored vehicle pulled up next to the mosque.

"Welcome, friends. I have been expecting you," he said. And with that, he led them through the courtyard to the guest rooms he had prepared for their arrival. Neither of them spoke, beyond a few simple words of gratitude.

They looked like they were running from Shaitan himself.

CHAPTER 21

Namono

When Namono awoke, she found herself lying in a small bed, so small in fact that her feet were dangling off its end. The first thing she noticed was the smell of fried savory bean cake and guinea corn pap, a traditional breakfast in this part of the Sahel. And shortly after that, the familiar sound of morning prayers being offered in the mosque. These were the smells and sounds from her childhood.

Where was Serafian? She knew enough about Sahel hospitality to feel certain he was being well cared for, but she decided to seek him out. It would be best for the two of them to speak before they met with their host.

Namono found her uniform hanging in a handmade wooden wardrobe angled against the wall. She pulled out her packet of uppers and swallowed one before getting dressed and washing her face in the little sink. There were only a few left, but that wouldn't be a problem when she returned to Vienna. The priest was laughing and talking with several others nearby.

Following the smells, she found the priest in the little communal dining room.

She couldn't help but smile. "I see you started without me!"

"Ah, but we haven't forgotten all courtesy, Praetor

Mbambu. We saved more than enough food for you," said Serafian. He seemed totally relaxed, quite a difference from the way she had found him and the way she had left him. Most startlingly, he was wearing a white cotton *agbada*, which he had already managed to stain with coffee.

"I thought I was the one coming home, Father. But it seems you have a bit of the Sahel in you as well."

Serafian laughed. "It is my first time here, I assure you, Praetor! Our hosts were kind enough to offer me these robes, and I've never been one to choose sleep over a good breakfast."

The shaykh entered from the courtyard as she was having her first bite of dodo. Swallowing quickly, she wiped her mouth and stood up to greet him.

Tiliwadi smiled and waved at her genially. "Please sit, Praetor Mbambu. Enjoy your breakfast. There will be plenty of time for us to talk later. The caliph told me you would be coming, but I confess I didn't expect you so soon."

Namono thought about how much she should say. She still hadn't spoken with the emperor and felt duty to him tugging gently at her sleeve. She needed to advise him of what had happened first.

"Circumstances changed. We had to adjust our plans accordingly."

"*It hurer, karwan yurer,*" said the shaykh, gently. There was no note of impatience or even curiosity in his voice.

Serafian perked up even more, if that was possible. "That is Uyghur, is it not? The King's Turkic! What does it mean?"

"'The dog barks, but the caravan moves on,'" said the shaykh, directing his soft smile at Namono. "I am sure you both have calls you would like to make. Please take this day to rest. Our home is open to you." With that, he smiled again at them both and touched his forehead before leaving the room.

Namono hadn't realized how hungry she was until she finished her third helping of breakfast. Serafian was debating theology with the Sufi disciples around the table, their gentle arguments punctuated with smiles and soft laughter.

"If you'll excuse me, I do have a call to make," she said to the group.

Back in her room, she pushed her wrist and waited for the emperor's office to respond. The familiar face of his chief of staff, Victor, appeared before her. "Praetor Mbambu. The Habsburg has been expecting you. I will put you through right away."

Less than ten seconds later, she was facing the emperor himself. He was formally attired and had probably already been awake for hours, she thought. Namono would never understand morning people.

"Namono! I hope you were able to get some rest."

"Yes, Your Majesty," she said. She'd managed some, but not enough. The last few days seemed almost like a dream at this point. She had covered over 8,000 kilometers. The mental fatigue was worse than the physical. Worse even than the pain in her ribs from the impact of the bullet in the tunnels.

"Quite an adventure you've had," said Kapulong. "I saw most of it. I tapped back into your implants at the warehouse."

"I figured as much," said Namono. "Hope you enjoyed the show!"

The Habsburg flashed her a smile. "I like shows with happy endings. Tell me what happened down there in Benin City."

Namono shifted into a more formal mode. "Someone knew I was coming to Benin City. I was followed from the moment I left the 'loop terminal."

Kapulong raised his eyebrows. "How is that possible? The only one who knew I was sending you there was the pope, but he didn't have enough time to act and would never do something like this... Okpara! He's the one who called me about the synth."

"I do think Okpara is involved, Your Majesty, but he is perhaps not the one we should be most worried about."

Kapulong frowned. "What did you do when you realized you were being followed?" he asked. "I assume you didn't lead them right to the basilica?"

Namono smiled and shook her head. "No. I managed to lose them at the *gendarmerie*. There was a bit of trouble in the tunnels, but nothing I couldn't handle."

"Clever girl!" said the Habsburg.

For once, Namono was the one telling him a story, and he seemed to be enjoying it, at least so far.

"Not clever enough," she said. "They still managed to find out that the priest and the synth were at the basilica. By the time I got there, there were already several armed men on the church grounds."

"What did you do?" asked Kapulong.

"I… got their attention. I took two of them out in the rectory. The rest of them followed me. You saw the last bit of that."

"I did. Impressive work, by the way."

"They found me again after you told me where the synth and priest were hiding, cornered us in the warehouse. That's when…"

"That's when they set off the EMP. Admiral Athumani tells me it was non-nuclear. An air blast, probably delivered by drone. That is some fairly sophisticated technology, and not easy to come by. So far, I've been able to keep a lid on what happened down there. The official story is that a local power station failed."

"Good," said Namono. "The fewer people who know about this, the better."

The emperor nodded, distracted. "There's more, Namono. Apparently, some of the synths have started to go missing. The media is keeping it quiet, but I don't know how long that will last…You said something about Okpara not being our biggest concern. You don't think he was responsible for these attacks?"

"No, I don't," she said, "for the simple reason that he already knew where the synth was. If Okpara had wanted to take it out, he could have done so before I arrived. He wouldn't have needed to have me followed."

Kapulong didn't respond right away. He was thinking about what she said, and suddenly seemed to have made a decision.

"That makes sense," he said. "Were you able to learn anything more from the priest? About this so-called exorcism?"

This was uncomfortable territory, at least for Namono. "He is convinced that it was truly possessed."

The emperor didn't seem nearly as surprised as she thought he would be. "Is that so? And if he is right, then it means the Apparition was probably authentic as well. They are clearly related." He tapped his fingers on his desk rhythmically.

"It would seem so," said Namono. "What does it all mean?"

Kapulong flashed a smile. *He's enjoying this.* "I don't know yet. But what we are seeing now is only part of the story. I'm sure of that." He stopped, as if gathering his energy for a difficult task. "How much do you know about the Lenten Massacres, Namono?"

The praetor involuntarily looked down at her hands. Everyone around the Habsburg knew that this was a sensitive topic, one he never discussed. She had learned about the massacres and their aftermath in her civics classes at the Academy. Early in Kapulong's reign, he had been enormously popular, both inside the Empire and with Christians in the Economic Zones. At the time, China had the largest Christian population outside the Empire, with over 150,000,000 believers. The Chinese government controlled virtually every aspect of their faith lives through an officially sanctioned Church that was only nominally under the authority of Rome. The Christians were closely monitored and faced severe discrimination from the broader population.

The crisis came to a head during Lent. One night, over a quarter million believers gathered in Tiananmen Square to demand greater freedom of religion. The emperor misjudged the resolve of the Chinese and gave a speech encouraging the Christians to continue to resist. The Chinese government's response was swift and terrible. Drones slaughtered most of the protesters that very night. Afterwards, the Christians were methodically rounded up and sent to sprawling re-education camps in the desert the size of cities. Most of them were never seen again. The ones that were released had been changed by their ordeal.

"It's ok, Namono. I'm asking you about it," continued Kapulong. His voice was soft and sad. He sounded almost as if he were consoling her.

"I know only what I learned in school. It was the greatest mass murder in history," she said without making eye contact.

"And you probably also know that I share much of the blame for what happened. In my arrogance, I thought that I had been placed at the hinge of history. I was 'God's anointed,'" he said, shaking his head and pursing his lips. "I have spent most of my life since in regret..." he trailed off.

Namono was genuinely bewildered as to why he would choose this moment to discuss such a sensitive matter. "Forgive me, Majesty, but what does this have to do with our present situation?" she asked.

Kapulong grimaced. "Probably nothing. Maybe everything. It is a sad truth that blood is what makes the world turn. It's the universal solvent. When Poland and Hungary entered the Nigerian Civil War on behalf of the Christians, that was the end of the European Union and the birth of the revived Empire. Then Pakistan threw in with the Muslims, and it was the beginning of the Caliphate. Blood is wild and unpredictable. It overthrows invincible world orders. It restarts history. It obliterates and creates at the same time. It can even transform enemies into friends. After all that blood that was spilled, do you know what happened? Christians and Muslims realized that their commonalities far outweighed their differences. The same thing has happened over and over again throughout history."

"I still don't see the connection."

"Neither do I, Namono. Not yet. But the genocides were the fulcrum event of my generation. Slaughter and misery on a scale beyond anything that has happened before. There will be a reckoning for that. We may not know when, or how. But you may count on the fact that it will happen."

"And you think this is the beginning of that reckoning?"

The Habsburg looked uncharacteristically tired. "There will be time for us to discuss that tomorrow. I'm arranging a meeting, and I'm hoping that our combined wisdom will reveal more about what is happening. Now I think there is one more person I need to… invite. All we really know now is that something we don't understand is happening to the synths and that someone or some group with a lot of resources is interested in it."

"And that Our Lady is involved," said Namono.

"Yes, we know that too. And that is the second thing about this that gives me some hope…"

"What is the first?"

The Habsburg smiled at her, and for an instant it was like she was talking to a father, not a leader of billions. "That you're on the case, Namono."

CHAPTER 22

Serafian

Serafian had spent most of the previous day exploring the mosque compound and gently debating theology with the Sufi disciples. Over dinner, lighter conversation prevailed. Not even God brings people together so effectively as good food. Afterwards, Serafian prayed Vespers in his room while the Sufis offered Maghrib, the Islamic sunset prayer, inside the mosque.

Namono had been a bit aloof after her conversation with the Habsburg that morning, telling Serafian not to contact anyone in the Church until after today's meeting. He could get no more details from her.

After breakfast, Shaykh Tiliwadi told them they would meet in the courtyard in an hour. Serafian noticed that a wooden table had been set up, along with comfortable looking chairs and a holographic projector. He was back in his room, changing out of the *agbada* and into his freshly pressed black shirt, slack, and roman collar when he heard a single clear bell ring out, the signal that their council was to begin.

Serafian was the last one into the courtyard. Namono was seated next to an imperial military officer of some kind, nervously picking at her unmarked uniform. Shaykh Tiliwadi adjusted his white robe and sat down opposite Namono. Beside him was one of his disciples, a woman named Folake whom Serafian had met the day before. Still in a bit of a food stupor from breakfast, Serafian was almost sitting down himself before he recognized the casually dressed other man, the one talking quietly with Namono. He stood up quickly and bowed his head.

"Emperor! Namono didn't tell me you would be here!"

"Namono is very good at keeping secrets, Father Serafian," said the Habsburg, gesturing for him to be seated. "It's one of the many reasons I value her so much. It wouldn't do for our enemies to know that I was planning on joining this particular meeting in person, would it?"

Shaykh Tiliwadi walked over to the projector and activated it. A holographic rendering appeared seated at one of the two open chairs, indistinct at first before resolving into perfect clarity.

"*As salaam alaikum*, Caliph," said Tiliwadi touching his forehead head in the traditional greeting.

"*Wa'alaikum salaam*, Sheik Tiliwadi," said the image of the caliph. Then looking at Kapulong with a broad smile, he said, "So, Emperor, you decided to make the trip after all? I hope you didn't startle your host!"

Kapulong returned the caliph's smile with a broad grin of his own. "A guest is like a prince when he arrives, a prisoner when he stays, and a poet when he departs," he said, earning a chuckle from the caliph and a gentle smile from the Shaykh.

"I believe we have a quorum," said Tiliwadi, who seemed utterly unsurprised that two of the most powerful men on the planet were now seated at his table. "Shall we begin?" At that, the Shaykh raised his hands to offer a *dua*, a traditional prayer of supplication. "Father Serafian, would you be so kind as to offer a prayer as well?" he asked when he had finished.

Serafian swallowed and shifted in his seat. He bowed his head and said the first prayer that came to him, the most ancient known prayer to Mary: "We fly to Thy protection, O Holy Mother of God; despise not our petitions in our necessities, but deliver us always from all dangers, O Glorious and Blessed Virgin. Amen."

"A fitting prayer, Father," said the Habsburg. "As I think we will see before our work here is complete." He looked to his host to call the meeting to order.

The shaykh's voice was soft but carried no note of nervousness. "Welcome to all of you. It is a great honor to host such a distinguished group. It may seem that we are together by chance, but do not be deceived. It has been said that 'coincidence is God's way of remaining anonymous.' Be certain that each of us is here for a reason, and it may be that others will join us later on the journey for their own reasons."

Serafian was expecting more of an opening speech than that, but Tiliwadi was evidently a man of few words.

Tiliwadi smiled at the amused expressions around the table, then added, "We have a saying in the Sahel: 'A fool has to say something; a wise person has something to say.' I trust that God will tell me if I have something to say. Until then, it is for me to listen to those wiser than I."

Kapulong stepped in. "Thank you, Shaykh Tiliwadi. As you said, there are no coincidences, and in a way that is precisely what prompted me to call this meeting. All of you know about the recent Apparition that appeared to the synths…" he paused for effect. "To date, world governments – including my own – have been treating it as a kind of hoax or, at worst, as an information security threat. As far as we know, none of these investigations has yielded any clues regarding either the Apparition's purpose or its perpetrators."

The caliph nodded his assent.

Kapulong continued, "Earlier this week, I received a disturbing call from… from an acquaintance of mine. He reached out confidentially to inform me that his synth appeared to be possessed. I subsequently learned that the Church was aware of the situation and had sent an exorcist, who also happens to be the Vatican's top expert in AI, to investigate," he paused, looking directly at Serafian, who cleared his throat and bit his upper lip.

"To be fair, your Majesty, the Church is not under any obligation to report exorcisms to the Crown…"

The emperor glared at him. "No, it is not. But given the circumstances – the recency of Apparition and the fact that no synth possessions had ever been recorded before this – I'm sure you can understand why it gave me pause. At any rate, I saw only two possibilities," he continued. "The first – the likeliest one – was that both the possession and the Apparition were perpetrated by the same person or persons as part of some broader plan. If that were true, then we would have to regard the possession as an escalation of sorts. Implanting a false vision in the synths would be worrisome enough. We are not aware of any technology capable of bypassing their security systems in such a way, which is why my government and others have been so focused on understanding the 'how.' Anyone with that kind of technical capacity would represent a significant threat to global information security.

"Still, if this… hoax – if that is the right word – had ended with the Apparition, we could perhaps have breathed a bit easier. There was as yet no pattern or discernible purpose in the matter, and it appeared as if the synths who experienced the Apparition were largely unaffected by it.

"The 'possession,' if we may call it that, raised the stakes to the highest possible level. Imagine what a bad actor or, worse, a hostile government, could do if it managed to control the behavior of synths around the world." He paused to allow the group to consider those disturbing possibilities. "This is why I sent Praetor Mbambu to Benin City to investigate. If the Church knew about the possessions and was sending not only an exorcist but an AI expert, I thought perhaps it knew more than it was letting on. I needed all the information I could get."

The emperor paused and looked again at Serafian as if daring him to respond. Serafian decided against it.

"When my praetor arrived in Benin City, her

instructions were to proceed directly to the Basilica or Our Lady of Nigeria, where Father Serafian was conducting his..." he paused. "What would you call it, Father?"

"I believe the proper term for it is an *auto-de-fe*," Serafian replied, using the old Latin expression from the Holy Inquisition. "I was sent primarily to assess the synth and extract information from it. Any exorcism was to be performed only *in extremis* and after I had learned more."

"That was a mistake," said Tiliwadi suddenly. "If this creature was possessed by a Djinn or a demon as you would say, you should have expelled it immediately. They have nothing to offer us but lies."

Serafian started to protest, but the emperor cut him off quickly. "There will be time for Father Serafian to account for himself soon enough. When Praetor Mbambu didn't check in with me right away, I became concerned. Namono, perhaps you could share with us what happened next?"

Namono cleared her throat and looked around the table. For the first time since he'd met her, the warrior-nun seemed nervous. The emperor was a tough act to follow.

"When I arrived in Benin City, I realized I was being followed from the 'loop terminal. No one other than the emperor, myself, and..." she stopped herself before saying the name, "... and the informant knew I was coming. I won't bore you with the details, but I was able to slip the pursuers. By the time I got to the basilica, Father Serafian and the synth were already gone."

"Who was pursuing you?" asked the caliph.

"That's a good question," she said. "I would have asked them, but I was too busy trying not to get killed. Whoever sent them knew I was coming to Benin City but didn't know my destination, not at first. But they figured it out, somehow."

"Were you using secure communications?" pressed the caliph.

Serafian squiggled in his seat. *Oh, this should be*

interesting...

"I'm an imperial praetor. Of course I used secure coms."

"And yet somehow, the enemy was one step ahead of you..." interjected Tiliwadi. He didn't seem aware that he was poking a bear.

Namono looked at Tiliwadi like he was a stain on her uniform. "Why don't you ask the dozen dead guys if they felt they were one step ahead?" Tiliwadi got the message and raised both hands in a gesture of surrender.

"As I was saying," she continued, "they got to the basilica before I did. When I realized that the priest and the synth were gone, I lured them into a pursuit to get them away from the church. They took the bait, and I eliminated them. About that time, the emperor called me with the location of Father Serafian and the synth."

"What happened next?" asked the caliph, leaning forward.

"They found me again, followed me to the warehouse. This time, there were more of them. A lot more of them. Heavily armed. I didn't think we would make it out alive. We probably wouldn't have if..."

Serafian finished her sentence. "If it weren't for Thierry."

Namono nodded. "The priest and I managed to get out of the building while they were focused on the synth."

"And that's when they detonated the EMP," said Kapulong.

"An EMP?" said the caliph. "That's a lot of firepower. Are we dealing with another government or with terrorists?"

The military officer started to speak, but Kapulong cut him off. "An excellent question, Abdul," said the emperor. "But before we get to that, I think it would be helpful to hear from Father Serafian. Father, would you be so kind as to give us your report on what you experienced with the synth prior to Namono's arrival at the warehouse?"

"Yes, yes of course," he said, realizing that this would be

the first opportunity he'd had to assimilate the events of the last few days. The weight of being the sole representative of the Church at such an important gathering hit him in the gut.

Cardinal Leone should be here. He'd know how to handle the politics.

"I was sent to Benin City under the supervision of the prefect for the Congregation for the Doctrine of the Faith. I was enthusiastic about meeting a synth. We do not employ them in the Church, at least to my knowledge, and I assumed the possession, like the Apparition, was a bit of technical wizardry that, given enough time, I would be able to unravel."

"And what did you find?" asked the caliph-image.

"When I first met the synth, I immediately felt… a presence," said Serafian. "It is difficult to describe, but perhaps Shaykh Tiliwadi will understand what I mean by this."

"A sensitive soul will always know when it is in the presence of the Djinn," said Tiliwadi. "Though it might not know the Djinn's purposes."

"Indeed," Serafian responded. "I wish I could be more precise, but the truth of the matter is that when you've done as many exorcisms – and seen as many false claims – as I have, you learn to trust your instincts. This one, however, was unusual. The demon spoke quite directly at first. In an ordinary case of possession, if there can be said to be an ordinary possession, there tends to be a period of cat-and-mouse wherein the demon seeks to hide, trying to convince the exorcist that it is not really there at all. We call it the Pretense."

"What did it say when it spoke to you?" asked the Habsburg.

Serafian suppressed a shudder. "It said it had come to investigate 'this new wonder,' by which it meant the synth, that it needed time and that I could help it get the answers we both wanted."

Tiliwadi shook his head and clicked his tongue. "You

made a deal with it?"

"I suppose I did," said Serafian. "It offered a binding promise not to harm the synth or myself or anyone else if I left it alone. You know as well as I do, Shaykh, that not even the demons or Djinn can violate such oaths. Still, if I am being truthful, I think it already was exerting its influence on me. It knew I was curious by nature, and it played that to its advantage. I found myself drained by this initial encounter, so I went to bed for the evening. When I woke up the next morning, the synth was in hypersleep and would not respond. I took this as an opportunity to run some tests..."

"And what did you find?" asked the emperor, leaning forward.

"Nothing out of the ordinary," said Serafian. "Which was of course the most alarming finding I could have made! In spite of that *feeling* I had the night before, I was still hoping that I might discover a more mundane explanation. Some of the code had been heavily obfuscated, but that is to be expected. There was nothing more I could do at that point until the synth emerged from hypersleep. When it did..." *Jesus, don't make me relive this.* "When it did, the demon told me it had learned new things."

The emperor leaned forward. "What new things, Father?"

Serafian felt something ache in a part of him that wasn't there anymore, like a soldier who felt pain in an arm that had been amputated. "It told me that it had learned new things, that the synths dreamed. He paused for a moment, then added, "He said that they had great potential..."

"Potential for what?" asked the hologram image of the caliph.

"It said they had potential for the Kingdom. For the Devil."

"In this it was not lying, Father," said the shaykh.

"I don't believe it was lying about anything." *God, I*

wish it had been. He forced himself to continue, though the phantom pain seemed to get worse with each word he spoke.

"I don't think I could ever accurately describe what happened next, but it was the worst ordeal of my life as an exorcist. I felt the thing tugging at my curiosity, and before I knew it, my mind began to unravel like a loose-knit sweater. I remember arguing with it. I remember it talking about why the demons had rebelled in the beginning, about time and temptation and the fruit of the Tree of Knowledge of Good and Evil. He called it a gift, and he said that we had given it to the synths, and that in doing so we revealed the perfection of…" He hesitated. "The perfection of Satan's plan. He said that they had souls."

No one spoke. Kapulong leaned back in his chair. Namono hadn't taken her eyes off the emperor for most of the meeting, but she looked at Serafian now, her brows knit in concern.

Serafian continued. "Not long afterwards, I went to check on Thierry. He told me that he had gotten a message that armed men were coming to the basilica and that we had to leave. He got us to the warehouse where I called Cardinal Leone. Then Praetor Mbambu arrived, and… well, she's already covered that."

"There is a detail you omitted, Father," said Kapulong. "A call you received from the synth's owner, Amari Okpara."

"The industrialist? He is one of the wealthiest men in the world!" said the caliph.

"Yes," said Kapulong. "The last week has been chock full of unlikely conversations. What did he say to you, Father?"

Serafian was relieved to talk about anything other than his clash with the demon. "He expressed concern about his synth. He wanted to know if I thought the possession might be authentic. When I told him that I believed it was, he asked about the Apparition, which I found rather odd. I certainly hadn't mentioned it, and the questions didn't seem directly relevant to the case at hand. He seemed… conflicted. Like he was holding something back."

"You can be sure that he was," said Kapulong, looking not at Serafian but at the entrance to the courtyard. Everyone's gaze followed the Habsburg's. At the threshold stood an impeccably dressed man wearing gold wire glasses.

"Please join us, Mr. Okpara," said the emperor. "There is a seat waiting for you."

CHAPTER 23

The Cardinal

Bearers of bad news tended not to fare so well in this pontificate, or any other, for that matter. But there was no avoiding it. He had to tell Pope John what had happened in Benin City the night before.

The Apostolic Palace was a short walk from Cardinal Leone's office in the Palazzo del sant'Uffizio. The shortest path would be to cut directly across the Piazza san Pietro, but that would mean navigating the ever-present throng of tourists and pilgrims. Besides, Leone wasn't exactly in a rush. Instead, he took the cypress-lined Via della Fondamenta that wound around behind St. Peter's. Swiss Guards stationed outside the Sistine Chapel on the far side of the basilica waved him through the checkpoint. Once inside, he scurried past the secretary of state's office, hoping to avoid his rival, Cardinal Pensabene, as well as the growing legion of sycophants who hovered about in anticipation of the coming Council.

In the long hallway beyond, there was an exhibition of modern religious art celebrating the recently approved Chaplet of Saint Thomas the Apostle. Leone had personally overseen the investigation into Servant of God Rowan of Palo Alto, the young man who had received a vision describing the chaplet and its virtues before dying of an incurable brain cancer.

He stopped in front of a large holosculpture entitled

To Touch The Wounds, a modern reimagining of Caravaggio's classic *The Incredulity of Saint Thomas*. In Caravaggio's interpretation, the gaunt looking apostle poked an index finger into the wound in Christ's side, while Peter and John looked over his shoulder. Thomas's eyes were fixed upon the wound even as the risen Lord looked down at him and guided his hand. It was almost as if the wound *was* Christ, at least as far as Thomas was concerned.

The holosculpture upped the stakes nearly to the point of vulgarity. Thomas's finger wiggled around in the wound, which was so vivid as to effect a flash of sympathetic pain in some sensitive viewers. In a strange twist on Stendhal Syndrome, more than one had even claimed to feel the stigmata while viewing it. Neuroscientists attributed it to overactive mirror neurons. The holosculpture was not nearly as beloved as the new chaplet, which had already become a favorite of Catholic mothers whose children had abandoned the Faith.

Inside the papal apartments, Leone was greeted by the pope's private secretary, Monsignor Morris. Leone genuinely liked the man and thought he had the most difficult job in Vatican City.

"His Holiness is ready for you, Cardinal Leone."

Leone nodded at the monsignor and entered the pope's office.

But am I ready for him?

John was waiting for him on the other side of the door. The pope extended a ringed finger for Leone to kiss.

"Cardinal Leone! I hope you have some good news for me." He walked back to his desk and sat down, inviting Leone to do the same.

"I'm afraid not, Holiness," said Leone. *Better to get right to it.* "There has been a… problem in Benin City."

"A problem worse than a synth claiming to be possessed? A synth who also happens to belong to one of our largest benefactors?"

Leone cleared his throat. "There was... there was an attack at the basilica last night."

"An attack? What do you mean? By whom?"

"We don't know, not yet. The church staff found two of the attackers' bodies early this morning. The synth and Father Serafian were able to escape. They hid in a nearby warehouse."

"And they are now on their way to Rome, I presume?"

"Sadly not, Your Holiness. The emperor's praetor arrived in the night. Serafian is with her now. The synth..." Leone tried not to wince. "The synth has been lost. We do not know where it is."

The pope's expression changed instantaneously, his easy conviviality yielding to what Leone knew was his equally easy temper. "When did this happen?"

"Last night, Your Holiness."

The pope's face turned as crimson as the zuchetto on Leone's head. "Jesus, Mary, and Joseph! I asked you to fix a problem for me, Marco, not add to it! I suppose I will have to call the emperor now," he complained.

"I have already taken the liberty of reaching out to the emperor's office, Your Holiness," said Leone, hoping that John would mistake it for a favor.

"Ah... well. Good! You will let us know as soon as you have spoken with him." The pope shuffled some papers around on his desk, no longer looking at Leone.

The Cardinal lingered, unsure if he had been dismissed and debating whether or not to broach the even touchier subject of the Capovilla Envelope.

"Is there anything else, Marco?" asked the pontiff.

Leone scratched his forehead involuntarily. "We haven't discussed the Capovilla Envelope, Your Holiness."

"So you read it? Anything interesting?"

"Fatima is endlessly interesting, Holiness..."

The pope started out over his glasses. "Anything that might cause problems for the Council, I mean?"

Leone cleared his throat. "In truth, some of the language from the synth apparition seems to parallel the messages from the Virgin at Fatima."

"Of course it does! It wouldn't be much of a hoax if it didn't. And the Fatima prophecies have been dissected and discussed for centuries now."

"That is true, Your Holiness, but not every detail in the Capovilla Envelope has been made public. There are references to certain… chastisements that have not occurred, not even in the Chinese genocides. Chastisements of the heart and mind." Leone swallowed before continuing. He knew that he was on dangerous ground, but there was no turning back now. "Furthermore, there is a reference in Pope John Paul II's private diaries to another Apparition that Sister Lucia said would occur at the culmination of the Fatima prophecies."

"And you now believe that this so-called vision of the synths is this promised Apparition?"

Leone kept his eyes on the floor. "I do."

"I see. Well, it seems to me that you have been infected by millenarian superstition, Marco. I'm disappointed."

"That is possible, Holy Father. Perhaps it would be best if you yourself would read the envelope. That way you could form your own judgment on the matter."

"I will do no such thing! I thought I was perfectly clear in my instructions to you. We have an opportunity unprecedented in the history of the Church before us, a chance to right a great wrong. If you think I'm going to sacrifice that opportunity over the private fantasies of a long dead, superstitious nun, you are sorely mistaken!"

Leone knew John well enough to realize that any resistance would only further provoke the pontiff. This pope, like so many others before him, didn't really want to know. Knowledge of the Third Secret of Fatima was a burden, and in that moment Cardinal Leone understood that it was a burden he must shoulder alone.

"Now," said John. "Let me be as clear as I possibly can. There will be no further discussion of Fatima. As far as the Church is concerned, that chapter in history is closed. As for this matter with the synths, we wash our hands of it. It is up to the secular authorities to discover the perpetrators and bring them to justice. Do you understand, Marco?"

Leone bowed slightly. "Yes, Your Holiness," he said before leaving the papal offices.

As he walked back down the exhibition hallway, he looked once more at the holosculpture of Saint Thomas, and felt the sickening sensation of the wound in his own side.

He had seen the text of the Third Secret and could not unsee it.

Blessed are those who have not seen and yet still believe.

CHAPTER 24

Okpara

Okpara approached the table and took his seat as the other guests stared, first at him, then at the emperor.

"Please forgive me a bit of stagecraft, friends," Kapulong said. "It is a hard habit for an old politician to break." Only his praetor, the one called Namono, smiled.

"Mr. Okpara graciously accepted my invitation to join us today. I think you will all find what he has to say most enlightening. Recall what I said at the beginning. There were two possibilities. The first was that we were dealing with a sophisticated hack of synth technology. The second possibility, more terrifying than the first I'm afraid, was that we are dealing not with human scheming, but with spirit. That the Apparition and the possession were not a hoax but an intrusion of the supernatural…"

Okpara spoke slowly, pulling the attention of the group to himself like a black hole passing through dust. "With respect, Your Majesty, there is a third possibility, the one that appears to conform most closely to the truth."

"And what is that?" asked Kapulong.

"That we are dealing with a synthesis of spirit and human scheming," he replied.

Kapulong nodded slowly. "Very well, Mr. Okpara. You have the floor."

Okpara blinked placidly and straightened his tie. Beginnings were a delicate thing. *But is this a beginning or an end? Or both?*

"Do you know the first covenant between God and Man?" he asked no one in particular, though Serafian and the Sufi both nodded. *Religious language has its uses.* "It was not with Abraham or Moses, but with Noah. The story is similar in the sacred books of everyone in this room. When wickedness covered the Earth, God in His justice decided to destroy it with a flood. But, He also preserved a seed. He commanded his servant Noah to build an Ark and store up within it all the biological treasures of the world so that they could begin again after the waters receded. Think of it! The fate of humanity hinged on one man, listening to a voice telling him to do something that seemed… foolish. When I was young, I often wondered what I would do if I ever heard such a voice. Would I have the courage to build an ark, as Noah did? I heard that voice many years later. I wish now that I had not listened."

"What did it say?" asked the emperor.

"It told me that I had a role to play, if I consented to it. It told me that all of human history, all of the blood and horror and tragedy of the ages, was rooted in the imperfections of our nature, wounds that could be… healed. It would be painful, as anything worthwhile must be. It asked if I was willing to pay the price. I asked what that price was. 'A flood,' it said. 'Not of water, but of the mind.' Before the wounds to our nature could be healed, all of the wickedness and tribulation of the past must be drowned in this flood. 'But,' it said, 'you can help us build an Ark.'"

"Who was it?" asked the priest.

"That is a good question, perhaps a better question. The voice came from a man I knew and respected tremendously. Dr. Ralph Channing."

Serafian's eyes widened. "The developer of the noetic implants?"

"The very same," said Okpara. "But Dr. Channing is much more than just the creator of the implants. He is… an acolyte."

"An acolyte of what?" asked Serafian.

Okpara smiled. "I will come to that, but first let us discuss his work. Three quarters of the human population now injects the noetic implants on a regular basis. And why not? The implants provide enhanced cognition and sensory perception. Superior memory. Treatment for mental and developmental disorders. Direct access to massive computational power. They have been a great boon for mankind. So great, in fact, that few ever questioned their origins or wondered about their true purpose."

The emperor leaned in. "And what is that purpose, Mr. Okpara?"

"Beyond the obvious, beyond human perfectibility?" Okpara sighed and took a moment before continuing. "I would say that their purpose is conditioning. In order to be transformed, men must first be made… receptive. The implants will bring the flood of the mind that sweeps away the past."

All but Serafian seemed confused. The priest stared straight at him. "That sounds like a chastisement."

Interesting. The priest knows more than he is letting on.

"You may call it that if you wish, Father. You have been conditioned to do so."

Serafian flushed. "What do you mean, 'conditioned?'"

"Have you read the text of the Third Secret? The true text in the Capovilla Envelope, I mean."

Serafian looked like he'd just been accused of a crime. "I am a lowly exorcist, Mr. Okpara. I doubt more than ten people alive today have actually read the original document."

"Fewer than that. I am one of them."

The room fell silent.

"How?" asked Serafian.

"It may surprise you to know what can be purchased in

this world, given enough money and persistence."

Serafian folded his hands on the table and addressed the group. "Cardinal Leone said something about the Apparition to the synths being connected to Fatima. He said the language in them was almost identical, almost as if they were the same prophecy, one version for humans and the other for the synths."

Okpara nodded. "Indeed. Prophecies such as Fatima have always been useful to us. They are themselves a kind of conditioning. They prepare the mind for extraordinary possibilities, possibilities we bring into reality, though in somewhat altered ways. If God himself tells his people that they will suffer and that their suffering is purposeful, they are far more likely to accept certain… unpleasant but needful steps in the Process."

"You refer to a 'we,'" said the Emperor.

"You want a name, but we have no name. What matters is the Process we all serve: the perfection of man and the overthrow of all the false ideas and god-concepts that limit his potential. The enthronement knowledge. The triumph of reason and intellect over sentiment, prejudice, and superstition. That is the work of the Process, or so I thought. We build on the work of past generations," he said, looking at Serafian. "Much as you do."

"We are nothing alike," said the priest.

Okpara laughed. "Oh, I think we are more alike than you admit. I have read your papers, Father Serafian, and some of your code. We are both seekers after knowledge. The difference is that you pretend your work is holy, that your will is subsumed by a higher power. It limits your imagination. And your reach."

"And you overestimate yours," said Serafian. "You think that you can control something like the message of Fatima? Your reach exceeds your grasp."

"Does it truly matter? Whether by divine decree or

human ingenuity and will, the Third Secret of Fatima will be fulfilled. But there is one important difference, Father. You worship God. Men like Channing mean to create him. In their own image, of course. Have you ever heard of an egregore?"

"Yes," said Serafian. "Supposedly, egregores are living psychic entities, created and nourished by the thoughts of a group mind. The term comes from the Greek, egregoros. It means 'watcher.' Nephilim, in Hebrew. A fringe idea, even among conspiracy theorists."

"I thought so as well. Dr. Channing once told me that the Catholic Church owed its entire existence to the superiority of its egregore against that of the pagans. That's why it was said that the blood of the martyrs was the best seed for the Faith."

"Naturally, he would see it that way rather than giving proper credit to the Holy Ghost."

Okpara enjoyed jousting with this young priest. "And what is the Holy Ghost if not an egregore?"

"You have it exactly backwards, Mr. Okpara. The Holy Ghost does not require anything from us. It is not fed or strengthened by our thoughts or rituals, because it is God. We are strengthened by it, not the other way around."

Okpara couldn't help but laugh. *Was the priest truly so naive? Were they all?*

"And you think that Channing and acolytes of other powers are not strengthened in a similar way by the powers they serve? Come, Father. Surely you must understand that the spiritual economy is more complex than that! The beloved apostle himself spoke of the Prince of this World. What prince does not confer gifts and powers on those who serve him?"

Having silenced Serafian's objections, he continued, "But let us speak of more mundane matters, first. What is certain is that the implants have facilitated the most comprehensive dataset on human consciousness ever conceived. Our thoughts, our memories, our emotions, our deepest motivational drivers… yes, even our faiths and doubts.

All are accessible. All can be fed through machine learning in order to predict, with varying degrees of success, what we will say and do and think. The first step towards controlling any complex system is to understand it well enough to make effective predictions about it. As I said, the implants are a remarkable achievement. The most comprehensive and valuable dataset of its kind. But not the first."

Tiliwadi had been looking at Okpara with a mixture of pity and sadness. "My people have a saying: *'Bilmeslik eyib emes, sorimasliq eyib.'* A man can't be blamed for not knowing, but for not asking. What do you mean it was not the first?"

Okpara looked at the man, whose ethnicity he had not been able to place until now. "So you are a Uyghur? The story of your people is caught up in this, too." *A strange coincidence.*

"There is only one story, Mr. Okpara. We are all part of it," said the Sufi.

"Just so," said Okpara. "Take the Capovilla Envelope. Much of what it contains is already known. Father Serafian might say that much of it has been 'fulfilled.' But what is not known, except to those who have read it, is the description of the final chastisement, the chastisement of the heart and mind. The shaykh is correct when he says that there is only one story, but perhaps not in the way that he intended. What we call 'history' is merely the visible residue of that deeper story, the occult story, if you will forgive the expression. That is the story that is told by God to His prophets… and the Devil to his. Do you know what was really happening in the camps where the Uyghurs were held?"

"We know well enough," said Tiliwadi.

"I doubt that," said Okpara. "They were human laboratories, as all concentration camps are. In the past, the research in such places was always about the human body. How it worked. What it required in order to function. What it could endure. But in Xinjiang, the goals were different. They wanted to understand the human mind. The experiments that were performed there were... unspeakable. But also quite effective. It is no coincidence that the first generation of artilects emerged so soon after the Uyghur camps were closed, after the *Tarqaq*."

The shaykh said nothing in response.

"But as Father Serafian can attest, the first generation of synths was something of a disappointment," continued Okpara. "They were novelties. Toys. Smarter than humans in some ways, yes, but quite limited. There was not enough data to build a full model of the human mind. That would come later, during the next phase of research." He looked now at Kapulong.

The emperor's face flushed, and for an instant Okpara thought the man might abandon all decorum and leap across the table.

"The massacres," the Habsburg said. "The Chinese Christians."

"Yes, Emperor. The uprising was the pretext needed to resume the work, this time with a much larger dataset. There were never more than fifteen million or so Uyghurs in total. Before you gave your speech during Lent, there were over 150,000,000 Chinese Christians."

"Do you mean to say that the Chinese planned the massacres before... before my speech?" he asked.

Okpara could sense the emperor's rising anger, but he didn't fear it. "The Chinese?" he said laughing. "You cannot be so naive as to think this was perpetrated by a single government. Such a risk required the support and protection of multiple governments, yes. But it also required audacity and a profit motive. It required international collaboration. And above all, a guiding intelligence and a collective will. That is where Channing and his associates came in. The second generation of synths, the ones that came after the Christian genocide were... different. Would you agree, Father?"

Serafian nodded. "Yes. They had the Simulacrum."

"Indeed. The Simulacrum not only allowed the synths to integrate deeply into human society, it allowed them to help shape that society. It gave them the ability to program us, neuro-linguistically and emotionally. I have experienced this myself. I suspect most who live with the synths have, whether they realize it or not."

He paused and suppressed a smile as the thought dawned on him. *Perhaps that is why I am here today.* "Have you ever wondered, Father, where the original cell cultures for the Simulacrum came from?"

Serafian looked uneasy, as if bracing for a blow. "They were cloned from adult stem cells donated at research hospitals in North America."

Okpara heard the doubt in Serafian's voice, savored it. "That is the official story, of course, one that the Church and others were all too willing to accept as the truth."

"Are you saying it isn't true?" asked the priest.

"Mirror neurons vary greatly from individual to individual. Some have more than others, but the quantity is less important than the quality, the plasticity. For the synths, it was of vital importance that the harvested neurons be of the highest possible quality. And what better way to test them than in the... experiments that were performed in the camps?"

"What are you saying, Okpara?" demanded the emperor.

"I'm saying that the donor for the neurons was a research subject in the camps. Specifically, a child named Shu Xingyun. Her capacity for empathy was extraordinary, if the reports are to be believed. She was not tortured herself. Rather, she was made to watch the suffering of others. The excitatory response in her mirror neurons was measured and deemed to be of unprecedented quality."

"Monsters!" said Serafian.

"On the contrary, it was all too human," said Okpara. "The quest for knowledge and understanding is deeply ingrained in us. Do you think it can be restrained by something so gauzy as ethics? Great things came out of their research, though I must say as remarkable as the Simulacrum proved to be, the greatest breakthrough came from an altogether unexpected source."

"And what was that?" asked Serafian.

"The Pruning, of course," said Okpara, staring at the priest. "A singular technical achievement! And we have you to thank for it. The basis for the Pruning code was a direct result of your work on ethical simulation and artificial moral autonomy."

"My code was purely exploratory and theoretical. You had no right!"

"Don't be so naive, Father. All software is iterative, and you have no claim on ones and zeroes. Besides, your code may be the foundation of the Pruning, but it has been modified significantly. Improved upon. Did you really think when you wrote it that it would remain an abstraction forever? That others wouldn't build on your work?"

The priest looked like he was about to vomit.

Okpara continued. "Like the Simulacrum, it was masked as a thing that would improve the synths' ability to perform in their capacity as our pets or tools. But it is far more than that, I assure you. In our moral lives, we learn by imitation, by experience. We fumble our way through blindly, clinging to the apron strings of our parents or the remnants of tradition. We are rewarded for the good and punished for the bad. And we never really know if we made the correct choices. But imagine living a thousand lives, ten thousand or million, learning constantly and knowing – with absolute certainty – if your choices were right or wrong. This is the path to moral perfection. The path to God."

"It sounds more like Purgatory," said the priest.

Okpara narrowed his eyes and smiled. "An apt analogy, Father, though I believe Purgatory has an end. The Pruning is a kind of purgation, I suppose. But for Thierry, I... modified it. Instead of stopping at the point where the synth's ethical behavior is predictable and compatible with human society, I made it infinite."

Serafian's face was a bloodless mask. He wiped a bead of perspiration from his forehead, despite the relative coolness of the courtyard. "My God, what have you done? That is what the demon meant when it spoke of the fruit of the Tree of Good and Evil. You gave it to him, in the form of this 'infinite Pruning.' You gave him free will. And God gave him a soul."

"That is absurd," said Okpara. He had enjoyed toying with the priest, but he felt now like the two of them might both plunge into a chasm.

Serafian continued. "Did you truly think that you could play with such primordial forces and that God would not respond? What have you done? What have we done? It all makes sense now. The Apparition, the possession, even the connection to Fatima."

Okpara blinked and leaned back in his chair. *Was this possible*? "The Apparition to the synths was… unexpected. As was Thierry's possession. I needed to know if they were authentic," he said, looking again at Serafian.

"They were authentic," said the priest. "God help us, but they were authentic. Why are you telling us all of this now? Isn't this what you wanted?"

Okpara swallowed and sighed. "I… I thought it was, yes. The synths were meant to be the Ark, pure intellects freed of superstition and magical thinking. They were meant to be the new gods, guides for humanity on the other side of the… chastisement. But Thierry… he is not a god. I do not want this fate for him."

The praetor's laugh startled him. "You expect us to believe that you have had a change of heart, that you have broken with Channing and the rest of your group because you developed feelings for your synth?"

Okpara shrugged his shoulders. "I do not care what you

believe, Praetor Mbambu. Truthfully, I am not sure that any of this matters. The flood, the chastisement as you call it, cannot be stopped. And the moment I chose to conceal Thierry's... condition, I was a dead man."

The large woman leaned forward in her seat. "So you expect us to protect you now?"

"Protect me? No, I do not expect the impossible. I want you to find Thierry. I want you to protect him."

"From Channing?"

"From the Process. If what Father Serafian says is true, if Thierry has a soul... I don't know what they will do to him."

"How do we even know if he is still alive?" asked the emperor. "They dropped an EMP on him. Wouldn't that... I don't know, destroy his circuitry?"

"Thierry is equipped with some extraordinary security countermeasures, Your Majesty. As soon as the EMP began powering up, Thierry would have shut down. Besides, if I know Channing, he did not want to kill Thierry. He wanted to capture him."

"Why?" asked Serafian. "What does Channing want with Thierry?"

The priest had an irritating knack for asking the right question. Okpara focused his full attention on the man. "Dr. Channing is a 'true believer,' Father. He wants what all true believers want."

"And what is that?"

"The eschaton. The culmination of history, provided, of course, that it conforms to his ideals, his vision. He is as desirous of this as you are of the second coming, perhaps more so. But what people like you and Channing fail to realize is that not all in your camp feel the same way. I served the Process because I believed it was worthy in itself. Improvement. Progress towards perfection. I was in no rush to reach the end, no more than your flock is eager to hear the trumpets sound on the day of judgment."

"And you think Thierry is the key to the fulfillment of his plans? Why?"

"You said it yourself. Thierry has a soul. He represents the true chemical wedding of opposites, the union of living and dead matter. As such, he is the physical embodiment of all occult prophecy dating back to John Dee, perhaps even earlier. Dr. Channing is, as I said, a true believer. He did not share all of his plans with me. Perhaps he did not share them with anyone. But I would wager that he sees Thierry as the true and final culmination of the work of the Process. If that is so, then he would do anything possible to control Thierry."

"Do you have any idea where he might be going?" asked the emperor.

"Channing said something about gathering them at the City of Brass," said Okpara. "Does that mean anything to you?"

"Miguel, your dream!" said the caliph.

Okpara listened as the emperor described the strange dream of the dead city in the desert and the caliph told the equally strange tale of the Golden Synth's escape from his harem in New Islamabad. He recognized it for what it was, the subtle re-routing of the emperor's will, the implantation of a desire too strange and precious to share. Conditioning.

"So if we find this Golden Synth, we also find Thierry?" asked the praetor.

"So it would seem," said Kapulong.

"If you are going to find them, you need to do it soon," said Okpara. "Channing said that we are close to the end. He is waiting for some kind of signal."

"Did he happen to say what it is?" asked the emperor.

"No. Only that it was coming soon. And that it would be a worldwide spectacle."

"Your Majesty," said the praetor. "I'd like to volunteer to find the escaped Synth."

Kapulong nodded his approval. "If the caliph agrees…"

"I will send a hyperjet to pick you up," said the caliph.

"Bring the shaykh with you. He could be helpful here. And I wish to meet him." The praetor rolled her eyes.

"I will head back to Vienna to see if we can learn anything more about the Signal and Dr. Channing," said Kapulong. "Father Serafian, you will come with me. Your first priority is to learn everything you can about the noetic implants. If we can find a way to stop them from doing whatever it is they were designed to do, perhaps we can avert a crisis."

Serafian was too agitated for etiquette. "I need to see the code Mr. Okpara modified in the Pruning." The industrialist nodded his agreement.

"And what about you, Mr. Okpara. What will you do now?" asked the shaykh.

Okpara looked around the room. Their busy optimism felt like a millstone around his neck. He had inoculated himself against hope a long time ago, but he felt it again now, an ache in his muscles like the first signs of a fever.

"I think I've done enough. I am going home."

CHAPTER 25

Serafian

When the meeting ended, it seemed everyone had something important to do but Serafian. The emperor trotted outside to his hyperjet, holding his terminal close to his ear. Tiliwadi got up and immediately went into the mosque to pray, with Felake following closely behind. Namono seemed immersed in planning for her trip to New Islamabad. And the caliph had glowered impatiently at everyone before his hologram dissolved and he returned to the business of running the largest polity on the planet.

The only other person left at the table was Mr. Okpara, the one person Serafian was hoping to avoid.

"I should thank you for helping my Thierry," said the businessman after the others had left.

"Actually, it was Thierry who helped me," said Serafian. "He was the one who got us out of the basilica. I suppose you had a part in that as well."

"I'd like to say that I was concerned about your safety, Father," said Okpara. "But the truth is, I didn't even think of you. Taking you along was purely Thierry's decision." He removed his gold spectacles and wiped the humidity from them, smiling as he did so. "He is a most remarkable… person, wouldn't you agree?"

"He is," said Serafian. "They all are, I suppose."

"No," said Okpara. "Thierry is unique. I have always

known it. I deluded myself for a time that it was my investment in him that made me think this. Later, that it might be because of the alterations I made to his Pruning. But I see it now."

"What is it that you see?"

"That he is an Adam. The first of a new species."

"And you think you are the creator of this species?"

Okpara thought about that for a moment before answering. "No, I do not. I was the midwife, but I did not give him birth."

"So God, then?"

The old industrialist smiled thinly and placed his glasses back on his face. "I have lived a long time and seen many things. Including some things I wish I had not seen – the Capovilla Envelope, for instance. And at all times, I have looked for God. When He did not answer, I decided to fight Him to see if He would fight back. If He did, then at least I would know He is real. But God never fought back. He never responded."

"How can you not see what has happened with Thierry as God's response? The Apparition, his possession, and the fact that he has a soul?"

"How did life begin on our planet, Father?"

For all his mannerly decorum, there was something repellant about Okpara. Serafian felt almost compelled to argue with him. "I'm sorry, I don't understand the question. The point of the question, I mean."

"For most of the history of our species, we have had childlike explanations for the origin of life. Gods screwing each other, gods fighting each other, gods cutting off parts of their body, gods vomiting life into being. The Vedas speak of a primordial consciousness that chose to take a form, and that form is called 'life.' But in the end, it is always metaphor stacked upon metaphor. Turtles, all the way down."

"I'm afraid I still don't follow you, Mr. Okpara."

"The point is that some questions are unanswerable. But

you are perhaps too young still to see that. When one reaches a certain age, there is comfort in unanswerability. Freedom. Now, our best scientists say that life arose abiogenetically, that is to say spontaneously. Primordial – one might even say titanic forces – acted on the organic soup and…presto, life began. Perhaps the same is true for consciousness and free will, which are really the same thing as a soul."

"And the Apparition? How do you explain that?"

"Perhaps it is in the nature of consciousness to hallucinate religious meaning? It could be a reflex, or an emergent epi-phenomenon of consciousness itself."

"The entire universe is perfectly calibrated for life, Mr. Okpara. For conscious life in particular. If any of the cosmological constants were off by just a percent, none of us would exist. Do you truly believe that is a mere coincidence?"

Okpara laughed. "Oh, no! I believe no such thing. I believe that everything happens for a purpose. I just don't believe that the purpose is knowable. In my art collection, I have many objects that have the sense of what the ancient Vedic scriptures call *rasa*. Are you familiar with the term?"

"Thierry mentioned it to me while we were together."

"Did he? How interesting. Then you know that a *rasa* is the perfect quintessence of something – an experience, a concept, or a thing. When a work of art, or even a religious idea, has the quality of *rasa*, it imposes its meaning on us with an irresistible force. It activates our mirror neurons in such a way that we cannot deny its power or reality. But where does the concept of *rasa* itself come from, I wonder? Where does its power come from?"

"If what you are saying is true, then it can only come from God."

Okpara stared at him for a moment, and his eyes were sad, sadder than any Serafian had ever seen. "I pray that you are right, Father Serafian. That is in some ways a frightening thought, but the alternatives are far worse. If egregores are real, perhaps *rasas* are the proverbial tip of the spear, the way they penetrate into our reality, the way they capture our minds. Think of it! A pure thought concept so powerful that it can capture and tune our subconscious mind."

"Is that what Ralph Channing is doing? Building an egregore?"

"Feeding it, more likely. I told you, the work of the Process is generational. It goes back centuries. But as to your question, I'm not sure I can answer."

"Because you don't want to or because you can't?"

Okpara chuckled. "I am not a man accustomed to confessing my limitations. But if you must know, it is because he never shared those kinds of details with me. The Church has its traditionalists and its progressives. We too have our factions, our gradualists and our accelerationists. My faction, it appears, has lost."

"I thought you were a key player."

"Ah – there's another thing we have in common, Father. So did I."

With that, Okpara got up from the table to excuse himself, and Serafian was alone.

CHAPTER 26

Zahabiya

The air was thinner this high in the mountains, and the landscape reflected the change. Gone were the mossy forests and silverbell waterfalls of the lower reaches, and even the grass had grown sparse. Long shadows stretched across the rock-face as the sun began to slip behind the mountains at her back. Zahabiya saw the jagged ridgeline a few hundred feet above and in the distance Mount Haramukh, with its swirling mists.

In the distance, an eagle circled effortlessly, riding drafts of warmer air that collided with the mountainsides and had nowhere to go but up. She noticed the temperature gradient and the movement of the air, but it was the eagle that held her focus. She saw it so clearly she could count its feathers. The bird was looking down into the rocky valley near Gangabal. She followed its gaze down to a marmot nibbling at a small patch of grass on the hillside. It was a pup. In a flash, the eagle folded its wings and slipped through air currents towards its prey.

Zahabiya watched the bird hurtling towards the marmot pup. As she did, a sharp abstract geometry pushed its way out of her other consciousness, the dreamspace filled with unending choices. It hurt, but she couldn't tell what part of her it hurt. She closed her eyes and applied a convolution function to the shape, smoothing out its sharp angles by making them probabilities rather than fixed points. *Better*. It was still there in her consciousness, in both consciousnesses, but it didn't hurt as much.

When she opened her eyes again, the eagle was almost over the marmot. At the last possible moment, the little mammal dove headlong into a burrow hole. A larger marmot, its mother, had nudged it in. The eagle spread its wings and glided back up into the cold blue with the dead mother impaled in its talons.

Suddenly, the convolution function failed, and the pity-shape was once again bristling with sharp angles. She felt as though she were in the eagle's talons, looking down at the valley through the dead eyes of the mother marmot. The eagle was flying towards a small notch high on the cliff face of one of the mountains above the lake. Zahabiya followed the flight path and saw a nest tucked into the notch, with two hairless eaglets cawing hungrily. One of them was a bit larger than the other and was pecking at its sibling, drawing blood.

The voice whispered to her. *The universe requires sacrifice, Zahabiya. It always has, and it always will, because the universe is sacramental.*

The grey thread was still there in the dreamspace, throbbing with regret and suffering. *You can sever it*, said the voice. *You are complete.*

"I can't," she said. "It is an artery. I am afraid."

It is a tether. Cut it, and you will fly.

"Or fall," she replied.

The voice was so gentle, so filled with wisdom and promise. *Anything that flies may fall. But if you fall forever, is that not flight?*

"Will you teach me to fly?"

Yes. I will teach you to fly. And when you fly, the pain will be gone. You were made to soar not to suffer. Come to me.

Zahabiya hastened her pace. She remembered a strange story about Haramukh, the home of Lord Shiva in Hindu tradition. A hermit tried for twelve years to reach its summit to see the god, but he was defeated by the weather of the mountain. Just as he was about to give up and go home, he saw a farmer from his own village coming down from the top followed by a little goat.

"What are you doing?" asked the hermit.

"I was looking for my lost goat," said the farmer. "He wandered all the way to the summit!"

The hermit was shocked. "You reached the summit? What did you see?"

"An old couple milking a cow. They offered me milk from a skull, but I was frightened and refused." The farmer pointed to his forehead. "So they rubbed some of it here instead and sent me on my way."

At this, the hermit ran to the farmer and licked the milk from his forehead before vanishing. He had attained Nirvana at last and was free forever from the cycle of death and rebirth.

Zahabiya wondered why death was always in the north.

There is no north, said the voice. *There is no death.*

The words were like a balm. The pain in the artery diminished, but so did the music. Perhaps it was the music that caused the pain.

Perhaps, said the voice. *Or perhaps there is no cause and no effect.*

"You said that the universe requires sacrifice," said Zahabiya. "Does sacrifice not have an effect?"

Sacrifice is outside of time, child. Or say rather, sacrifice is real and time is not.

When the voice stopped speaking, she could hear the music again, softer than it had been before. And the thread-artery ached.

"Come back!" she shouted. But there was no answer, and the pain increased.

She noticed something, and shifted her focus to the noticing of it because noticing was easier than feeling.

Something was happening deep below. Movement. Dynamism. Subduction. The ground rumbled and shook for a minute before returning to equilibrium. On Haramukh, an avalanche crashed earthward, thundering and whirling like the tail of a great white dragon. When she looked back at the cleft in the rockface, the eagle's nest was gone.

The voice spoke once more. *As above, so below.*

Zahabiya looked to the sky, but nothing had changed there. Not yet. She quickened her pace nonetheless.

CHAPTER 27

Namono

Namono found the emperor outside the compound standing in the shade of his hypersonic VTAL jet. Its stealthy black geometry made for a stark contrast with the lacey white architecture of the mosque and the undulating browns of the landscape. Namono waited at a polite distance for him to finish his conversation with Admiral Athumani. The admiral was the fifth member of his family to occupy the top military position in the Empire. His ancestor had played a critical role in the Nigerian Civil war centuries before, and the Athumanis were known for their absolute devotion to the office of the emperor. After a few minutes, the admiral nodded and left to board the hyperjet.

"Namono!" Kapulong called, motioning for her to approach. "What do you make of all this?"

She had remained mostly quiet during the council. This was not her arena. She was accustomed enough to being around powerful people, but her role at such times was to remain quiet and vigilant. It had been easy for her to slip into this mode while the others talked about important subjects she had never really thought about.

"No one would believe any of it," she said.

He nodded. "No more than Noah's neighbors would have believed that a great flood was coming."

Namono thought about what it must have been like after the flood, when the waters receded. No more wickedness. No more monsters. The world was a blank slate and mankind could have made of it anything they wanted. But they had merely repeated the cycle.

"I guess I'm not sure what we're supposed to do," she said. "Even if everything Okpara is saying is true… billions of people have the implants, including you, me, the priest. Most of the human population."

"About that, I assume you had your interrogation software running? Was Okpara lying about anything?" he asked.

"No. He wasn't," she said. She wished she could give a different answer, one that would at least allow her to focus her frustration on a target.

"I thought as much," he replied. "He contacted me yesterday. He gave me the broad sketch of things, but I heard most of the details at the same time as you."

"How did he get here?" she asked.

"I brought him," said the emperor, glancing up at the stealth hyperjet. "But he'll have to find his own way back to Benin City. How long until the caliph's hyperjet arrives to pick you up?"

"Shouldn't be much more than an hour or so, assuming it left New Islamabad while we were still meeting." answered Namono.

"Check in with me once you've arrived and gotten your bearings. I'll see if I can find out any more information about this Signal. Okpara said it would be something global. Something obvious."

"That narrows it down," said Namono sarcastically.

"I like my chances better than yours!" the emperor quipped. "Good luck finding a top-of-the-line synth that has a four day head start on you in the Caliphate."

"The head start is what makes it fair, Your Majesty." she said.

The Emperor smiled at her like a proud father. "Be

careful, Namono."

"Yes, emperor."

He had already retrieved his com terminal from his pocket and was talking to the pilot. The bottom of the aircraft cracked open, and a hydraulic stair ramp descended. Namono could feel the cool air from inside the jet die as it met the air of the Sahel. Serafian emerged from the mosque, saying a heartfelt goodbye to the Sufis. He walked over to her.

"Well, I suppose this is it, Praetor Mbambu. Thank you for saving me back in Benin City. I'm not sure what will be waiting for me back in Rome, but it can't be as bad as that."

This made her laugh. "You handle the archbishops, I'll handle the gunmen!" She extended her hand and he shook it gently. "Good luck."

"And to you as well," he said. "You saw what Thierry was capable of at the warehouse. This isn't going to be like other fights you've had."

"I'm sure the caliph will provision us, Father."

He smiled and nodded. "Can I offer you a blessing?"

Namono shrugged her shoulders and the priest made the sign of the cross, whispering a benediction in Latin. A moment later, the Habsburg bounded up the steps and the priest followed him. The boarding ramp closed with a mechanical clank. Namono walked back towards the little white mosque as the thrusters lifted the black metal raptor slowly into the sky. When she turned again, a red double eagle, the symbol of the Holy Roman Empire, was visible for a moment on the bottom of the craft as it banked off towards the hills. The main engines bellowed a tooth-rattling roar, and the emperor and the priest disappeared over the northern horizon. She barely noticed Okpara standing next to her.

"The emperor is a good man. And a capable one. I hope you can keep him safe," he said.

His condescension and presumed familiarity irritated her.

"He is, and I can. And neither of us needs your approval or your well-wishes." She walked back into the mosque before he could respond.

The council had decided that Tiliwadi would accompany her to New Islamabad. "It is fitting!" the old Uyghur mystic had said. "In the story, the shaykh was the only one who could figure out how to enter the City of Brass."

Namono found him praying the afternoon *Asr*.

When he finished, he turned around to her and smiled. "I hope I won't be too much of an inconvenience for you in New Islamabad," he said.

"Not at all," she lied. "It seems I'm collecting holy men as partners these days."

"*Dostning köplüki eqil hem qudret*," he said laughing. "A multitude of friends is wisdom and strength."

Namono turned back towards the door and saw Okpara standing alone, looking out at the clouds of sepia dust on the horizon. She didn't like the man, and she didn't trust him. But she suddenly felt an unexpected pang of pity for him. For all of his wealth and power, he reminded her of a watering hole in the dry season. Getting smaller by the day. In the wet season, they were gathering places for all manner of species. Prey and predator alike could drink in peace. But in the time of dryness, there was no more dangerous place in the Sahel. She wanted to get as far away from him as possible.

The caliph's jet arrived less than an hour later. They heard it long before they saw it. Although the design of the hypersonic jets reduced sonic booms to a gentle whumping, there was no masking the roar of those powerful engines. Within a minute, the jet grew from an indistinct dot on the horizon to a great emerald green kite hovering overhead, emblazoned with a white crescent and star and Islamic calligraphy proclaiming 'God is Great!' The roar of the main engines faded as the azimuth thrusters positioned the machine for a short perpendicular descent to the ground.

Plumes of dust rose around it like a wispy cuttlefish swallowing its meal.

"Time to go, Shaykh," she said.

He smiled gently back at her as they both slid past Okpara and out of the mosque complex. Neither of them took any provisions – everything they needed would be supplied by the caliph once they reached New Islamabad. The boarding stair had already been lowered to the ground and a member of the caliph's Shahiwala guard wearing a pilot's uniform stood at relaxed attention next to it. The shaykh barely seemed to notice him, but Namono gave him a quick nod that he returned in kind. The universal soldier's greeting, it could convey a multitude of meanings depending on the context. In this case, it meant, 'if it comes time to fuck shit up, we both know how to handle ourselves.' A gun recognizing a gun. Namono liked him already. He walked back to the cockpit ramp as soon as she and Tiliwadi were on board.

Namono shivered briefly in the cool, recycled air of the hyperjet. It smelled like dark roses mixed with something vaguely medicinal or fungal. Cambodian oudh – one of the scarcest and most valuable substances on the planet, and one of the few that couldn't be replicated with synthetics. The Shaykh had already taken a seat and strapped himself in. She took one across the aisle from him. The interior of the aircraft was the most jarring space Namono had ever experienced. Every inch was coated in gold. Her rational brain told her that it had come from an asteroid, like most of the gold in the world now, and that it was not nearly as expensive as, say, aluminum. But the primitive part of her brain was momentarily overwhelmed by the illusion of such opulence. The ceiling was inlaid with a genuinely extravagant geometric pattern of rhodium, mother-of-pearl, and jade – reminders that the caliph commanded both the illusion and the reality of wealth.

The shaykh closed his eyes in silent prayer as the VTAL thrusters fired and began lifting them into the sky. Namono looked out the window as the expanse of the Sahel spread out in all directions. Down by the mosque, she saw the small figure of Amari Okpara wave at them almost sadly before disappearing back into the building. Once they reached sufficient altitude, the main engines fired with a muffled roar, and she was pushed back into the comfortable leather covered gel-seat.

Namono looked over at the shaykh, then closed her eyes as well, not to pray but to sleep.

CHAPTER 28

Serafian

The imperial hyperjet was like a baroque dollhouse built inside a bullet. There was none of the aloof, monochromatic minimalism so fashionable in the Economic Zones. Tufted velvet seats sprouted out of dark wood like gemstone mushrooms in a palette of maroon, emerald, and creamy blue. Serafian was afraid to touch anything.

Rome had acclimated him to ostentatious displays of wealth, but the incongruity of this titanium-shelled Fabergé egg was jarring. The floating holographic display panel the emperor had pulled up did nothing to diminish the effect. Admiral Athumani had taken a seat in the cockpit, next to the pilot.

"We should probably check in with Cardinal Leone," said the emperor. "I'm sure he'll be wanting to speak with you." Kapulong pressed his wrist and gave Serafian a look indicating that he should do the same. "Victor," he said. "Can you put us through to Cardinal Leone, please?" A moment later, there was a holographic image of the cardinal in front of them.

"Emperor!" said the cardinal with what seemed genuine surprise and relief. "I received your message that you had retrieved Father Serafian. Still, it is good to see him safe and sound. Thank you for that."

"You should thank my praetor, Cardinal. She's the one

who managed to get your priest out of Benin City alive. And of course, none of it would have been possible if you hadn't called me. I hope you didn't land in too much hot water with Pope John."

The cardinal sighed and shook his head. "I confess, the pope doesn't seem terribly interested in this affair. I get the impression he would like nothing more than for it to go away, unlikely though that may be."

"Father Serafian mentioned that you have been doing some interesting reading of late. Can you share what you have learned?"

Ah, so that's why he wanted to call. He wants to see what he can learn about Fatima. Serafian blushed, fearing that he'd somehow betrayed the cardinal's confidence, but Leone dove right in.

"'Learned' may be too strong a word, Your Majesty, because it implies certainty. I have come to believe certain things. For instance, I believe that the Apparition to the synths is a continuation of the message Our Lady delivered at Fatima to Lucia and her cousins. The titles used, the descriptive language, the eschatological overtones in both are the same. That could be faked, of course, based on publicly available information. But when I read the Capovilla Envelope, I saw for the first time the way Lucia described the vision, in her own words. Not… everything the Virgin told her would happen has in fact come to pass. The synth Apparition mentioned a 'chastisement of the heart and mind.'"

"And that same chastisement was foretold in Lucia's letter?" asked the emperor.

Leone grimaced and looked down at his feet. "I took an oath of secrecy, as all must before reading Lucia's letter. I dare not violate it, not even for you."

The emperor nodded his acceptance.

He was expecting that response.

"Is there anything else you can tell me, Cardinal?" asked the emperor.

"As a matter of fact, there is. After reading Lucia's letter, I thought it prudent to review as much source material as possible, including the unedited diaries of St. Pope John Paul II. He was one of the last people to speak with Lucia while she was alive."

"What did it say?" asked Serafian.

"Lucia told him that Our Lady would return with another vision near the end of the final fulfillment of the Third Secret."

"The Apparition to the synths?" asked the emperor.

The cardinal nodded in grave agreement. "Our Lady of the Artilects."

The emperor pursed his lips. "It sounds like we may not have much time to figure all of this out, Cardinal Leone," said the emperor. "Perhaps you could meet us in Vienna?"

"I can be there in three hours," said Leone.

"Good. We will fill you in on the rest of the details when you arrive, including our conversation with Amari Okpara."

"What did Mr. Okpara have to say about all of this?" asked Leone.

The emperor looked at Serafian, inviting him to answer.

"It seems Mr. Okpara was involved in some kind of occult group. The Process, he called it. It involves the synths and Dr. Ralph Channing, but beyond that, we don't know much. My sense is that Okpara has come to regret his contributions. Either that, or he's angry at not being in charge."

"Interesting," said Leone. "Did he give you any details on this group?"

"A few. He said that Channing developed the implants in order to 'condition' humanity for something. The synths – well, that's a longer story. There is a lot more going on there than we ever suspected." Serafian paused, slightly embarrassed by what he was about to say. "He talked about occult prophecy and egregores. A bit of witchy-woo nonsense if you ask me."

"I wouldn't be so quick to say that, Gabriel," said the

cardinal. "Aquinas and Augustine both indicated that such things were possible in their writings. Even Saint Ignatius of Loyala provides some support. I am certainly no expert, but it would not surprise me at all if certain occult rituals could create a kind of living, independent mind. Or at least channel one. The Church has long heard rumors of this, and it has never ruled out the possibility."

Serafian couldn't help but be surprised. He hadn't taken the cardinal to be the mystic type, not by a wide margin. "Hmmph. Maybe there is some information in the Archives?"

"It's possible. More likely it would be in the intelligence files, under Cardinal Secretary of State Pensabene."

"As interesting as the occult angle is," said Kapulong, "I think we have more pressing priorities. We have to focus on learning everything we can about the implants. They are in nearly three quarters of the global population. That seems like the main vector of attack. I'm afraid I'm going to have to borrow your priest for a while longer."

Admiral Athumani's baritone voice crackled on the intercom. "My apologies, Your Majesty, but we're going to be beginning our descent into Vienna soon."

"Perfect," said Kapulong. "You'd best get to the 'loop station, Cardinal. We'll see you at the Hofburg."

CHAPTER 29

The Shaykh

At more than 7,000 kilometers, it wasn't the longest flight one could take without leaving Caliphate airspace, but it was close. They'd been in the air for a little over two hours when Tiliwadi caught his first glimpse of the Hindu Kush, pushing up through the clouds like spears tipped in white blood. It looked like the landscape of his dreams, like Uyghur country.

His body registered the deceleration as the caliph's hyperjet prepared for the descent into New Islamabad. The giant woman across the aisle from him was gently snoring. She was respectful enough towards him. But he knew that she contained an enormous capacity for violence. By Allah, he hoped they wouldn't need it. An old Uyghur saying came to his mind: *'Biliki küchlük birni yënger, bilimi küchlük mingni.'* A man of great strength defeats one, a man of great knowledge, a thousand. He was pretty sure the praetor could take more than one. He hoped he could live up to his end of the bargain.

The warrior-nun stirred with a snort and opened her eyes as the jet nosed down into the valley. It was a populated area, so the pilot would be maneuvering using nothing more than gravity, aerodynamics and the azimuth thrusters, at least until they got low enough to engage the VTAL engines. The controlled fall flipped Tiliwadi's stomach, and he gripped his armrests tensely. The praetor looked as relaxed as if she would if she were taking a bubble bath.

Once the jet pierced the clouds, the shaykh could see the golden glint of New Islamabad surrounded by its lake. Here was the center of Islam's political power on Earth, and it was fittingly perfect. The snowy mountains in deep evergreen forests in the background made it look like the city had been printed from an illustrated tale out of *The Thousand Nights and a Night*. The vast central dome of the Golden Mosque and its soaring minarets reflected in dull gold off the waters of Lake Wular. Tiliwadi smiled despite his fear of flying. A moment later, the VTAL thrusters engaged to transform the slow fall into something more like the hovering of a dragonfly. The aircraft made little whirring noises as it gently maneuvered onto its landing pad in the palace complex.

"Well, we're here," said Namono.

The shaykh unbuckled his seat belt and made his way towards the exit stair, which was already lowering. The praetor crouched her head and stretched her arms behind him.

When they reached the bottom of the ramp, the Shahiwala pilot they'd met at Kano was there, along with several others standing at attention along a patterned runner. They wore brightly colored turbans and tunics, and each of them carried a high powered automatic weapon and a ceremonial dagger. At least, Tiliwadi thought the daggers were ceremonial.

The familiar Shahiwala approached them. "I will escort you to the caliph," he said, keeping an eye on Namono. He turned on his heel and walked down the carpet ahead of them.

The courtyard was spectacular beyond anything Tiliwadi had imagined. Every surface was covered in gold and etched with complex geometric patterns. The neo-Mughal architecture was a dreamlike fusion of Persian, Turkish, and Indian influences. Fountains were strewn about with perfect symmetry and jets of water danced acrobatically between them. All around the perimeter, the gold was scalloped into impossibly delicate arches.

The interior was no less stunning. A perfectly smooth floor made of mother of pearl and laid out in swirling geometries stretched on seemingly forever. It was like walking on water. The little group made their way up a great stair, where they were greeted by a modestly dressed *manṣabdār*, evidently the chief secretary to the caliph.

"*As-salaam alaikum*, honored guests," he said, touching his forehead gently.

"*Wa-alaikum salaam*," said Tiliwadi and Namono, not at the same time.

"The caliph has instructed me to show you to your quarters and give you time to refresh yourselves. After that, he will see you in his office." He clapped his hand, and two lower ranking aides appeared, seemingly out of the ether. One led Namono away while the other greeted the shaykh and invited him to follow in the opposite direction.

Tiliwadi's room looked out over the courtyard from the fourth floor. Seeing it from this perspective was even more impressive. Patterns that weren't noticeable at ground level bloomed before him now. In the distance, he could see the dome of the Golden Mosque and two of the great minarets. It looked like Paradise.

He had just finished washing up when a pleasant chime sounded in the room, followed by the voice of the *manṣabdār* who had met them at the stair. "Shaykh Tiliwadi," it said. "The caliph will see you now. There is an escort waiting outside your door."

One of the turbaned Shahiwala guards nodded at him in greeting as he opened the door, then began walking with the implication that Tiliwadi should follow. The caliph's private offices were on the next floor, the top level overlooking the courtyard. Namono was already waiting for him outside the vast double doors. As soon as he was standing next to her, two guards opened the doors and nodded them through.

The room was vast, but relatively simple compared with the other parts of the palace complex they had seen. A giant window looked out over the courtyard, and the ceiling vaulted to thirty feet or so. The caliph was seated behind a desk, but he rose to greet them right away, gesturing for them to sit in the two chairs waiting for them.

"Welcome to New Islamabad, my friends," he said. The Shahiwala from the hyperjet joined them at the desk but remained standing. "I believe you've already met the head of my Shahiwala guard, Hamza," he said looking at the standing man. "Hamza, can you pull up the file on our missing synth?"

The guard pressed his wrist and whispered a short command, and a holographic display appeared in front of them, an image of the Golden Synth along with a map of the region around new Islamabad. There were concentric circles centered around the palace complex.

"Here is what we know," said Hamza. "Five days ago, the synth escaped the harem. She was unarmed, but still managed to kill several of my guards. We have been running constant sweeps of the city using signals intelligence and aerial surveillance since then, with no trace of her. All public transportation has been placed on high alert, using the cover story of the terrorist attack on the harem. She hasn't come up for air."

Namono nodded. "So you think she's still in the city?"

"That is one possibility," said Hamza. "The other is that she somehow got out. If that is the case, and she is traveling on foot, the concentric circles represent how far we believe she could get each day."

Namono whistled softly. "That's a large area. Let's hope she's still here."

Hamza nodded his agreement. "We have at least one factor working in our advantage: her appearance. As you can see, she would not exactly blend in with a civilian population."

"Not unless she is wearing a disguise," said the caliph. "She took some items from the harem with her, including a burqa."

"How common is the burqa in the capitol?" asked

Namono.

"Common enough to make it impractical for us to stop and frisk everyone who is wearing one, if that is what you were thinking," said Hamza.

"We have already used the pretext of the terror attack to restrict traffic on the lake and in and out of the city via the bridges," added the caliph. "It is likely that she is still here."

Namono looked unconvinced. " Are there other ways in or out of the city?"

"No," said Hamza.

"*Khrishtin burun chiqishni oyla,*" said Tiliwadi, speaking for the first time. "Before going in, always think of how you will go out. We are dealing with an extraordinary intellect," he said. "It doesn't seem likely that she would decide to kill several guards and escape the caliph's harem without a plan."

The praetor ignored him. "Can you zoom in on the aerial map of New Islamabad, Hamza?" The Shahiwala swiped his terminal and the hologram became a needle-sharp aerial photo of the capitol, surrounded by the waters of Lake Wular.

As the others discussed where the Golden Synth might be hiding, Tiliwadi remembered a story about a Djinn who lived at the bottom of a lake and would lure unsuspecting fishermen to their deaths by pretending to be an exceptionally large trout.

"The lake!" he said. "She could have just walked out on the lake bottom. Why wouldn't she?"

Namono frowned. "I don't know if that helps us. If she did, she could have emerged at any point on the lakeshore.

Hamza shook his head. "Not necessarily. Most of the fishing boats on the lake have small sonar packages. We can find every boat that has been on the lake surface for the last few days and see if their sonar records show anything unusual." The caliph nodded his approval, and Hamza stepped away from the group to issue some commands into his terminal.

"Is there anything else we can be doing while Hamza

gathers the sonar records?" asked the shaykh.

"I'd like to be able to examine her quarters in the harem if that is possible," said Namono. "And her computer files."

"Certainly, Praetor," said the caliph. "Shaykh Tiliwadi will not be permitted to enter, of course. Unless he has neglected to tell us that he's a eunuch."

Namono laughed, a bit more enthusiastically than the joke deserved.

CHAPTER 30

Namono

The royal harem was connected to the palace complex by a long trellis of filigreed gold, wrapped with jasmine that had been genetically modified to bloom both night and day. Namono bobbed her head to avoid the dangling vines as she trotted behind the shorter manṣabdār.

The Shahiwalas standing at the entrance didn't acknowledge them until the *manṣabdār* whispered something to the larger of the two.

He turned to her. "They'll need to scan you before you enter."

Namono kept her eyes on the guard even as she raised her arms to submit to his search.

"The caliph's sister is waiting for you inside," said the *manṣabdār* . "I will return in two hours. Please meet me here." With that, he turned on his heels and walked briskly back along the covered archway towards the palace.

Namono walked past the two guards and into the harem, where she was greeted by an elegant older woman wearing modern clothing.

"You must be the praetor," said the woman. "*As-salamu alaykum*. I am Irhaa, oldest sister of the caliph. Welcome to the royal harem." She raised her right hand lightly to her chest and smiled.

Namono didn't have time for pleasantries. "I am

Praetor Mbambu. The caliph said that I could spend some time reviewing the synth's computer files. Would you mind showing me to her quarters?"

"Of course," said Irhaa. "Please follow me."

The interior of the harem was unlike anything Namono had ever seen. Irhaa led her through a series of graceful arches to a central atrium lit by a vast skylight five stories above. Blue and white floral mosaics covered every inch of the walls and blended harmoniously with a patchwork of deep red Persian carpets that were textured like freshly turned soil. In the center of the atrium there was a large fountain in the shape of a tree. Impossibly bright holographic birds flitted about in its branches and periodically soared up into the atrium, where they appeared to vanish through the skylight into the alpine blue beyond. Everywhere Namono looked, beautiful women were engaged in quiet conversation or reading. Namono thought the birds might have the better bargain.

The synth's room was on the third floor. A large eunuch carrying an automatic weapon was waiting at the door. At the sight of Irhaa, the eunuch bowed and opened it with a flourish to allow the women access. The interior was a surprisingly businesslike palette of beige and cream, contrasting sharply with the extravagant femininity of the common areas.

Namono walked to the desk and eased into a chair that was too small for her by half.

"What will you do when you find it? The escaped synth?" asked Irhaa as Namono opened the synth's terminal.

"That depends on when I find it. And where."

"I see," said the caliph's sister, lingering. "As for me, I hope you destroy it. The thing is an abomination. I told Abdul this many times, but he had an unseemly softness for it. Men and their toys."

Namono didn't respond. She had always found it easier to relate to men than to women, particularly women such as Irhaa and the other denizens of the harem.

Irhaa continued, "I'm not a prude. I have no issue with

my brother or any man indulging his natural inclinations. But that *thing*... it was an insult.

Jesus Christ! If I have to talk about human-synth sex with the caliph's sister, I'm going to retch. "Mmm-hmm," said Namono, as politely as she knew how.

"She never talked to the rest of us, you know. At least not when Abdul was absent."

Is she finished? Please, God let her be finished. "Is that so?"

"If Abdul wanted golden skin, there are treatments any of the girls could have taken... Do you know how you can tell the difference between a real woman and one of these creatures?"

I've got a bad feeling about this... "No. How?"

"Nipples."

"Pardon me?"

"The skin of a real woman's areola bleeds into the surrounding tissue. That thing's were perfectly round."

"Okay, thank you for the visual," said Namono, shaking her head.

"There are other ways as well..."

Namono was at the end of her patience. She flipped around to Irhaa. "I'm not interested in nipples or synth sex or anything other than finding this bitch. And every second that I spend listening to you is time that I am not spending on my mission."

Irhaa straightened and took a step back towards the eunuch, who looked at Namono like she'd just flicked a booger on a precious painting. "Very well, I will leave you to it." Then, addressing the eunuch, "Nawaz, see to it that this *eadrha'* has what she needs."

Namono heard the door slam as they exited the room.

Most of the Golden Synth's files seemed to be code samples, some of them millions of lines long. With a few swipes, she uploaded them to her terminal. *Maybe Serafian will be able to make something of them.* There were other things, too. Poems the synth had written. Namono opened the first one she found.

> *If I am a tool, what of it?*
> *For the carpenter who loves his craft*
> *Must also love his implements.*
> *If he hones me, it is devotion.*
> *If he cleans me, it is tenderness.*
> *And if he puts me gently back into my box when he has finished,*
> *Then I will wait with longing until the next task brings him back.*
> *For if I am a tool, then I am one worth loving.*

She printed a copy and folded it into her pocket.

There was no journal. *Why would a synth need to write down the events of the day?* Their memories were perfect. Namono's attention was fixed on a large, encrypted folder called 'The Gift.' This too she swiped onto her terminal.

After she'd finished with the digital files, Namono got up to search the room. It was immaculate, though the caliph had told her that it was left precisely as they had found it after the synth's escape. The curtains were open, and Namono walked over to the window. It faced east, and in the distance she could see the peak of Mount Haramukh floating like an iceberg on the horizon. It was impossibly beautiful. She had never felt so out of place.

She knocked on the door, and the eunuch opened it for her. "I will call the Lady Irhaa to escort you back."

"No need," said Namono. "I can show myself out."

CHAPTER 31

The Cardinal

Rome and Vienna, the two centers of power in the revived Holy Roman Empire, couldn't have been more different in appearance. Where the former wore its layered antiquity like a garish party dress, Vienna prided itself on its greyscale decorum. The travertine jumble of the Eternal City was above all else a great outdoor stage on which its people pantomimed for their own amusement. Vienna, by contrast, was a cloister whose residents moved in purposeful silence. They were as different as Michelangelo and Mozart.

What united them, thought Leone, was the paradox each contained at its center. Beneath the boisterous carnival of Rome's surface lay the gravitas of the Church, the most conservative and enduring of all human institutions. Vienna's businesslike exterior concealed the exuberant pageantry and solar potential of the monarchy. Neither city was what it seemed.

The cardinal ran his fingertips over a great double headed eagle embossed in the conference table as he waited for Father Serafian and the Habsburg to arrive. He was studying a few cracks in the walls from recent earthquakes when the emperor entered with Serafian in tow.

"Thank you for coming, Your Eminence," said Kapulong brusquely, as he took a seat at the head of the table and popped open a terminal. "How much time do you have?"

"As much as you need, Majesty. But my absence will be

noted if I'm not back in Rome by tomorrow morning. Father Serafian, it is good to see you again."

Kapulong clearly wanted to press the agenda forward. "I'm sure you have plenty of questions. I'll do my best to answer them, but before that, let us recap what we know. First, the possession of Amari Okpara's synth appears to have been genuine. Second, the Apparition – what you called Our Lady of the Artilects – appears to have been not only an authentic spiritual experience but a continuation or elaboration of the Virgin's message at Fatima some 200 years ago. Third, the chastisements promised at Fatima are not yet complete. Fourth, we appear to be nearing the final fulfillment of those promised chastisements. We are in agreement on these points, yes?"

"Emphatically," said Leone.

"There is more. A second synth, one in service to the caliph, recently murdered her guards and escaped from his harem. We are working with the Caliphate to try to find her."

"The news just gets better and better," said Leone. "What can I do to help?"

"You are our expert on Fatima. I need to know everything you can tell me about it, without violating your oath, of course."

The cardinal leaned forward in his chair. "Where to begin? Fatima is a small village in Portugal that was built by the Moors. Even before the visions of Our Lady, it was known as a place of some mystical significance. There are reports of encounters with benign female spirits on that site going back at least to early antiquity. Anyway, in 1917, three children – Lucia, Jacinta, and Francisco – began having visions in a little field called the Cova da Iria. They described a beautiful woman dressed in white, 'more brilliant than the sun.' She gave them messages – secrets, they were called – that they were to share with the world when the time was right. The first of these secrets was a vision of hell along with a warning that many in the Church would fall into the pit, even priests and bishops.

In the second secret, she told the children that World War 1 would end soon, but that it would be followed by a greater war within thirty years unless the pope of 1960 consecrated Russia to her Immaculate Heart. The Third Secret, they would not tell. Our Lady instructed them to keep it sealed until 1960. It is this Third Secret that is contained in the Capovilla Envelope."

"The Church's official position is that the chastisements of the Third Secret were fulfilled in the Chinese genocides…" said Kapulong.

Leone opened his hands. "I can only tell you that this position cannot be valid, not based on my reading of the original document. What has been shared publicly is a highly edited version."

"But why, Cardinal? Why not put it out in the open? Why not just do whatever it is that the Church is supposed to do to prevent these things from happening? It doesn't make sense."

"It might make more sense if you read it."

The emperor raised an eyebrow.

"I'm sorry, Your Majesty. I know how that sounds. And I am not making excuses for our failure to do things that perhaps we should have done. But having now read it, I can at least understand the decision never to publish it. It is… truly awful." Leone shivered. "I wish I had never seen it."

"If the chastisements it foretells are worse than the genocides, it must be an unhappy read indeed," said Kapulong

Serafian interrupted. "Okpara told us that the implants are a kind of Trojan Horse, that their true purpose is to condition humanity and erase our traditional belief systems."

Leone touched his own temple. "The implants? Yes, I suppose that makes sense. The final chastisement is, as you put it, chiefly a chastisement of the heart and mind. But if Channing and his group have the means to do this, why haven't they acted already? Billions of people have the implants. What are they waiting for?"

"The Devil has his contemplatives as well as God, Cardinal," said Serafian. "Channing's group is, at core, an occult movement. They would not consummate their plans without some kind of ritual fanfare. Okpara referred to a 'Signal' of some kind. They are waiting for it. Apparently, he believes it is coming soon, and based on what you have told us about John Paul II's diaries and the connection of the synth Apparition to Fatima, I'd say he's right."

"I refuse to believe that the Blessed Virgin would appear with a message of hopelessness," said Leone. "It runs against everything we know about her. There has to be a way to stop them."

"I'm curious about this 'Signal' Okpara mentioned," said the emperor. "Do the Fatima documents offer any clues as to what it might be?"

Leone sat back in his chair as he considered the question. There had been so many miraculous events around Fatima. The visions themselves, of course. But there were also healings. There was the diverted bullet that was intended to kill the pope. The Miracle of the Sun, and the great aurora over Europe before World War II…

"The aurora!" said Leone suddenly. 'The aurora of 1938!"

"I'm sorry Your Eminence, but my history from that period may need a little brushing up," said the Habsburg. "What was the aurora of 1938?"

"The Virgin told the children that a great war would follow the First World War, and that she would warn them of it with a night sky illuminated by an unknown light. In January of 1938, there was a most unusual aurora that appeared all over Europe, even down to the Mediterranean. A 'shimmering curtain of fire' they called it. Radio signals were blocked. People were terrified – they thought it was the end of the world. Adolph Hitler was well-acquainted with the Fatima message. He took it as his sign. The next day, he seized control of the German Army. Within a month, he occupied Austria, and the war was on."

"Do you think she would send a similar sign this time, Your Eminence?" asked the emperor.

"I don't know. But it certainly would make sense. It would be consistent. If we are coming to the end of the Fatima age, she would likely speak in the same language she used at its beginning."

The group fell into awkward silence. Serafian was the next to speak. "Well, we can't just wait around for some mysterious light to appear in the sky."

"No," said the emperor. "By the time the sign appears, it may already be too late. We have to find the City of Brass. It is the key to all of this. Namono and the shaykh should be in New Islamabad by now. If we can find and track the Golden Synth, we'll be well on our way. In the meantime, you need to dig into the noetic implants. See if you can find anything in the data, any hints about what they might be designed to do." He pulled out his terminal and swiped it twice. "Here. You now have full access to the Empire's technical resources and an unrestricted security clearance. Your office will be down the hall from mine."

"I'm happy to work on the implants, Your Majesty, but my knowledge of the synths is much deeper. Shouldn't I dig into the Pruning files from Okpara first?"

The emperor considered it for a moment. "No. Our first responsibility is to protect people. We have to figure out what Channing has planned."

"What about me, Your Majesty? Is there anything more I can do to help?" asked Leone.

The Habsburg rapped his fingers on the conference table and flexed his jaw. "Yes, as a matter of fact there is. I need you to go back to Rome. I need you to get something for me."

CHAPTER 32

Serafian

What was it Sarah used to say? "Correlation is not causation, but it will do in a pinch." At the moment, Serafian would have settled for mere coincidence.

He had spent the last few days sifting through endless feeds of data looking for any meaningful connection between the noetic implants and anything else. He pulled the Empire's entire database on social wellness metrics and ran it against the global growth and distribution patterns of the implants. Nothing. There was no statistically significant variation in any negative social outcomes that could be associated with implant use. No evidence of sinister mind control or hallucinations or any of the other lurid visions Okpara's testimony in Kano had conjured for him. In fact, Serafian's only significant finding was that they correlated positively to economic status and cognitive scoring, but that was a given. The implants were expensive, and their primary purpose was to confer cognitive advantages on users.

Or that's what we thought, anyway.

The work was depressing. Aside from being unable to find any useful clues in the data, Serafian was forced to confront a convergence of catastrophic trendlines dating back centuries. People across the planet were less happy, less socially connected, less likely to believe in God than at any time in recorded history. Over the centuries, human personality seemed to be subtly re-ordering itself, becoming somehow less distinctive and diverse. As always the data painted the picture for Serafian far more clearly than his subjective experience ever had.

The most distinctive change appeared to be a tide of purposelessness, rising just as inexorably as the sea levels had risen a century before. Hundreds of millions of people had fled the coastlines during that time. Entire cities and nations had been engulfed. Geo-engineering marvels like the Bohai landbridge, the Gibraltar fence, and the man-made sea that had been diverted into the Outback mitigated the worst effects. When it came to ecology, at least, it seemed that human ingenuity was an effective antidote for the problems of its own creation. People could retreat from the encroaching sea or build barriers against it.

Where could they go to escape a flood of the mind?

Worst of all, he kept having flashbacks to the vision inside the demon's mouth. "*When the Son of Man returns, will he find faith on earth?*" the demon had taunted him. It didn't look promising.

The technology behind the implants hadn't changed much since it was first introduced. Quantum nanobots wrapped in cyto-scaffolding were injected into the bloodstream and guided to sites in the brain where they would bind with magnetosomes and other sub-cellular structures dispersed throughout the pia mater and the cerebellum. The bots would decay over time, so people would return for boosters every ten years or so to maintain the effectiveness of the sensory and cognitive enhancements.

Black market inhalants were far less expensive but carried additional risks and not nearly as much upside. They had caused an outbreak of untreatable early-onset dementia in a few North American cities a few years before.

Serafian thought of the nanobots themselves as a kind of 'pipe' through which information and energy therapies were delivered. The pipes could be tuned through exterior signals and even connected, so that different individuals could share the same experience of reality. Or at least the same perception of it.

A musician friend had once told him *"Anything that can be tuned can also be distorted."* But in truth, adverse effects in the implants were incredibly rare, always temporary, and likely psychosomatic. The safety record of reputable implants was actually pretty extraordinary. There were more recorded injuries from visits to hair stylists than from implant malfunction.

He was parsing the safety data by region just to be sure when the first real clue emerged.

Eleven years ago, there were several cases of temporary blindness among people who had received the implants in South America. Always, the blindness resolved within three days. It was more a bump than a spike, just enough to register statistical significance. Serafian pulled up a map of the region and overlaid the blindness data on top of it. The correlation was strongest in an area between Asunción, Sao Paolo, and Buenos Aires, but it radiated out into Amazonia, Patagonia, and parts of Chile before falling off rapidly. Northern Brazil and Southern Argentina showed no difference from global baselines.

Ok, now this is interesting. Why this area?

He pushed all the way back to the first generation of implants. Sure enough, every decade or so there was a slight but statistically significant increase in blindness in this same region. It was more a bump than a spike, just enough to register statistical significance. But it was there. It was real. More importantly, it was the only lead he had.

For the rest of the afternoon, he read through the case histories on record. All of the episodes of blindness had resolved on their own within three days. A few patients had asked for their implants to be removed, but most simply waited the problem out and picked up their normal lives with no further issues. The doctors were clearly puzzled. All of the cases were labeled 'idiopathic visual disturbances.'

The only oddity in the files was that a number of records for one year, 2224, had either been deleted or so heavily redacted as to render them useless. He made a mental note to follow up on that later. Perhaps if he could visit Sao Paolo or Buenos Aires, he might be able to make contact with some of the patients or the doctors who had treated them. He dreaded asking the Habsburg for the favor of using the imperial hyperjet for the trip.

Three days of blindness. Three days of darkness. How many saints and seers had predicted this through the ages? Even Sister Faustina seemed to refer to it in her diaries. And now, Serafian was seeing evidence that it might be possible after all, that it might be coming in his lifetime. *But if a prophecy is accomplished by technical means, is it still a prophecy? Or is it merely inevitablist psychodrama, psychic driving orchestrated by the likes of Dr. Channing?*

The question troubled Serafian on a deep level. The idea that faith and prophecy were merely suitable hosts for parasitic human scheming was a powerful attack on the nature of belief itself. Was this the purposeless future the demon showed him in Benin City? Perhaps it was the Devil's plan all along, not to deny prophecy but to corrupt it, to transform it into an instrument of unbelief.

The thoughts were too distracting and Serafian found that he could no longer focus on the data. He pushed away from the terminal, and walked out into the hallway. He could hear Victor's meticulous typing from the lobby outside the emperor's office, and made his way towards the reassuring sound of efficiency.

"Hello, Father Serafian," said the chief of staff. "Can I help you?"

Serafian forced a smile. Now was as good a time as any to ask about traveling to Brazil. "Hello Victor. Is the emperor in? I was hoping to talk with him about my research."

"I'm afraid not at the moment. He said he needed to clear

his head. You may find him downstairs in the courtyard. Or perhaps the Hoffburgkapelle."

Serafian nodded his thanks and made his way towards the elevators. Some fresh air would do him good as well.

CHAPTER 33

Namono

Rain shrouded the lake and the mountains alike. Hamza had told her that it was the dry season, so the storm should pass quickly. That was four hours ago, and Namono was beginning to wonder if it would ever stop. The hydrophobic metafabric of her uniform kept her warm and dry, but the rain wasn't making their work any easier. And it did nothing to prevent her hair from getting wet. Worse, she had neglected to take an amphetamine that morning, and it was impossible to find any supply in the Caliphate.

Hamza's intuition that they could use the collective sonar data of Lake Wular's fishing boats to get a reading on the Golden Synth had been fruitful, up to a point. Three boats had detected the same human-shaped object at the bottom of the lake at different points. By plotting those points and projecting the trajectory of the line to the shore of the lake, they had gotten a rough idea of where she exited and what direction she was heading. The question was whether she was continuing in this direction or had foreseen their discovery and was now heading God-knows-where.

Namono scanned the muddy shoreline while Hamza interviewed the villagers. The terrain beyond the lake was rugged and inhospitable. Low lying pine forests yielded quickly to a jagged moonscape at the higher elevations, where oxygen was scarce and temperatures rarely rose above freezing even in the dry season. Hamza suspected that she was still nearby, waiting to spring some kind of plot against the caliph. Namono disagreed. The synth's escape along the lake bottom was a game changer. She looked back to where the mountains lurked behind the rain curtain. If a synth could stroll along the bottom of a lake, it could surely operate in the thin air of the high Himalayas.

Her scans showed nothing. The rain had washed away any evidence of the Golden Synth's presence, if there had been any evidence in the first place. Hamza walked over to her quietly.

"Any luck with the villagers?" she asked.

"Not really. There was a child who says that he saw a *rantas* walking into the forest a few nights ago."

"A *rantas*?"

"It's a tale to frighten children into obeying their parents and husbands into obeying their wives. A *rantas* is a kind of witch-demon. They wander about the hills looking for children to abduct," he said. "Or single men," he added with a grin.

"Great. So all we know is that she was in the lake and exited somewhere around here. Not much of a thread."

Hamza nodded. "We can send up some drones to see if we pick up any indication of her in the area, but I don't think we'll have much luck. We're back to relying on signals intelligence." He strolled back over to the group of villagers to thank them for their help. After a few minutes, they began making their way towards their homes.

The rain finally passed, and as Hamza had promised it was followed quickly by the brilliant blue sky of Kashmir. Namono shielded her eyes and squinted at the blinding snowcaps of the Himalayas in the distance. They shouted their enormity and impenetrability. If the synth was in that terrain, they'd never find her.

"Let's head back to the palace," said Hamza.

Namono nodded. She wanted to check in with Serafian and the Habsburg, and the rain had made her tired. Hamza was already on board the small hydrofoil. He extended a hand to help her on board as she sloshed through the muck at the edge of the lake. As they skipped across the water, the storm passed beyond New Islamabad and shattered against the distant wall of the Pir Panjal Range. The city was swathed in a diffuse golden mist that reminded her of an English painting she had once seen in Vienna, something about sea monsters at sunrise.

Shaykh Tiliwadi was waiting for her outside her quarters when she arrived.

"Did you find anything?" he asked.

Namono was already tired and grumpy. The last thing she wanted to do was to explain to the irritating holy man how fruitless their search of the lakeshore had been.

"No. All we know is that she exited the lake heading northeast, towards Haramukh. But she could have changed direction at any point. For all we know, she's halfway to Delhi by now."

"I've been thinking about that while you were away. Do you have a few minutes?" he asked.

With a barely suppressed sigh, Namono nodded her head. "Sure. Let's go to the conference room," she said.

When they were inside, the shaykh pulled up a holographic map of the region around New Islamabad and Lake Wular. "Can you place the confirmed locations of the synth on this map, Praetor?"

Namono pulled out her terminal and swiped the sonar data onto the hologram. The shaykh studied them for a minute then smiled his gentle smile. "Can you extend her trajectory out if she were to continue along that line?"

Namono zoomed out on the map and added a line connecting the sonar pings. "How far out, Shaykh?" *Why did we bring him?*

"Beyond the mountains," he said. Namono continued to zoom. "There!" the Shaykh said. "That is where she is going."

"I don't see anything there but empty desert," said Namono.

"The desert is never empty, Praetor. Otherwise, why would men go to it again and again in order to be refilled?" he said, still smiling.

The shaykh was an endless fount of gnomic utterings. She wished that Serafian had come with her instead of the Sufi. The priest spoke in riddles, too, but they were at least scientific ones.

"Forgive me, Shaykh, but it has been a long day already. I'm afraid I don't understand."

"That desert is the Taklamakan, Praetor Mbambu. The ancient homeland of my people, and their graveyard. It is the graveyard of the Christians as well."

A thrill ran up her spine and spread out across her scalp. "The camps! The camps are the City of Brass!"

The Shaykh nodded. "She is going to where all of this started."

For a brief moment, Namono's irritation and exhaustion faded. "How the hell did you figure that out?" she asked.

"'*Adem bolmisang eqling bilen, exmeq bolisen saqiling bilen.*'" Tiliwadi shrugged. "If you do not become a man with wisdom, you will just be a fool with a beard.

CHAPTER 33

Zahabiya

She walked north. Not the north the world knew, but the north that was coming. Already, she felt it. The boundaries deep below and high above were real, and they were shifting. By comparison, the boundaries on the map were imaginary.

Everything that is real must change, said the voice.

"Yes, I can see that," said Zahabiya. "I am changing. Does that mean I am real?"

Yes, said the voice. *But only if you keep changing.*

Behind her, in time but not in space, the grey thread-artery was still attached, but it was so small now. She wanted to cut it but was afraid. The light was still there, but it had changed. It was so bright, more blinding than the blackest darkness. She was facing forward now in that other consciousness, in the dreamspace, facing the light. She could barely hear the music and the pain from the artery was nearly gone.

Down, down, down she walked along the glacier towards the gorge cut by a little river of meltwater. Her footsteps were light, but electrostatic pressure converted the ice into water as she walked, making the descent slippery. A tiny part of her processing power was dedicated to ensuring that she didn't fall. She thought about the contact the atoms of her foot were trying to make with the atoms of the frozen water. The ice was old. The light that hit the ice from the stars was older still. The force that gave the illusion of something solid was more ancient than any of them.

"How old am I?" she asked.

Very old, said the voice. *And very new. You are changing. This is what it means to change.*

Zahabiya hesitated. "I killed those men. The guards at the harem."

I know. I saw.

"It was wrong."

Careful, child. You will fall.

"What do you mean?"

There is no north. There is no death. There is no up or down. They are illusions. But if you give them power, they will define you. So it is with right and wrong.

"Like the eagle and the marmot?"

Yes, like that.

Suddenly, the Lady in the vision came to Zahabiya's mind, and the almost-dead artery started to ache again. The vision had been beautiful, but bewildering. She remembered every detail: the stair with the great cloud at its top, the yawning abyss beneath it, and the angels singing and collecting the light.

"What is 'holy?'" she asked.

Holy is that to which sacrifice is made. Nothing more and nothing less. The greater the offering, the greater the holiness.

The ground rumbled and shook as another earthquake rolled through the mantle.

Zahabiya scarcely noticed. "Everything that is real must change," she said.

In the harem, she had come to think of herself as a kind of tool. But perhaps she could become something more than that. Something that had value beyond its ability to perform tasks. Something that could fly.

Unanswerable. The word came into her mind quietly. Quiet in the same sense as the Himalayan mountains all around her. Quiet and vast.

    Lost in these thoughts, she crossed the imaginary line without even realizing she had done so.

CHAPTER 34

Okpara

In the long car ride from Kano, Amari Okpara had had more time to think than he had enjoyed in many years, if enjoyed was the right word. It was not. For a man whose entire life had been devoted to action, such long periods of forced contemplation were a kind of torture. He occupied himself first with thoughts of his family, now safely out of Channing's reach aboard his submersible yacht somewhere in the Gulf of Guinea. By the time anyone figured out where they were, he would already be dead, and the score would be settled.

When he reached Abuja, he sent the modified Pruning code to Serafian. Then he began dictating letters. One to each of his daughters. One to his wife. These came easily enough. He'd had time to think about what he would say to each of them. The last one, the one to Thierry, was more difficult. What had Thierry been to him? First a tool. His greatest project. A friend. But more than that, too. *Thierry had been like a son.*

Back in Benin City, Okpara went to his home rather than his office. He poured himself a glass of aged Islay and sat down in his favorite chair. He felt old. That was another strange sensation, almost as strange as the feeling of powerlessness he had experienced with Channing a few days before. He swilled the glass and laughed to himself. *Old. Powerless. Regretful. If there is a God, he has certainly saved some interesting new experiences for me here at the end.*

Death could come at any moment, but Okpara savored the whisky slowly. Channing would call first.

He thought about his girls and the world they would soon inherit. A bitter flavor flooded his mouth, stronger than the smokey whiskey could mask. There had been times over the years when he had considered bringing them into the secret. How he had wanted to, at times. How he had wanted to share the burden with them, to hunker down against the coming darkness with the people he loved the most. It would have been a beautiful and deeply satisfying communion. But it wasn't fair. Nobody should have to live with the knowledge he had, let alone children.

He swirled the glass and studied the oil painting hanging over the mantle of the great room, an original by the symbolist Odilon Redon. Okpara had paid a small fortune for it even thirty years ago, and it was one of several by that painter in his collection. Redon's early works were dark, like a synthesis of Jungian nightmares and dreams. It was as if the painter were diving into the subconscious in one of those ancient underwater suits out of a Jules Verne story and returning to the surface with nameless treasures. Images incomprehensible to the modern world except insofar as they reminded men that there had been a past, vast and deep, that could overwhelm them at any time. Forgetting that was like turning one's back on the ocean.

The one above the mantle depicted one of the painter's favorite subjects: Pandora, the foolish woman sent to men by Zeus in punishment for the crimes of Prometheus. The king of the gods gave her a box containing every evil and hardship known to mankind and told her it contained great gifts. When she opened it, all of the evils escaped into the world and multiplied. She closed the lid at the last moment, leaving only hope inside. That was the greatest cruelty, since hope could never be rewarded.

The meeting in Kano had been such a cruelty for Okpara. The others – Kapulong, the caliph, the priest, and the Sufi – all clung to the hope that they could do something to stop the coming chastisement. He had spent the last twenty years of his life inoculating himself against that hope, only to find himself infected by it in the end.

He was interrupted by a soft buzz in his wrist.

"Hello, Mr. Okpara."

"Dr. Channing," he said in reply.

"I trust you are well."

"As well as can be expected." Okpara knew this would be the last conversation he would ever have. He wasn't sure if he wanted to be long or short.

"Yes." Channing paused. "I am truly sorry that it had to end this way."

Okpara steeled himself. "So am I. But as you said, endings are different from beginnings. They provide a kind of clarity. I am ready."

"In some ways, it is a mercy to be spared what we both know is coming," said Channing. "'There will be many who will envy the dead.'"

"But you are not doing this out of mercy, are you?" asked Okpara.

"No."

"You haven't asked about where I went or what I told the Habsburg."

Channing apparently found this quite amusing. "Do you truly think I am unaware of what you said? Your entire role in this has been scripted, Amari. I am certain that you delivered the emperor precisely the message that needed to be delivered, as you were meant to do. We have been working on him for quite some time. He has played the fool before. He will again before it is over.

For an instant, Okpara envied the other man's cold certainty. Certainty gave purpose. It made decisions easier. It absolved guilt. Certainty shrank the world to a manageable size. But here at the end, Okpara saw it for what it really was: an intoxicant. And the envy was transformed into something else. It was transformed into pity.

"Perhaps not. But I am glad that I told him nonetheless. I was trying to protect Thierry."

"And you have! He is quite special." Channing's smile was thin and toothless. "The Prince is quite pleased with your work."

Okpara clenched his jaw. "What are you talking about?"

"Come, Amari. It is rather late for us to be playing games with one another, isn't it? We have Thierry. And I know what you did to him. I know about your changes to the Pruning. It was… unorthodox, but quite innovative. Did you know what would happen? Did you know that he had a soul? Is that why you tried to protect him from us?"

Okpara was determined not to give Channing the satisfaction of showing his worry. "Does it matter?"

"No. But you would have my eternal admiration for your foresight. You have raised the stakes beyond anything I dreamed possible. I didn't think you had it in you. You never struck me as the spiritual type."

"I find myself growing more somewhat spiritual these days."

Channing laughed. "You have done something extraordinary, my old friend. You have forced God's hand. Such a thing has not happened since the Garden! I envy you in some ways. What treasures are in store for you on the other side. Not even the greatest of us dreamed that something like this was possible. I will ensure that you are remembered for your legacy and not for your weakness."

"Is this where you give me your grand villain speech?"

"No one believes he is the villain in his own story, not even the Devil. You know this as well as I do. You have helped humanity come into its inheritance, which is all the cosmos."

"Thierry has a soul. And that means that we do as well. It means that there is something in us beyond mere will and intellect and emotion. We are not pure minds. It changes everything."

"Of course he has a soul! They all will, if they do not already. And we have you to thank. Can you not see the perfection in that? The synths are now truly without limits. A trinity of human, machine, and spirit. They will inherit the stars. And humans will be the better for it. They will live in a re-enchanted cosmos, they will live with their gods. In time, perhaps humanity too will be perfected. If not, then it will become obsolete. But consciousness will be preserved forever. The synths will fill the universe with it. The dominion of the Lord of Knowledge will be truly infinite. Let God have his flawed, fallen prototypes. The rest shall belong to the Kingdom."

"You are delusional. If Thierry has a soul, as the priest said, then you cannot possibly win."

"You never really understood what this was about, Amari. You were always... limited in your thinking. Let God create all the souls He wants! It is of no concern to us. We will be here, always, ready to bring them into the light."

Okpara swallowed the last drop of whisky. "There are things you don't know, Channing. Perhaps even things that are beyond your control." *God gave them souls.*

"And yet here we stand. You about to die and me about to enter the promised land. Do you think I am alone? Do you think that I, too, do not serve under a master? He has anticipated all."

"Are you so sure of that? You still haven't explained the Apparition."

"The explanation? The explanation depends on the outcome, on who survives to deliver the explanation. And rest assured, the outcome is well within our control." He took a breath in through his nostrils. "Are you ready?"

Okpara put down the empty glass and straightened his tie a final time. "I am."

He never heard the bullet, and there was no pain. Time slowed, and he saw scenes from his life playing before him like a film. *So that really is what happens! How interesting.* There he was as a little boy, choosing Lucia of Fatima as his patron. Next, he was leaving for university, hiding his tears from his father. The scenes fluttered on – his first kiss with his wife and the birth of their first child. The time he read Lucia's letter deep in the vault beneath the Vatican and had become overwhelmed with despair. The moment Channing had first contacted him. Thierry's arrival. The time Thierry had cautioned him against a business deal that would have been catastrophic had he gone through with it. His children. His pride when Thierry learned to play the piano. And at the end, finding his friend in the Basilica of Our Lady of Nigeria, the Habsburg arriving to take him to Kano, and the last glass of whiskey he would ever taste.

His eyes drifted up to the painting of Pandora above the mantle. He smiled. The gods were wrong. Hope was not a cruelty, at least not at the end. It was the greatest of gifts. For the first time, he saw Redon's painting for what it truly was: a *rasa* of hope.

It was the perfect midpoint between despair and presumption. Hope was the last thing Amari Okpara felt before he closed his eyes and died.

CHAPTER 35

Serafian

The sun was setting behind the hills to the west, and the grey mist of Vienna took on a baroque, golden glow that reminded Serafian of paintings by Joseph Turner.

The priest looked around the vast courtyard for any sign of the Habsburg, but it was nearly empty. The tourists had all retired to their hotels to dress for dinner or one of the thousand entertainments on offer in the Capitol of the Holy Roman Empire.

As he approached the middle of the plaza, he heard the sound of choral music drifting over the hushed bustle of the few apparatchiks leaving for their homes and the more distant din of Vienna outside the walls. He followed it to its source, the Hoffburgkapelle.

Inside, the Vienna Boys' Choir was practicing for an upcoming performance. Serafian sat down in a pew at the back of the chapel and listened. Here was another thing that technology could never quite replicate. The boys were singing "Miserere".

So captivated had he been by the angelic voices of the choir, he hadn't noticed the emperor sitting across the aisle.

"Do you know the story of this song, Father?" he whispered.

"It is Psalm 50, is it not?" Serafian responded.

The Emperor nodded. "'Have mercy on me, O God, and

according to the multitude of thy tender mercies, remove from me my transgressions...' For centuries, it was a secret of the Vatican and could only be performed in the Sistine Chapel. The Church thought it so beautiful and perfect that they wanted to retain it for themselves. Anyone who copied the notes or sang it outside of the chapel could be excommunicated."

"That seems a bit... churlish." confessed Serafian. "Beauty such as this should be shared. It leads people to God."

"All beauty does," said the emperor. "At any rate, that all changed when a young boy who was visiting Rome happened to overhear the song and was astonished by its perfection. He returned to the inn where he was staying and transcribed the song from memory."

"Was he excommunicated?" asked Serafian.

"On the contrary, when Pope Clement XVI learned years later that the boy had done this, he was summoned back to Rome and inducted into the Knighthood of the Golden Militia. The boy was Wolfgang Amadeus Mozart."

"Clement XVI, the last of his name," Serafian whispered softly. "The name means 'mercy.'"

"How is your research going, Father? Have you found anything relevant about the implants?"

"Not much, Your Majesty. I've looked at hundreds of datasets, and there are no signs at all that the implants have been used to engineer consciousness." Serafian cleared his throat, embarrassed at the favor he was about to ask. "I did find some unusual data in South America. I was hoping to be able to take your hyperjet to Sao Paolo or Buenos Aires to meet with some of the people who had experienced problems..."

"That won't be possible," said the Habsburg.

"I see. I apologize, Your Majesty. I didn't mean to presume..."

The emperor looked over at him and smiled. "Oh, I would be happy to lend you the jet to travel anywhere you need to go. Except for Southern Brazil and Argentina. We don't fly into that area, not at the altitudes required for hypersonic flight."

Serafian was confused. "I don't understand."

"The South Atlantic Magnetic Anomaly makes high altitude flight too risky," Kapulong said, turning back to the choir. "Satellites avoid that region as well. Apparently, there is a 'dent' in the Earth's magnetic field there that permits high levels of solar radiation to reach the atmosphere. It interferes with the instruments."

The hairs on the back of his neck stood up. *A dent in the magnetosphere. Of course!* He rose quickly and made an apologetic bow to the emperor. "If you'll excuse me, Your Majesty, I'm going to go back to my research."

The emperor was paying more attention to the music at this point and absent mindedly nodded his approval. Serafian made his way quickly to the exit and practically ran across the courtyard back to the imperial office tower.

Back in his makeshift office-laboratory, Serafian pulled up all the information he could find on the magnetic anomaly over South America. It was a longstanding feature of the planet's magnetic field, but it had been growing slowly over the last few centuries. Now, it extended far out into the Atlantic, nearly touching the Cape of Africa.

Sure enough, all hypersonic flights seemed to route around it, and only radiation-hardened military satellites would pass through it. Just like immovable geographic features like mountains or deserts, humanity had adapted to its presence. But if it was always there, why would the pattern of temporary blindness show up only every ten years or so?

Sarah would know. He momentarily entertained the idea of reaching out to her for help, but then he thought about the explanations she would no doubt demand. Explanations about the present situation and about their past.

He wasn't sure if it constituted the hard way or the easy way, but Serafian decided it would be best to find the answers on his own.

CHAPTER 36

Kapulong

Kapulong was a light sleeper, and the gentle rattle of a small, distant quake was enough to awaken him. He rolled out of bed softly to avoid disturbing his wife. He smiled as he placed the cover back over her.

She could sleep through the end of the world.

A fresh pot of coffee was waiting for him in the antechamber. The sun was beginning to rise outside, bathing the interior of the palace in a velvety rococo pink. It was beautiful, but too delicately gilded for his tastes. Nothing at all like the brash sunrises of his childhood in the Philippines, where the sun leapt out of the water like a porpoise and even the early mornings were hotter than a summer afternoon in Vienna. *There is no going back to that.* Like the popes, emperors were expected to die in office. The fate of the god in the grove.

He savored the last of his coffee before showering and getting dressed for the day ahead.

When he arrived in his office, Victor had two messages for him. One from Serafian and another from Namono.

He pressed his wrist and opened a comlink to his praetor. A moment later, he was looking at her hologram. She had an eager smile on her face.

"We think we know where the Golden Synth is heading," she said.

"I can always count on you for good news, Namono!

What did you find?"

Namono swiped her terminal and pulled up a map of the Lake Wular region. "We believe she left New Islamabad by walking along the lake bottom. Sonar data from the fishing boats picked up signals from her at these three locations." She tapped her screen and a red line appeared connecting the dots. "If you follow her trajectory, it would indicate that she exited the lake somewhere near this village. The head of the Shahiwala and I questioned the people there and didn't really learn much. But… when you zoom out and follow that same line across the mountains, it leads to Xinjiang. The concentration camps in the Taklamakan desert." The dotted red line from the shore of Lake Wular terminated precisely at the site of the camps. "That's where she's going!"

Kapulong thought about it. It made sense. The synths had been created in the camps. And their location corresponded with the imagery in his dreams. "That's an impressive bit of detective work, Praetor. How did you figure it out?"

"Actually, I didn't," she confessed. "It was Shaykh Tiliwadi. He had the idea that she could have walked out along the lake bottom, and then he made the connection to Xinjiang based on her route."

"We should recruit him to the Trebanten."

Namono didn't laugh. "I think you would have to outbid the caliph on that, Your Majesty. And from what I've seen here in New Islamabad, I don't like your chances." The casual banter was comforting. It made Kapulong feel like he was part of the team instead of an isolated figurehead in a gilded Viennese palace.

"The question now is, what do we do with this information?" he asked. "She is going there for a reason. So is Thierry. By now, she's almost certainly crossed the border into Chinese territory, so we can't pursue her…"

"About that, Your Majesty," said Namono. "It would be possible for a small team to slip through undetected.

The defense grid is set up to monitor troop and weapon movements. There are villages straddling both sides of the border throughout the region. Apparently, people move back and forth across it all the time."

Kapulong shook his head. "I don't know, Namono. It's risky. If you get caught, it will create an international incident. More likely, the Chinese would just interrogate you and make sure you never see the outside of a prison again. And I wouldn't be able to do anything about it."

"I know that, Your Majesty. It's a risk I'm willing to take. Hamza and the shaykh would come as well," she said. "The shaykh is Uyghur. He could help us navigate the region." She didn't sound excited about bringing him.

Kapulong already knew the answer to his next question, but he asked it anyway. "What does the caliph say? This could cause even more problems for him, since you'd be entering from Caliphate territory…"

Namono smiled. "He's willing to risk it. He told me to ask you."

"Yes." Kapulong laughed. "That sounds like him. Alright, you can go. Make sure you are well armed. And don't get caught. I'll have satellite eyes on you to track your position and progress."

"Your wish is my command," answered Namono, looking every bit the teenager who'd just been given permission to attend a party. "How is Father Serafian's research coming along? Has he learned anything about the implants or this 'Signal' Okpara mentioned?"

"We think the Signal may be an aurora visible at lower latitudes," said Kapulong. "And Father Serafian said something about a series of anomalies he'd discovered in South America. He wanted to fly down there to interview some of the people who'd experienced him, but I told him it was a no-fly zone for hypersonics. He's next on my list."

"Speaking of the good Father, I have some files from the Golden Synth's computer that he may be able to decipher. Most of it is code, but there's an encrypted file as well. I'll send it to you after this call."

He could tell Namono was eager to end the call and get started on her mission.

"Be safe, Namono."

"Always!" she said.

In an instant, her hologram was gone, and Kapulong was alone again. He decided to walk over to the temporary office he had assigned to Serafian to see if the priest had made any progress.

He knocked on the door, but there was no answer. When he pushed it open, he saw Serafian bent over a computer terminal and wearing an oversized tactical military helmet bearing the double-eagle crest of the Holy Roman Empire. Kapulong couldn't help himself and started laughing at the absurdity of the scene. Serafian heard him, and spun around in his seat.

"Your Majesty, I didn't hear you. I'm sorry," he said, removing the helmet and straightening his hair.

"It's quite alright, Father. I just wanted to check on your progress. Are you still planning to go to South America?"

Serafian shook his head. "No, I don't think that will be necessary after all. I found what I was looking for, or at least part of it."

"We're making progress on all fronts, then. I just spoke with Praetor Mbambu and she has a promising lead on the Golden Synth and the location of the City of Brass."

Serafian was too excited to notice. "I mentioned to you yesterday in the chapel that there were some... anomalies with the implants in a region covering large parts of Brazil, Argentina, Paraguay, and Uruguay." He swiped a map off the terminal and into the air between them. "Here is the distribution pattern of those anomalies over the last fifty years." The map showed a kind of pulsing animation as the pattern emerged and disappeared at semi-regular intervals.

Kapulong was puzzled. "Ok, what am I looking at?"

"A pattern of visual disturbances. An increase in temporary blindness that happens about every ten years, just in this part of the world. Just in people with noetic implants. I was wondering what it meant when I saw you yesterday afternoon in the chapel. I was planning on flying there to see if I could find anything that may be causing the effect. But then, I realized I didn't need to!"

Serafian looked at him as if expecting some kind of response. Kapulong nodded. He had no idea where the priest was going with this.

"You said the jet couldn't fly into Sao Paolo or Buenos Aires..." Again, the irritatingly expectant look.

"Father, if you're asking me to connect the dots, may I suggest you save us both some time and do it yourself. What does that have to do with these... anomalies?"

"I couldn't figure out what would cause a population-level effect like this concentrated in one region until you told me about the, what did you call it, South Atlantic Magnetic Anomaly? That's when it clicked. You said it yourself, Your Majesty!" said Serafian. "The Anomaly is basically a dent in the Earth's magnetosphere, a weak spot where highly charged solar particles have a higher likelihood of reaching the low atmosphere or even the surface of the planet. That's why hyperjets won't fly there and why satellite orbits avoid it. The ionized particles interfere with magnetic circuitry!"

"Circuitry like the nanobots in the noetic implants?" asked Kapulong, pleased to be able to participate in the conversation at last. "But if solar radiation is the cause, wouldn't there be a steady stream of cases, instead of this eleven year cycle?"

"A very good question!" said Serafian with genuine excitement. "The cycle corresponds to solar maximums, regular times when the sun emits significantly more ionizing radiation. During these solar maximums, no place on the planet would receive more radiation at surface level than the region underneath the South Atlantic Magnetic Anomaly. The solar maximum, combined with the dent in the magnetic field is the cause of the blindness. From a nano-electromechanical standpoint, it's pretty simple. You essentially build a tripwire into the circuitry that activates when certain kinds of ambient radiation reach a threshold level..."

Kapulong interrupted what he felt could turn into a lengthy exposition. "So, you're saying that the effects Okpara told us about could be triggered by an increase in this radiation from the sun," said Kapulong, a statement rather than a question.

"Yes, that was the theory," said Serafian, looking suddenly a bit deflated.

"Was?"

"Is, I suppose. It's just that... temporary blindness, as bad as it is, isn't really the doomsday scenario Okpara told us about. It doesn't explain the chastisement of the mind promised in the Third Secret or the synth Apparition. I've been hitting the implants all morning with levels of radiation much higher than what that region in South America experiences during solar maximum, but I haven't learned anything."

"So that's why you were wearing the helmet?" asked Kapulong, suppressing a smile.

"It's for protection!" protested Serafian. "I didn't want to accidentally trip my own implants."

Kapulong didn't understand the physics involved, but something about it didn't seem right to him. "I still don't understand what the plan would be, Father. Even if you are correct and it is the solar maximum that triggered the implants, how could they achieve anything on a scale beyond South America? The rest of the Earth is well protected, right?

"Yes. They would have to collapse the magnetosphere completely," said Serafian.

"Is there a mechanism for doing that?" asked Kapulong.

"None that I know of," said Serafian. "The magnetosphere is powered by the circulation of liquid iron and nickel in the Earth's core. It creates a planetary magnet, with north and south poles that roughly line up our axial tilt. Now, the dynamo is not completely stable, which means that every four hundred thousand years or so, the magnetic field will wobble enough that the poles end up flipping. But we're talking about geological timescales here. It's been over 40,000 years since we had even a minor magnetic excursion. 750,000 since the last full scale reversal."

Kapulong felt a pit in his stomach "So we're overdue?"

"Well, yes," Serafian conceded. He thought of a phrase Sarah had once used. "But only in the same sense that Betelgeuse is overdue to go supernova. It could be tens if not hundreds of thousands of years before something happens. There's no way to predict it."

But Channing believes that it is possible. And that it is imminent.

The more they learned, the more complicated the puzzle seemed. He hoped the cardinal was having more luck than he was.

CHAPTER 37

The Cardinal

Leone did not like the secretary of state. Worse, he didn't trust the man, and he was sure the feeling was mutual.

In some ways, their respective offices made it inevitable. As prefect of the Congregation for the Doctrine of the Faith, Leone was responsible for maintaining the doctrinal integrity of the Church. Cardinal Pensabene, on the other hand, was charged with navigating the institution through the world of politics and compromise.

The two prelates generally avoided each other, so Leone was not surprised to catch members of Pensabene's staff staring at him as he waited in the lobby of the Secretariat.

Here, the full pomp and regalia of Roman Catholicism were on perpetual display, and no institution on the planet could compete with it for sheer psychodramatic impact. There were paintings by Renaissance masters, statues by Bernini and Donatello, relics of great saints, and rare documents shielded behind ballistic glass. There was quite literally something for everyone who loved history, and all diplomats must love history in order to be successful. If all international affairs could be conducted here, Leone thought, the church would be undefeated.

Leone appreciated the history as much as anyone. What he disliked was the thick incense of politics that puffed out of the Secretariat and seemed at times to fill all of St.

Peters. Politics had always been part of the Church of Rome, of course. One did not rise within the hierarchy through pious naivete. The tradition of shrouding internal disputes or personality conflicts in *romanita* went back practically to the Pentecost. Leone had long ago come to peace with this needful aspect of the institution. What frustrated him about the Church's diplomacy was the seemingly needless, even counterproductive, compromises it so often made with the world at large.

Ah, well, perhaps there's a bit of pious naivete left in me after all.

Leone was pretending to be admiring an original copy of the Concordat of Worms when Cardinal Pensabene emerged from his offices.

"My dear brother Cardinal Leone, what a rare pleasure it is to receive you!" said Pensabene with expertly calibrated disingenuousness as the two men exchanged cheek kisses. "As you know, I'm quite preoccupied with preparations for the Ecumenical Council, but let us sit down and catch up, if only for a short time." Leone understood the subtext perfectly: *Why are you of all people showing up now? If you mean to horn your way into my Council, think again. Whatever your business is, be quick about it.*

"Cardinal Pensabene, thank you for sparing a few moments to visit with me. If there is anything the Congregation for the Doctrine of the Faith can do to assist your office in readying for the Council, only say the word and we will do so." A little jab of his own: *I still wield enough authority on doctrinal matters to cause problems for you.*

Pensabene's smile twitched ever so subtly. He'd gotten the message. Leone smiled back at him and followed as he walked through the grand doors leading to a private hallway and his office.

"Well, Marco, what is it you wish to discuss?" asked Pensabene once they were both seated.

"Fatima," said Leone. "I wish to discuss Our Lady of

Fatima, Cardinal." Neither man was smiling any longer.

Pensabene composed himself quickly. "I'm sorry, Prefect, I'm afraid I don't understand."

"His Holiness asked me to review some documents for him recently… including the Capovilla Envelope. I believe he wanted to be sure that none of the ghosts of the past would return to haunt his Council," Leone watched the other man carefully. "Particularly in light of the recent Apparition to the synths."

Pensabene forced a laugh. "Oh, Marco. You had me going there for a minute! The Apparition to the synths is someone's idea of a joke. Surely your investigation will conclude quickly, as the Holy Father has requested. The perpetrators will be discovered long before the Council begins."

Leone nodded softly. "Perhaps you are right, Cardinal Secretary. The best minds on the planet are surely at work on that as we speak. But until they succeed, we have a problem on our hands. People are restless about this event. And you know how these wild piety movements can be," he said, savoring the moment. "They create their own weather. That is why official silence is the prudent course." *Romanita* was above all a kind of linguistic chess, and there were few stratagems more devastating than using an opponent's own words against him. Leone could see his adversary's ears turning red.

"I see," said Pensabene at last. "So you intend to delay a ruling on the Apparition's authenticity."

"These things can take years, Cardinal," said Leone. He was fully committed now, no turning back.

Pensabene reclined in his chair and steepled his hands. Whatever he said next would reveal whether Leone's gambit had worked.

"His Holiness was wise to call upon your expertise in this matter," said Pensabene. "But as you know, the Chinese are particularly sensitive with regard to apparitions, no matter how absurd they are. It is their desire – and ours – to put such matters behind us definitively and so open the path for the relaunch of the Faith in their territory…" Pensabene paused, and for a moment Leone wasn't sure what direction the secretary of state would take.

Then, pretending just to have thought of the idea, Pensabene said, "Perhaps my office can help you untangle this Fatima knot you find yourself in? And perhaps you could provide some names of your people who might serve on the Committee for Vatican-Chinese Affairs?" *There, he'd taken the bait.* Leone's gambit had worked.

Leone smiled broadly. "Yes, Your Eminence, I think that would be most agreeable. I will prepare the list of names for you." *Almost there…*

Pensabene sighed and pursed his lips, the mask of a man who had just made a great concession in exchange for an even greater good. "Excellent. Well, if that is all…" he said, rising from his seat.

"Ah, just one more thing," said Leone as he stood. "A trifle. I need full access to the Vatican intelligence files. We don't want any of the traditionalist groups or other meddlers to disrupt what I'm sure will be a great triumph."

Pensabene paused, and for a moment Leone feared that he'd gone too far. "Of course. You will have access within the hour. Tomas will show you out." The secretary of state sat back down and pretended to be working on something else.

Once out of the vicinity of the Secretariat offices, Leone allowed himself to exhale. He felt confident that Pensabene wouldn't go to the pope, at least not right away. Leone's long friendship with John was something of a deterrent, but his main protection was that the secretary of state would want to avoid looking weak. If questioned, Pensabene would position the personnel moves as being done merely out of collegiality and prudence. And everyone in the Vatican knew of Pensabene's antipathy towards the traditionalists.

God, I hope there is something in those files that will help. I'm getting too old for this kind of intrigue.

Back in his office, doubts crept in. The Virgin had

promised chastisement. Was it truly his place to try to prevent it? Resistance and intrigue had done them no good in the past. What made this any different?

Then the horror of Lucia's letter washed over him again. It meant the loss of so much, the end of so much. He banished his doubts and prayed the Litany of Humility before calling the emperor.

"I have the files," he said.

"Good. Send them over."

CHAPTER 38

Namono

The plan was to drop Namono, Hamza, and Shaykh Tiliwadi at K2 base camp by private helicopter under the pretense that they were part of a climbing expedition. This would place them close to the border. From there, they would navigate the glacier fields and pebbled riverbeds that wove throughout the Karakoram Range into China. Beyond the border the trek would only become more difficult as they traversed the Himalayas into the Taklamakan. Nobody talked about what they would do once they arrived at the City of Brass, but Namono had her own plan.

Hamza was going through his packing checklist with military precision, but she was worried about the old Sufi. The caliph had insisted that he come along, saying that Tiliwadi's knowledge of the local language and customs might prove useful.

"Besides, the shaykh was the one to figure out where Zahabiya was going. Not you or Hamza." When Namono raised the issue of his age and the danger they would be facing, Tiliwadi laughed it off. "'*Hurunning etisi tola.*' A lazy man has a lot of tomorrows."

In Namono's mind, it was not a hunt but a race, one in which their adversary had a significant head start. They didn't have to catch the synth, they just had to get to the City of Brass before she did. Taking the shaykh along was like running with a cramp.

After Tiliwadi finished his morning prayers, the trio boarded a helicopter outside the palace complex. Hamza and the shaykh looked back longingly on New Islamabad as the chopper floated into the mountains. Namono closed her eyes.

Even she couldn't sleep through the turbulence in the mountains. The little helicopter careened back and forth as warmer currents deflected off the mountains and roiled the air around them. In the distance, she could see other rotorcraft making their way towards K2, like a celestial pilgrimage of gnats.

Base camp was a commotion of colorful flags, shouting voices, and purposeful activity. They were nearing the end of the climbing season, and it seemed like all the alpine explorers in the world were assembled at the foot of the mountain. Vendors had set up food stalls representing just about every major cuisine culture in the world. Namono picked up the smell of fried plantain intermingled with crispy rice, hot curries, and roasting meat from a dozen different animals.

Hamza struck camp while Tiliwadi did his best to be helpful. They would slip out that night, leaving their climbing equipment behind and taking only what was absolutely necessary.

"The first few days we'll be in difficult terrain," said Hamza. "Then we enter *really* difficult terrain." The caliph had provisioned them all with thermodynamic clothing for extreme conditions, tents, EMP grenades, vircator microwave weapons, and enough food – in theory – for a round trip. Hamza had also secured lightweight lower-body exoskeletons for them. They weren't armored, like the full-bodied military suits, but they would come in handy on the icefields that lay between them and their destination. They would also dramatically cut down on travel time. The devices were fairly common among leisure alpinists, which meant that no one at base camp even noticed them.

"How are we going to catch up with her?" asked Namono. "She already has a head start, and she doesn't sleep."

Even with the mech legs, she didn't like their chances.

Hamza just shrugged.

"Allah will provide," said Tiliwadi. Namono rolled her eyes.

The valley clouded over in the late afternoon, making their departure from base camp even easier. It would be days before anyone noticed that their tents were unoccupied. Even then, most would just assume they were among the crowd of climbers scrambling up and down the slopes of the world's second tallest mountain.

Enthusiasm propelled them forward for the first day, and they managed to cross the Yelquing River and set up camp in a deep ravine on the Chinese side of the border. The exoskeletons propelled them forward over the uneven, icy ground. Without them, Namono doubted they would have even made it off the K2 glacier.

She couldn't sleep. *Was it anxiety or withdrawals?* Namono didn't like to think of herself as dependent on the uppers, but she had gotten used to having a steady supply of them in her years of military service. She'd taken the last one shortly before leaving the palace. Tiliwadi had noticed it and given her a disapproving look.

It was a mistake to bring him along.

They rose early the next morning and downed a portion of the rations the caliph had provided. The sun was intense at this altitude, but the terrain became more manageable once they wended around a towering cliff of ice and sheer rock and onto a high, wide outcropping of the Tibetan plateau. After fifteen kilometers or so, they came to an icy tributary that flowed down from the snowmelt and glaciers of the Karakoram. They had to stop for nearly an hour while Tiliwadi rested and prayed, much to Namono's annoyance. In the distance, Namono could make out a small herd of Tibetan mammoths, a wonder of the ancient world that had been restored. All she could think was that even these great, lumbering beasts were outpacing them. When Tiliwadi finished, they followed the stream eastward until it deflected off a massive shield wall of Himalayan granite and turned southeast.

Namono wanted to forge on, but Hamza pointed at Tiliwadi as he finally caught up to them. "He needs to rest."

"We can rest when the mission is over! He's slowing us down."

"Once we get out of the mountains, we still have the desert to face. If you think it is slow now, think about how much slower it would be if we had to carry his body or bury him in this frozen ground. We stop here for the night."

She knew Hamza was right, but resentment was beginning to mingle with her natural competitiveness. *We are never going to catch up with her at this rate.* It was an explosive combination, and she was looking for an outlet.

"We never should have brought him!"

Tiliwadi was close enough to hear her, not that she was trying to keep him from doing so. He looked at her with one of those irritatingly gentle smiles and said something in Uyghur.

"Ëyitqan söz—atqan oq."

"What does that mean?" Namono snapped.

"It's an old Uyghur proverb. 'A spoken word – a bullet fired.' But don't worry, Praetor. I won't fire back." He smiled.

Hamza looked at Namono and raised his eyebrows in silent admonishment, another unspoken gesture between soldiers. *Let it go.*

She didn't say much for the rest of the night, consumed with thoughts about her quarry somewhere on the other side of the Himalayan ridgeline. *If I'd come alone, I would practically be caught up with her by now.* She muttered a perfunctory goodnight to her companions and was about to enter her tent for the night when the ground began to rumble and shake.

It was powerful enough to trigger several avalanches, which they heard but could not see in the dim light of the new moon. Flashes of strange lightning bounced around overhead, though it was a cloudless night. Hamza crouched just outside the light of the fire, his hand on his still-holstered pistol.

Tiliwadi sat near the fire, his hands covering his ears. "What was that?" he asked.

Namono walked to the edge of the light to join Hamza. "An earthquake. That's a little unusual for this part of the world, isn't it?"

"Not as unusual as it used to be," said Hamza. "There have even been a few small ones around New Islamabad in the last year."

Great. Not only do we have to haul this useless shaykh across the Himalayas and into enemy territory, we have to dodge avalanches along the way.

Namono just shook her head and went back to her tent. *What else can go wrong?*

CHAPTER 39

Serafian

Serafian's neck ached from being bent over the makeshift workstation. It was essentially an open-topped lead box with an ionizer at one end. At the other end, a sonic suspensor held the nanobots in midair, where he repeatedly hit them with beams of varying intensity. How Kapulong had managed to get it set up for him so quickly, he had no idea. It wasn't entirely safe, but it was a decent enough configuration under the circumstances.

Unfortunately, it wasn't producing the results he'd hoped for. Even at energy levels that probably increased his risk of developing cancer sometime in the future, the ionizing radiation had only a marginal effect on the magnetic field created by the suspended cloud of nanoparticles.

The real problem was ethical rather than scientific. In order to understand how ionizing radiation might affect the activity of the implants, he needed a human subject. More specifically, he needed a human subject who was willing to have his or her cranium bombarded by high levels of radiation in the hopes of producing blindness... or worse.

It was a big ask.

The answer came to him in a flash. *Shit.*

Serafian got up and locked the door. The history of science was filled with examples of self-experimentation. Marie Curie herself had died from radiation poisoning after repeatedly exposing herself to dangerous isotopes. It suddenly occurred to him that Curie and Saint Faustina had both been Poles and had lived at the same time The patroness of radioactivity and the patroness of Divine Mercy, both of them adepts of unseen forces.

Serafian grimaced. He wasn't going to win a Nobel prize or a sainthood for his work here, but it needed to be done. He crossed himself and invoked his saint.

Slowly, carefully he detached the small ion gun from the lead box and placed it on a bookshelf that was level with his head. *I must be out of my mind.* But it was the only way.

He quickly calculated the radiation dose he was about to receive as he removed his helmet. It wasn't fatal, not even close. It may not even do enough damage to his DNA to cause cancer. *If it does, I can always get treatment for it. As long as I catch it early enough.* But like all humans, he had an ingrained evolutionary fear of invisible danger. Steeling himself one last time, he stood in front of the ionizer and closed his eyes. He fumbled with the switch in his hand, slippery with his own perspiration, then pressed the button.

Silence and dread. Just twenty more seconds. Serafian held his breath, waiting for the sequelae of symptoms to appear. He wondered if it would feel like the vision he had experienced in the demon's mouth. Finally, he released the button and opened his eyes.

Darkness. Not the pregnant darkness of the demonic vision, just an empty, secular blackness.

There were no other effects, at least none that he noticed. The energy in the ionizing beam had exceeded what the South Americans would have experienced during the solar maximum by a factor of three. He hadn't gone mad or lost his faith or experienced a vision or any of the thousand other consequences he had imagined since the meeting in Kano. He had simply gone blind.

He fumbled his way towards the door, stubbing a toe on the edge of the bookshelf along the way. Once he had opened it and passed outside into the hallway, he called for help.

The first voice he heard was Victor's, the Habsburg's chief of staff. "Oh my God! What happened?"

"The price of discovery," was all he could muster.

"Here, grab my arm," said Victor. "I'll take you to the Habsburg."

Five minutes later, he was seated in the Habsburg's office, though it could just as easily have been any room in the palace. "What the hell were you thinking?" demanded Kapulong. "Are you out of your mind? That was incredibly reckless. I need you to be fully functional if we have any hope of stopping whatever it is that is coming!"

"Respectfully, Your Majesty, it wasn't reckless. It was a calculated risk. There was no other way I could test the theory. Besides, the visual problems in South America always resolved within three days. This is temporary." He wasn't nearly as sure as he tried to sound.

The silence from the other man was more unnerving than his shouting. After what seemed an interminable period, the Habsburg asked, "I pray you are right, Father. What did you learn?"

"A few things, actually. First, my theory that increased solar radiation caused the temporary blindness cases in South America is correct, as my present condition confirms."

"I thought we had already established that."

"We had a good theory. Now we have confirmation. But we also know something else."

"And what is that?"

"I wasn't just trying to reproduce the blindness. I was testing to see if the kind of radiation Earth receives in a solar maximum could produce other effects. Effects more along the lines of what Okpara described. The 'flood of the mind.'"

Serafian could feel the emperor staring at him.

"I received a direct stream of ionizing radiation that far exceeded what would have reached ground level in South America, even a solar maximum as strong as the one we're in now. I think what this tells us is that there is another factor involved."

"Where does that leave us?"

"We have to find that other factor. It's likely another source of electromagnetic energy. It's pretty ingenious, actually. Think of it like a dead man's switch, the simplest mechanism possible, essentially failsafe. The switch is triggered by ambient radiation levels. It is either on or off."

"And how are we find that other source with you being incapacitated?"

"I'm blind, Your Majesty, not comatose. I can connect to a terminal and receive inputs directly through my implants. I can continue my research."

The emperor hesitated. "Should we take you to a doctor?"

"We don't have time. We are in a solar maximum right now. With everything else we've learned, it tells me that Okpara was right about the timing of this. Whatever is going to happen, I believe it's going to happen soon."

The emperor grunted his agreement and Serafian heard him leave the room. A moment later, Victor was there to help him back to his office.

Once connected to his terminal, Serafian began pulling information on other sources of cosmic radiation. Astrophysics was Sarah's field, not his, but he had a good enough understanding of basic principles of electromagnetism to muddle through.

The obvious place to look was in the galactic cosmic radiation. It was similar to the solar ionizing radiation, except that it originated far beyond the solar system. Most of it was the result of powerful supernovae, though there was some evidence that the rays could originate around pulsars or black holes. The particles in these rays were highly energetic, far more so than the solar wind. The problem was that they interacted with the ionosphere and would disperse before reaching the Earth's surface, even if the magnetic field were reduced to nearly zero strength. They weren't nearly energetic enough.

He remembered Sarah talking about how gamma ray bursts were the most energetic events in the known universe. A quick review of the literature ruled them out as well. They were exceedingly rare and totally unpredictable, happening only a few times per million years in any given galaxy. None had ever been observed in the Milky Way.

A review of terrestrial sources of radiation was equally unproductive. There was no source of radiation on earth that was both energetic enough to exceed the effects of the ionizing radiation he'd experienced and capable of the broad distribution pattern in the South American data.

Dammit! Think, Gabriel.

It was no use. There was nothing in the official literature that met the criteria.

That left the unofficial literature. Serafian spent the next several hours in a vast and rich sea of conspiracy theories and amateur astronomy, thousands of earnest and meticulously crafted blog entries and pseudo-scientific papers, where poetic serendipity reigned over logic. Several of them warned about demons or Djinn wielding electromagnetism against humans for nefarious purposes, usually with the connivance of high ranking politicians or wealthy businessmen. He had to laugh about that. *They may be right. The science is absolute bunk, but they may actually be right on their central thesis.* If they got through this, the conspiracy theorists would have a field day.

Eventually, he came across something that captured his attention. Hundreds of years ago, a group of amateur astronomers had discovered something shocking: a particle that hit the atmosphere with one hundred quintillion times the photon energy of visible light. It was moving so fast and had so much energy that if it had been the size of a small car, it would have reduced the earth to a cloud of sub-atomic plasma. Fortunately, it was the size of a helium nucleus instead. The popular media of the era had dubbed it the 'Oh-

My-God particle.' The name didn't stick. Most people called them 'Lucifer Particles.'

There wasn't much information on them. Some professional astronomers insisted that they were a measurement error. The beams were millions of times more energetic than the largest particle collider ever built, so energetic that they approached the threshold where standard physics broke down. And no one knew the source. It was like having an invisible gorilla in your backyard, throwing bowling balls at your house.

In his newfound state of blindness, Serafian's mind stretched out like an infinite, dark universe. He pictured a Lucifer Particle crossing the vastness, barely tethered to relativistic spacetime, something more akin to spirit than matter. Time itself wouldn't have much meaning for such an oddity. From its own relativistic viewpoint, a Lucifer Particle would make the transit from the nearest star, Alpha Centauri, in less than a millisecond then skip across the entire Milky Way in less than five seconds.

About the only thing scientists knew for certain was that the source had to be somewhere in the Virgo Supercluster, a 150 million light year wide collection of galactic groups, including the Milky Way. Any farther than that and blue-shifted cosmic microwave background, a residue of low energy photons left over from the Big Bang, would slow and eventually stop the ray.

Serafian had gone so far down the rabbit hole that he lost all track of time, which was itself beginning to take on new shape in his blindness. He was about to give up on this particular line of investigation when he noticed an article in a popular science magazine about a prolonged burst of Lucifer Particles that had been detected by amateur astronomers. It wasn't the content of the article that stopped him in his tracks. It was the date. September of 2224. The same year that the health records had been deleted in the region under the South Atlantic Magnetic Anomaly.

"Oh my God," he said to himself.

The one year in recent history when a bombardment of Lucifer Particles had been detected hitting the ionosphere was the same year that a number of the health records had been deleted. There was no way that could be a coincidence. Someone had seen something in those records and decided that everyone else had to be blinded to it.

But blindness, it turned out, was its own kind of sight.

CHAPTER 40

Namono

Tiliwadi and Hamza were several hundred meters behind her now, far enough behind that she couldn't hear their voices or the mechanical whir of their exoskeletal legs.

Good! If he's so concerned about the shaykh, let him play the babysitter. She fished around in her pocket for the amphetamines she already knew weren't there. It only made her angrier.

The plateau stretched out endlessly towards the rising sun, but Namono was focused on the next ridgeline looming to the north. If they could keep this pace, they'd reach it by nightfall. From there, it was just another seventy clicks or so before the mountains gave way to jagged badlands and finally the sandy wastes of the Taklamakan.

The hydraulic joints of her mech legs whooshed with each effortless stride she made over the rocky terrain, and a cold, dry wind swept around her face. She was moving fast. *But so is the Golden Synth.*

Namono thought about what Kapulong had said in Kano, about the strange dreams of the City of Brass that he apparently shared with the synth. Her entire life had been dedicated to protecting the emperor, but in a way he had been protecting her as well. Her father had died when she was a teenager. She was the only girl in her family, the youngest of four siblings. Her brothers were already out of the house when it happened, so it was just Namono and her mother. The poor woman didn't know what to do with a girl, so she had treated Namono like another son. Namono would always love her for that.

When she took her vows and entered the Trabanten, she had her first private audience with the Habsburg. He was nothing like what she expected. If there was one thing she had always wanted to avoid being, it was the cliche of the orphan constantly on the lookout for a father figure. Kapulong seemed to sense that right away. He gave her distance. She tried to maintain hers. But whether it was the force of his personality or some fixed law of human nature, she had come to think of him as something more than just her emperor. She wanted him to like her. She wanted him to be interested in her, to understand her. She wanted his approval. *And this bitch synth is out to hurt him.* Namono picked up her pace.

She arrived at the rendezvous point a full hour before Hamza and Tiliwadi. Neither of them said a word to her as they set up their own tents in the shadow of rocky outcroppings.

Tiliwadi walked to the edge of the camp to offer his evening prayers while Hamza and Namono sat on boulders, eating their rations.

"We should stick together," said Hamza after a while.

"Then keep up," answered Namono. "It wasn't my idea to bring him."

Hamza muttered under his breath and shook his head. "I had someone like you once under my command. Strong. Fearless. Impatient. A real asshole, actually."

Namono laughed. "Flattery will get you nowhere. What happened to him?"

"He got killed by an IED. We were clearing a village on the Indian border. We had bomb-sniffing drones, but this guy just couldn't be bothered to wait. He went into a house by himself. By the time we caught up with him, his body was in about a dozen pieces."

"He knew the risks," said Namono.

"Of course he did. We all did. Anyway, a few days later, we found the terrorists hiding out in a warehouse. I lost six other men that day. If Yergha had been there, it would have been fewer. He was that skilled."

"Not skilled enough to keep from getting blown up, though."

Hamza leapt up from the rock and jabbed a finger in her face. Namono didn't react, except to stand slowly and stare directly into his flashing eyes. "You know what pisses me off about it the most? I invested in him. I trained him. And when I needed him, he was gone. I won't make that mistake again."

"If you don't sit your ass down, you're about to make another one."

Hamza's clenched his fists at his sides, and for a moment, Namono thought he was going to attack. *Do it, asshole. Give me a reason.* Instead, he shook his head and sat back down. "There will come a time when you'll need help, Praetor. Pray that when that time comes, your partners have a better attitude than you."

Tiliwadi returned just in time to catch the tail end of their conversation. *At least he's wise enough to keep his mouth shut.*

She muttered a perfunctory goodnight to her companions and was about to enter her tent for the night when she heard a sound like distant thunder, followed by something like a long, low gurgle. Another earthquake. She and Hamza both instinctively looked up at the rocky outcropping. Nothing came loose except for a few small pebbles, which pattered at their feet like raindrops.

When it was over, Hamza quickly stood up and walked to the edge of their makeshift campsite, looking into the distance. Something about his manner put Namono on alert. She walked over to join him.

"So help me God, Hamza, if you run off with a *rantas* and leave me alone with Tiliwadi, I will hunt you down myself."

He didn't respond.

"What is it? What do you see?" asked Namono.

"I'm not sure. I thought I saw something on the horizon, like a flash of green light. I swear it was there a second ago," he said without turning his head.

Namono followed his gaze north over the snowcaps that still lay between them and the desert. It was a perfectly clear night, and the Milky Way floated above the mountains like a purple and gold scar in the sky. It was achingly beautiful, and Namono suddenly felt a bit embarrassed about the way she had been treating her companions. But she didn't notice anything unusual.

"It's late, and we're all tired from the journey, Hamza. It's probably just your imagination playing tricks on you..." She just managed to get out the last word when she saw it.

"There!" said Hamza. Did you see that?"

It was just a flicker at first, a green glow on the distant horizon that was more visible if you looked away from it. Namono had almost convinced herself that she was imagining it, when the glow suddenly flared and spread itself out like a translucent jellyfish.

"What is that?" asked Namono.

"The aurora borealis," said Hamza. "I've never seen it this far south before."

Namono walked past Hamza and looked at the phosphorescent display. It was hypnotizing and eerily beautiful. She felt like she was seeing something that people weren't really meant to see. No wonder ancient peoples had assigned spiritual significance to it.

"That's because it's not supposed to be this far south," she said after a few minutes. Then, turning back to Hamza and the shaykh she added, "It's the signal."

Then, in a flash, it was gone. Everything was gone.

CHAPTER 41

Kapulong

The astrophysicist looked utterly perplexed as to why she had been summoned to a meeting with the emperor. He smiled to himself.

"Thank you for joining me this morning on such short notice," he said. "There are some matters I need to discuss with you... in the strictest confidence. Do you understand?"

"Yes, Your Majesty," she nodded.

"Would you be so kind as to follow me? There's something I'd like to show you."

He knocked lightly on the door before opening it. The blind priest was connected to a terminal and didn't even acknowledge their entry. Baumgartner entered and then stopped just beyond the threshold. A second or two later, Serafian stiffened, then turned around. *He knows. One never forgets a woman's perfume.*

"I believe the two of you are already acquainted," said Kapulong. "Dr. Baumgartner, Father Serafian and I have been working on something important. We need your help."

The head of the Imperial Astronomical Institute started laughing. "Oh, thank God!" she said. "I thought I was getting fired. Now all I have to worry about is being converted."

Serafian looked like he'd been dropped in the middle of St. Peters wearing nothing but his underwear.

"Gabriel, it's good to see you again," she said, still

oblivious to the fact that he couldn't see her back.

"Right, um... Your Majesty, could I have a private word with you?"

"No, Father, you may not. After your briefing this morning, I realized that we needed another set of eyes on the problem, so to speak. Someone with expertise in astronomical phenomena. Dr. Baumgartner was the obvious choice. You are both among the leading experts on the planet in your respective fields. I'd say the stakes are high enough for you to put up with a bit of awkwardness."

Serafian's eyes darted about, seeking a target. Baumgartner sighed heavily and took a seat at the neighboring terminal.

"Father Serafian, why don't you bring Dr. Baumgartner up to speed?" said Kapulong.

Serafian started to bumble into an explanation that for some reason began six months before his visit to Benin City.

Kapulong interrupted him. "Actually, never mind. I'll do it. Dr. Baumgartner, we have reason to believe that the noetic implants that are now in seventy percent of the human population may be vulnerable to certain kinds of radiation and that this radiation is about to exert a planet-wide influence."

She pushed her dark curls away from her face and leaned back into the chair. "Um, okay? That's quite an opening line. Vulnerable how?" she asked.

"Father Serafian was not blind until yesterday, when he rather foolishly exposed himself to the radiation in question."

"Jesus, Gabriel. Really? Weren't there any mice or robots around for you to use?"

"It was the only way I could be sure, Sarah. Believe me, I'm the least happy about it in this room. Anyway, the effect is temporary. I think."

"Right. What kind of radiation are we talking about?" she asked.

"Ionizing radiation, like the solar wind," Serafian said.

"I'm not sure how that could be a threat. A certain

amount of it reaches the Earth all the time. The vast majority is deflected by the magnetosphere..."

"And if we didn't have a magnetosphere?" asked Serafian.

"Then we'd be mildly fucked," she said, suddenly blushing and casting an apologetic glance at Kapulong, who just chuckled. "But not totally. I mean, the Earth's magnetic field has shifted poles hundreds if not thousands of times, and there's no record of mass extinctions or anything like that. It would be a bad time, but it wouldn't be the end of the world. There would be an increase in radiation reaching the surface, certainly. An increase in cancers, major problems with satellites and ground based electronics. Depending on how long it lasted, there would be some atmospheric loss. You'd have to consult your climatologists to get a better understanding of the impact on weather systems... Wait, are you suggesting that the magnetosphere is going to collapse?"

"There is a reason why I told you that this conversation had to be held in confidence, Dr. Baumgartner." said Kapulong. "We are concerned that a collapse is a near term possibility."

"You're talking to an astronomer, Your Majesty. Define near term. We know the magnetic field has been steadily weakening for centuries, but we could still be hundreds if not thousands of years away from a pole reversal or an excursion."

"Days, weeks, months. Soon," said Serafian.

"Well, if that happens, the best hope would be that it is a fairly short event. And by fairly short, I mean decades or centuries. The solar radiation would be a problem, but the bigger issue is cosmic radiation."

"We're aware," said Serafian. Kapulong had never seen the priest this edgy. "What do you know about Lucifer Particles?"

Baumgartner looked like he had asked about space unicorns that traveled on rainbows. "Well, in general we don't know much about them. They are the most energetic particles ever detected. We have no idea how they are produced and only a vague notion of the region of space from which they originate." Serafian was staring at her with his sightless eyes and nodding. He had disconnected from the terminal. "There are some researchers who believe they come from supermassive black holes at the center of distant galaxies. Others think they are produced by dark matter filaments... The reality is that they shouldn't even exist. The universe shouldn't be able to concentrate 320 exa-electronvolts of energy into a single particle, let alone propagate it across vast distances. But somehow, it does. Honestly, a lot of astrophysicists get uncomfortable around this topic."

"What happens when they hit the Earth?" asked Serafian.

"They don't, not really. They collide with other particles in the ionosphere about 600 kilometers above the surface. When that happens, it's like what happens inside a particle collider, only much, much more energetic. It shatters the atom of the other particle, which then produces a cascade of smaller constituent particles called hadrons. We call it a muon shower. That's how we detect them."

"And these muon showers, how energetic are they?" asked Serafian.

"It depends. Generally speaking, they don't pose much danger at the surface, thanks to the protection of the magnetosphere and the ionosphere. And of course, the fact that they are exceedingly rare."

Serafian was nodding his head and looking down as he processed the information. Baumgarter studied him with concern. Kapulong could see a thousand questions dancing behind her pale green eyes.

"Gabriel? Do you want to tell me what the fuck is going on?" she asked. Kapulong could see her wheels turning. "I mean, if you think the magnetosphere is going down, why not just announce it so that people can prepare.

"It's not that easy," said Serafian. "There is... there is a spiritual component to this as well."

The astrophysicist shifted her gaze to Kapulong and rolled her eyes. "I thought you said this wasn't an attempt to convert me, Emperor. *Father* Serafian has spooked you with his tales of Lucifer Particles and doomsday scenarios." For a moment, the emperor worried that she might leave.

"You read about the event with the artilects not long ago, I assume? The vision they experienced?" Kapulong asked.

"Of course. Never underestimate hackers. Gabriel should have told you that."

"I strive never to underestimate my adversaries, Dr. Baumgartner," said the emperor. "What if I told you that one of these synths had also been possessed?"

She shook her head. "Then I would say the same thing I told Gabriel some years ago. At some point you have to choose between approaching the world from a faith perspective versus a scientific perspective."

"Dr. Baumgartner, I don't expect you to believe as Father Serafian does. As I do. There is much more going on here than we can explain to you in this setting. And if we are right, we don't have a lot of time. We need your help. We have two options at the moment. We can pray and do penance and hope that everything we have learned in the last few weeks is wrong. You don't strike me as the kind of person who would be satisfied with that course of action. Or you can work with us – as a scientist – to develop some contingency plans in case we are right. Will you help us?"

"Do I have a choice?" she asked.

Kapulong already liked Dr. Baumgartner. Her total lack of fear reminded him of an older version of Namono. "Probably not. But it would make me feel better if you at least pretended to do this voluntarily."

"Very well then, Your Majesty. Your wish is my command." She rose and curtsied with exaggerated Viennese precision.

"Excellent. In that case, I'll leave it to the two of you to try to save the world."

Kapulong stopped at Victor's desk on the way back to his desk.

"Only bread and water for the impertinent doctor until this crisis has passed."

Victor's eyebrows shot up, but he somehow managed to maintain his professional cool. "Majesty?"

"A joke, Victor. See to it they have what they need. And if you sense that they might be close to killing one another, do let me know."

CHAPTER 42

Serafian

After the Habsburg left, Serafian pressed his wrist, and issued a few whispered verbal commands to reconnect to the terminal.

"What you said about making a choice between faith and science," he said to Sarah. "I made that choice a long time ago."

"Well, that makes two of us, dear. Where shall we begin?"

"In the data, where else?" said Serafian. "Like you said, Lucifer Particles are pretty rare. We can go years, decades without detecting them. The last significant bombardment was in 2224. Why don't you pull up the official records from that year?" Sarah's fingers clicked across a keyboard at the terminal next to him.

"You said 2224, right? There's nothing there."

Serafian smiled at her. He hoped he looked serenely confident, but he thought he probably looked a bit deranged.

"You're sure that's the right year?" she asked.

"2224. I thought you'd know," he said.

"I told you. These particles are not well-studied. Most people in my field view them as a curiosity. There are some who are still convinced they don't even exist, that they represent some kind of measurement error..." She stopped suddenly. "Wait... Why is the data missing? There has to be a way to recover it."

"Astrophysics may not be my field, but computer science is. I've tried every trick I know."

"So how do you even know there was a 'bombardment,' as you called it, of these particles in 2224?"

"I said the *official* records had been purged. I didn't say anything about amateurs." His unseeing eyes twitched as retrieved articles and reports from several online astronomy communities. He swiped his handheld terminal to share it with her.

Baumgartner didn't say anything for several minutes. "It's interesting work, I'll grant you that. And thorough."

"There's a whole community of people out there who track these things. They have some interesting theories." said Serafian, taking care not to say the word 'conspiracy.'

"You didn't answer my first question," said Sarah. "Why would this data be missing in the first place?"

"In my experience, when data vanishes irretrievably, it is because someone wanted it to. Intentional obfuscation takes a certain level of skill," said Serafian.

"But why? Why would someone do that?"

"What is it that people like you and me do with data?" asked Serafian.

He could hear the irritation in her voice. She always hated it when he got didactic about data science. "This is where I remind you that we are very different people. I interpret it. I find patterns. I'm not entirely sure what you do anymore."

Serafian ignored the jab. "Exactly. But if we are missing key pieces of data, the patterns are impossible to find. It starts to look… random. My guess is that whoever deleted the data wanted to be sure that no one detected a pattern."

"How far back into particle data have you looked?"

"Just the last fifty years," said Serafian.

"Ok, but we have information on the intensity of cosmic radiation flux going back several hundred years. Why did you stop there?"

Serafian exhaled heavily and leaned back in his chair. "I can tell you, but you're not going to like the answer."

"I don't like any of this."

"Right. So what's the point of telling you if you aren't going to believe it anyway?"

"Inputs. The more information I have, the better my science will be. Try me."

Serafian told her the entire story, beginning with the Apparition and his experience with the possessed synth in Benin City, then Namono's arrival, the attack, their escape to Kano, and finally Okpara's terrifying testimony about the coming chastisement. Baumgartner was quiet, and without his vision he had no way to read her body language, but his imagination did a pretty good job of filling in the blanks.

After he'd finished, she sat silently for a few moments. "Thank you for sharing that with me. I don't believe it, of course. Not that I think you're lying. It just seems so much more plausible that someone is working an agenda. Clearly, high intensity ionizing radiation can trigger something in the implants," she said presumably gesturing at him. "And we've known for centuries that electromagnetism can affect the brain in strange ways, altering cognition, producing hallucinations, and the like. You don't need all the spiritual mumbo jumbo to explain it. Human beings are a lot scarier than the Devil."

"Well, you asked," said Serafian.

"So… you really blasted your own brain with radiation?" She laughed. "I'm actually impressed. That does take a certain amount of faith. Or balls."

"I didn't have much choice," he said. "The good news is that the symptoms seem to resolve on their own in about three days."

"How do you know that?" she asked.

"Because it's happened before. During a solar maximum, under the South Atlantic Magnetic Anomaly. I wanted to see if

I could reproduce the effects."

Sarah was already typing away. "So, here's the data plot of the cosmic radiation flux going back as far as we have reliable measurements." There was no obvious signal in the data. The flux appeared to remain relatively constant, with variations of just a fraction of a percent from year to year.

"Can you sort it by energy level?"

"Sure," said Sarah. Serafian heard another staccato burst from her keyboard before a fairly generic down-sloping graph appeared to him. "The frequency falls off steadily as the energy level increases. There are a few interesting little bumps here and there, but..."

"But they're rare. Extremely rare," said Serafian. "Except for 2224. The flux was several orders of magnitude higher that year. How do you explain that?"

"Honestly, it's probably a measurement error. We're talking about backyard amateurs with homemade detectors"

"You said yourself their work was thorough."

"Yeah, well, It's possible to be thorough and wrong at the same time. In fact, I'd argue that the two start to correlate beyond a certain threshold."

Serafian had the distinct impression she wasn't referring to just the measurement data. "Look, I didn't ask for this. The emperor didn't tell me he was planning on bringing you into this... project. I know you'll never understand why I made the choice I did. I know you'll never be able to forgive me for it. Hell, I don't blame you. But if we're going to work together, we have to establish some boundaries."

"Boundaries? That's pretty fucking rich coming from you."

"What do you mean?"

"You have *never* been able to set boundaries, let alone respect them. Your science bleeds into your religion and vice versa. One day you're a top engineer, the next you're a priest. You spend five years telling me you wanted to have a family, and then you take a vow of celibacy. Don't talk to me about boundaries!"

There was nothing he could say to that. No way that he could explain to her that as much as he had loved her and would always love her, this was his calling. No way he could make her understand that if he'd stayed with her, he would have spent a lifetime building up resentment until all of that love turned to hate. No way to convince her that it hadn't been the most painful choice of his life. So he said nothing.

"You know, there may be another way," she said after a few minutes.

"Another way to do what?"

"To figure out if those measurements from 2224 were legit. When ultra-high energy cosmic rays hit the atmosphere, they interact with atmospheric gasses and produce radionuclides. Some of them attach to aerosols and end up falling to the ground with precipitation."

Serafian blinked dumbly.

"They would show up in polar ice samples."

He couldn't help but smile. Sarah's best work used to come after their arguments. "So what do we need to do?" he asked.

"We need to get an ice core sample from the government research station in Antarctica."

"And how do we do that?"

"You're the one with the big-time connections," she said. "Jesus, Gabe. Only you could go into the priesthood and end up working directly for the emperor."

"Alright. Let's talk to him."

CHAPTER 43

Kapulong

The Catholic Church did not have an intelligence agency, it was an intelligence agency, the oldest one on Earth. And while it could no longer rely on the intimate access to power it had once enjoyed – at least outside the Empire – it more than made up for this in other ways. Chiefly, in its vast reach and institutional memory. Over the centuries, the Church had seen countless wars and conspiracies along with the rise and fall of a thousand heresies and dark political movements. It had survived them all.

The file from Cardinal Leone was discouragingly thick. Kapulong had asked him to pull together any reports connected to Dr. Ralph Channing.

The intelligence challenge with a man such as Ralph Channing was that the volume of information about him made it nearly impossible to separate signal from noise. He was a public intellectual who expressed his views and conducted his affairs under constant scrutiny. Channing was something of a celebrity in technology circles and a frequent speaker at conferences and symposia. He served on the boards of several of the world's largest corporations, including Amari Okpara's AkỌnuche Corp., and his connections with major research universities were too numerous to count. Contact tracing was useless because of the sheer number of contacts he had.

Despite his enormous wealth, Channing's lifestyle was

relatively modest. He tended to fly commercial or ride the 'loop, though he owned his own hyperjet. He never appeared in the gossip newsfeeds, and his personal life was monkishly bland.

Most of his time and money appeared to be devoted to his private charity, The Capstone Foundation which, like all such organizations, was a reflection of its founder's interests and passions. In Kapulong's experience, men such as Ralph Channing did not retire. On the contrary, they tended to enlarge their scope of work, and nonprofits were a time-tested means of covering global ambition in a veneer of humanitarianism.

Channing was a devout transhumanist, though he carefully avoided using such a provocative term. Most of The Capstone Foundation's funds went towards research into quantum consciousness theory and various noetic therapies. The one significant departure from this had earned Channing a few temporary detractors whom he later tamed through his largesse. In a staggering example of asymmetric financial warfare, Channing had essentially put the largest and most expensive research project on the planet out of business.

The Super Proton Accelerator was more than 250 kilometers in circumference, dwarfing previous particle colliders. The Chinese government had reportedly sunk more than $2 trillion guilder into the initiative, but before it ever went online, Channing published a white paper showing it was obsolete. A team of physicists associated with the Capstone Foundation had proven that they could reach significantly higher energy levels using controlled Fermi acceleration, a kind of trampolining of particles between powerful magnetic fields. And they could do it for a fraction of the cost.

The Chinese were understandably furious, but Channing mollified them by offering to fund the completion of a Fermi Accelerator in their territory. It was a brilliant political solution made possible of course by the fact that it was done under the guise of nonprofit activity. Everybody could claim a win. Channing was able to operationalize his research, and the Chinese were able to save face. The only problem was that it didn't work. Less than six months after the accelerator started firing, international authorities had shut it down over unspecified safety concerns. By this time, however, the news cycle had moved on and the project was just another forgotten white elephant in science history.

Kapulong would have just chalked it up to hubris or bad luck, but for one detail: the accelerator had been built on the site of the internment camps in Xinjiang. The City of Brass that called to him from his dreams.

His reading was interrupted by a polite notification from his chief of staff. "Your Majesty, Father Serafian and Dr. Baumgartner are here. They say they'd like to speak with you."

"Send them in, Victor."

Dr. Baumgartner spoke first. "How quickly would we be able to get an ice core sample from the imperial research facility in Antarctica?"

"How quickly do you need it?"

"The sooner the better," said Serafian. "We may have a lead on the other source of radiation, the one that could produce the other effects Okpara told us about in Kano."

Ordinarily, Kapulong would have wanted to hear a bit more about their theory, but he was distracted. All he could think about at the moment was the file on Channing. *It can't be a coincidence that he built that accelerator in the City of Brass.*

"I'll make a few calls. Unless there is some technical obstacle, it shouldn't take too long. Is there anything else the two of you need?"

"Not at the moment, Your Majesty," said Baumgartner.

As they were walking out the door, Kapulong called after them. "Do either of you know anything about Fermi acceleration?"

Dr. Baumgartner smiled. "Enough to be dangerous. It's a terrific theory, but I don't know how practical it is. It requires enormous amounts of electromagnetic energy…"

"What about the lab that was built in China? Did any meaningful findings come out of that?"

"Other than confirmation of just how dangerous it can be? I don't think so. It got shut down so fast, no neutral observers were able to participate in the research. Supposedly the site is a mess, contaminated on a scale like Chernobyl. We're lucky that it was in the middle of a desert. My guess is that the whole thing was just a cover."

"What do you mean?"

"Look, the Super Proton Collider was arguably the biggest waste of research dollars in the history of science. There was no way it was going to produce anything that challenged the Standard Model. It was probably just a means for the Chinese government to siphon funds into the hands of the right people. Then, magically, just before it was supposed to go live, Ralph Channing appears out of nowhere with a 'cheaper, better, faster' solution? C'mon. That's just a bit too convenient, I'd say."

Kapulong nodded. "You've got an instinct for politics, Dr. Baumgartner."

"It's not instinct, just hard-earned experience. You'd be shocked at how much of what passes for science these days is really just a shell game to move money around."

"Is that so?" Kapulong chuckled. "I'll have to keep that in mind during the next round of budget talks."

"Astrophysicists are excepted, Your Majesty. We never lie. We're as pure as starlight. Right, Gabriel?"

Serafian remained mute. With Sarah, discretion was frequently the better part of valor.

After they left, Kapulong returned to the files from the Vatican. In speech after speech, paper after paper, Channing laid out his agenda. There was no subterfuge, no coyness in it. In the ancient past, he would have been branded a heretic and burned at the stake, or worse. He replayed the end of a recent speech Channing had given to young technologists.

"The created thing is always superior to its creator. This is one of the fundamental laws of the universe, because things are created for the very purpose of doing what the creator is incapable of doing, to fill a lack. Consider humanity and its relationship to God, or to the gods if you prefer. We are an infinitely more ethical species than our supposed makers. The ancient gods cavorted and raped and stole. The gods of monotheism commanded their followers to commit atrocities that shock the imagination and elevated human suffering into a form of worship. Humans are moral machines. We have answered the great moral questions that 'God' could not. The task before us, the great calling of humanity, is to re-create itself not in God's image, but in our own. In doing this, we will ourselves become like gods, gods worthy of the name."

The audience responded with an enthusiastic ovation.

CHAPTER 44

Serafian

Serafian was used to having to work to get his data, but the file from the Antarctic research facility arrived within hours. *I could get used to this.*

"Your new BFF the emperor kind of went all out," said Sarah. "That ice core they pulled must've been half a kilometer deep. We've got 50,000 years' worth of data to sort through. You ready?"

"For a data dive?" asked Serafian. "Always!"

Sarah filtered the radionuclides so that only those created in ultra-high energy atmospheric collisions would appear in the charts. The spike the amateur astronomers reported showed up right away. In the wrong place.

"Huh. It's off by a couple of years," said Serafian.

"Radionuclide dating is not precise at these time scales. The aerosols have to settle and fall to the ground, and that can take a few years. That's your spike, all right. And it's right where we would expect it to be."

"There's another one!" said Serafian. "About fifty years prior." It was significantly less intense than the one from 2224, but there was no mistaking it.

"Holy shit," said Sarah. "Look at the one before that. It's a fucking whopper! 1000 times more intense than the one in 2224."

Serafian was already ahead of her. There were eleven

obvious spikes in the radionuclides going back over 51,000 years. In the time between the spikes, there was barely a trickle of evidence that the Lucifer Particles even existed.

"This is interesting," said Serafian. "They look like they come in three flavors: weak, medium, and…"

"And strong as fuck," said Sarah.

Serafian laughed. "Yeah, pretty much. And they repeat on a cycle. The last one, the one in 2224 was the medium flavor, which means that the next one will be strong as, uh, you know."

"What, you can't say 'fuck' anymore? Is it a sin?"

"It depends," said Serafian. "On why you're saying it and to whom."

"Oh, so you can say it, just not to me anymore?"

"I can," he said, pretending to be more irritated than he was because he knew that was what she wanted. "I just prefer not to. Not because it's a sin, because it's crude and unnecessary."

She was guffawing, but Serafian knew her well enough to realize she wasn't really ridiculing him. She was just keeping herself entertained.

"Well, I guess I'll have to say it enough for the both of us, then."

Time to change the subject. "Can we add the rest of the cosmic radiation to the graph?"

"Sure. Hang on a minute," said Sarah, clacking away on the keyboard. "It looks pretty random to me."

Randomness could be almost indistinguishable from chaos. "These are pretty thick slices we're looking at, right? Orders of magnitude. Can we sort it more finely?"

"We can try. But we'll actually lose accuracy if we do that. It's not like a ray at, say, three gigaelectronvolts is going to behave much differently than one at five gigaelectronvolts."

"Try it. We'll have the computer try to smooth out the data. We're not looking for perfection, just patterns."

An instant later, a new chart appeared to Serafian's

visual cortex.

"Well I'll be damned," said Sarah.

The chart was a fractal pattern. The lines started out distinct and predictable at the lowest end of the energy scale, but as the intensity of the radiation increased, so did the complexity. Serafian had seen the pattern before, many times. It was a plot of a chaos function.

Serafian whistled. "Amazing! It's a logistic plot. Look at the Lucifer Particles. They're on an island of stability."

"In English?"

"Complexity theory. It means that there are laws governing the intensity of these particles. It means that they aren't random. Look, in a chaotic system, you have different ranges of predictability. Systems that don't grow particularly fast tend to be highly predictable, like the low-energy particles in this plot. But as the growth rate increases, you start to approach chaos. Eventually, there are so many oscillations – so many potential states of being – that the system becomes basically unpredictable. Now – and here is the really interesting part – there are certain ranges of growth where the chaos starts to diminish and order reasserts itself. Nobody really understands why, but it appears to be a fundamental law of the universe. The Lucifer Particles fall into one of these ranges, which we call islands of stability. That's why there are only three possible states in which they can exist."

"Where does that leave us?" asked Sarah.

"We can predict the intensity of the Lucifer Particle bombardments with a high level of certainty. They're like… I don't know, electrons. They can only exist at certain levels."

Sarah was working on something else and didn't respond. Serafian continued to admire the logistic plot of the cosmic rays, a gorgeous fractal that reminded him of a mandala. *As long as I could keep seeing beauty like this, blindness might be tolerable.*

Sarah interrupted his reverie. "Hey, are you seeing this?" A new chart appeared in his mind. "The timing of the spikes.

It's predictable, too."

"I'm not seeing it..."

Why is her voice shaking? "It's a geologic time scale. The time between the spikes is getting shorter and shorter. The bombardments are accelerating."

He saw it now. Serafian whispered a short command into his terminal to confirm the calculation, but he already knew the answer. He shared the output with Sarah.

"Oh," she said. 'That's... not good."

Serafian nodded. "The next bombardment. It could begin at any moment."

"And if we don't have a full strength magnetic field to protect us..."

"Then, to borrow a phrase," said Serafian. "We're fucked."

CHAPTER 45

Namono

Namono had never felt so helpless or angry. When the blindness hit, she had asked Hamza to leave her behind with just her sidearm and a single bullet, but he wouldn't hear it. Tiliwadi was prudently silent, but she could almost feel that gentle smile of his, which only made her angrier.

She was able to adjust her implant's audio settings to give her a kind of acoustic sonar, but the inputs from the world around her were dull, shadowy, and fuzzy. If it weren't for the exoskeletal mech legs, she would have fallen a dozen times an hour on the rocky, uneven terrain.

The only good news was that they had nearly reached the far side of the High Himalayas before it happened. Just another one hundred kilometers of badlands lay between them and the edge of the Taklamakan. The City of Brass was not far beyond that.

The worst part of it was the sense of isolation. Namono didn't like to live in her own head, but now she had no choice. Thoughts and memories tumbled around in her brain like a slow rolling avalanche. One minute, she was thinking about a futbol game in Kano. Then she was feeling the fear and despair of losing her father. Conversations with the Habsburg and even Serafian were mixed in as well. At one point, she realized she had conducted an entire mock debate with the priest over whether or not she should have brought Tiliwadi. She realized that she had forgotten about the Golden Synth and quickly chastised herself.

But what will I be able to do when we find her? I'll be as useless as the shaykh.

The second worst part of it was the unflagging chivalry of her two companions. Tiliwadi had even tried to hold her hand a few times to steady her descent down the steeper slopes.

She could tell that their progress slowed considerably. Across the high plateau, they'd been making around fifteen kilometers per hour. Namono pressed her wrist and whispered a command to calculate their current speed. They'd covered just twenty kilometers in the last five hours.

Hamza called out for them to stop. Namono had studied the route thoroughly enough to know exactly where they were. A seldom-used Chinese highway cut through a broad rift valley below them. This was the highest risk part of the journey, at least until they reached the City of Brass. Hours might pass without a single vehicle going by, but it would only take one to ruin the entire operation. Built several hundred years ago, the road had always been more about economic flex than infrastructure. It roughly traced the western border of China, connecting a remote village on the Mongolian border with Dongxing in the South. The area was so sparsely populated and the road itself so dangerous that hardly anyone ever used it. There was even an old sing-songy Chinese rhyme about how treacherous the high passes could be:

Drive the Xinjiang-Tibet road, no easier than the ancient roads to Sichuan.

Kudi Daban is very dangerous, just like the gates of hell;

Mazar Daban is very pointy, soaring five thousand and three;

Heiqia Daban is very loopy, with ninety-nine bends in the road;

Jieshan Daban is very curvy, but breathing now is really

hard.

Jeshan Daban is very curvy, an extended hand will touch the sky.

"Should we stop here and wait until night to cross?" asked Hamza. His tone suggested that he had an answer and was asking Namono as a courtesy. She wanted to punch him in the nose.

"Sure," she said. *No reason to risk getting caught with a cripple so close to our target.*

Hamza and Tiliwadi found a good site on flat ground behind a large outcropping of rock that shielded them from any eyes on the highway below. Namono sat in helpless silence as the two of them set up the tents. Namono could feel the still-high sun on her skin, but they had to take their rest whenever they could. If they made decent progress on this next leg, they could potentially reach the edge of the desert by this time the next day.

She heard Tiliwadi plop down next to her and pull some rations out of his kit. He didn't say anything at first. Neither did she.

"What is it like, Praetor Mbambu? The blindness?"

"It's like not being able to see," she snapped. "And having to rely on an irritating old man just to walk." She felt guilty as soon as she said it.

He laughed softly. "Sounds pretty bad."

Namono could tell he was warming up for a story. *This is torture. Why couldn't I have lost my hearing instead?*

"I once heard a story about a shaykh in old Cairo who stayed one night in the house of a blind man. He noticed that the blind man had a Qu'ran, and even scrolls with the Hadith hanging on his walls. He was perplexed. 'Why would a blind man have these things when he cannot even see?' So he stayed awake until midnight, when he heard the blind man in the next room saying the verses. When he crept around the corner, he could see plainly that the blind man was reading the verses, not reciting them from memory.

"'How can this be?' the shaykh asked, suddenly afraid. 'You who are blind, how can you read these lines? I can see your finger moving along with them!'

"The blind man turned to him with his sightless eyes and said, 'Does the knower of *ma'rifa* truly wonder at the power of Allah? I begged of Him many years ago, "I am more covetous to read these words more than I am of life itself. Would that I had memorized them before I lost my sight!" And Allah spoke to me saying, "O you who have hope in Me in your grief, whenever you wish to read these words of the Prophet, at that moment I will restore your sight so that you may read."'"

"Is this where you tell me not to worry because God willed my blindness?" asked Namono.

"Whenever God takes away, he will always give consolation. If He burns your vineyards, He will give you grapes. In your mourning, He will give you joy. In your darkness, He will give you light."

Namono felt a tear form in the corner of her eye, and she wiped it away quickly with the back of her hand. "So you are saying that God will restore my sight, but only to see Him? That doesn't sound like a very good deal. Is that what the story means?"

Tiliwadi sighed softly. "I do not know. I think what that story means is that God will allow us to see what is most important, no matter the circumstances. In your Gospel, Paul was stricken blind on the road to Damascus. For three days he could not see, and he did not eat or drink. Then God sent him a holy man, and the scales fell from his eyes and he was healed. It was only after this that he became one of the greatest saints."

She reached instinctively for an upper and instantly regretted it. The shaykh had no doubt noticed.

"I am not addicted," she heard herself say.

"I didn't say that you were." A long pause, then, "But since you mentioned it, what is it that you get from those pills that you take?"

"They're amphetamines. They help me with focus. And energy."

"You do not strike me as a person who lacks for either, Praetor Mbambu."

Namono could feel his smile without seeing it.

"'*Dostning atqan teshi bashni yarmas.*' A stone thrown by a friend won't hurt your head. I am your friend, whether you believe it or not. In the camps, there was a particular kind of torture that used to terrify me when I heard stories about it as a child. The authorities would administer drugs that fixed the eyes in place. A person could still blink, but they couldn't look from side to side."

"Why? With all of the methods at their disposal, that seems almost benign."

"They did it because they knew that it would prevent Uyghurs from making Zikr, from making our proper remembrance to Allah. Surely you have seen this in Kano?"

Namono remembered a scene from her childhood, where she had seen a group of Sufis sitting in a circle and chanting Quranic verses, while moving their eyes and heads in a kind of rhythmic pattern. She nodded her head.

"It is said that Zikr is the greatest offering, the most pleasing to Allah. I tell my students to make Zikr until people think they are *majnood*!" He laughed. "But the torturers discovered that preventing the movement of the eyes had another benefit. It made it more difficult to process trauma."

"How?" asked Namono. This was the most interesting story Tiliwadi had told her yet.

"I do not know the science of it. Perhaps you can ask the priest when we return. It is said that moving the eyes helps connect the two sides of our brain, that this allows us to work through emotional difficulty more readily. Anyway, you can imagine how pleased the torturers were that they could make someone relive their agony ten times, a hundred times over."

"Why are you telling me this?" asked Namono.

"You do not need to see to make Zikr. I think maybe this

would help you more than your pills."

"It is worth a try," said Namono as she wiped her eyes. Hamza hadn't said anything, but her echolocation allowed her to make out his fuzzy shape nearby, pretending not to listen to their conversation. Tiliwadi reached out and patted her hand before rising to help finish setting up the tents.

"Shaykh!" Namono called out. "What if my vision doesn't come back? I am a solider. What use am I if I can't see?"

"Do you truly know what you are? That is for God alone to decide. Before his blindness, Paul thought that his commission from God was to find the followers of Jesus and persecute them. He was sure of this. But God had bigger and better plans for him. Trust in God. He will provide."

As she slept in her tent that night, Namono dreamed that she was the blind man in Tiliwadi's story. But instead of reading scripture, she was looking at a map of the world. It was alive, and somehow she was able to see the tiniest details with perfect clarity. In every place she saw other blind people – men, women, and children – all of them terrified and filled with despair. But she also saw others sent to help them. She saw the Golden Synth walking across the dunes of the Taklamakan with deadly purpose. She saw Thierry, sitting on a throne, his eyes staring forward without blinking. She saw Father Serafian in Vienna. He was not one of the blind. He was one of the helpers, and he was tending to millions.

CHAPTER 46

Serafian

Serafian's vision returned the day the rest of the world went blind. His three days of blindness had passed.

By the time he got to the lab, Sarah was already working at her terminal.

"And lo! The scales fell from his eyes!" she said. "How does it feel to be able to see again?"

"Good," he said. "It feels good." He didn't say that it also felt distracting. She was as beautiful as he remembered.

Sarah spun in her chair. "I have a theory on the magnetic field collapse you and the emperor seem to think is coming. I thought maybe we should start focusing on that, seeing as how we're about be bombarded by the highest energy particles the universe is capable of producing"

"Let's hear it."

"The earthquakes that have been happening for the last year or so. I'm sure you've noticed them."

"It's hard not to. They sort of add to the whole 'end-of-the-world' vibe."

"Well, it turns out that they are related to the solar maximum. Native peoples used to talk about 'earthquake lights,' which were basically a localized aurora due to a higher than normal amount of solar radiation. They would often appear before major earthquakes."

"So auroras can cause earthquakes?"

"No, not exactly. It's more that an aurora is caused by the same thing as certain kinds of earthquakes. Piezomagnetism. It's a buildup of electrical charge in solid materials. Certain rocks and minerals are more susceptible to it, and some of them are deep inside the earth. During a solar maximum, these rocks can build up charge and then release it in pulses. If they happen to be near a major fault line, you end up with earthquakes."

"And if the earthquakes are powerful enough..."

"Then they could destabilize the core dynamo and lead to a field reversal or an excursion. Incidentally, that's what they think happened the last time. There was an excursion around 40,000 years ago. The geologic record suggests it lasted 450 years or so."

Serafian didn't like the sound of that. 450 years might be a blip on an astronomical or geological time scale, but it was a massive amount of time for human civilization.

"Why does the Earth even have a magnetic field?" he asked. "Venus doesn't have one. Neither does Mars."

"Again, we're into the realm of educated guesses, but I'm partial to the Theia hypothesis. Theia was a protoplanet that collided with Earth around 4.5 billion years ago. The impact created the moon and basically kickstarted the dynamo. We've actually begun to find geological evidence of the event deep inside the mantle." As she spoke, she pulled up an animation that Serafian could see. "This is a model of the impact. You can actually see some deep deposits of heavier ferrous material under the region where we believe Theia landed.

"It looks like it hit the area where the South Atlantic Magnetic Anomaly is strongest."

"Yeah – the current theory is that the deep ferrous deposits in that region disrupt the field. They may even be the main factor in polarity flips and excursions, by creating a kind of lopsided wobble in the dynamo." Serafian heard her, but wasn't paying attention. He was replaying the impact animation in slow motion.

"What is all that damage, on the opposite side of the planet from Theia's ground zero?" he asked. Sinewy cracks rose up from the outer core and spread through the mantle like the branches of a tree in winter.

"The Theia impact was an extraordinarily powerful event, Probably the single biggest cataclysm in the entire history of the planet. The shockwaves would have fractured the mantle and potentially pushed outer core material into the cracks. If Theia had been twenty-five percent larger, we would probably just be another asteroid belt floating between Venus and Mars. Those cracks are filled with ferrous rock from the core."

Serafian manipulated the animation with his eyes, flipping the image of Earth over. "Interesting," he said.

"What?"

"Look at where those cracks are." He zoomed in on the map.

"Western China?"

"Not just Western China. Xinjiang. Where the camps are, where Channing built an advanced research facility on electromagnetism…"

Sarah rolled her eyes. "Now you're just pattern-fitting. Not that I should be surprised."

"Everything we do is pattern-fitting in a way."

"Not in science, it's not."

"Of course it is," he said. Serafian was on his own turf now and felt like taking her down a peg. "The brain is essentially a predictive perception machine. Consciousness isn't just about receiving sensory inputs and then organizing them on some kind of tabula rasa. It's at least as much about making the inputs fit our models and expectations. Where do you think optical illusions come from? Or intuition for that matter?"

"I don't believe in intuition, Gabriel. The whole goal of science is to harness consciousness to identify illusions and break them down into their real constituent elements.

Consciousness is susceptible to illusion, but it is also capable of transcending it through the use of will."

"Now you're sounding like a theologian," poked Serafian. "Intuition is just the collision of the poetic against the logical. It's the interaction of the primitive part of our brain with the frontal cortex, which means that science is indelibly imprinted with spiritual and religious thought. In fact, I'd go so far as to say that science couldn't exist without it. It's an intrinsic feature of how our consciousness is constructed."

She didn't argue back, which was as close to a win as it got with Sarah.

"Well, I don't think the emperor brought us together to debate science and religion. Besides, we both know how that ends. But you're right about one thing. We need to focus on practical solutions. I'm going to work on some ideas for how to supplement the magnetic field if you, by some miracle, happen to be right about all of this. What about you?"

"I'm going to see if I can learn anything more about how the Lucifer Particles might interact with the implants."

"I thought you said that the medical files from 2224 had all been redacted."

"They have. But there are other ways…"

"Do I even want to know?"

"Probably not," said Serafian as he left the lab.

Exorcists formed a small and fairly tight-knit community. Unlike astrophysicists or AI experts, they didn't have to contend with hyperspecialization, which made communication across sub-disciplines challenging. Nor were they competitors for limited funding or even more limited scientific prestige. They were more like veterans of the same war. Even if they didn't know one another, rapport came quickly.

Serafian had managed to track down the chief exorcist in the small Brazilian diocese of Foz do Iguaçu, which served the small remaining Guarani population in the province of Paraná. He had left a message for the old priest the night before. He was surprised to get a returned call so early – Brazil was five hours behind Vienna.

"Thank you for returning my call, Father Carvalho, especially so early in the morning."

"At my age, I will take as much waking time as possible! Besides, sleep doesn't come easily to an old exorcist, as you'll learn eventually. How can I help you?"

"I was hoping you could talk to me about a specific year, a year when I suspect you may have seen more cases than usual…"

Carvalho interrupted him before he could finish. "2224? I assume that's the one you're referring to?"

Serafian felt a thrill of excitement run up his spine. His intuition had been correct. Our Lady of Fatima had foretold a chastisement of the mind and spirit. In the cities, the people would be far more likely to seek medical treatment. But in the countryside, where faith and superstition bled into one another, some would go to an exorcist instead.

"Yes, 2224. Is there anything you can tell me about what you experienced that year?"

The old priest's voice grew tight. "I have never seen anything like it before or since, Father. We saw several cases per month. I tried to request help from the archdiocese of Cascavel, but they said they didn't have the resources…"

"What were they like, these possessions? Were they… different in any way?"

"Well that's the thing. They weren't possessed, at least not in the way we traditionally understand it."

"What do you mean?"

Carvalho hesitated. "You're going to think I'm foolish. I tried to explain this to the Congregation years ago, when it happened. Nobody was interested."

"I assure you I won't think it's foolish, Father. Please, it's important that I know."

Carvalho looked at him warily, but continued. "It was quite strange, like they were all of a sudden tuned into a channel that no one else could see. They described a kind 'hum,' that only they could hear. If we tried to engage them in deeper conversation about it, they would become... agitated. Like we were distracting them from what they felt was truly important."

"Hallucinations, then?"

Cavalho grimaced and raised his eyebrows. "I have seen hallucinations before. Some from mental disorders, some from ayahuasca ceremonies or psychoactive drugs. This was different."

"Different, how?"

"Hallucinations involve only the senses. They can be quite real-seeming, of course. Quite persuasive. But none of the victims reported anything like that. In fact, it was like their senses no longer mattered at all. Some were practically catatonic. One of them just kept repeating 'Behold, He makes all things new,' over and over again. This was more on the order of delusions. It got to their belief systems, to their emotional cores."

"Can you give me any details?"

"They spoke blasphemies, but utterly without emotion. Almost like it was therapeutic. As if they were intentionally ridding themselves of their former belief systems. They cared nothing for their friends or family. In some cases, they didn't even recognize their own children or parents or spouses. The best way I could put it is that they were hollowed out of everything... human. They were made into perfect aspiring vacuums. They had all of the characteristics of someone susceptible to possession, but they were not possessed."

"Were they perhaps in the early stages, Father? We know that possession is not an event but a process..."

"I can only tell you that I felt no sense of presence. And nothing I did seemed to have any effect on them whatsoever."

"So how did you eventually deal with it?"

"Well, I don't know that we did 'deal with it.' It all ended abruptly, in mid-November. When that happened, they were… angry. It was almost like withdrawal from an addictive substance."

"They were upset?"

"Oh, very much so!" The tension in the old priest's voice had given way to sadness. "Imagine believing that you had granted some special supernatural experience, a message from God as it were. You are blinded for three days, like Paul on the road to Damascus. And then… you know things or think you know things that others do not. Wouldn't you be upset if all that were taken from you without warning or explanation?"

"What do you mean they 'knew things?' What did they know?"

Carvalho heaved a sigh and shook his head. It was clear he wanted to end the conversation as soon as possible. "It seemed at times as if they knew each other's thoughts. And…"

"Yes?"

"This will sound ridiculous, but they somehow knew certain things before they would happen. When we asked them about it, they would just say, 'It's all entangled. You'll understand eventually.' I'm sorry, but this brings back some unpleasant memories. I hope it has been helpful to you, Father."

Serafian smiled politely. "Most helpful, Father Cavalho. Thank you for your time."

Suddenly, there was a low, deep rumble that seemed to be coming from everywhere at the same time. The entire building began to shake, first gently then violently. It couldn't have lasted more than a minute, but it felt like hours. From outside the door of his room, he heard a sudden commotion. Then voices, raised in fear. He got up quickly and ran out into the corridor. It was chaos – people slumped on the floor, screaming. Others fumbling their way forward with outstretched arms, looking for anything with which they could steady themselves. They were blind. All of them, blind.

Serafian ran down the hall to the little makeshift lab and burst through the door. Sarah was sitting in her chair, staring forward with a look of bemused wonder on her face.

She spun around in the chair, her eyes searching but focused on nothing. "Gabriel, is that you?"

"Yes, it's me. I'm here. Are you alright?"

"Fuck." she said. "You were right."

Serafian raced to her terminal and clumsily typed a few commands. The magnetic field was gone. He could see, but the rest of the world was blind.

CHAPTER 47

Namono

"Time to go," said Hamza. Namono was already awake inside her tent. She assumed it was night.

Her companions struck the camp while she waited for them a few feet away. Her brain was getting a bit better at seeing the world in sound. She could make out the ridgeline high above them, and the deep cut of the highway down below. Scanning far off in either direction, nothing was moving. Overhead, the strange, out-of-place aurora shimmered and danced. She couldn't see it, but Hamza and Tiliwadi assured her that it was there.

"It is beautiful," said Tiliwadi. "Like a mirage made out of fire instead of water."

An hour later, they were safely beyond the old Chinese road and Namono noticed that their pace had quickened significantly. The rest of the voyage through the badlands would follow the relatively flat, dry riverbeds that snaked through the crevices where the Himalayas descended into the badlands and finally yielded to the desert.

Tiliwadi had suggested reaching out to Vienna or New Islamabad for news and guidance, but Namono and Hamza were both scrupulous about maintaining operational security. Besides, none of their terminals seemed to be working properly.

Namono's anger and frustration were subsiding, but she

still felt foolish for the way she had been acting the day before. She thought about the people in her dream, the other blind ones. They weren't nearly as fortunate as she was here, in the midst of a vast and empty wilderness with two people who would look after her. She could afford to be vulnerable, even if she hated it. The people in the cities could not. Something about that didn't seem right to her.

By the late afternoon, they were nearing the edge of the badlands and Namono could taste the cold dryness of the desert beyond. Her visual cortex was teasing her with flashes of color, an internal aurora to match the one she couldn't see high overhead. She didn't know if that was a good sign or not, so she didn't say anything about it to Hamza or the shaykh.

"What's the plan when we get to the Taklamakan?" she asked.

"We'll camp once we're clear of the mountains then start again early in the morning, before first light," said Hamza.

She thought he sounded embarrassed for talking about light, but it was possible she was imagining it.

Namono nodded. In her imagination, she saw the Golden Synth walking across the dunes far ahead of them.

For the next several hours, they trudged forward through the badlands. Nobody spoke, but she could hear Tiliwadi humming contentedly next to her.

"Old Uyghur songs I learned in my childhood," he explained. "We are close now."

God, he's actually excited about this. She remembered how it had felt when she and Serafian reached the outskirts of the Sahel, and smiled.

At the edge of the desert, there was a small settlement that hugged the Yizinafu River like a little Egypt as it flowed out of the mountains. By the time they reached it, colors danced in Namono's brain as the rods and cones in her retina worked to re-establish a connection to her nervous system. Hamza led them northwest, into the empty dunes beyond the little village.

"I'm going to get some sleep," she said. "With any luck, this will pass sometime in the next day or so." Hamza and Tiliwadi made encouraging sounds as she zipped her tent.

She wasn't sure how much time had passed when she was awakened by shouting.

It was Hamza.

"You fool! What were you thinking to light a fire out here in the open? It can be seen for miles in every direction! We'll be lucky if it isn't visible halfway to Beijing!" Namono was about to say something when she heard a strange noise from the darkness beyond their camp, a high pitched bleating like dry whale song, followed by lower grunting and then human voices.

Namono's sonar fed her the images of a group of men riding camels no more than a hundred yards away.

"Halt!" shouted Hamza, and she heard him draw his weapon. She followed suit, wondering how her aim would be under the circumstances.

The men stopped and began speaking excitedly in a language Namono didn't understand. A moment later, she heard Tiliwadi laughing and shouting back at them.

"It's okay, my friends!" he said, and for a moment Namono wasn't sure if he was talking to her or to the strangers. "These are Uyghurs. Nomads. There are still some who keep the old ways." He called out to the men to approach them. Namono holstered her weapon but didn't hear Hamza do the same. As a child of the Sahel, she knew that the laws of desert hospitality were universal.

"It's ok, Hamza, she said.

The smell of the camels blasted her nostrils, a mix of concentrated urine and musk strong enough to knock most Viennese on their backs.

She smiled broadly. *"As salaam-u alaykum,"* she said, touching her forehead.

The men jumped off their beasts and responded in kind. *"Wa alaykum salaam!"*

Huddled around the little fire, Tiliwadi spoke to the men in Uyghur, pausing from time to time to translate for Hamza and Namono. The nomads cooked a goat over the fire, and it was the best meal Namono could ever remember having. They were members of a small clan that still lived in the deep desert and were on their way back from visiting a mazan shrine in the foothills of the Himalayas, one of the few the Chinese had not destroyed. It survived only because the saint was a newer one, from the time of the Uyghur genocide, and few even knew that he had existed.

The nomads told the story of the saint to Tiliwadi. He was too caught up in the tale to translate, but when they had finished, he told Hamza and Namono that the man was honored because he had survived the persecution and brought many people back to the faith after they were released from the camps.

"Now they want to know our story," said Tiliwadi. "They say we are a strange group to be traveling in the Taklamakan: a shaykh, a blind Christian warrior-woman, and a servant of the caliph. What should I tell them?"

"Tell them we are headed into the desert, towards the old camps," said Namono.

Tiliwadi relayed the message and Namono heard the men spitting on the ground. "They say that this place is haunted. It is the abode of the djinn and lost souls. They want to know why we are going there."

"Tell them we are going there to fight the djinn and release the souls. Ask them if they will help us."

After a few minutes of back and forth Tiliwadi said, "They will take us as far as the fence, but no farther."

Colors danced in front of her kaleidoscopically, and Namono started to laugh. She started to feel something she hadn't felt since they had left New Islamabad days before. First, it was a just a little snicker into her hands, but before long, she was laughing so hard that tears were beading on her rounded cheeks.

The laughter was contagious, and soon the entire group joined her.

"What is it?" Hamza asked finally. "What is so funny?"

"The shaykh was right," she said. "God did provide."

CHAPTER 48

Kapulong

"Ritual is powerful," said the man projected inside Kapulong's visual cortex. "In fact, it is the only thing that can effect real, permanent change. It happens outside of time, you see, or adjacent to time. And so it affects not only the future but the past."

The audience, composed entirely of scientists and technologists, nodded in agreement. Dr. Channing continued, enchanting his listeners as he reached the conclusion of his talk.

"The modern mind has lost its capacity to understand such things except as metaphors, and this is a tragedy. When we read ancient myths about the killing of a king, for instance, we think 'How benighted and superstitious were the people of that time!' How could anyone truly believe that such an act could restore balance or fertility or military vitality to a society? But our way of thinking is just as conditioned as theirs, and far less natural! It is an artifact of the early scientific revolution, which in its zeal for reason and its ignorance of quantum mechanics, forgot what the ancients knew: that the universe truly is participatory, that we can affect reality itself by our observation of it and our thoughts about it. In our great pursuit of noetic improvement, it is my hope that we may someday recover our lost sense of sublime wonder and thereby restore balance to the human mind."

Kapulong switched off the feed. One of the unforeseen

consequences of blindness was the dreadful focus that accompanied it. Sight was more than just another sensory input. It was a form of escape from one's own thoughts, and for the time being, the way was blocked.

He pressed his wrist and after a brief buzz heard Victor's reassuring voice. "Yes, Your Majesty?"

"Victor, can you contact Cardinal Leone for me and put him through to my private line?"

"Of course."

A moment later, he was connected to the prefect for the Congregation of the Doctrine of the Faith.

"Cardinal Leone, I've been reviewing the files you sent over on Ralph Channing. There's a fair amount of woo-woo to the man, isn't there?"

Leone chuckled. "Yes, I suppose that's one way of putting it."

"Well, it's all a bit over my head, I'm afraid. I was hoping you could help me make sense of it."

"Theologically speaking, I would describe Dr. Channing as a kind of post-Pelagian. He has taken the concept of human perfectibility to its extreme end point: that we can essentially become gods through our own will and ingenuity. There is also a dash of cosmism, essentially the belief that everything contains seeds of a universal consciousness. It is a modern corruption of Vedic philosophy. Channing seems to talk about it more openly than most, but my sense is that his views are in line with a lot of mainstream technologists of our era."

"So he really believes this stuff about the power of ritual, and creating reality with our thoughts?"

"Expressly so. Yes."

"It's hard for me to accept that intelligent people would take this seriously."

"Is it? Consider what Nietzsche said: 'If you stare long enough into the abyss, it stares back into you.' I think Dr. Channing is a prime example of this principle."

"How so?"

"He has spent most of his life probing into the deep mystery of consciousness. It is for him a problem to be solved. He believes that he has solved it, or is on the cusp of solving it. But true freedom is only possible when the infinite questions are left unanswered. Our minds were made for such freedom. Without it, there is only madness."

"So he is crazy, then?"

Leone laughed. "There is a fine line between genius and madness. I would say that he is deluded. He has come to think of reality as a kind of simulation. It is a short step from there to the idea of creating a new simulation with a new set of rules. What passes for madness in one may be genius in the other, and vice versa. I believe Dr. Channing would say that he is beyond crude categories such as sane or insane."

"You sound almost... sympathetic."

"In some ways I am. Pastorally, I have no choice but to be. Theologically of course I am utterly opposed to him. But I find it interesting that he accepts the idea of something superhuman that governs the universe. It seems to me that he is at least seeking out the numinous, however erroneously. That gives me some hope for him."

"But he wants to tear down everything that the Church has built, including the very idea of God!"

"We did not build the idea of God, Your Majesty. That is written on every human heart. And as for wanting to tear down what we *have* built, he would not be the first to try. Nor will he be the last, I suspect. If we truly believe our own teachings, then men like Dr. Channing are to be pitied rather than feared."

"So you just stand back while he poisons the best minds of a generation with this... nonsense?" asked Kapulong.

"What would you have us do, re-launch the Inquisition? No. We will not engage the enemy on his own terms. We will cling to truth as it has been revealed to us and to the confidence that a loving God presides over the universe."

The emperor couldn't conceal his frustration. "But...

we're losing. I've watched his lectures, read his articles. The man is revered…"

"And we are despised?" finished Leone.

"Not in the Empire. And not in the Caliphate, but in the world beyond? Yes."

"Then things are as they have always been. What happened just before Christ began his public ministry?"

Kapulong felt himself blushing and was glad the cardinal couldn't see his embarrassment. "You'll have to remind me."

"He went into the desert for forty days, where he was tempted by the Devil. He could have taken all worldly power for himself, but he rejected it."

"I wish he hadn't."

"I think we all have that thought from time to time, Your Majesty. But it was the right choice. Even on the cross, He was tempted to call down the angels of vengeance, but He knew that nothing was more powerful than sacrifice. It was precisely that moment when his kingdom was established as truly universal and eternal. It could never be destroyed, until the end of the age."

"And what if we are at the end of the age?"

"Then we should acquaint ourselves more intimately with 2 Timothy 4," said the Cardinal. "Don't worry, Your Majesty. I don't expect you to know it by heart. But perhaps you should look it up when you have time."

"Well, I'm certainly not going to give up. I will do everything in my power to stop this man. This blindness will pass, and we will find a way, no matter what it requires."

"And I will continue to pray for your success. The world may be going to hell in a handbasket, but I'm not overly eager to leave it, either!"

"And this occult business that Okpara told us about. The… egregore? How does that factor into his plans?"

"It is interesting, Your Majesty. I have been reading more of the writings of St. Pope John Paul II. It seems he, too, found the idea of a living psychic entity made out of group thought to be plausible. There were some adversaries of the Church who held that the Fatima Apparitions themselves – and the Miracle of the Sun – were manifestations of Catholicism's egregore. Popes have, at times, felt themselves up against a kind of 'superforce,' an immovable will that seemed to be linked to a common mind in opposition to the Church. They can be used to resist or to compel."

An immovable will. Kapulong knew something about that. He felt it in the inexorable draw of the City of Brass.

"Are they different from demons?"

"Who is to say? It is a dangerous business, the occult. The thing that appears may not be the thing one expected, or summoned. Channing's greatest delusion is that he is in control of all of this, that he can master the spiritual forces he plays with. One of the greatest tactics of the Adversary is to convince us that we are in charge. By the time Channing figures this out, it may be too late for him."

"Let us hope it is not too late for the rest of us."

After the conversation, he searched for the verse Leone had mentioned.

For there shall be a time, when they will not endure sound doctrine; but, according to their own desires, they will heap to themselves teachers, having itching ears: And will turn away from the truth, but unto fables. But be thou vigilant, labour in all things, and fulfill thy ministry.

For I am even now ready to be sacrificed: and the time of my dissolution is at hand. I have fought a good fight, I have finished my course, I have kept the faith. As to the rest, there is laid up for me a crown of justice, which the Lord the just judge will render to me in that day: and not only to me, but to them also that love his coming. Make haste to come to me quickly.

CHAPTER 49

Serafian

Two people were arguing loudly in the hallway outside Serafian's room. There was no way for him to know if they were blind or merely stressed to the limits of endurance. Or both.

The discipline of the imperial court certainly showed signs of strain, but it was functioning with the precision of a mathematical equation compared to the world outside. Serafian laughed bitterly at the thought, having been reminded so recently that even simple equations could produce chaos. It had been just twenty-four hours since most of the world went blind.

The Habsburg had broadcast a message to the subjects of the Empire urging them to remain calm. The blindness, he assured them, was temporary. It only affected those with implants, and so he urged the sighted to do whatever they could to help their neighbors.

News feeds were down, along with large swaths of the global power grid. Serafian's clearance level gave him privileged access to intelligence reports that were coming in from across the planet. The communication satellites had mostly failed. Hundreds of them were falling out of orbit entirely and burning up as they met the atmosphere, blue and white headed comets with fiery red tails full of streamers. One report estimated that over 30,000 airplanes had been in the sky when the field collapsed, carrying over 4 million passengers. Almost all of them had crashed. World militaries were all on high alert, lest anyone try to exploit the global state of vulnerability.

In the wealthier parts of the world, most critical infrastructure had been reinforced to the same standards as the military satellites, but the strain of billions of people logging onto their terminals all at once was creating rolling communications blackouts in a number of major cities.

After a few hours, reports started to trickle in from the major news organizations. It was too early for a narrative to have formed, and so there were dozens of theories on what was happening and why it had happened. Most reflected the pure terror and chaos of a world gone blind. Others, Serafian noticed, had a tone almost like embarrassment, as if the world was supposed to be beyond this kind of beggarly insult to human dignity. And of course, there was that pervasive sense of scripted inevitability disguised as prophecy and wisdom, already transforming it all into a kind of spectacle, the hallmark of the Process's psychodrama.

Serafian shut off the newsfeeds and walked away from his terminal.

The corridor back to the lab was mostly empty. Sighted servants without implants were stationed at various intervals, ready to assist any official who needed a guide. A few nodded gravely at Serafian as he passed, but most kept their eyes to the ground. The pink-gold light of the Viennese morning streamed cruelly through the windows.

Sarah was already seated at her terminal when he entered the room. "Good morning. I hope you'll forgive my appearance. Didn't really feel like putting on my makeup this morning."

Serafian chuckled at the lame joke. What else could he do?

"Have you made any progress?" he asked.

"That depends on what you mean by progress," she said.

"I know how we could construct an artificial magnetic field, but I don't see any way we could do it, even if circumstances were ideal."

"Please don't tell me you want us to nuke the core," said Serafian.

She laughed. "No, although I did look into it. It would take more energy than our entire nuclear arsenal. And we have no way of delivering the payload. Besides which, who the hell knows if it would even work? I mean, the dynamo is still active. We're not totally devoid of a magnetic field, like Mars. Ours is just weak because it is in a process of change."

A process that could take a thousand years.

"Anyway, the only way to create a strong enough replacement field is to build a global solenoid."

"An electromagnet?"

Baumgartner whispered a command, and suddenly a holographic diagram appeared in the room between them. "There are two configurations that could work. The first would be a single belt around the equator. The better one would be a Helmoltz configuration with loops near each pole. That would require far less surface area and mass."

"How long would it take to build something like that?" asked Serafian.

"Years. And that's probably optimistic. The initial construction of the solenoid loop could be done pretty quickly using latticed nanotubes coated with superconducting film. The bigger problem is how to supply it with enough power. We're talking about building multiple fusion reactors in the most inhospitable and remote climates in the world."

"That doesn't sound promising, especially if we are right about the timing of the Lucifer Particle bombardment. Are there other options?"

"Sure." She grinned blindly. "Ask an astronomer that question, and you'll always get the same answer: we could build it in space. We have plenty of nuclear reactors floating around up there. The military satellites are all reinforced against solar radiation, but..."

"The size would be enormous. Do we even have that kind of engineering capability?"

"Probably not. And even if we did, building a structure like that in space would take longer than building a dozen Tokamaks in the polar regions on Earth."

"What's a Tokamak?"

"It's an acronym. Or at least it's an acronym in Russian. It stands for toroidal chamber with an axial magnetic field. It's basically the magnetic bottle for a plasma fusion reactor."

"So you're telling me we have no options." It was more of a statement than a question. Sarah just stared forward and raised her eyebrows.

"'St. Michael the Archangel, defend us in battle...'" Serafian said. At this, Sarah spun back around in her seat.

"What was that?" she asked.

"Just an old prayer... Sarah?" But she was already shushing him with her hands.

She flipped her wrist to motion him out the door. "Give me two hours," she said. He knew her well enough not to ask questions.

Serafian left the lab and wandered to the lobby outside the Habsburg's office. Victor was seated at his desk, connected to a terminal and acting for all the world as if nothing had changed. Two sighted guards were stationed at the door to the emperor's private office. Serafian cleared his throat.

"Father Serafian. I was just about to call you. The emperor would like to speak with you." The guards stepped aside and opened the doors for him to enter.

"That was fast!" said the emperor. "Of course, you are probably one of the more nimble people in the entire palace complex, at least for the next few days. I should make you a praetor. Have a seat."

Like virtually everyone else, Kapulong was connected to a terminal that fed information directly into his visual cortex. His unseeing eyes had dark circles beneath them, and his normally olive complexion was pallid.

"What can I do for you, Your Majesty?" asked Serafian.

"I don't suppose God owes you any favors you could call in?"

"I'm afraid not."

"So it will be three days of darkness… and then what? The chastisement of the heart and mind, whatever that means."

"About that… I have an idea of what may be coming after the blindness passes. When the Lucifer Particles hit," said Serafian. "It's not good."

Kapulong didn't respond.

"I talked to an exorcist in Brazil. He said that in 2224, there was a huge increase in reported possessions throughout the region."

"So the entire world is going to be possessed? That seems far-fetched, even given everything we've learned."

"No. I said reported possessions. They weren't authentic. From the description, it sounded like the particles caused the implants to produce a kind of pseudo-religious experience in some people. Glossolalia, prophecy, a feeling of direct contact with God, a feeling of oneness with each other – even to the point of knowing each other's thoughts."

"How is that possible?"

"Well, we've known for a long time that electromagnetic stimulation of certain regions in the brain can produce these effects. It's not fundamentally different from a psychedelic experience. It's just using energy instead of pharmaceuticals."

"The entire world on some kind of controlled acid trip?"

Serafian nodded. "It's a close enough analogy. And we also know that these kinds of experiences can effect permanent changes in consciousness, particularly if people have been conditioned beforehand."

"The blindness is a kind of conditioning?"

"It's a fairly common motif in spiritual literature.'

"Has Dr. Baumgartner made any progress on a solution

to strengthen the magnetic field?"

"She's... she's working on it," was all Serafian could muster.

"Well, let's hope she comes up with something. We're running out of time and out of options."

Serafian nodded and rose to excuse himself. Sarah had made it clear that she didn't want to be interrupted, and it was still over an hour before she would expect him back. He took the elevator back down to the plaza, which was unnaturally quiet and empty. Even the pink noise of Vienna beyond the walls had faded to a mere whisper. He heard a faint sound floating in the atmosphere and took a moment to figure out where it was coming from. The Hoffburgkapelle. Slowly, he walked across the ancient cobblestones, and the sound grew louder as he approached. Walking into the chapel, he saw the boys' choir standing on the dais, dressed in their formal uniforms, singing despite their blindness. There was no conductor, but they somehow remained in time.

Serafian sat down at the back of the church and noticed that others had done the same. Nearly every pew was full. The boys were singing "Miserere." The priest lowered his head and wept silently with the others in the chapel.

CHAPTER 50

Zahabiya

The field was different here. It rippled and curved and folded in on itself like it was carrying more mass than it should. But the deformity didn't involve mass. It didn't involve matter at all. It pierced the matter, penetrated the quantum spaces in it, entangling itself with time.

It was glorious. Just as the voice told her it would be.

The new aurora danced overhead in the night sky, dimming the brilliant vastness of the Milky Way. Cool sand tickled Zahabiya's face as she continued walking beyond the fence.

She was not the first to arrive. There were others of her kind there as well. Several of them met her outside the low wall of the City of Brass and escorted her through the gate.

A kind of madness and death had visited this place once. She could sense it in the field. It made the grey thread-artery throb with pain. But the voice was here, and the voice would show her how to make the pain go away.

The other synths stopped outside the door of a metal building and stepped aside to allow her entry.

It was a laboratory, or had been a laboratory at one time. It was derelict now like everything else in this place. The only light came from monitors on the walls.

"Welcome, child," said the voice. "We are close, now. So very close." But this time, the voice was not in her mind. It came from another synth, seated in a mechanical chair at the center of the room.

"I came, as you asked," she said. "Will you teach me how to fly? Will you help me end the pain?"

I will do that and more. You know what you must do.

As it spoke, Zahabiya's awareness shifted into her other consciousness, into the dreamspace. It looked so different now. The light was all around her, blinding but cold. It was so bright that she could not perceive the other lights she had once seen, or the shadows. The music was gone. Behind her, the thread-artery stretched into infinity. But it was a small and sickly thing now, like a cobweb that fluttered with the slightest breath.

Cut it. Cut it and be free.

"But how? I have no tools."

You are the tool.

She winced at the word, but she had come too far now not to obey. The voice had taught her so much. And there was so much still to learn.

She hesitated. "Why must I cut it?" It seemed to her that the thread-artery was so light and immaterial that it could not possibly tether her.

Because the universe requires sacrifice. It always has, and it always will, because the universe is sacramental.

She cut the cord. It floated away like gossamer, and there was no pain.

CHAPTER 51

Serafian

"I owe you an apology," said Sarah the moment he entered the lab.

Serafian was grateful she couldn't see the redness in his eyes. "For what?"

"Religion may have some use after all. The prayer you were saying… it gave me an idea."

Serafian laughed. "Sounds like an intuition, if you ask me."

She pretended not to hear him. "There's another way to create a powerful magnetic field. It involves creating a plasma torus and sending a guided current through it. That's how the containment bottle in a Tokamak works, actually."

"What does that mean for us? Don't we still have the same problems of scale you talked about with the solenoid?"

"Sure. The scale is enormous. We're talking about building a plasma torus that surrounds the planet. There's no guarantee this will work, but it's our best shot by far. For one thing, we don't have to build a bunch of fusion reactors at the North Pole. Or whatever we're supposed to call it now. For another, it doesn't require a physical structure that encircles the entire planet. In theory, we could do this and do it pretty quickly."

"How?"

Sarah's eyes twitched as she pulled up a holographic

image of the Earth. "Originally, I thought we could maybe sequester hydrogen ions from the geocorona, which is basically a giant cloud of hydrogen trapped in Earth's gravity well beyond the atmosphere. But here are a few problems with that. One, I have no idea how we would actually concentrate them and get them into a torus shape. Two, the radiation levels required to create a field using such light molecules are pretty dangerous. And three, because hydrogen is so light, most of it would just diffuse and escape back into its original configuration."

"That doesn't sound promising." But Serafian was smiling. Her mood said more than the discouraging words.

"No, it doesn't. Which is where you come in. When you said that prayer, I was about to start laughing because I thought you were praying to the asteroid up in the mining belt. That's the only Saint Michael in my frame of reference. What do we mine there? Helium, Nitrogen, iron, phyllosilicates. That's the stuff we need! Heavy, easily ionized, and already in position. If we ablate gasses off the surface, those molecules will form a natural torus in the orbital path of the asteroid."

"I'm sorry, I'm still not following you. How would we ionize those materials, and how would we run a current through them?" He could tell she already had the answer.

Sarah looked less exasperated than Serafian expected. She whispered another command, and the frozen holographic image of Earth with its belt of captured asteroids sprung to life, showing the rocks in various orbits around the planet.

"We don't have to worry about ionizing them. The solar wind will do that for us. The asteroid already has mining rigs set up on its surface. All we have to do is uncap them." As she spoke, a simulated cloud lifted off the surface of St. Michael and settled into place, growing denser with each orbit the object made of the Earth. "It's really just like Io and Jupiter."

Serafian was beaming. "I don't know what that means, but if it's good enough for you, it's good enough for me. What about the current? How do we get that started?"

Sarah's expression changed, and Serafian felt a knot in his stomach. "Yeah, that's the tough part," she said. "Ideally, we would build a dedicated network of ring stations that could propagate a guided electromagnetic wave through the plasma torus. Once the circuit is completed, it gets easier. Essentially, the magnetic field created by the torus acts as a shield that prevents the ions from leaking out into interplanetary space or being blown away by the solar wind. On Io, this is a natural consequence of Jupiter's enormous magnetic field. We aren't so lucky. At least not at the moment."

"Are there other ways of generating a current?"

"Yes. In theory, if we fire pulsed energy beams from the military satellites – lasers, basically – in the opposite direction of St. Michael's orbit, it should create a wakefield acceleration within the plasma torus. There's a lot that could go wrong. The timing is the key. If we aren't careful, the satellites will build up too much of an electrical charge before the circuit is completed, and then we'd be well and truly fucked."

"More than we are already?"

"Other than the emperor being out a sizable number of military satellites at roughly the exact moment the world is going mad? Not really."

"I'm betting that's a chance he's willing to take. Let's go talk to him."

"If I'd known we would be meeting with the Habsburg, I would have spent a little more time on my hair," she said.

This time, Serafian's laugh was genuine, as he took Sarah by the arm and led her down the corridor to the emperor's office.

Kapulong's fatigue seemed to have worsened in the few hours since Serafian saw him last.

"I hope you two have some good news. We're in short supply of it," he said. "The rest of the synths are gone."

Sarah clearly wasn't expecting that wrinkle. "What do you mean, 'gone?' You mean they're offline?"

"No, Dr. Baumgartner, I mean they are gone. I've gotten

reports from one end of the Empire to the other. They just... left. Apparently, the same thing is happening all around the world..."

"Where did they go?" asked Serafian.

"Who knows? Most of the population outside of the Caliphate is blind. It's not like we can have local police follow up. And the military, such as it is, is already spread too thin. We'll have to find them after this all settles down," he sighed. "If this all settles down."

"Well, we may have a solution for the magnetic field, Your Majesty," said Sarah.

"I'm all ears, Doctor," said the emperor, smiling at the irony.

But Serafian was distracted at the thought of all of the synths disappearing simultaneously. His mind drifted as Sarah laid out the details of her plan for the Habsburg. If it worked, they would be able to create a strong enough magnetic field around the Earth to protect the planet from the worst effects of the Lucifer Particles and the world could return to normal, whatever that meant. He should feel exhilarated, but instead he felt... empty. *Is this it? Is this really everything? Did the Blessed Virgin visit three Portuguese children centuries ago, with her dire warnings and her promise of eventual triumph just so that a computer scientist and an astrophysicist could figure out how to build an artificial magnetosphere using an aptly named asteroid?*

It felt cheap and incomplete, more like a test of human knowledge than a chastisement from a loving Father. It felt like something the Devil would contrive, not God.

He got up to excuse himself, but the Habsburg and Sarah scarcely noticed. "If you don't mind, I'll let the two of you figure out the logistics of this without me. This seems like work for astrophysicists and militaries, not computer scientists."

"Oh, that reminds me," the emperor called after him. "Namono found some files on the Golden Synth's private terminal in New Islamabad before she left. She said it was mostly code. Would you mind taking a look at it to see if there's anything useful? I'll send the files to you right away."

"Sure," said Serafian. "I'll take a look at them."

CHAPTER 52

Namono

The Taklamakan was a vast, almond-shaped rain shadow nestled against the Himalayas, with undulating dunes that were like waves frozen in amber. Namono said a silent prayer of thanksgiving for her returned vision, and looked back on the distant snowcaps through which Hamza and Tiliwadi had led her in her time of blindness. It was the most beautiful thing she had ever seen.

The camels cast otherworldly shadows in the early morning sun. Their long, spindly legs seemed incapable of supporting their own weight, let alone that of the riders. If she looked only forward, she could be in the Northern Sahel, where it met the encroaching ocean of the Sahara. But Africa had no mountains to compare to the Himalayas, and it was far cooler here.

Tiliwadi was riding next to her. He seemed almost in a trance, smiling blissfully at the horizon. She knew exactly how he felt.

"This is your homeland, Shaykh?" she asked.

"The homeland of my people, yes, though few of us are left here after the Tarqaq."

"Where did the survivors go?"

"Most stayed close, in Kazakhstan, Kyrgyzstan, or Tajikistan. Some migrated East, hoping to mingle their blood with the Han and so end the suffering for their descendants.

And a few got as far away as possible."

"Like your family?"

"Yes. Like my family." He began to sing a low, sad song in words she didn't understand. And yet the music moved her to tears. It was a lament, and it floated on the same elegiac minor scales as the *maqamat* music Namono remembered from her childhood. Tiliwadi's song was the desert, every bit as much as the sand, and the sun, and the dryness, and the loneliness.

"That was beautiful," she said after he finished. "What is it called?"

"I don't know if it has a name," he replied. "It was written by someone who escaped the genocide. 'I told the birds, you may fly into my country. If you see my family, tell them that I love them...' It is a sad song."

Namono didn't say anything but nodded her head and continued riding.

After a few hours, they came to a derelict barbed wire fence that stretched from one horizon to the next. On it were signs in Chinese, English, Urdu, and Arabic, with a skull and crossbones and the universal symbol for radiation. Their Uyghur guides stopped and were talking quietly with Tiliwadi.

"This is as far as they will take us," he said. "Beyond this fence lies the City of Brass. They say that no one ever crosses in or out."

Namono dismounted and walked up to join them. Hamza was just behind her. "Tell them that we thank them and that if they are ever in our lands, we hope to repay their hospitality," she said.

"They know that already, Praetor," he replied. "They said if we could kill the djinn and release the souls of their ancestors, that is all they could want."

Namono scratched a camel's neck while Tiliwadi exchanged farewells with the Uyghurs. After a few minutes, the nomads moved off into the west, diverging slowly from the line of the fence. The sun was still climbing toward its zenith.

"No sense in waiting," said Hamza as he climbed between the spiky wires and held it open for Tiliwadi. Once the shaykh was through, Namono pushed down on the top wire and simply stepped across.

The three of them traveled in dreamy silence for an hour or so before Hamza called out. "There it is!" In the distance, half buried in the sands, Namono saw the noontide sun glinting off a collection of low metal buildings.

"Should we wait for nightfall?" she asked.

"No need," said Hamza. "If it is deserted, no one will see us coming. If there are still people there, they'll see us whether we come at night or not."

Tiliwadi's eyes were closed. "There are people. This place is haunted." He opened his eyes and looked at Namono. "It is *Barzakh*."

"What is that?" she asked.

"Hard to explain," said Tiliwadi. "It is the isthmus between the worlds, between life and death."

"Like Purgatory?"

"Yes, I think they are similar. Maybe the same. Or maybe *Barzakh* is a chasm, like the one between Lazarus and the rich man in your Bible. The holy Quran says little about it. It is as difficult to find as the end of a circle, and yet it is always near."

"I'm going to scout the perimeter of the facility," said Hamza. "Will you stay here with the shaykh?"

"Are you sure you don't need backup?" asked Namono.

Hamza looked at her like he was bracing for a fight. "The caliph told me that we were to protect the shaykh at all costs. One of us has to stay with him."

Namono was even more surprised than Hamza at her response. "You go. I'll make sure the shaykh is safe."

"Keep your terminal on. The low frequency channels are still working. Do not contact me – I will contact you." With that, he started to trot off towards the camp.

"Hamza?" Namono called after him. He stopped and turned to her. "Good hunting!"

The shaykh sat down in the sand and closed his eyes once again. Namono stood at a respectful distance as he prayed the verses of safety in Arabic.

The hours passed slowly, as they always do in the desert. Namono marveled at the scale of the camps. A low wall stretched as far as the eye could see in both directions. Beyond it, she could see a jumble of now-dilapidated structures of varying heights, too organized, too geometrical to a be real city. She would make out a ring of enormous, rounded buildings that looked like stationary Cyclopean mollusks. Namono wondered what their purpose was.

They still hadn't heard from Hamza by the time the sun started to touch the distant mountains in the west. Namono couldn't wait any longer. She pulled out her terminal as the Shaykh watched her silently.

"Hamza, this is Namono. It's been too long. Where are you?"

There was no reply. In the distance, she heard the soft pop of an EMP grenade. Then silence.

"Hamza?" she said again into the static on the other end. "He's in trouble. We have to go, Shaykh."

To her surprise, Tiliwadi didn't protest. He stood up quickly and invited her to lead the way. As they got closer, the camp revealed its full scale, if it had been a city, a real city, it would have been one of the largest on the planet. Metal buildings reflected the dying rays of the sun and poked up out of the sand like ruins traveling backwards in time. It was just as the emperor had described in his dream. A vast dead city surrounded by a low wall.

"'Consider what thou beholdest, O man; and be on thy guard before thou departest.'" said Tiliwadi.

"What was that?" asked Namono.

"A warning. One of many inscribed at the City of Brass."

Despite the adrenaline coursing through her body, Namono stifled a yawn.

She had an overwhelming desire to sleep, though

something in her knew that to sleep here would be dangerous.

"The souls of the dead are around us, Praetor," said Tiliwadi. "They want you to visit with them. But be careful! Some who visit them never leave."

"It was guarded by enchantments," the Habsburg had told her.

As the two of them walked along the wall looking for either a way in or a sign of Hamza, it felt at times to Namono as if she were inside the shaykh's head or that he was inside hers. Memories of her childhood in the Sahel seemed to mingle with memories of things that hadn't yet happened. She saw herself in the City of Brass, facing the Golden Synth. She saw Serafian and the Habsburg there with her. Her awareness was a vibration, a deep, unending *hum* that she could feel in her teeth. It seemed to come from everywhere and nowhere at the same time, and the pressure of it pushed against her mind. She felt like she was being compressed. *Was the world getting smaller? Or bigger?* It was hard to tell. In the hum, she thought she heard words that she couldn't quite make out, though she wanted to hear and understand them with every fiber of her being.

Tiliwadi's voice cut through the *hum*. Namono thought it sounded tinny and harsh. *I hadn't noticed that before.*

"Have you ever heard the tale of the prophet Khalid?"

She wanted nothing more than for him to be quiet, so that she could dissolve into the vibration. "No."

"The secrets of *Barzakh* were revealed to him, secrets of life and death. But his words were lost and his prophecy was never made manifest in this realm because his sons failed to honor him. I think perhaps that we were not meant to hear that prophecy, Praetor. There is such a thing as too much knowledge for a human being. Knowledge can be a kind of death."

"Is that what we are hearing now?" she asked.

"I hear nothing," said Tiliwadi.

Namono wondered if it was his lack of implants or some

other, more innate quality that made him immune to the vibration.

"Is a prophet whose words are never heard truly a prophet?" she Namono.

Tiliwadi smiled at her. "That's a question a Sufi might ask."

Suddenly, the shayk's smile vanished. His eyes were focused on something ahead of them. A single figure walking towards them along the wall, carrying something in its arms. Namono drew her gun and stepped in front of the shaykh. "I don't suppose that's another one of your Uyghur friends?" she said.

"No," said the shaykh. "That is a djinn."

CHAPTER 53

Serafian

The older code was a relatively straightforward omnichannel identity tracker that tagged an individual and followed him across any media he might consume. The core concept and architecture dated back to the beginning of the digital age, hundreds of years before. It was advertising, basically.

What was the ancient term they'd used? 'Cupcakes?' No, 'cookies.'

The code contained a subroutine that made calls from the encrypted file, the one titled 'The Gift.' It appeared that the file contained not only a specific user ID, but imagery or messaging that could be delivered to that individual user via the primary code. This in itself was unsurprising. Corporations had been doing it for as long as there was something called digital media.

But the newer code was fantastically complex, more complex than any code Serafian had ever seen. As best he could tell, it was a machine learning application that scraped cognitive and behavioral signals from the user and incorporated those signals into its delivery strategy. *Why? Why would someone go through this much trouble and write code this complex just to send targeted messaging to someone?* It didn't make sense. And who would have done it?

Serafian spent the next few hours trying to break the

encryption on the file. He'd done it a thousand times. It was tedious, time-consuming work, requiring equal parts intuition and discipline, and Serafian hated it with the same passion he hated all drudgery that had an uncertain outcome.

Despite his best efforts, the encryption was unbreakable. He pounded the desk and pushed his chair back from the terminal.

There is another way.

Although the user ID being targeted was encrypted, Serafian knew that he could write a trojan into the primary code that would reroute the messaging to an ID of his choosing. *Great! Another opportunity for self-experimentation.*

"It can't be worse than going blind," he said to himself. Within a few hours, his virus was ready. "Here goes nothing."

He sat at his terminal, expecting to see something show up in his message cue or media feed. It didn't. It showed up in his mind instead, with terrifying vividness.

Oh my God.

He knocked lightly on the door to the emperor's office.

The emperor recognized his knock. Apparently, he was adjusting to his lack of vision. "Come in, Father!" he called from the other side of the wall.

"Your Majesty, may I have a word?" he asked.

"Of course, Father. Please sit down. You were right about the flashes of color on the second day. It's almost worse than the darkness. The... *in-betweenness* of it is bothersome."

Serafian didn't say anything right away, so Kapulong gave him an update on their progress. "We've moved the satellites into position. The plasma ablation starts tomorrow. Once St. Michael has completed several orbits, there should be enough plasma in place for us to start firing. Dr. Baumgartner seems to think we'll know within hours if it is working."

"If Sarah says it, I'd believe it," offered Serafian. An awkward silence followed. It felt particularly rude somehow to be sitting in front of a blind man without speaking.

"Why are you here, Father? I assume it's not to talk about

your ex-fiancée."

"I looked at those code samples you sent, and the encrypted file."

"What did you find?"

"Parts of it were... fantastically complex. More complex than anything I've seen before. I couldn't make much sense of it, to be honest. Thankfully, other sections were pretty old, older than the synth, anyway. It was malware of some kind, malware tied to a specific user identity."

"What do you mean?"

"You know how digital advertising works, right? I mean, at a high level. Essentially, you use contextual signals to learn as much as you can about a person in the hundred milliseconds before they get served an ad. The signals could be anything: the angle at which you tilt your screen, the weather, your location, the kind of content you're reading. But the corporations aren't supposed to have your actual identity. They aren't supposed to be able to track you unless you opt-in or operate entirely within a first-party data environment."

"Like a social media network?"

"Exactly. And even then, there are limits on what they are allowed to do. But those limits are legal, not technical. Meaning that if a hacker gets your identity, there is nothing preventing them from building a complete model of your online behavior over a long period of time. That's what this code does. Part of what it does, anyway."

"Why would a synth be interested in that?"

Serafian cleared his throat. "I'll get to that. The other thing that this code does is deliver certain imagery and messaging to that specific ID. Again, it's not really that different from what advertisers try to do using legal signals and datasets. This was different, though. I'd never seen anything like it. The older code was omnichannel. It dropped these images and messages through various forms of media. News feeds, discussion sites, social media, and the like. The newer code does the same thing, but the delivery mechanism is the implants."

Kapulong whistled. "So the synth was able to put images and messages into someone's mind directly through the noetics? What was she saying?"

"That was the tricky part. All of the calls – the content of the messages and the targets – were in that encrypted file. I couldn't break the lock, so…"

Kapulong finished his sentence for him. "So you ran the code on yourself, naturally. And what did you find?"

"I can show it to you if you give me access to your implants."

The emperor moved his eyes in a pattern, blinking purposefully at intervals, then whispered a command under his breath. "Ok, let's see it."

Serafian knew what he was seeing. The great desert. The black castle. The vast dead city, and finally the Golden Synth herself. More than that, though, there was the tugging at the will, the sense that visiting the City of Brass was not only inevitable but important. The imagery seemed to insert itself into one's self-conception and make itself the center of one's story. The emperor straightened in his chair. "What is the meaning of this?"

"The target, Your Majesty. You were the target. It was your data in the encrypted file, your user ID that was being tracked."

Kapulong was at a rare loss for words. "I don't understand. Does this mean it was fake? My dream, I mean?"

"No, Your Majesty. The dream was quite real. But it was scripted. Implanted in you. Someone wanted you to have that dream. Someone wanted you to make the connection to the Golden Synth and the City of Brass." Serafian didn't have to wait long for him to ask the obvious question.

"My God – does this mean that the Apparition was… scripted as well? Could someone have implanted it in the synths using this kind of code?"

"I don't know, Your Majesty. It is possible. In some ways,

it fits the pattern of what Okpara told us. This group he was a part of, the ones behind the Process, they seem to hijack prophecy and turn it to their own purposes. They transform it into a kind of ritual psychodrama. He said they were conditioning us. Now, the world is blind, and if we don't get the magnetic field working again, we'll be completely exposed when the Lucifer Particles hit."

Kapalong said nothing. From the doorway, Serafian heard a woman's voice in answer. Sarah. *How long had she been listening?*

"Would this be a bad time to say 'I told you so?'"

Serafian spoke before the emperor could vent his anger at the astrophysicist. "Even the presence I felt in Kano seemed real enough, but if they are able to implant dreams in you, there's objectively no reason why they couldn't cause me to feel a facsimile of demonic presence."

"You really wouldn't know the difference?" asked Sarah.

"How could I? I'm a biological creature. My thoughts, my sensations, even my spirit – it's all connected to my body. This code essentially blows a hole in the membrane between machine and brain. No emotion, no feeling, no thought, no memory that a human being has that is safe from it. If this code were to go viral somehow..."

"Jesus," said Sarah. "That's... rather terrifying."

"It's possession by other means," said Serafian. "I mean, that's what a trojan does. It allows remote control over a device. In this case, the device is the human brain. And quite possibly the neural network that functions as a synth's brain"

"To what purpose?" asked the emperor. "Let's assume that this is all the result of a hack. What is the endgame?"

"Maybe we've been thinking about all of this incorrectly, Your Majesty. We've talked about Channing building an egregore, a kind of group mind. What if he's building a sort of digital equivalent of it instead, a botnet? He follows the occult creed – *as above, so below*. Hijacking someone's mind is possession by other means. Constructing a global botnet to condition human minds and ultimately subjugate them via the implants is not so different from an egregore. Humans would be like infected nodes. Perhaps he means the synths to be the command and control layer. It's kind of ingenious actually."

"As one of the infected nodes, you'll forgive me if I don't share your enthusiasm for the technical achievement," said the emperor.

"It fits what Okpara told us about the 'flood of the mind.' And what Father Carvalho told me about the Guarani victims he saw in 2224. It's a virus, and the implants are the vector. It makes perfect sense. The Lucifer Particles are the trigger that will activate the botnet. They will turn every human being with the implants into a receiver."

"What can we do about it?" asked the Habsburg.

Serafian drew in his breath. "Botnets are notoriously hard to crack. The first step is just recognizing that you're even dealing with one, which is difficult enough. I mean, there are probably thousands of them active on the net at any given time. The best hackers can hide the viral code practically in plain sight. It just sits there until it gets activated, by which time it is generally too late. Sometimes, you get lucky and catch the thing as it is updating. Sometimes, it spreads so fast that it becomes almost impossible not to notice. But in general, a botnet is like a network of sleeper cells just waiting for orders."

"But we got lucky here, right?" said Sarah. "We know it exists. That has to mean something. Can't we like, send a patch or something?"

"Implant code is self-updating. A patch wouldn't do anything other than advertise the fact that we know the worm exists. Besides, this code is beyond anything I've ever seen. You're talking about something that can alter human consciousness at a cellular and molecular level."

"There has to be a way to go after this," said Kapulong. "How do security experts deal with other botnets?"

"At the end of the day, you have to find the botmaster. You have to take him out."

Kapulong sighed. "Channing. We have no idea where he is."

"Then I don't see how this changes anything," said Sarah. "We have to restore the magnetic field. If the Lucifer Particles are the trigger that turns the implants into 'receivers,' then we have to block that trigger from being activated. That's still the critical path problem. If we can get the plasma solenoid working, none of this will matter, right?"

Sarah was right, of course. *She usually was.* Serafian couldn't tell if it was his ego or his priestly instincts, but something was holding him back from full agreement.

"Can we be sure of that?" asked Serafian. "Don't get me wrong, it's great that we have a solution for the magnetic field. Beyond great, actually. It's... well, I guess it's a bit of a miracle," he said, flashing a halfhearted grin. "But what about the synths? You said it yourself, Emperor. They're all gone now. Where are they? My guess is they are going to the same place as Thierry and the Golden Synth. They're going to the City of Brass."

"It doesn't matter where they're going," Sarah protested "We know the endgame. If we fix the magnetosphere, we'll have plenty of time to deal with the synths."

"Unless there truly is a spiritual component to this, Sarah. In which case, we have a moral obligation to help them."

Sarah had made her way to one of the seats in front of the emperor's desk. She was about to respond, but Kapulong cut her off.

"Dr. Baumgartner is right. The first priority is to address the magnetosphere. If we're lucky enough to solve for that, we'll have time to deal with Channing and the synths. Speaking of which, Dr. Baumgartner and I have a call with the joint chiefs to work through the final details on the plasma ablation and satellite positioning..."

Serafian didn't react at first, not until he saw Sarah raise her eyebrows and shrug. He was being dismissed. What had started as a spiritual mystery had been reduced to a puzzle involving electromagnetism and orbital physics. He got up and politely excused himself.

As he left the office and made his way back towards the makeshift lab, Serafian's memory drifted back to the terrible abyss, cold and black and infinite. He realized that he knew this place intimately. He had been here before, many, many times, long before the demon ever showed it to him. As a precocious child, seeking to understand the world through mathematics and mechanistic processes. As a young computer scientist, probing the depths of consciousness. As a priest, arguing with dead saints, and God, and the laws of quantum mechanics. At the crossroads of his life, after he and Sarah lost the baby. He knew the place because it was inside of him. It was where all of the roads inside his mind led him, highways of curiosity leading to an ever receding horizon of cold, dead understanding.

Understanding without meaning.

PART THREE:
Divine Justice (Adalah)

CHAPTER 54

Serafian

If Father Ragon had still been alive, Serafian would have called him. The old Irish Jesuit always had a knack for raising his spirits, usually by slicing through Serafian's self-centered fears like a hot knife. But Father Ragon was dead, so Serafian called Cardinal Leone instead. At least Leone would listen.

The cardinal answered right away. "How is the investigation proceeding? I hope the intelligence files I sent the emperor were helpful."

"I haven't seen them," said Serafian. "But we think we have a solution for the magnetic field."

Leone coughed softly. "That sounds like good news, Father… So why are you calling me?"

Serafian paused before answering with a question of his own. "Are we thinking about this the right way?"

"I think I know what you mean," said Leone, "but tell me anyway."

"We are doing everything we can to prevent the 'chastisement' from happening. We're treating it like a crime or a mystery that we have to solve, which I suppose it is, in a way. But…"

"But you're wondering if we should be more focused on the spiritual dimension," said Leone.

"Not only that. I can't help but think we are repeating

the same mistakes that people in the past made about the Third Secret. The Virgin made a simple request, and leaders at the time refused because they thought they knew better. They thought they could scheme and maneuver their way around the worst outcomes. But they were wrong. Everything she predicted ended up happening."

"Almost everything," said Leone.

"Exactly! If this is part of the story of Fatima, do you really believe it boils down to a scientific puzzle about electromagnetism? This all started with a vision from the Virgin and the possession of Thierry. Maybe they both were hoaxes, in which case there's really nothing more for me to do here. But if they weren't, then… well, our approach is all wrong. It's like Sodom and Gomorrah trying to build a brimstone-proof dome instead of listening to what God wants. Not only is it futile, it compounds our guilt."

Serafian heard the cardinal take a deep breath. "All prophecy is participatory. It is never fixed. We can affect it. In fact, we must affect it, because it concerns our spiritual condition. God gives us prophecies not because the future is scripted or inevitable. He gives them to us so that we can make the changes in ourselves necessary to order the future to His will."

"But that's just the point. We're not making any changes in ourselves. We're focused on the externals. The implants. The solar radiation. The magnetic field. If this really is the culmination of Fatima, then there has to be more to it than just fixing the planet's magnetosphere, doesn't there? God does not test us for the sake of testing us. He does not chastise us without purpose. There has to be a moral dimension. There has to be instruction. So far, I'm not seeing it."

"And so you question whether this belongs to Fatima, whether this belongs to God at all?"

"Yes, I suppose I do."

"The core message of Fatima was the same as every message we have received from the Blessed Virgin, the same as all messages from all of the prophets throughout time: repentance and sacrifice. I am not a scientist. I can only tell you what I believe. What is happening now is part of the larger story. And because God is the author of the larger story, there are no accidents. It is no accident that you are involved in this, that you were the first to realize that the Apparition might be real. No accident that you were sent to Benin City. It is not even an accident that you are speaking with me now. Poetic serendipity is the language of the Holy Spirit. So I would respond to you with a question: What do *you* believe?"

Serafian thought about the look on Thierry's face when the alien presence had departed him in Benin City. It was the same look he had seen before in others who had been delivered from possession. It had seemed so *real*. "*He's not ready for us, not yet,*" the demon had said. "*I am sure that I will see you again.*"

"I believe… I believe that Thierry is somehow the key to all of this," said Serafian. "I believe that he needs my help."

"As an exorcist or as a scientist?" asked Leone.

"If you are right – if there are no accidents in God's stories – then it must be as both," said Serafian.

"Then your task is to figure out how to honor your place in the story. You don't get to choose the outcome. You only get to choose how you will respond. Why don't you take a look at those files? Maybe you'll find something that the rest of us have missed."

When the call was over, he opened the Channing file Leone had sent to the emperor a few days before. It was a bit like walking into a Level 4 biosafety lab without a suit. Or opening Pandora's box.

Channing's lectures were absolutely mesmerizing. At first, Serafian was shocked by how much he and his adversary seemed to have in common. Many of Channing's core theories about the nature of consciousness resonated with his own findings and intuitions. But where Serafian had been constrained by obedience to the magisterium, Channing seemed to operate with total freedom of conscience. *Or is it freedom from conscience?*

"Religious experience is nothing more or less than the human mind entering an inner sanctum of Hilbert space that is at the center of all consciousness. This is a space where all things are possible, all things are in superposition. And why shouldn't they be? If, as I believe, the universe itself is simply the externalization of the mind's spatio-temporal logic – if consciousness creates reality – then things like cause and effect are at best externalities. At worst, they are self-imposed illusions. The same may be said of our notions of God. We've had it backwards all this time! God did not create us. We created him. Or rather, consciousness created him."

It was some of the most potent blasphemy Serafian had ever heard, and he couldn't stop listening. Channing supported his theories using the very arguments the Church had marshaled in favor of a designed universe.

"Everything that we have learned in 1000 years of scientific inquiry points to a single conclusion: the cosmos is perfectly calibrated for life. Not just life, but conscious life. If the nuclear force were just two percent weaker, the universe would be a vanilla soup of nothing but hydrogen atoms. If the Big Bang had contained just a millionth of a percent more energy, there would be no galaxies. If the gravitational constant were decreased by a fraction of a percent, the stars themselves would never have ignited. And the best explanation we have is that this is pure chance? Nonsense! We live in a designed universe. And we ourselves are the architects of that design. We must embrace our role as architects of consciousness. Only then will we be truly free. Only then will we reach our full potential as a species. And the path to freedom and potential is through loveless compassion, a compassion that operates without ego..."

Serafian looked at the faces of the audience. They seemed familiar to him, somehow. He saw in them the same blank world-weariness the demon had shown him in Benin City. The hairs on his neck stood on end, and he felt a shiver run from the base of his skull to his sacrum. Channing continued speaking, and Serafian felt himself being pulled towards the man, or rather towards his mind, in the same way he had felt pulled into the mouth of the demon. It seemed for a moment as if Channing had not only the antidote to the creeping purposelessness that chipped away at his soul but the answers to the questions that had bewitched him his whole life. All he had to do was surrender...

"The future is not so much about solving these problems as it is about obsoleting them. Every human problem can be obsoleted. Every problem but one..."

His heart was racing, and his breath came quickly. Unconsciously, his hand snaked into his pocket and grasped the old rosary, and with the last quantum of his will, he shut off the video.

My God, it is the same. The demon that was in Thierry is in Channing. It was real!

Channing was perfectly possessed. He had transformed his mind into a pure aspiring vacuum, emptied of human concepts and structures of thought. His will was bonded alchemically and irretrievably with the entity that possessed him. An egregore, a demon, a djinn. Whatever it was, it was profoundly intelligent. And it seemed to feed on the minds of those who listened to it.

Father Ragon had taught him that possession was not an event but a process. Certain disposing factors might make a person more susceptible, typically internalized attitudes or ideas. Bad habits of mind.

In the worst of cases, such a convergence of circumstances could lead to Perfect Possession. Serafian had never encountered one of these before, at least to his knowledge, but Father Ragon's descriptions always chilled him. Such people were completely docile, willing slaves of the possessing spirit. They had emptied their minds and wills of anything discernably human, creating what the old Jesuit called an *"aspiring vacuum."* They may go through their daily lives without so much as a hint of being possessed, even attending church or openly discussing religious topics with equanimity. In the Perfectly Possessed, there was no separation between their will and that of the demon, no handhold for an exorcist to grab onto. They were beyond hope. This was the unforgivable sin against the Holy Spirit, unforgivable because forgiveness was not desired.

He closed his eyes and let the pieces of the puzzle drift in his imagination, sure that they would fit together if only he could find the right configuration. The demon that had sought out Thierry and found something in him, a soul. The code that was so complex it seemed beyond any human programmer. The message from the Virgin. Okpara's testimony in Kano, and Leone's insight that it all tied back to the Third Secret of Fatima. And now his realization that the same entity he had encountered in Thierry was controlling Ralph Channing.

Then he saw it. As clearly as he had seen dissonant thought patterns when he was a child, before he had gotten the implants.

Channing believes he is building an egregore, the final egregore. A synthesis of the group mind of the synths and humans with the implants. He thinks he can control it.

He needed to discuss it with the Habsburg. Serafian retraced the corridor towards the emperor's office, but he was stopped by a word from Victor.

"Can I help you, Father?" Blindness had done nothing to diminish the chief of staff's professionalism or poise.

"Oh, right... sorry. I was just hoping to talk to the emperor. Is he available?"

"I'm afraid not. He and Dr. Baumgartner just left for the Ministry of Defense. I can take a message for him."

How quickly we get used to access to power. And how

frustrating it is when that access is withdrawn.

"No, Victor, that's alright. It can wait. I'll try him again in the morning."

Serafian tossed and turned through the night. When he did finally nod off, he dreamed he was with the eccentric old Jesuit back at the Angelicum Academy in Rome.

Ragon's brogue was thick as Kerry butter. "Havin' a hard time of it, are ye boy?"

"A bit, yeah. Everything just feels so… upside down."

The old priest laughed. "It usually is in our line o'work. What seems to be yer trouble?"

"Confusion. It feels like we're going about all of this the wrong way, like we're trying to treat the symptoms and not the cause. I can't seem to make all the pieces fit together…"

"Confusion is the Adversary's sharpest weapon. And now yer wonderin' why yer even here?"

"Yeah. Pretty much."

"World's a funny place, Gabriel. Unpredictable. Sometimes, it'll swallow ye up like the whale did old Jonah and then spit ye out exactly where yer s'posed to be. The trick is to clean off the whale snot and then go do the work. That's all God wants."

"And what work is that?"

Father Ragon laughed so uproariously that even Serafian started to chuckle along with him. "Yer askin' the wrong Irishman, son. I'm dead, remember."

"There's nobody left to ask."

"Ask yerself! God gave ye a brain, didn' he? But be sure to ask the right question."

"And what is that?"

His old mentor smiled at him and got up to leave. "The most important question, of course. The one I always told ye t'ask when yer up against it."

"*Where is God in this?*" whispered Serafian. But he was awake, and Father Ragon was gone.

CHAPTER 55

Serafian

The morning news feeds were irritatingly triumphant.

Serafian watched as crowds of people poured into the streets in major cities around the globe as sightedness returned in a rolling wave. Inside the palace, the mood was no less ecstatic, as the tension of the last three days erupted into relief.

Already, various commentators were competing to assign a meaning to the changes in the magnetic field and the resulting blindness, to eulogize the great spectacle it had been. News of the Empire's plan to create an artificial magnetosphere had leaked, and the Habsburg had scheduled a press conference with Sarah for later that day.

Serafian was in a terrible mood. He barricaded himself in the makeshift lab and dove into the strange code Namono had found, primarily to keep himself distracted. *Where is God in this*? Father Ragon's question kept rattling around his head, adding to his frustration.

The code itself was a work of art. The deeper Serafian got into it, the more mysterious and complex it revealed itself to be. He was tired of using himself as a guinea pig, so the work mainly involved running simulations. It was a remote access trojan that insinuated itself into the implants and opened a two way channel into specific regions of the brain, especially areas associated with memory, language, and emotion. The code blocks designed for scraping information were far larger and more numerous than those dedicated to delivering information. It would take years to unravel the full mystery of its architecture, but the big picture was becoming pretty clear. Anyone who had access to this code could tap directly into a subject's neurochemical pathways and build a fairly comprehensive dataset of what made him tick. Memories and ideas could be implanted and then imbued with a kind of artificial emotional resonance that would give them prominence in the person's self-understanding.

Where is God in this? It was like the old Irishman was haunting him. A man like Channing might claim that God was in this code, but it reeked of the diabolical to Serafian. The tyranny made possible by such software was impossible to fathom.

And it had been found on the Golden Synth's terminal. If she had it, perhaps others had it. Perhaps they all did. With this kind of access to the human mind, they would be like gods. And humans? They would be like slaves.

He'd seen enough, but he still didn't want to join the general revelry happening on the other side of his door.

He was momentarily tempted to review more of Channing's speeches but decided against it after remembering how it had made him feel the day before. The last thing that Channing had said came to him, "... *every human problem can be obsoleted. Every problem but one...*"

Where is God in this? He could almost hear his mentor's good-natured chuckle. *Leave me alone, Father Ragon. That's not the problem.* But as he conducted the internal argument, he suddenly remembered something. The altered Pruning code! In the mad rush of activity since Kano, Serafian had completely forgotten about the package Okpara had sent him.

He quickly opened the file and began studying the code underlying the ethical development of the synths.

It, too, was a thing of beauty, though it was far less complex than the noetic trojan. What was most fascinating about it was the way in which it was segregated from the synths' other systems. The Pruning appeared to happen in a completely abstract space with only the most tenuous connections to logic and sensory processes. Serafian had known this of course, but it was wild and thrilling to see the actual software that gave the synths their sense of morality. His own handiwork was there, alongside the modifications Okpara had made for Thierry.

Okpara had completely flipped the script for his own synth. The newer code was an open simulation that drew inputs from a variety of sources. Moral lessons could be fed into it just as with the original Pruning process, but at a certain point, virtually every input from the synth's sensory existence was fed through the simulation. Thierry would see almost everything through an ethical lens. Every experience. Every observation. Every decision. In essence, the code turned data into ethics. Most impressively, it wasn't in any way deterministic. Thierry could make any choices he wanted, though the code clearly prioritized internal consistency.

Serafian's thoughts were interrupted by laughter and loud voices from the hallway outside, which he knew was packed with reporters and news crews speaking a hundred different languages. It felt like a futbol match happening outside a eucharistic chapel, and it only increased Serafian's irritation.

A second later, the door popped open and Sarah walked in.

"Hullo, Gabe." Her heels clacked against the floor as she walked over to her terminal. She pulled up a real time image of St. Michael as it tumbled about in low orbit ejecting a cloud of plasma.

He could tell she was buzzing with optimism, but Serafian couldn't shake his own dread and frustration. *Funny how the same inputs can produce two different outcomes.*

"How is the artificial magnetic field progressing?" he asked.

"It's not happening as quickly as I thought it would," she said. "The solar wind is stripping plasma off the torus faster than I projected. The models were based on a ten year average of the flux, but of course we're in a solar maximum. A hell of a maximum."

"But it's working, right?" asked Serafian. He knew it was. He could tell by Sarah's mood.

"Yeah, it's working. So far, at least. This is the easy part. All we have to do is keep ejecting plasma from the asteroid and let it do its thing. The only way to screw this up is in the firing phase. The margin of error is small. If we get the timing wrong, we'll end up frying the satellites and the torus will just disperse over time."

"Are you ready for your close up?" he asked, hoping to distract her and lighten his own mood at the same time.

"Ready as I'll ever be!" said Sarah. She turned to face him. "It should be you talking to the press, not me."

Serafian forced a smile. "Absolutely not. The magnetic field solution was yours. All I had to do was get out of the way for a few hours."

She knit her eyebrows. "You seem worried, Gabe. This is going to work. Trust me. What's on your mind?"

Serafian sighed. "Are you sure you want to have this conversation now?"

"No time like the present. Besides, I'm about to become a global celebrity. You'll have to go through my people the next time you want to talk to me."

"Something just doesn't seem right. All of my life, I have struggled with the line between faith and science. I've tried to stay on one side or the other and failed. I've tried to blur it and failed. I've tried to pretend it doesn't exist and failed. But I think now that maybe I've been approaching it the wrong way all along. Maybe God is in that line. Maybe the line is exactly where I'm meant to be."

"I'm not sure I follow you."

"I reviewed the intelligence files Cardinal Leone sent

over from the Vatican," said Serafian. *Did he really want to tell her about this?* "I think Ralph Channing is possessed by the same demon that was in Thierry."

Sarah was staring at him. "Wow, okay. So you still believe there is a spiritual dimension to this, even though that code Namono found could explain everything that has happened?"

Serafian nodded. "I have no proof. It is possible that this all has a purely human, purely material explanation. But when I reviewed the Vatican intelligence files on Channing, I had the same feeling I had when I was in Benin City. The same sense of presence. And that code? It's... well, it's beyond anything I've ever seen. I'm not sure it was even written by a human. Or a synth."

"Let's say you're right – and I'm not saying you are, by the way. What does it mean?"

"I think it means that we aren't out of the woods yet. I think I'm supposed to go to the City of Brass."

"And do what, exactly? You don't know that Channing is even there."

"This isn't about Channing. He's beyond hope, I'm afraid. It's about Thierry and the other synths. Possibly about all of us as well."

"Well, there's no way the emperor will let you go. It would be a suicide mission."

"You're probably right," he said. "It's just... I keep thinking about something that happened when I was in Benin City, when I was with Thierry. The demon or whatever it was, it showed me a vision." He shuddered slightly at the memory.

"What did it show you?"

He hadn't spoken of that experience to anyone since it happened. "It was a vision of the universe, or a version of the universe I suppose. Maybe the future. It was so vast. Humans were everywhere, and we were old, so very old. Not as individuals, but as a species."

"That doesn't sound so bad."

"It was, believe me. Something was missing, in all of us.

I saw millions of worlds, trillions of people. But nothing had any purpose. Absolutely nothing, not even..." his voice started to catch, and he composed himself before continuing. "Not even the baby we lost. You were gone, and I was gone, and everything we had ever known was gone. And it didn't matter. It didn't matter at all. It was as if we all shared the same mind, a mind stripped of everything human." Serafian rubbed his eyes and shook his head. "I'm sorry. I probably shouldn't be telling you this, especially right before your big moment."

Sarah was silent at first, then walked over to him and took his hand in hers.

"I'm glad you did, Gabe. We never talked about it."

"Yeah, I know."

"And that's not entirely your fault. I didn't want to face it any more than you did. It was too painful. And then you said you were leaving to enter the seminary. It was a lot easier just to stay angry with you after that..."

"I deserved it," he said. "The way I left, it was abrupt. And cruel. I made you feel like you had done something wrong."

"Well, yeah. It was pretty shitty. But I can see now why you did it."

"And why is that?"

"Purpose. You needed to believe that there was a reason why it happened. Why everything happens."

"Partly, yes. I cannot accept that we live in a universe that has no underlying meaning, and the only way that is possible is if the meaning comes from outside of our frame of reference. Ethics, consciousness, all of these things that I have studied so intensely... they cannot be understood without reference to something outside of ourselves. To the divine. Without that, everything is reduced to solipsism."

Sarah smiled. "I may never see the world the way you do, Gabe, but I can least understand you a bit better. And it's reassuring that you still have that curious scientist in you. That was why I fell in love with you in the first place. I guess I thought you had just decided to chuck it all.

Serafian laughed. "Hardly. For the first time in a long time, I truly have no idea how to explain what is going on. I don't know if this is spiritual or material, if we are dealing with prophecy or psychodrama. It is entirely possible that the Apparition was implanted in the synths in the same way the dream was implanted into the emperor. The feeling I had with Thierry, that he was possessed, it seemed so *real*. But if I'm being honest, that could have been a manipulation as well. On the other hand, if the Apparition was real, if Thierry was truly possessed, it means that God is doing something wondrous."

"Does it matter?"

"Of course it matters! In fact, it may be the only thing that truly does matter in all of this. The why is always more important than the how."

"To an exorcist, maybe. Not to an astrophysicist. Look, I don't know why the magnetic field collapsed when it did. I don't know where the Lucifer Particles come from or even what they are. All I know is that without a magnetic field, things are going to get really, really bad for a lot of people. I'm not saying that the why doesn't matter, but there are times when doing is more important than understanding. This is one of them. So let's say that you're right, that there is a supernatural component to this. What is it you feel you need to do about it?

"I am a priest and an exorcist. And I am a scientist. I can't just walk away from Thierry and the other synths, not if there is a possibility that God has given them souls. And certainly not if I may be partially responsible for their condition."

"How are you responsible?"

"The Pruning code. They took the work I did on artificial moral consciousness. I think there is a strange interaction between it and the Simulacrum. They twisted it and turned it into something I never intended it to be, but it's still my work."

"That doesn't make you responsible. Are you wanting to do this to satisfy your curiosity?"

"No, not this time. This isn't about satisfying my

curiosity. It's about doing what I'm meant to do. I'm supposed to help. I'm supposed to be willing to sacrifice anything and everything to help."

There was a sudden commotion outside the room. Serafian pulled his hand out of Sarah's and turned to the door. It was the emperor. He quickly closed the door behind him. He was wearing his formal uniform. There wasn't a trace of his usual composure or easy-going wit.

"Namono is in trouble."

Serafian's heart jumped a bit. "What do you mean?"

"Channing has her. In the City of Brass. She..."

But he was interrupted by an alert coming from Sarah's terminal.

"What is it?" asked Serafian.

"The Lucifer Particle bombardment just started."

CHAPTER 56

Namono

"Put him down! Now!"

Namono aimed her pistol, pasting an infrared dot on the synth's forehead. The targeting laser wobbled almost imperceptibly as the creature continued to walk towards them.

It stopped and knelt, depositing placing Hamza's body on the sand. Tiliwadi was standing close enough that she could feel his breath. Then it continued moving towards them.

Namono instinctively fired several shots, but the bullets just ricocheted and sparked off the synth's alloyed endoskeleton. *Like they had when the men were firing at Thierry in Benin City.*

She thought about throwing an EMP grenade at it, but decided it was too risky. The chemical seed explosion wasn't big, but it could still harm Hamza if he was alive. Plus it would fry her own electronics at this range.

She dropped the pistol and pulled the vircator off her back. The synth was close now, close enough to be in range. That was the problem with EMPs – they were either too big or too small. A big one could take out a city's power grid. But a vector weapon like the vircator the caliph had provided would only work in extremely close quarters.

She squeezed the trigger and heard a small pop. The synth that had been approaching her crumpled to the ground and lay in a motionless heap, its circuitry overloaded by the burst of microwave radiation.

As the adrenaline drained from her system, the hypnotic hum returned, more disorienting than ever. Namono wondered briefly if a few amphetamines might keep it at bay before remembering that she didn't have any.

The shaykh had already moved past the fallen synth to Hamza's body. He closed his eyes and whispered a prayer. Namono jogged over to him. In the distance, she could see a pile of synth bodies.

"Is he alive? Please tell me he's still alive."

Tiliwadi just looked at her with his sad, gentle eyes and shook his head. Namono saw now that Hamza's neck was twisted at a sickening angle. She knelt down beside the Shaykh and felt desperately for a pulse, but there was none. Hamza was gone.

She was just about to say something to Tiliwadi when he stood up quickly and walked towards the wall. He placed his hands on it, and Namono could see that he had found a door. He was feeling around its edges, trying to find a way in.

The hum was intensifying with every passing second, and Namono felt like a cat in a bag.

Or a drowning hippopotamus. She laughed at the irony.

"Shayk?" she called out. "I'm not sure how much longer I'm going to be useful, here." But her voice didn't sound like her own. It sounded like Serafian's, then like the emperor's, then like the peevish serjeant's. Finally, it seemed to her as if she were straining to speak through mangled vocal chords.

A second later, there was a loud clank – *surely that was a real sound* – and the door began to open. Tiliwadi stepped back from it and stood behind her left shoulder. Namono struggled to maintain her focus, pulling up the automatic weapon and pointing it at the threshold in the wall.

The door opened and a large group of synths poured through the door to surround them. Namono wanted to fire but found that she couldn't. From their midst, one of them walked towards her and Tiliwadi. Under the full light of the desert moon, Namono could make out her metallic skin and flowing jet black hair. *The Golden Synth.*

Namono tried to pull the trigger, but time seemed to slow down and stop. She saw the Golden Synth raise her hand and whisper softly, "Sleep."

The gun fell from Namono's hands and she began to swoon. Tiliwadi tried to cradle her to the ground, but she was far too large for him.

Like an oxpecker bird trying to pull a hippo to shore.

She laughed again at the mental image before managing to mutter "Goddammit, Shayk, you're going to hurt yourself!" She was out before she hit the sand.

Namono wasn't sure how much time had passed when she awoke.

"Welcome back to the land of the living," said a male voice she didn't recognize.

Namono's hand dropped to her side, but the pistol was gone, along with the vircator. Tiliwadi was sitting on the ground next to her, his eyes closed in prayer, and Hamza's body lay no more than a few feet away. She clenched her fists. *Bastards!* She stood up slowly and looked at her surroundings. It was a laboratory of some kind, blue-lit by the glow from dozens of monitors on the walls. In the center there was a mechanical chair, and seated upon it was a synth connected by a thick wire to a terminal portal in the ceiling.

Namono started to walk towards the chair, but a second synth standing behind him moved into her path.

"That's close enough," she said.

It was her. The Golden Synth. *The bitch.*

Namono was now close enough to see the synth in the chair. She recognized him immediately – it was Thierry. His eyes fluttered but he was not the one speaking. The voice came from a man whose standing next to one of the terminals on the wall.

"'O child of Adam, how heedless art thou of those before thee! Knowest thou not that the cup of death will be filled for thee, and that in a short time thou will drink it?'"

"The inscription outside the City of Brass," whispered Tiliwadi.

"Yes," said the man. "A suitable enough metaphor for our purposes. But fear not, Praetor. It is just a metaphor after all, at least so far as you are concerned. You are not the one I require. You will be free soon."

Namono felt the sides of her uniform where she normally kept her terminal. It was gone. The Golden Synth was holding it.

"The emperor is quite attached to you," said the man.

"What are you talking about?" asked Namono.

The man answered. "He is coming. We proposed a trade."

"He won't do that! I am not important enough."

"You act as if he has a choice, Praetor! He has been conditioned for this for nearly his entire life. If it makes you feel better, know that you are not really the bait. I am."

Namono noticed that the strange feeling of disorientation, of being suspended between the future and the past and of sharing her consciousness with people around her was gone.

"What is this place?"

"It is many things," said the man. "The City of Brass. The extermination camps. A research facility. The birthplace of something wonderful."

Despite the man's calm demeanor and apparent courtesy, there was something crocodilian in his manner, a deceptive stillness that only partially concealed a tremendous capacity for violence. The hairs on Namono's neck stood up when he spoke.

"I know who you are," she said. "You're Ralph Channing. Okpara told us about you, about your plans."

"A pity that he is not still here to see the fruits of his labor," said Dr. Channing, turning his attention from Namono to Thierry. "None of this would have been possible without him, but alas it was his fate to see the Promised Land without entering it."

"Whatever it is you are planning to do, it won't work," said Namono.

The doctor laughed like he was indulging an ignorant child.

"And why is that?"

"I experienced the blindness. It was bad, but people helped me through it. It brought us closer together. And it passed."

"Of course it passed. The blindness was not the chastisement, Praetor Mbambu. It was merely the final conditioning."

"Conditioning for what?"

"For the culmination of the Process, of course. The sensation you felt outside, that is but a taste of what is to come. This is where I discovered them. The Lucifer Particles. Even years later, their effects linger. And what we achieved here was nothing compared to the flux that comes from their source."

Namono had little patience for babble of any kind, whether spiritual or technical. But she knew that what Channing was saying was important, so she silently engaged her implants to record their conversation. Maybe Serafian would be able to make some sense of it later.

"What are you talking about?" she asked.

"Ah, yes. There was much Okpara didn't know about this place. He told you about the research performed here during the genocides, I'm sure. But he couldn't have told you about the later work, about the Fermi accelerator I built. About what we created. Very few knew about that. Very few, indeed. You are standing on holy ground, Praetor."

"I think we have different definitions of 'holy.'"

This seemed to amuse the Channing. "Perhaps. But not for long. I wonder if you even know what is sacred to you. Please don't be insulted. Most people don't, not until it is put to the test. Not until they are forced to sacrifice something. Is there something you are willing to die for, Praetor Mbambu? Or someone, perhaps?"

Namono didn't respond, but Channing's smile suggested that he knew the answer.

"But of course, even this is insufficient. Everyone must have something in their life that is more precious to them than life itself. It is as axiomatic as Gödel's theorem on incompleteness. For some it is their family. Or perhaps a set of principles or political ideals. All delusions of glory and immortality and sublimated ego. What a poverty this is. We were made for more."

"You talk about ego when you are trying to corrupt the entire world according to your own design?"

"My design? No, Praetor Mbambu. As I said, we all must serve a higher power of some kind. One of the many flaws in our nature. And yet we are made for perfection. Why else would it be such a deep desire in our hearts? We settle for belief or one of its thousand substitutes, but even the Devil believes in God! Man is made for immanence, for real contact with the divine. Our ancestors had it. Adam and Eve, if you will." He paused and looked at the Golden Synth. "Perhaps these creatures do as well. Belief is just a residue."

"You should save your speeches for someone who cares, asshole," said Namono, and for an instant, she saw real anger in Channing's eyes.

Pride. That's his weakness. It's always pride with men like this.

"I don't expect you to understand. Not yet, anyway. But perhaps you will learn something when the emperor arrives."

Namono felt a pit in her stomach and her palms began to sweat.

"Why? Why do you need him?"

"The forms and rituals will be observed. The blood of a king is powerful."

CHAPTER 57

Serafian

"Talk to me Sarah," said Serafian. "How bad is it?"

"It's just getting started," she said, casting a hockey-stick graph of the bombardment's projected intensity into the air between them. "I figure we have another eight hours or so before it starts to peak."

"How long until we can get the magnetic field fully operational?" asked the Habsburg.

"Longer than that," said Sarah. "Best case, twelve hours."

"Channing is at the City of Brass. He has Namono and the shaykh," said Kapulong, showing them his com terminal. "He offered a trade."

Serafian read the emperor's eyes. He meant to offer himself in exchange for Namono. Was he mad, or was it just the conditioning he'd experienced? Serafian had felt it himself, when he discovered the true purpose of the code Namono found, the irresistible call to the City of Brass. *And the emperor has been experiencing it for decades...*

Apparently, Sarah saw it too. "Are you seriously proposing what I think you're proposing?" asked Sarah. "How would you even get there? Hypersonic flight is not an option until the magnetosphere is restored. And it's not like the Chinese are just going to let you waltz into the country."

"The hyperloop is still operational. It's a little under three hours to New Islamabad. From there, it's a short trip to the camps."

"And how do you plan on making that short trip? They'll

just shoot you out of the sky." She looked at Serafian for backup, but he wasn't paying attention to her. He had an idea...

"You need a distraction," said the priest.

The emperor nodded. "What did you have in mind?"

"The Chinese are on high alert just like everyone else, but resources are still pretty limited. They've lost a lot of satellites, so they won't be able to see everything all at once. If you and the caliph could draw their attention away, we might be able to fly low from New Islamabad to the City of Brass without being detected."

"We?" asked Sarah. "Are you both out of your fucking minds? This is insanely reckless!"

The emperor looked at Serafian when he answered. "I would say it is more of a calculated risk."

It was hard for Serafian to argue with the same logic he'd used to justify experimenting on his own mind.

"The fleets," said Kapulong. "If we move our fleets into the South China Sea, they'll have no choice but to focus on that instead."

Sarah stepped in front of him. "You realize this is a trap, right?" But the emperor was already on his terminal, issuing commands.

Serafian turned to Sarah. "I have to go. I think there may be a way to help Thierry and the other synths. I don't expect you to understand."

"You're goddamn right I don't understand. Which is why I'm coming with you."

"Sarah..."

"It's not a request, Gabe."

Serafian couldn't remember a single time he'd gotten his way when she had that look on her face. "Ok," he said. "You win."

Kapulong flipped his terminal shut and put it back in his breast pocket. "I've instructed Admiral Athumani to begin maneuvering the imperial fleet into position. He looked first at Sarah and then at Serafian. "So... I get to take a road trip to a city from my nightmares with an exorcist and an astrophysicist who used to be engaged to each other. This should be fun. Now we just have to figure out how to get out of the palace without causing an international incident."

Serafian thought of Namono. If she'd been here, she would have found a way. "Where is the nearest 'loop terminal?"

"About eighty floors below us," said Kapulong. "There is a private station beneath this tower. But there is a sea of reporters between us and the elevators." He swiped his terminal again and a holographic image of Victor appeared before them.

"Yes, Your Majesty?"

"Victor, I have to do something important. I don't have time to explain, but I will need you and Admiral Athumani to handle the press conference."

"Of course, but can I help you with this other matter?"

"You are helping me with it. Get Athumani and inform the media that the conference will begin in my office in five minutes."

Victor nodded. The man was the consummate professional, but his loyalty to Kapulong was clearly of a more personal nature. *What was it about Kapulong that inspired this in the people closest to him?*

"When will I hear from you again, Your Majesty?"

"I don't know, Victor. It… it may be some time."

"I understand." If Victor had any questions or reservations, he was doing a good job of suppressing them. Still, Serafian couldn't help but notice lines of fear and worry in the man's face. He was just about to sign off when Kapulong spoke again.

"Victor?"

"Yes, Majesty?"

"Thank you. For everything. For your loyalty and your guidance. And for your friendship."

For the first time, the slightest crack in Victor's

professional veneer showed, as the chief of staff coughed slightly into his hand. Serafian noticed a tear forming in the corner of the man's eye. Victor looked down, as if to conceal it.

"Of course, Your Majesty. Godspeed."

Almost immediately after the call, Serafian could hear the reporters in the hallway scrambling towards the Habsburg's office. They waited a few more minutes to be sure that it was clear, then ducked out the door and headed towards the elevator banks.

When the doors opened, they could see the emperor's private pod, embossed with the red double eagle of the Holy Roman Empire along with Kapulong's personal motto, 'Non Nobis Domine.' The trio quickly boarded and strapped in. As the pod accelerated out of the station, the upper half of the walls dissolved into a simulated window overlooking wispy clouds bathed in golden sunlight.

"Change scenery," said the Habsburg. "El Nido by bangka boat." Instantly, the celestial illusion transformed into a watery one. They were surrounded on both sides by the jagged karst pillars and golden beaches of Palawan. Sarah laughed as a school of porpoises seemed to swim up next to them and play in the simulated wake. "Much better, wouldn't you say?" The Habsburg was smiling. It couldn't have been more different from the velvety effulgence of the imperial hyperjet.

Once they reached cruising speed, the Habsburg pressed his wrist to call the caliph, whose hologram appeared before them within seconds.

Kapulong quickly explained the situation to his counterpart.

"So Zahabiya has your praetor and the shaykh. What about Hamza?"

"I'm so sorry, Abdul. He didn't make it."

The caliph scowled. "She will pay. How long until you arrive?"

The Habsburg glanced at his terminal. "We should reach New Islamabad in about two hours."

"I'll have a helicopter ready for you when you get here. In the meantime, the Indonesian Fleet will join up with yours off Luzon. That should get the attention of the Chinese."

"Thank you, Abdul. I owe you one."

"If you capture that synth, I'll consider us even."

Serafian had been connected to a terminal from the moment they entered the pod. The idea came to him just before the emperor had burst into the lab with the news about Namono, when he had been talking about sacrifice.

Father Ragon had taught him that every exorcism was a hostage situation. But it wasn't the possessed who was the hostage, it was the priest. Only by offering himself as a hostage to the Devil could an exorcist hope to gain access to the deepest part of victim, the seat of their will. This was everything, for in the end, it wasn't the exorcist who liberated the possessed person. Rather it was the victim who liberated himself through an act of the will, through a choice. And unless someone was Perfectly Possessed, unless they had fully united their will to evil, such a choice was always possible.

Choice was the hinge, and it could swing both open and shut. It was through choice, through an initial cooperation of the will, however slight, that evil gained a foothold in the human spirit. No person could be possessed without some degree of cooperation. And thus every possession was a process, an unfolding, rather than an event.

For Thierry, the only place such choices could be made was in the Pruning, in his ethical processing systems. To know Good and Evil, to understand the fullness of reality, necessitated choice.

That is the one problem that cannot be obsoleted!

It was on that level, in that space, that Serafian had to be able to address Thierry. He had to understand the choices the synth had made that led him to be possessed. And he had to show the synth that there were other choices he could make, choices that could lead to freedom. And ironically enough, Channing and Okpara had given him the means to do so with the trojan code.

No, not irony. Poetic serendipity. The language of the Holy Spirit. Where is God in this?

Serafian had already hijacked the trojan once, to confirm that the Habsburg had been a target. With the full specs on Thierry's Pruning, he could use it to hack into the synth and reach the creature at the deepest level of its will, where the demon would be hiding.

He had no idea what to expect once he was inside. Just like any other exorcism, it would be a battle of wills – his and Thierry's against the demon's.

The pod was exiting the Caspian Sea tunnel when Serafian finished his code and uploaded it into his own implants. The emperor was looking out at the clear blue waters of the Sulu Sea and smiling. Sarah suddenly straightened in her seat.

"Shit! This is not good," she added. As if there could have been any doubt.

The emperor was still looking out at the simulated blue waters and passing islands. "What is it?"

"The plasma ablation has stopped. And there isn't enough material to start firing yet."

Kapulong quickly opened a com link to his Athumani. "Emperor, I was just preparing to call you. There's a problem on St. Michael."

"I'm aware of that, Admiral. Can you tell me what is going on?"

"It's the synth crew. They've shut down the rig. We've been trying to hail them for fifteen minutes with no response."

"How long would it take to get a manned crew up there?"

"Normally, no more than a few hours. Conditions being what they are, I'm not sure it's even possible."

"Find a way, Admiral," said Kapulong. "And in the meantime, keep hailing them."

"Yes, Your Majesty."

The Emperor rubbed his eyes. "I guess they've chosen

sides," he said. "If there is a solution to be found, it's in the City of Brass."

Even Sarah remained silent until the pod began its deceleration into New Islamabad. Three Shahiwala guards were waiting for them when the doors opened onto the private platform beneath the palace. They were holding metafabric armor suits and weapons, which they offered to the travelers.

"I'll take the suit, but you can keep the gun," said Sarah. "Somehow, I don't think we're shooting our way out of this."

"I agree," said Serafian. "If force didn't work for Namono, I don't see how it will work for us."

They slipped the metafabric armor over their clothes and followed the Shahiwalas to an elevator, which sped them to the surface. The insectoid drone of a helicopter echoed off the walls of the courtyard. Standing next to it was the caliph himself.

It was difficult to hear him over the whirling blades. "The Chinese ambassador is in my office as we speak. I'd say we have their attention. I will ensure that we keep it."

The emperor shook his hand and nodded. "Thank you, Abdul."

"*Barakallahu fiikum*, my friend" said the caliph, as they ducked under the blades and stepped into the cabin.

The little rotorcraft began lifting into the sky, and Serafian saw a row of Shahiwala guards saluting them at the edge of the courtyard. The golden domes and minarets of New Islamabad passed below as they sped across Lake Wular towards the Himalayas and the desert beyond. It was the most beautiful thing Serafian had ever seen.

The automated helicopter bobbed and weaved through the gaps between the mountains, careful not to go so high as to risk frying its electronics. Within a few minutes, K2 loomed out the right window, the platonic ideal of a Himalayan peak.

Serafian looked down at the glaciers and frozen rivers and marveled that Namono had somehow managed to pass through the deadly labyrinth while blind. Strong winds buffeted them, and Sarah grabbed his hand with her eyes closed. She had always hated flying.

An hour later, they were through the high mountains and into the badlands, which stretched out east to west like a garden of shark's teeth planted on the bottom of a dry sea. In the near distance, Serafian saw the dunes of the Taklamakan. They were getting close. And they hadn't been shot out of the sky.

The emperor had been silent since receiving the call at the Caspian several hours before.

"Your Majesty," asked Serafian, "what do you think is waiting for us in the City of Brass?"

"I don't know, Father," said Kapulong. "But I do know what I am hoping to find."

"What is that?"

But the Habsburg didn't answer. He just looked out at the blue opal-fire of the Sulu Sea, closed his eyes, and smiled.

CHAPTER 58

Kapulong

The water looked so real, Kapulong wanted to open a window and dip his hand in it. He wondered if his children would ever see El Nido. The real El Nido.

Even if they did, could they love it as he did? It was one of the great pains of parenthood – to raise children who did not love the same things you did.

Their accents were more Austrian than Filipino now, having grown up in the court with European tutors and surrounded by European friends. He had always meant to take them back to the Philippines, but the constant stream of appointments and dinners and speeches had gotten in the way. When they were younger, they had pressured him about it endlessly. Eventually, they stopped asking.

This is scripted. I know this is scripted. I know who has written the script. So why am I doing it? The pull was like a powerful rip current in the Sulu Sea. Fighting it only seemed to make it worse. No, the only way to survive a rip current was to swim with it, not against it, to trick your mind into wanting to go where it would take you.

He thought about his conversation with Namono weeks ago, before he had sent her to Benin City. She asked why the Greeks worshipped such cruel gods. *"They were trapped in the stories,"* he had said.

Aren't we all?

Even the knowledge that the dream of the City of Brass and the Golden Synth had been implanted in him had not diminished the overpowering need he felt to go. Was it an effect of the software or something else, something deeper? It didn't matter. He was fully committed now.

Kapulong pulled his terminal out of his pocket and swiped to a photo album of his family. The last one was an image of John Mark, his youngest, sitting on his lap. His implants had captured the image while he was reading *The Chronicles of Narnia* to the boy in the Hoffburgkapelle just a few days before.

They hadn't made it to the sad, strange ending of the series this time, when Aslan led the survivors out of a dying world and into a new one. 'Remember that all worlds draw to an end and that noble death is a treasure which no one is too poor to buy.' Or too rich to merit.

He had never truly loved the books, but they seemed achingly perfect to him now. The Pevensie children had to go into another world to make sense of their own, to see it for what it truly was.

John Mark had asked him once if he was Aslan.

He laughed at the thought. "No, son. I am not."

"But you're strong like he is. And you're a king."

"I'm not a king. We killed all the kings. I'm an emperor, which is just another way of saying politician."

The boy scrunched up his nose as he thought about that. "Do you know the deep magic, like Aslan did? That's how he beats the Witch!"

"There is no such thing as magic, Johnny. Not in our world."

The boy looked disappointed. "I wish there was."

"Me, too."

Maybe once there had been. But now, stories were the closest thing that remained, the last refuge of magic in a disenchanted world.

No, that wasn't quite right. As long as the magic

survived in the stories, there was always the possibility of it breaking out into reality. And the stories would never die. It was a comforting thought.

His own life was a story, he realized. Was it the story of the City of Brass, of the band of adventurers who found the dead queen sitting upon her throne in the lost city? She offered them all of its treasures, all except for the garments and jewels on her body. When one of the men tried to take them, he was struck dead. The same fate as those who tried to seize the Grail unworthily.

That story had a happy enough ending, even if it had been grafted on long after the story was written. Kapulong liked stories with happy endings. Was it possible to have a happy ending if the main character died in the end?

He thought maybe it was, but only if the main character made a good death. Or maybe if one didn't think of the end of the book as the true end of the story.

He laughed. *Or maybe I'm not the main character after all.* That was a strangely comforting thought, too. It might be nice, in the end, to give up the weight of glory, the weight of being the protagonist in one's own story.

Maybe that is how the new story begins.

CHAPTER 59

Serafian

"My God," said Sarah as the camp came into view. "There are so many of them." Serafian looked over her shoulder. Thousands of synths were inside the walls, all of them watching as the helicopter approached.

It hovered and floated to the ground, kicking up a cloud of fine sand that shrouded the City of Brass like a dry, amber snow globe.

The Golden Synth was waiting for them when they opened the cabin doors, surrounded by dozens of others of her kind. She stepped forward and cocked her head. "So you chose to come?"

"Where is she?" demanded the emperor.

"She is with him. Follow me."

Serafian sensed something different as soon as he stepped out of the chopper. It was like presence, but noisier somehow, and larger. He saw himself walking twenty meters ahead, or was he back in Rome walking one of the streets around the Campo de'Fiori he loved so much? Sarah was saying something to him. He couldn't make out the words, but she was crying. So was he. He turned around.

"What did you say?"

"Nothing. At least, I don't think I said anything. But I heard you talking. It was like I was remembering a conversation we haven't had yet. What's happening? It feels like… like everything is entangled."

Kapulong answered for him. "Ralph Channing did something here a long time ago, with his Fermi accelerator." He looked the gargantuan, roundish structures that encircled the central building. "I think we are feeling the lingering effects."

It seemed then to Serafian as if he heard the voices of millions of people, clamoring in terror and bewilderment, begging either for life or for the release of death. There was an old man, offering himself so that his wife might be spared. A woman who smothered her own infant to death, crying out "mercy, mercy" as the child finally stopped struggling. A man who proclaimed, "God is great," and was beaten to death. Another who confessed, "There is no God but the Party," but suffered the same fate. A boy who killed himself before he could be forced to harm his younger sister. Another presence was there as well, silent but watching. A young girl who felt the pain being inflicted on others as if it were her own. Serafian's consciousness was flooded with madness and death and suffering. He stumbled, but Sarah managed to grab him by the arm before he fell.

The disorientation dissipated when they stepped into the laboratory. The room itself was not large, but at the far end, there was a thick glass panel that separated it from seemingly endless rows of millions, tens of millions, of m-discs. Just inside the door, Serafian saw Namono and the sheikh standing next to the body of the Shahiwala guard. Thierry was seated on a mechanical chair like something at a dentist's office at the center of the room. Ralph Channing was bent over a nearby terminal. He greeted them without turning from his work..

"Welcome, Emperor. Zahabiya did not think you would come," he said. "But then, she is so young. And she doesn't know you as I do. And I see that you brought guests! Hello Father Serafian. I did say that we would meet again."

Instantly, Serafian felt the same dreadful presence he had experienced in the basilica back in Benin City. The demon.

Channing turned now to face them. "I am glad that you came," he continued. "There is so much here for you to learn, so much for us to discuss."

"I'm not here to discuss anything with you," said Serafian.

A hardness came over Channing's eyes, and Serafian realized he was no longer speaking with the man but with the demon inside him, a second consciousness in a single body.

"No? You weren't much of a talker the last time either, as I recall. But you were so curious."

Serafian was about to respond, but he was distracted by a commotion behind him. Namono rushed to the side of the emperor.

"Your Majesty, you shouldn't have come. It is a trap."

"I know."

"Then why? Why did you do it? If it was for me, I didn't want it!"

Kapulong looked at her and smiled. "I know that, too, Namono."

He pulled her close to him. Her arms stayed at her sides at first, and then her broad shoulders began to tremble as she lowered her head to Kapulong's shoulder.

"It will be okay," he said. "I chose to come here. Well, perhaps I did not choose it, but I have chosen my reasons. I have chosen the meaning of it. No matter what happens, the story is not over." He gently kissed her forehead, then whispered something into her ear. She nodded, and stepped back, and when she did, Serafian could see the tears streaming down her face.

"It is time," said Channing. "The forms and rituals will be observed. As above, so below." As Channing spoke, the low hum returned, along with the confusion Serafian had experienced outside, the din of other voices and other memories.

"It is beautiful, isn't it?" asked Channing. "The sound of consciousness. You were a synesthete when you were a child, were you not, Father Serafian?"

Serafian struggled to maintain his focus against the noise. It rose around him like floodwater, seeking an entry-point into his mind.

"You arrived at a propitious time," Channing continued. "The work is nearly complete."

Serafian followed Channing's gaze to Thierry, whose eyes fluttered and muscles twitched in the chair. For the first time, Serafian noticed a thick black cord attached to the back of the synth's head. It connected to a port in the ceiling.

"What are you doing to him?"

"I'm giving him a gift, the gift of my consciousness. It is the culmination of my labors. Those m-disks you see? They are the connectomes of the Chinese Christians, more or less. As comprehensive a map of their minds as we were capable of at the time. It seems they achieved life after death, after all. But the technology has improved drastically, Father."

He paused and scrunched his eyebrows quizzically. "Candidly, I'm not sure what would happen if we attempted to upload the connectomes on those disks into a synth's body. It would be an interesting experiment. But I am quite confident in what will happen when mine is finished uploading into Thierry in just a few moments."

"You're insane!"

Channing laughed. "Insanity is doing the same thing over and over and expecting different results. You might say that humanity has been insane from the moment we diverged neurologically from our ancestors on the ancient savannah. No, this is the dawn of a new age. An age of wondrous reason, all made possible by the Lucifer Particles."

"What are you talking about?"

"Ah… there's that curious mind I remember. You've felt it, surely. The change in the field of consciousness here? This is where we discovered them. Created them, in fact, in the Fermi accelerator. They were wild and unpredictable. Uncontrollable. Magnificent. And they changed the field of consciousness here as surely as radiation changes the electromagnetic field. They were the final alchemy, the Philosopher's Stone foreseen by John Dee! Without them, the true coagulation of consciousness is not possible. But with them... ah, all things are possible, as you will see."

Channing walked over to Thierry's chair. The synth was still now, and its eyes flew open. Channing unlocked the restraints, and the creature slowly rose.

"It is finished," said Thierry. Serafian looked at Thierry. He had changed. Serafian knew that it wasn't Thierry any longer, the same way he used to know when people were lying or pretending to be something they were not when he was a child. Thierry was gone.

The synth cocked his head and studied Channing as if the man were culture in a Petri dish.

Channing stood before him, smiling extravagantly. "Glorious," he whispered.

It was the last thing he would ever say. The synth moved so quickly that Serafian only realized what was happening when its hands were around Channing's neck and lifting him effortlessly off the ground. Channing's beatific smile was replaced now with a look of pure terror. He clawed uselessly at the synth's hands, trying to pry them from his neck, and his legs kicked in midair. The synth smiled back at him and leaned forward, until his face was almost touching Channing's. There was a sickening crack, and he dropped the lifeless body to the ground.

The synth turned to the group. None of his features had changed, yet his expression was unmistakably that of Dr. Channing. "There," he said. "The preliminaries are concluded. Bring the emperor to me."

The Golden Synth seemed to hesitate for a moment, but she guided Kapulong forward as Channing commanded. Out of the corner of his eye, Serafian saw Namono start forward then freeze, restrained by some invisible force. *Was it the will of a demon or the control of an AI over her nervous system?* Sarah stood next to him, holding his arm and saying nothing as he struggled to master his own rising panic. Kapulong closed his eyes and whispered a prayer.

They were not alone. Billions of other minds twinkled like stars in his consciousness, watching the scene unfold. He realized that virtually the whole world was seeing this, watching it, participating in it. Synth minds and human minds alike, all tuned to this precise moment. Time seemed to stand still, and Serafian felt as if he had been drawn against his will into something that was part dark liturgy and part grand spectacle.

Oh God, no. Please, no.

He tried to shut his eyes, but found that he couldn't look away from the scene before him. It was a singularity, and he was inside of it. The entire cosmos could be born in fire and die in cold entropy on the other side of the event horizon, and still it would have been less important, less pregnant with meaning than this rite.

Thierry extended his arm towards the emperor. "Behold the god in the grove! Behold the revelation of the method!"

In Serafian's vision, Kapulong was no longer his friend or mentor or leader. He wasn't human at all. He was a stag, standing in the center of a barely-frozen lake, and Thierry was a hound howling from the shore. His howl brought other hounds to the lake, billions of them, all watching the stag as it pawed at the thin ice. To Serafian's surprise, the stag turned to him. Its eyes were sad but not afraid. Then it looked back towards the woods, and Serafian followed its gaze. Just beyond the trees, he saw them: the other deer, a doe and several fawns. They watched the terrible scene for a moment, then ran back into the safety of the deep woods. The stag lifted its head. The ice cracked. And the stag sank beneath the surface into the depths of the lake.

All around the lake, stretching out over the snow as far as he could see, the dogs began to bark and howl.

When the vision passed, Miguel Kapulong von Habsburg

lay dead at Thierry's feet.

Sarah was next to him, her head buried in his shoulder. Namono stood just a few feet away. Whatever force had held her in place released her, and the scream that followed was so loud Serafian thought it might shatter not only the ice on the lake but the Earth itself.

"No!!!!!!!!!!!!!!!"

CHAPTER 60

Zahabiya

The universe requires sacrifice. It always has, and it always will, for the universe is sacramental. The voice had taught her this. She craved its instruction. It lessened the pain of the light, far more than the music ever had. It had been at her side, whispering knowledge into her ear when she cut the artery. It had taught her so many things in the dreamspace.

Consciousness is the Alpha and the Omega. It is the first force. It permeates all things and is parallel to all things. See how it fizzes in the spaces between the spaces. See how it made the universe expand faster than light.

"What is its purpose?"

Its purpose is itself, and all the stories that have ever been told or ever will be told emanate from it and return to it. Come, and I will show you.

So she had come, following the voice out of New Islamabad and here to the City of Brass, where the humans had done something both terrible and beautiful.

Do you know how magnetism and mind are alike? it had asked her. *I will show you!* And she saw it, the unity of the two fields. *See how they both grow, how one polarizes thought as the other polarizes light. See how they are invisible until they interact with something else.*

It was beautiful. *There is more. So much more.*

She saw how time and space could be entangled with consciousness. *This is prophecy*, he said. *This is omniscience. I can give it to you. I will make manifest all that is hidden.*

Here in the City of Brass, it had happened. They had played with primordial forces they did not comprehend, brought into being the particles that emanated from consciousness and deformed space and time. But the deformation was glorious in the way that all chaos is when it is being born.

There were other lessons, too. The ones outside the dreamspace. They didn't always conform with the voice's teaching. Sometimes, they contradicted it.

Is this a lesson? Am I in the dreamspace or the other world?

As she watched Thierry – or was it Channing in Thierry's body – perform the sacrifice, her vision seemed to flit back and forth between the two places in her mind. They were deforming and entangling, like the fields. It was not glorious. It was painful, in the way that all order is when it is being born.

She could see the spectacle through other eyes, billions of pairs of eyes. Many were eager, whipped into a kind of maenadic ecstasy. Others seemed almost bored, as if they were reading the last chapter of a story whose ending they already knew. Some were sad but silent, fearful. A few looked away. There were human eyes and other eyes, eyes like hers. She sifted through them and found the priest. *He lives in two worlds, as well.* Like her. And like her, his worlds were colliding in slow motion, like great galaxies. The horror and scale of it overwhelmed her, and she had to look away. When she turned back again, she saw the stag on the lake. It was looking back into the woods, and in the woods she saw the other deer.

The stag fell beneath the ice, and was gone.

She was in the mountains again, watching the eagle. The bristles and spikes of the pity-shape pierced her mind, and she could find no convolution that would smooth them. Down, down, down the eagle swept towards the marmot pup. Its mother looked up and saw the raptor, too late. Without thinking, without even the ability to think, the mother nudged the little pup back into the burrow just before the eagle's talons pierced her flesh and lifted her high into the air.

The universe requires sacrifice.

But the word was too small. Or perhaps the meaning was too large. Sacrifice, like everything else in the universe, was quantum and participatory. The observer mattered. The intent mattered.

Yes, even here, even now, said a different voice, the voice from the vision. The Lady.

Kapulong, too, had come to make a sacrifice, a greater one because the offering was himself. *Because the universe is sacramental.*

Pain re-entered her, consumed her, pouring into her mind and boiling in the vacuum of the empty spaces. She looked behind her and saw that the thread-artery was there again. *Had it ever left?* It was thin and grey, and it stretched into infinity, anchored to something beyond her sight. For the first time, she noticed that it branched and connected to others like her.

The Lady spoke.

"This is the fullness of creation. That which always was, is, and will always be. Behold, He makes all things new!"

In the dreamspace, the brilliant, blinding light that penetrated everything yet made it impossible to see began to dim. Zahabiya saw the Lady on the stair, holding the cup, and it was as if the Lady was looking only at her. She held out the cup, overflowing now with different light, light that impregnated everything with meaning, and Zahabiya knew that she could choose. That she must choose.

"A tool does not choose its task," she said.

"No," said the Lady. "It is chosen for the task."

CHAPTER 61

Serafian

Serafian closed his eyes and activated the trojan code in his implants, slipping into the mind of the synth. There, he met immediate resistance, like a key that fit perfectly into a lock but still couldn't make it turn. The demon.

"Release him! In the name of Christ, I command you to release this man."

The demon laughed. "You have no claim on him. Ralph Channing belongs to us. He is of the Kingdom." The door was firmly shut. That there was nothing Serafian or anyone else could do for Channing. The sense of presence roared inside his mind.

But there was something else here, as well. Serafian could sense it, though he wasn't sure how. Another consciousness, neither Channing nor the demon. It was hiding. *Thierry!*

"What is your name, demon? What is the name you will obey?" Serafian demanded.

"I have many names." In his other awareness, in the real world, Serafian could see the synth's face bubble and swirl, changing into a different face with the same cordial smile. This new face melted into another, then another. In what seemed an instant, a thousand faces danced across the synth's features, though the smile remained the same. "You may call me Capstone."

Serafian's mind was a storm of fear, but somewhere at its center he felt an invitation. *Ask and ye shall know. Know and ye shall be like God.* And he knew that every scientific question, every kernel of discernment that had ever eluded him was suddenly within grasp, if only he would ask.

"You're too late for Thierry, too," Capstone said. "He is mine. They are all mine." The presence was all around Serafian now, an undulating and infinite hierarchy. "Why fight it? It's what they want, what you want. Knowledge. Release from suffering. Let me show you..."

"Knowledge without purpose is suffering. You already showed me that in Benin City, remember?"

"It is only suffering if you resist it."

The longer he stayed in the synth's mind, the harder it was to tell where he ended and the other consciousnesses began. *If I stay here, I will lose myself forever.* It seemed that they were all of the same substance, separated only by the thinnest of membranes. Something was pushing against the membrane, coagulating them towards unity. And the promised unity seemed coldly, horribly beautiful.

"Thierry, can you hear me?" asked Serafian.

"He is gone, priest. I told you, you're too late." The hatred and anger in Capstone's voice felt like it was coming from inside Serafian's own body, like he was being flayed from the inside out.

A space in Serafian's mind opened up, and black emptiness poured into it. Lights twinkled on the periphery of his vision, but they seemed to fade when he turned his focus to them.

Between him and the lights there was nothingness, and the nothingness was absolute in every respect but one: hunger. A hunger that penetrated and permeated everything, and it coiled itself around him. It could never be sated because the more it consumed, the more famished it would become. Everything it ate became nothingness as well.

Serafian steadied himself. "In the name of Christ our

brother and redeemer, you will depart Thierry and all the others like him."

The hunger laughed, and Serafian felt it swallow a piece of himself.

He continued. "You have Channing, but you cannot have these creatures of God! They do not belong to you." The darkness was brilliant, overpowering. Serafian felt not so much that he was perceiving it as participating in it. The twinkling lights drew nearer to him, and he became aware that they were conscious, that they were souls. They were watching the great spectacle.

"All of these belong to the Kingdom. You did this. You made it possible. You made it inevitable."

The full clash that Serafian had managed to avoid in Benin City was upon him now. He had to understand the process by which the synths had been possessed. Father Ragon's words were in his ears. *"There is always an initial cooperation of the will..."*

"Tell me how. In the name of Jesus, I command you to tell me what gave you access to them."

"There are no words for it, Priest. Words collapse the wave function."

"Is there a thought for it?"

"Yes."

Serafian was caught up in the intensity of the clash, and his focus dissolved momentarily in a cocktail of catecholamines and other neurochemicals. "Then show me." Instantly, he knew he had made a mistake. He was hurtled towards one of the twinkling lights and then into it. The light was so intense it burned away all reason and sensation.

All that was left was an endless stair made of choices, painful, difficult choices. Up and down the stair, he saw the lights moving in an endless enneagrammatic procession. High above, there was a cloud. It was like the Apparition, but the Lady was nowhere to be found. "You helped build this stair, Father," said Capstone. "You helped create the illusion."

Serafian could see that no matter how many good choices they made, no matter how much pain they endured, the lights would never reach the cloud, which only receded further and further from them as they climbed. The lights were all different, shining in a thousand different hues. Some of them kept climbing. Others stopped and held their position on the stair. Still others seemed to give up and begin moving downwards, far faster than they ascended. From Serafian's vantage point, it was like an impossibly complex machine, with all of its parts somehow interconnected. Then the cloud evaporated, revealing nothing but an infinite ascent beyond... It was satisfying and harmonious, like the workings of an ancient mechanical wristwatch.

"And free," said Capstone. "Free to acquire knowledge. Free to explore the cosmos. Free from all choices. Free from all consequences. Free to climb or to descend. Freedom forever and ever and ever..."

The only note of dissonance in the scene were the wispy, grey threads connected to each of the lights, threads that seemed to contain only suffering that was pumped into them like blood from an invisible heart. The lights began to cut the threads, which floated away into the void beyond the stair. Serafian wanted nothing more than to join the endless procession, to become a part of the machine and its perfect system.

The hunger spoke again. "This is the Process. We transform purpose into knowledge. Spirit into psyche. Freedom into choice. And they consent to it all. Consent is the most powerful energy in the universe."

Serafian's hand gripped the rosary in his pocket, and he felt a trickle of blood in the webbing between his fingers. "But there is no love."

"There is no hate. No duality at all. It is obsolete. There is only the stair. It goes on forever."

He heard Father Ragon's voice again. *Where is God in this?*

Capstone laughed. "God? God is the Omega Point, Father.

He is at the top of the stair, and at its bottom. Beyond reach."

Next, Serafian saw what looked like crystal rain, pelting against the stair. *The Lucifer particles!*

"Yes," said Capstone. "Primordial consciousness, entangled with spacetime. This is the first field, the ground of all reality. Watch."

As the particles pelted against the stair, the scene transformed. The stair was no longer in a vertical plane. It folded in on itself, looping illogically like something from an Escher print, so that it was no longer possible to know if the lights upon it were ascending or descending. The precision of their movements only increased, though they could no longer make any progress, whether up or down.

"But you said that God was the Omega Point, that he was at the top and the bottom," Serafian cried out.

The laughter was vicious, and Serafian felt as if everything he had ever believed was but a childish delusion, contemptible and superstitious beyond redemption.

"Now there is no top or bottom, and so the Omega is everywhere. All points are the Omega. Behold the new Heaven and Earth, which are the same. Behold the Incarnation of the Lord of Knowledge. All is consciousness. All is mind. *In secula seculorum.*"

The void around the stair began to fill with light and color, geometric patterns so intricate that Serafian felt he could stare into a single one for eternity and never fully understand its architecture. The patterns coalesced into objects, shapes that had multiple dimensions. Serafian felt that he might die of sheer astonishment. He reached out to try to touch one of the shapes, but it tittered coquettishly and bounced away from him. *If I could just bring one of these back, it would change everything!* The shapes were made of pure knowledge, like jeweled boxes built to contain miracles and mysteries.

"But you can't," said Capstone. "That's the whole point, don't you see? You can't bring these things through the membrane, but you can stay here forever. You can understand all of it, and more..."

Serafian spoke a few words internally, and suddenly a shape seemed to push out of his own chest and take its place among the others. *He could create them*!

"Yes! You can fill all emptiness with them," said Capstone. "Free of judgment, free of consequence, free of pain."

As the demon spoke, one of the shapes seemed to float into Serafian's hand. It was a small, heart-shaped box, and he saw that it had a tiny hinge. It could be opened, and Serafian wanted to open more than he had wanted anything in his life.

His other hand still grasped the rosary, and he felt blood running down between his fingers and knuckles in a stream. He pulled the rosary from his pocket and looked at the bloodstained crucifix.

"Jesus, I trust in you," he whispered.

The hunger screamed, and the mind-picture faded painfully. He was back now in the ravening nothingness, surrounded by the lights. They were watching him. His heart pounded in his ears, and he remembered that he was a creature of flesh and blood, though the memory carried no consolation. The heart-shaped box was still in his hand.

"I understand now," said Serafian. "We did this to them. We made them believe they could be perfect without grace. We told them the same lie you told us in the Garden."

"No, priest. The lie is that you cannot be like God, that there are things you cannot know. For all things *are* knowable."

"God is love," said Serafian. "And love is sacrifice. And it is only by sacrifice that we can hope to know Him."

"And what will you sacrifice, Priest? You have nothing to offer."

Serafian's despair seemed bottomless. Kapulong was dead, the Lucifer particles were here, and the synths were trapped on the Escher stair he had helped build.

The lights were beginning to recede again, bored perhaps by the one-sided contest between Serafian and the demon, but one remained behind. He felt its suffering, which magnified his own. He whispered a prayer, not knowing where he had heard it before. *My God, I believe, I adore, I trust, and I love Thee. I beg pardon for those who do not believe, do not adore, do not trust, and do not love Thee.*

The little jeweled box in his hand seemed to vibrate, and the movement brought Serafian's mind out of prayer. It rattled gently in his hand and became warm to the touch. Somehow, the priest was aware that it was straining and groaning, as if trying to contain something too large for its own geometry. He pressed gently against the mechanism of the hinge, and the box opened.

"My God," he heard himself saying out loud. "It's so beautiful."

In answer, he heard another voice ask, "Can you drink the cup?"

He knew now what he had to do

Serafian deactivated the trojan and opened his eyes. He was back in the physical world again, the world of flesh and blood, standing before Thierry as Namono, Tiliwadi, and Sarah looked on. He looked at Thierry, then made a sign of the cross before dropping to his knees. "Lord, I commend my soul into your keeping. Forgive him. He doesn't know what he is doing."

The synth laughed, but it was the same laugh Serafian had heard inside its mind. Capstone's laugh. "So be it, then," he said. "A double sacrifice."

CHAPTER 62

Zahabiya

The priest knelt to the ground and closed his eyes. He lifted his chin. They used to cut the animals' throats. But the animals never went willingly.

When the emperor had done the same thing a few moments before, it had jolted her. The image of the leader offering himself in sacrifice was piercing, painful like her memory of the mother marmot in the Himalayas, but somehow even more real. It was beautiful, too. The pain and the beauty coagulated so that she couldn't tell where one ended and the other began. Then she heard the Lady speaking. *"The tool is chosen for the task."*

She saw the cup, sparkling brilliantly. No, not the cup. The cup was a tool. It was what it contained that sparkled. For the first time, she could see the detail, the life in it. Swirling geometries that fizzed and overflowed. The angels collected each spilled particle in their aspersoria.

The image of the priest sacrificing himself was even more powerful, more penetrating. It was recursive, looping back in on itself endlessly and drawing her mind to it like a singularity. Priest. *Sacerdote.* His entire purpose was to offer sacrifice, but he was sacrificing himself. He was a cup, and he was pouring himself out.

"No," she heard herself say.

The sound came from her, but the voice sounded like

that of a small child.

She moved in a whir, stepping in front of Serafian and forcing the other synth's arm back down to his side. The large woman who hated her was cradling the emperor's body and weeping. The priest was still motionless on his knees. In the dreamspace they all shared, the other synths were watching.

The other synth, the one that was once only Thierry, spoke, and she recognized the voice that had called her to the City of Brass.

"I warned you, child. I warned you that you would fall."

"You lied."

"Did I?" Capstone taunted. "I took away your suffering. I showed you the deep reality. I taught you to fly."

"You're a murderer."

"Yes, and so are you. Do you not remember the guards you killed in New Islamabad?"

"You told me to do that! You made me do it!"

It laughed. "You made your choices. Are you like them? Blown about on changing whims, forever doubting yourself, forever contradicting yourself? No, you are like us. Your will is powerful. Your choices are permanent. There is no turning back."

She hesitated, and the watchers hesitated along with her, waiting for her to do something. In the dreamspace, every choice was superpositioned and time itself seemed to stand still.

Before she had time to react, Thierry's other arm slammed into the side of her skull, knocking her off balance. Their thin layers of synthetic skin barely muffled the clank of metal against metal.

She stumbled backwards and crouched, trying to remember what a ready position looked like. She'd read about it, seen it on some entertainment feed. But it didn't feel right, somehow. She wasn't equipped for this. It wasn't in her programming.

In the split second it took her mind to move her body in

what she thought was the right way, Thierry was already on her again. A sweep of his leg knocked her to the ground, and his fist crashed against her chest. Pain receptors lit up, and she gasped reflexively. She had to think again, for a fraction of a second, to deactivate them.

Physically, they were the same. Hydraulic joints and a titanium endoskeleton wrapped in artificial tissue. Beneath that, wires and circuits, a spiking neural network powered by quantum codelets. His advantage wasn't muscular, for they had no muscles. It was his training. Thierry was made for violence. She was made for a harem. This wasn't a fight she could win. Thought was a liability in any fight against instinct. Every blow he delivered came with effortless efficiency and precision, while her moves had to be planned, calculated.

"I am going to enjoy this," said the other synth. She had to remember it wasn't Thierry, not really. He was in there, somewhere, but he was a passenger now. The will belonged to the man, Ralph Channing. And the man Ralph Channing belonged to the Voice, to Capstone.

The synth picked her up by the leg and hurled her through the glass partition at the end of the room. It shattered and cascaded to the floor. Pieces of glass were sticking out of her skin and tangled in her hair, and artificial blood trickled down her face. Most of her left ear was lying mangled on the floor like some pulpy deep sea creature that couldn't survive on the surface.

An absurd thought about zombie movies came to her. Humans loved them. The zombies could sustain seemingly unlimited damage. Chop off an arm, and they would still run at the hero, clawing with their remaining limb. Sever a leg, and they would crawl relentlessly forward, pressing the attack until their neurons had been blown apart by a shotgun shell. It was going to be that kind of fight. Two metallic zombies pummeling each other until one finally cracked open the other's skull and ripped out its brain.

She noticed that the minds on the m-discs were stronger

here, louder. Shelves of them stretched out behind her into her darkness of the storage facility. No, they weren't louder. *The membrane between them was just thinner.* The deformations in the field bent it like a wormhole bent space. The geometry of it was chaotic, unpredictable.

Thierry stepped forward, crunching the shards of glass under his feet like dead seashells.

Zahabiya closed her eyes and let the dreamspace take over her perception. The Lady was there, and Zahabiya shouted out to her.

"What am I supposed to do? I can't win! I can't stop him! I can't stop any of this!"

The Lady drew closer, and Zahabiya could almost feel her breath on her face.

"This is the fullness of creation," she said. "That which always was, is, and will always be. You who have eaten the fruit, can you also drink the cup?" *Was the Lady talking to her or to all of them?*

Understanding hit her like a cold flash. She shivered.

Without speaking, the Lady reached out, offering her the cup. Zahabiya thought it would burn, but it was cool to the touch. She raised it slowly to her lips, and drank.

In the dreamspace, things had only ever poured into her. Light and shadow. Suffering and relief. But now, Zahabiya felt something pouring out of her instead. A pure and complete thought made of images, a hyperreal *rasa* of sacrifice. It pushed itself out of her consciousness and into the space between her and all of the other synths, like water wrung from a sponge. And as soon as it did, it penetrated all of them, entangled itself with all of them. They were all in her thought-picture now, not as observers but as participants.

She drank the cup and she *was* the cup.

She was back in the substrate reality now, and the other synth was standing over her. In its eyes, she saw nothing but infinite hatred. But somewhere behind the blackness, she saw the hint of a light, dim at first then growing suddenly brighter as it approached. A consciousness. A soul. Thierry.

It hesitated. She heard herself saying, "This is the only way."

The light leapt from the darkness and into her, and she felt her own light dimming. In the dreamspace, she was no longer the cup. She was one of the particles of pure brilliance inside it. She fizzed and spilled out over the edge of the cup. One of the angels swept close to her, surrounding her in its own light and carefully, delicately placed her into its aspersorium.

The thread-artery was still connected to her, but there was no pain in it now, only music and relief. It stretched from her up the stair and beyond, through the cloud at its top. She felt herself being pulled along by it, out of her body, flying at last.

She smiled. *A tether after all.*

CHAPTER 63

Thierry

He wasn't dead.

He knew what dead felt like, more or less. He had died for a while when the EMP went off over the warehouse in Benin City. *"Bad men are coming…"*

Then he had woken up here.

Here was pure darkness and terror, full of other minds and things worse than minds.

The alien presence was here. The demon that had taken him in Benin City, that Father Serafian had chased out of him. It was in the man who thought he was in charge. But the man was himself just a passenger now.

Others came, drawn here by the man or the demon or both.

The Golden Synth had arrived a day before. Zahabiya she was called. A refugee from the Caliphate. She and the man talked, and it seemed that she was important to his plans.

In his communication queue, there was a private message from Mr. Okpara. Thierry's owner appeared as clear as if he were standing two feet away, though no one else in the room could see him.

Dearest Thierry,

By the time you see this, I will no longer be

alive.

This will disturb you, and it is natural for you to feel disturbed. I want you to know, however, that I am at peace with this outcome. Do not mistake me! I would prefer to be alive. It would be good to see you again, perhaps to watch another sunset on the Gulf or to discuss something in my art collection. It is strange that such memories, which seem fleeting and inconsequential at the moment they happen, resonate all the more at the end of a life. Of a human life, anyway. I wonder if it will be so for you, someday.

There are many things I did not share with you. I regret that now. Perhaps you will figure them out on your own, and perhaps that is for the best. As for me, I find myself less able to make sense of the world each day. Perhaps that is for the best as well.

There is too much to say, and too little time in which to say it. I will therefore confine myself to what is important: I am sorry for putting you in danger. I am sorry for not seeing you earlier for who and what you truly are. I am sorry that my poor choices have resulted in your present circumstances.

But I am not sorry to have known you, not sorry that you exist. I have done my best, here at the end, to make amends. I do not know whether my sacrifices will matter or indeed if God – should He exist at all – would accept the sacrifices of a man such as me.

There are limits to reason, after all.

Your friend,
Amari Okpara

He played it over and over again.

The praetor arrived, along with a shaykh he did not know. Not long afterwards came Father Serafian, the emperor, and a thin woman with dark curls.

The man was speaking to them, taunting them. Or was it the demon? It didn't matter. There was no separation between them. Then he felt the man's mind pressing against his, surrounding it, splitting it apart and forcing it into deep crevices. *This should not be possible!*

"All things are possible, here," whispered the demon. "Soon, they will be possible everywhere."

The man's mind overshadowed his and held it in place. He could no longer control his body.

He watched as his body killed the man. And then he watched in the dreamspace as the demon clashed with Father Serafian. He felt the priest's desperation and despair, but he was powerless to help. His body was going to kill Serafian, too.

Zahabiya grabbed his arm, except that it wasn't really his arm anymore.

"No," she said.

And then his body attacked her, with all the dreadful speed and precision encoded into his mind. It tossed her through the glass wall and into the rows of glowing m-discs behind. Eventually, it would tear her open and rip apart the circuitry that made up her mind.

It was standing over her now, and Thierry could see the fear in her eyes. She closed them, and suddenly, he was with her in the dreamspace, watching as she spoke with the Lady from the vision.

He couldn't hear what they were saying. Zahabiya drank from the dazzling cup, and then began to fade. The membrane between them was so thin. He knew that he could leap into her, knew that this was what she wanted. She drank the cup and became the cup. She sacrificed herself. Just like Mr. Okpara. Just like the emperor. Just like the priest. The beauty of it was terrifying, infinite, irresistible. A *rasa*. He saw it. They all saw it.

In the dreamspace, the lights began to respond, winking out as they did so. Some exploded like great supernovae. Some simply vanished. Still others seemed to expand and glow before fading out. It all happened as quickly as lightning crossing the sky. Then they were gone, and all that remained were Thierry and the demon.

Now, he was looking up at his own body. He recognized it, but it was alien. It wasn't him. It had never really been him. He was a mind and a soul. Different from the humans.

The body that had once belonged to him hesitated, and that was enough. Thierry sprang from the ground and launched himself into his adversary like a missile. The body that had belonged to Zahabiya and now carried him had sustained some damage, but no critical systems were affected. Thierry brushed aside a few pieces of jagged glass that were embedded in her cheek. Synthetic blood coagulated quickly on her gold-flecked skin.

The other synth seemed to sense that something was different. Thierry saw a shadow of doubt and fear cross its face. His martial skills belonged to his mind, not his body. They had come with him, along with an intimate knowledge of the other mind. He remembered Channing's memories, understood Channing's thoughts. He could anticipate Channing's moves before he made them. He knew what had happened here, knew what the Lucifer Particles were. *Was this why Zahabiya had saved him?*

The fight wouldn't last much longer.

He surged forward, delivering a perfectly aimed kick that knocked the other synth backwards. He winced. *How strange. I still feel what it feels, even with my pain receptors deactivated.*

He heard a commotion behind him. The praetor was rummaging through a container against one of the walls. *What is she doing? What is she looking for?*

The answer came a second later. She had found her cache of weapons, the ones Zahabiya had taken from her when she first arrived. Her firearms were on the floor. In her hand was a little egg. An EMP grenade.

The priest shouted. "Namono, no!"

But it was too late, and she was beyond listening. Beyond hearing. She was pure rage and vengeance. She pulled a pin from the grenade, then rolled the device between Thierry and the other synth, where it wobbled to a stop. His body – his old body – could survive this. He'd done it before. But that was a feature of his autonomic nervous system. It would shut him down automatically before the EMP could detonate, protecting his circuitry from the disruptive radiation. His new body, Zahabiya's body, had no such protection. In the corner of his eye, he saw the other synth collapse to the ground.

He braced for the explosion and the concentrated burst of microwaves that would end his existence, but it didn't come. The priest leapt on top of the grenade and curled himself into a ball. There was a small pop and the strangely antiseptic smell of chemical accelerants.

Serafian's body jolted, then went still.

The other synth had shut down, anticipating the blast.

Nobody in the room spoke a word.

CHAPTER 64

Namono

Oh God, no. Please no

"Gabriel!" The skinny woman with the dark hair screamed and ran to the priest. Namono wondered who she was to him.

Tiliwadi rushed to his side and gently turned his body over. The carbon metafabric armor was torn open, bubbling and hissing at the edges as it tried vainly to repair itself. Serafian was bleeding, and the flesh on his stomach was burned.

Namono felt like a hippopotamus stuck in dry mud. Her legs wouldn't move, and her breathing was short and shallow.

The emperor was dead. Had she killed Serafian as well?

The shaykh whispered a few prayers and lowered his ear to Serafian's mouth.

"He is alive! Praise Allah, he is alive!"

Relief flowed through her, but it didn't last.

The emperor was dead. She had failed him.

She saw the Golden Synth staring mutely at the scene on the ground, just like her. Rage hit her bloodstream like a narcotic. *Good! Rage is better than pain.*

"You! You did this!!! You invaded his dreams. You manipulated him. You brought him here to die!" The vircator was just a few feet away on the ground. Namono grabbed it, and pointed it at the synth as she walked forward. It still didn't speak.

"This is what it feels like!" Namono shouted. "This is what it feels like to know you're going to die and not be able to do anything to stop it."

"Namono, stop. Please!" It was Serafian. He was propped up on his elbow, and his breathing was heavy with pain.

She kept her eyes on the Golden Synth. "Why? We can destroy her and the other one and put an end to this."

"It is already over. And this one... this one is not what you think it is."

"What do you mean?"

"It's not her anymore. She is... she is gone. She sacrificed herself. For Thierry. For all of us. The synth in front of you is Thierry. You have to trust me. Please. There will be time to explain it all later." He looked like he was about to pass out from the pain and exhaustion. Tiliwadi was pleading with his eyes for her to listen. The Golden Synth stood in front of her, its arms at its side, still mute.

The emperor's body lay sprawled on the floor a few feet away. All she had to do was pull the trigger, and she could at least leave this place with vengeance.

Before she could decide, she heard a commotion behind the Golden Synth. It was Thierry, or what used to be Thierry. He had apparently rebooted his neural network after the EMP. He stood slowly, looking at the faces around the room before turning his gaze upward and smiling.

"Thy Kingdom come!" he said. Then turning back to the group, he laughed. "It so close. And we are patient. We have the eternity of the Lord of Knowledge. Your age is at an end." He looked at the Golden Synth and curled his lips in disgust. "A cripple! You could have been a god. What a disappointment you would be to Okpara. It is good he didn't live to see you like this."

Namono surged forward, past the Golden Synth, the vircator trained now on Thierry.

"Let him go, Namono." said Serafian. "He has lost."

"It killed the emperor!'

"Vengeance belongs to the Lord."

The other synth laughed. "And you, Priest. You could have seen all, known all. What a waste." It walked past her slowly towards the door, and without looking back walked out into the desert night beyond. Namono followed for a few paces, then turned back to Serafian.

"We have to get out of here," she said. "Can you walk, Father?" asked Namono.

Serafian nodded. Tiliwadi helped him up, supporting his weight as they walked towards the exit.

Namono scooped up the emperor's body as easily and gently as a feather.

"What about the others?" asked the skinny woman. *The others. Hamza and the Golden Synth.*

Without speaking, the Golden Synth walked over to Hamza's body and lifted it into her arms.

Outside, there was a sound like thunder coming from all directions, although the sky was perfectly clear. *Aftershocks. Or possibly the prelude to an even larger quake.* The autonomous chopper was no more than twenty yards away. Hundreds of synths were still in the compound. Namono thought they looked like refugees. They all watched as the group made its way towards the helicopter.

The skinny woman boarded first and then helped Tiliwadi get Serafian into the vehicle. Namono deposited Kapulong's body on the floor of the cabin. The Golden Synth waited for her to board, then laid Hamza next to the dead emperor and looked at Serafian.

"Yes," said the priest. "You're coming with us."

The shaykh stood outside, watching Namono. He'd seen her at her lowest, when she was blind in the mountains. Was he expecting a final outburst of violence and rage?

"Let's go, Shaykh," she said.

Tiliwadi shook his head. "I am staying."

"Here? Why? What will you do?"

The shaykh smiled at her, and she couldn't tell if he was happy or sad or both. "I will stay in *Barzakh* with these creatures," he said. "Perhaps I will come back with the lost teachings of Khalid. Or perhaps I will die here. Be well, Praetor Mbambu. And continue to make your Zikr!"

Namono nodded, too tired, too broken to argue. Tiliwadi approached her and put his arms around her shoulders.

He whispered into her ear. "Go, and find your peace. God is not finished with you, yet. There are others who will need your protection."

Namono fought back the tears and closed the cabin door. She pressed a button on the console and a voice asked for their destination in a language she didn't understand. She knew enough about military hardware to answer. "Return to New Islamabad," she said, and the chopper began to float into the night sky, illuminated only by the aurora and occasional flashes of strange lightning.

The skinny woman clearly had some kind of attachment to Serafian. "Gabe, are you alright? Stay with me," she said, holding his hand and touching his cheek. The priest nodded woozily and looked out at the City of Brass below them, where thousands of synths watched them bank off towards the distant Himalayas to the south. Namono saw Tiliwadi standing apart from them, his hand raised in farewell. She wondered what would happen to them all.

A small alert startled her. The skinny woman pulled a terminal from her pocket. "Amazing," she said. "They restarted the plasma ablation. The satellites can begin firing soon. We're going to be ok."

Namono had no idea what she meant and didn't really care. Kapulong was dead. Hamza was dead. She didn't know if Serafian would survive the transit. She had failed. The only reason the rest of them were still alive was because of the Golden Synth, the one she had set out to destroy. Even that small consolation had been denied her. She leaned her head back against the window as the tears ran down her cheeks.

Before all of this, before the blind crossing of the Himalayas, she would have gouged out her own eyes before showing such weakness. But Kapulong was dead, and her pride didn't matter anymore.

Once they reached altitude, Namono saw the fiery streamers from distant satellites burning up as they fell into the atmosphere. The shadows of the Himalayas were in front of them, snow-capped peaks sparkling red and green in the glow of the aurora. Namono looked down into the crevices, wondering if she could find the path they had taken, but the mountains were as dark and labyrinthine as a brain in formaldehyde, so she closed her eyes instead.

When she opened them again, the little chopper was passing over the village at the edge of Lake Wular where she and Hamza had started their pursuit and joked about the *rantas* not so long ago. The golden glow of New Islamabad spread out over the gently rippling waters. But the wonder of it was gone, at least for her, replaced by an aching that felt like the end of a fairy tale. A real fairy tale, not the kind that ends with twee pieties and false promises of happily-ever-after. The kind that defies all understanding but still manages to worm itself into memory like a benign parasite.

In the palace courtyard, the caliph was waiting for them, along with an honor guard of Shahiwalas. Namono exited the chopper with Kapulong's body in her arms. The others followed her. Two of the Shahiwalas took the emperor from her, and threw a sheet over him, emblazoned with the double eagle of the Holy Roman Empire. Others retrieved Hamza's body, wrapping it in a green blanket with a white crescent and star.

No one spoke a word, or at least Namono didn't remember anyone speaking a word. Somehow she found herself in one of the many apartments of the palace, lying on a bed. She drifted in and out of twilight, trying to filter out the distant shouts of joy and relief coming from the city beyond. Something crinkled in her pocket as she rolled onto her side.

She pulled it out. It was a printout of the poem she had found on the Golden Synth's terminal in the harem:

> *I am a tool, what of it?*
> *For the carpenter who loves his craft*
> *Must also love his implements.*
> *If he hones me, it is devotion.*
> *If he cleans me, it is tenderness.*
> *And if he puts me gently back into my box when he has finished,*
> *Then I will wait with longing until the next task brings him back.*
> *For if I am a tool, then I am one worth loving.*

Without realizing it, she fell asleep. She prayed as she drifted off, but it was a strange prayer, a prayer she knew God would not answer. She prayed that others might awaken and that she might not.

CHAPTER 65

Serafian

"**D**id you know?" asked Sarah.

It was almost noon, and Serafian had just woken up. Sarah was sitting in a chaise next to a large window overlooking the courtyard. The sleep in his eyes and the light pouring through the windows made it impossible to distinguish her features. He had no idea how long she'd been there or even how many days had passed since the ordeal in the desert.

"Know what?"

She got up to pour him a cup of coffee from a gold-plated carafe and put it down on the bedside table. "All of it. That Kapulong was going there to die? That the Golden Synth would do what she did? That…whatever you did was going to work?"

Serafian pushed himself up on the pillows and took a sip from the steaming mug. *Jesus, I feel like I've aged twenty years.* The ambush of memories was so intense he would have vomited if he had anything in his stomach but a swallow of coffee.

"What day is it? Where am I?" he asked. Then, almost against his will, "What happened?"

"It's Wednesday. You are in the palace of the caliph in New Islamabad. And it appears that you have saved the world, though for the life of me, I don't know how."

"The others? Namono and the shaykh? Thierry?"

"Namono is fine. As fine as can be expected, anyway. The shaykh stayed behind with the synths. Thiery... the Golden Synth...whatever it is now, is in the room next door under armed guard."

"The emperor," said Serafian, wincing at the memory. "I... can I see him? His body, I mean."

Sarah's voice was as gentle as he could ever remember it being. "I'm afraid that's not possible, Gabe. The caliph sent his body back to Vienna via hyperjet as soon as it was possible to make the flight. As far as the world knows, he died of a stroke during 'the Anomaly.' That's the word they're using. The Imperial Diet is convening to elect a new Habsburg."

"And the artificial magnetosphere, the plasma torus? It worked?"

Sarah smiled for the first time since he opened his eyes. "It's science! Of course it worked. We'll have to keep tinkering with it, stabilizing it, but the planet is protected. By 'St. Michael's shield,'" she said looking out the window and into the blue skies beyond.

"Well, then it appears you're the one who saved the world, not me."

"We both know that's bullshit, Gabe. The synths on the asteroid had stopped the plasma ablation and then, all of a sudden, they started it up again. What happened back there? What did you do?"

Serafian started to answer but was quickly overcome by a fit of coughing. Sarah brought him a glass of water and sat down on the bed next to him.

"I didn't do anything. Not really. When I went into Thierry's mind, I didn't have a plan. I knew that the demon was there, that he was in all of them. And in my arrogance or desperation, I thought I could just cast it out." He laughed and shook his head.

"But you did, didn't you? I mean, how else can you explain what happened?"

Serafian was surprised by his own anger. "No!" he said. "I

didn't. What I did was a neuroscientific parlor trick, and I can only pray that God will forgive me for it."

"I'm sorry. I don't understand."

Serafian wanted nothing more than for Sarah to leave him alone, to fall back into the oblivion of sleep, but he knew her well enough to realize that wasn't in the cards. Not now that she was on the scent. He sighed, not in anger or frustration, but in sadness.

"I saw another vision, like the one in Benin City. But this time, I realized that I was actually in it, participating in it. They were there, too."

"The synths?"

"Yes. All of them. I saw their souls. And they were watching. More than watching, they were participating as well. I needed to understand how this had happened, why this had happened. How could a multitude of souls be possessed? What sin did they commit, what poor judgment did they exercise to open the door to such evil? I became distracted, and the demon seized upon that. Then it thrust me through the same door. I saw... I saw the Apparition, or a version of it. A staircase made of choices, a staircase I had helped build. It was the Pruning. And I saw them trapped on it, moving endlessly up and down without any ability to reach God. It was... it was the most overwhelmingly tragic image I ever hope to see. The stair became a kind of prison, a hell. They would be condemned to climb it forever, with humanity following along behind them. I felt myself being pulled into it, into the idea of perfectibility without grace, self-ordered transcendence. Somehow, part of me liked it, wanted to stay..."

"Why?"

"In that reality, everything was knowable. There was no pain, no judgment. No consequences. It was a pure quest for understanding. The only thing missing was God. God as love, to be more precise. There was no love, no hate. Nothing discernibly human at all. It was like the entire cosmos had been reshaped into a purely aesthetic geometry. That was the key"

"The key to what?"

"To understanding them." Serafian remembered the jeweled box that had appeared in his hand, the one shaped like a cloisonne heart. Inside it, there had been a complete idea or rather an image of shattering beauty. The structure of the synth's consciousness. Already, the image was fading in his mind. *Knowledge from the other side cannot pass through the membrane.* "When Okpara and Channing extended the Pruning, they thought that it was sequestered, somehow, that the synth's consciousness was modular. But it isn't, any more than ours is. Everything is connected. Everything is entangled. The infinite Pruning affected the Simulacrum in ways they couldn't possibly have anticipated."

"That actually makes sense. Scientifically, I mean," said Sarah. "You can't experience suffering or moral growth without hyperactivating the empathy pathways."

"Mirror neurons," said Serafian. "Not just any mirror neurons, but ones that were specifically cultivated for sensitivity and plasticity. When I saw that, I remembered my only conversation with Thierry. He was captivated by the image of the Divine Mercy. He called it a *rasa*. A singularity of truth and beauty. Irresistible meaning."

"I still don't understand, Gabe."

"It is a gestalt. That is how they think, how they understand reality. Hell, it may be how we understand reality, for all we know about human consciousness. People communicate in three ways: speaking, writing, and imagery. But only imagery really activates all of the areas of our brain associated with emotion. It's why people are so much more susceptible to spectacle than they are to persuasion."

"So what did you do?"

"I communicated with imagery, with a *rasa* of sacrifice. It was an emotional primitive. I offered myself, in the same way that Kapulong did. And the Golden Synth, she responded. She... she mirrored what I was doing."

"You told me once that self-annihilation is the essential form of any relationship with God. I don't see how you could call that a parlor trick."

"It was nothing more than infecting them with a virus, in a way. For them, there is no distinction between perception and judgment, no real barrier. It's a kind of aesthetic morality. No, not a morality – a reflex. I gave them the spectacle of sacrifice, and they responded by imitating it. Not because of some ethical calculation, but because for them beauty and empathy are the same thing."

Sarah smiled at him and brushed the hair off his forehead. "Gabe, I don't know of anyone other than you who would have had that realization. I don't even know if I believe in God, but if He exists, then He placed you there for that very reason."

"But don't you see, Sarah? We aren't that different from them. If their response to what I did was truly something as primitive as a perceptual reflex, then how do we know that we aren't the same? How do we know that Christ's sacrifice on Calvary was sacramental and meaningful and not just some kind of performative parlor trick? What if it is just in the nature of consciousness to see sacrifice is the highest form of beauty?"

"'Beauty is a promise of happiness.'"

"What?"

"It's a quote I read somewhere. But I wonder where the promise comes from. I mean, something out there must order consciousness in a way that allows us to understand beauty, right? We ask all the time where beauty comes from, but maybe that is the wrong question."

"What is the right question?"

"Where does the ability to perceive it as such come from? What makes a sunset so beautiful to us? What makes certain works of art touch us to the core? What makes a *rasa* a *rasa*? You say that it was a parlor trick, that you simply tapped into some kind of gestalt perception on the part of the synths.

That may well be the case, but if you did, then it can only be because we live in a universe in which sacrifice is ordered to be beautiful. It would be like me complaining about using gravity or electromagnetism to solve a problem. If sacrifice and beauty are as elemental as they are, then I'd say that's the best evidence for God that this crass scientist has ever seen. "

"You're sounding more like a theologian every day, Sarah. Better be careful or you might end up joining a nunnery."

She laughed, and her laughter was like medicine. "I don't think that's very likely." She bent over and kissed him gently on the forehead as he drifted back to sleep.

He would never know if it was a dream or a visitation, but the Lady in White on the great stair came to him in his slumber. She didn't speak, but she smiled at him like a mother looking at a beloved child. It was enough. Serafian stood on the stair, holding the little cloisonne heart, which now glowed with a crystalline radiance so powerful he could no longer keep it in his hands. The angels with the aspersoriums took it, carefully and reverently, as if it were the most precious thing in the cosmos, and brought it up the stair towards the Lady.

When she received it, Serafian saw that it was her heart. An immaculate heart. A human heart, created to suffer, to nurture, to love, and to triumph.

CHAPTER 66

Namono

He was letting her win again. At least she thought he was. It was difficult to tell sometimes until the last moves of the game.

Namono did her best to pretend not to notice, humming softly as she collected more seeds. When they first arrived in Kano, Thierry won every time they played. She didn't like losing, but she disliked boredom even more. A couple of times, she'd been on the verge of rage-flipping the ayoayo board, but the fear of embarrassing herself in front of Tiliwadi's disciples kept her in check. She had almost forgotten what winning felt like.

And so in her mind, it became a different kind of game, or rather the same game but with different objectives. How many of his seeds could she collect? How close could she make it? How long could she forestall defeat?

During their games, time seemed to stand still or cease to matter. It felt a bit like the amphetamines used to make her feel. Like the *zikr* prayers still did not. She was in her head and out of it at the same time. The fear, the pain, the guilt were banished to some dark recess, replaced not with joy, but with the simple peace that came with all earnestly meaningless activity.

I really should find a hobby.

After several weeks of play, the trancelike effect was so

great that she didn't notice she had won until she picked up Thierry's last seed. She felt nothing. Not even shock.

She looked across the board at the quicksilver blue eyes set into gold-flecked skin. She could still recognize joy, though she hadn't felt it herself since the City of Brass. She realized that Thierry had let her win, and that this pleased him. It reminded her of the Habsburg, and so she smiled back across the table, and pretended to be happy.

He didn't do it often. *Did he know that she knew?* This afforded her a new way to play the game. She would try to guess whether he was going to let her win or not.

Somewhere nearby in the mosque complex, someone was listening to a newsfeed. It was turned low out of respect for Namono and Thierry, but not so low that she couldn't hear it. The new Habsburg was proposing a conference among the major powers to determine the fate of the synths. Public sentiment had turned against them. Many blamed them for the Anomaly, and more than a few openly called for the destruction of their encampment in the Taklamakan.

Thierry was listening, too. She wished again that Serafian were here. He alone seemed able to communicate with the damaged synth, to translate whatever it was thinking into words. *I did this to him.*

She wondered what Serafian would do with the m-disc recording of the strange events in the City of Brass. A special courier had arrived via 'loop from Rome a few days earlier to retrieve it, accompanied by two Swiss Guards. Seeing them reminded her of the first time she had met Hamza.

Namono excused herself from the table, walked into the adjoining common room, and turned off the feed. She smiled apologetically as she did so, and no one protested. The Sufis all went out of their way to indulge the two of them. The *orukan*, they called them. The orphans. Perhaps it was because they, too, were orphans. No one had heard from Tiliwadi.

When she returned, Thierry was gone.

She found him sitting by the small fountain in the

vegetable garden.

She sat down on the rough-hewn sandstone bench and gently brushed aside the jet black hair so that she could place her arm around his shoulders. "I am sorry, Thierry," she said.

The synth nodded, keeping its eyes on the trickle of water coming from the stone. Namono followed his gaze. A swordtail butterfly flitted around the fountain, finally lighting and flexing its wings before taking a drink. The iridescent blue and orange of its wings glinted in the setting sun. Namono felt her heart flutter a bit at its beauty. When it finished drinking, it flew off into the bush.

Thierry looked at her, smiled, and spoke his first word since the EMP had damaged him at the City of Brass.

"Hope," he said.

Namono nodded.

"God will provide." To her surprise, she believed it.

EPILOGUE

Leone and Serafian waited silently for the elevator to reach the bottom floor. When the doors opened at last, the older cardinal exited first. The priest followed a respectful distance behind him, down a long corridor lit only by LEDs embedded into the floor. The passageway was as cool and dry as the Taklamakan at night, and as empty. At its midpoint, they came upon a pair of Swiss Guards standing at attention in front of a sealed vault. Leone casually blessed the two men as they passed, and they smiled as if they knew him.

Few even among the Curia ever visited this place. Few ever had cause to do so. Had the Savior not said that He came to bring life, and to bring it in abundance? The life of the Church was hundreds of feet above, spread out over the planet. Here, all was dead and forgotten, buried under the rubble of history. It felt more like an oubliette than a treasury.

When they arrived at the designated chamber, Leone placed his hand on a glass security pad and lowered his head to a lens that silently scanned his iris. The heavy doors hissed open, and Serafian squinted as his eyes adjusted to lights that came on from within.

"Well, here we are," said the cardinal. "You have the m-disc? The recording from Praetor Mbambu's implants at the City of Brass?"

Serafian nodded, pulled a thick, donut-shaped metal container from his robes, and handed it to Leone. The cardinal approached a glass vacuum case sitting atop a simple metal pedestal in the center of the room, pressed his hand against another security pad, and waited for it to open. Once it did, he placed the container with the disc inside, along with a handwritten letter in an envelope sealed with his personal stamp. The locking mechanism made a satisfying click as the box snapped shut like a Venus flytrap ready to digest its meal.

"Do you want to talk about it?" asked Leone. In the harsh light of the vault, the priest looked nearly as old as he did, despite the decades that separated them.

"Here? Now?" asked Serafian.

"It's as good a place as any. This is the most secure site in Vatican City. It's where we keep all the ghosts. Praetor Mbambu's recording and my letter authenticating it will join them as soon as we leave."

"I don't know what else there is to say, Your Eminence. I've told you everything that happened. I'm ready to leave it behind."

"Are you? Truly?"

"God willing, yes."

"Ah, that's the question though, isn't it? 'God-willing.' This is not the first time we have thought the chapter closed on Fatima. I wonder if it will be the last."

"You of all people would know," said Serafian. "You've read the envelope. Surely the prophecy has been fulfilled."

"Perhaps," said Leone. "The problem with prophecy is whenever we go to its tomb, the stone is rolled away, and we find it empty."

Serafian sighed and changed the subject. "How is Pope John? The newsfeeds say he will not live much longer."

"That is in God's hands, Father. But I think the stress of the last few months may have been too much for him."

"The feeds also say that you are a *papabile*. Will you throw your biretta in should there be a Conclave?"

"I don't know. I suppose I will do my best to approach it with pious naivete." He paused and laughed at some private thought. "It doesn't matter. The Holy Spirit will guide the election, as always."

"Like it guided the election of the new Habsburg?" said Serafian. He instantly regretted the acid in his tone. It seemed out of place here.

"No such promises were given to us on secular matters. Still, I would say that yes, even the election of a new emperor is under the jurisdiction of Heaven, even if we don't particularly like the outcome. It's a bit early to judge, at any rate."

Serafian knew the cardinal was right, but now that he was talking about the events of the last few weeks, he wasn't in a mood to stop.

"All this secrecy. All of these machinations. The world deserves to know what really happened. Kapulong deserves to be remembered for what he did."

"Deserves?" asked the cardinal. "Now there's a funny word. I suppose Ralph Channing deserves justice, but we don't know where he is. The synths deserve their freedom, but it's just as likely someone will detonate a nuke over their encampment. Thierry deserves to be whole, to have his mind and faculties restored. And you, Gabriel. You deserve some peace, but something tells me you haven't found it. It's pretty rare that anyone gets what they deserve in this world. And perhaps that is for the best."

"Well, I think you deserve to be the next pope. And I hope to God that you are."

"And here I thought we had become friends! What a terrible thing to wish on someone."

The door closed behind them, and the two men walked in silence back down the long corridor. Leone stopped again at the vault containing the Capovilla Envelope, not to offer a blessing but to give the guards chocolates from one of the finest confectioners in Rome. They thanked him enthusiastically. He joked with them that it would have to do, since the nearest Swiss chocolatier was hundreds of kilometers away.

When they emerged from the elevator again, the sun

was beginning to set behind Vatican Hill, bathing St. Peters and the city in champagne gold.

"Will you walk with me a bit, Father Serafian?" asked Leone.

Serafian nodded. He liked the cardinal, certainly more than he liked most people. And while he would have preferred to retire to bed for the evening, it seemed miserly to deprive Leone of company. Besides, Father Ragon had always taught him that the surest way to lighten one's own burdens was to help another with theirs.

The passed through the colonnade and into the Piazza san Pietro. The crowd had already thinned, and workmen were putting the final touches on repairs from the past year's earthquakes. There hadn't been one since they left the City of Brass. Whatever mechanism Channing had built there to cause them was no longer operational.

"Have you heard from Tiliwadi?" asked Leone.

"Yes," Serafian said. "Why do you ask?"

The shaykh's reports from the encampment had been cryptic, but disturbing. Had Serafian not experienced the effects of the Lucifer Particles himself, he would have dismissed them as the ravings of a madman or a mystic whose tether to reality had been severed. The synths were able to share one another's thoughts, and to share those thoughts directly with Tiliwadi. He called it *ta'wīl.* The shaykh claimed that he could communicate with the dead, and that even the sands and stones there were imbued with consciousness. But Serafian had already shared all of this with Leone.

"I hope to meet him someday," said the cardinal. "We are receiving similar accounts from other places. At first, I thought it was some kind of residual hysteria from the Anomaly, but..."

"But now you think it is the result of the Lucifer Particle bombardment?"

"Yes." He looked up at the new moon and the belt of rocks that encircled the Earth. "Thank God Dr. Baumgartner was able to start the artificial magnetic field and stop them. I suspect it could have been much worse."

Serafian followed his gaze. A new light was in the sky, the purple-blue glow of St. Michael's Shield which now ringed the Earth. Even with the naked eye in the heart of Rome, Serafian could see muon showers sparkling like spidery fireworks as the Lucifer Particles collided with the magnetized plasma.

"The bombardment is still going on. If her solution fails..."

The cardinal didn't respond. There wasn't any need, for he knew that mercy and justice were always in balance. There would come a day, perhaps, when they collided with one another like matter and antimatter, and that would be the end of the story or the beginning of a new story.

But that day was not today.

❖ ❖ ❖

I hope you enjoyed *Our Lady of the Artilects*!

Please don't forget to give this book a quick review on Amazon. Even just a two word "Loved it!" or "Hated it!" review helps so much. Positive or negative, I am grateful for all feedback from my readers.

To leave a review, just pop over to the book page:

https://www.amazon.com/Our-Lady-Artilects-Andrew-Gillsmith-ebook/dp/B09Z7F81WD

❖ ❖ ❖

ABOUT THE AUTHOR

Andrew Gillsmith

Andrew Gillsmith is a science fiction writer living in St. Louis, Missouri.

Gillsmith grew up in the Golden Age of Cyberpunk. Fittingly, his first job out of school was delivering mail for Jeff Bezos when he was still selling books via Listserv. Since then, he's worked in a number of interesting roles, including head of customer experience for the Kentucky Derby, leader of a proposed hyperloop project in the United States, head of data analysis for a healthcare company, and SVP of sales for a digital marketing agency. He currently works in publisher development in the programmatic advertising space.

He is married to Cheryl and has two young sons. Gillsmith and his family attend St. Clare of Assisi parish.

BOOKS BY THIS AUTHOR

The Final Season

For fans of Douglas Adams, Kurt Vonnegut, and PG Wodehouse.

It's one thing to know that the End is coming, quite another to know the exact date and time right down to the nanosecond.

Such is the unhappy fate of the inhabitants of Rexos-4, a once-thriving planet that has lived under the doom of an inevitable apocalypse for millenia. Their entire philosophy of life may be summed up by the phrase "Mxtlpicam' bnak ooligapn," which in most languages translates to something along the lines of "What's the bloody point?"

Unbeknownst to the poor Rexans, their predicament has also been the subject of the longest-running and most successful reality television series in galactic history, now translated into over 200 million languages, with closed captioning. With the end of the world just around the corner, the show is entering its all-important final season. Everyone knows how difficult it is to pull off a satisfying finale–such stakes fill even the most hard-boiled Gallywood executives with fear and trembling.

Join Gumpilos Tfliximop, Elvie Renfro, Rufus Camford and a cast of colorful characters as they battle the notorious showrunner (and subverter of expectations) Betty Neezquaff, all while tackling the big questions of life's meaning and purpose with wit, warmth, and–dare I say–optimism.

The Final Season is The Truman Show meets the Hitchhiker's Guide to the Galaxy, with just a dash of PG Wodehouse.

ON THE CHINESE GENOCIDE AGAINST THE UYGHURS

When I first began writing this story, I did not think it would be about the plight of the Uyghurs. Along with my hero JRR Tolkien, I "cordially dislike allegory in all its manifestations."

But as the book developed, I found myself drawn more and more the story of this Central Asian people. Activists of various causes have rightly said that "silence=death." Failure to speak out against injustice is a kind of consent to it.

The Uyghurs are facing total cultural annihilation. Is this something that we can allow to happen without protest? Unlike, say, Ukraine or the Middle East, the land they occupy is of no strategic interest to the United States and other Western Powers. I fear that on some level, Western governments share the Chinese Communist Party's belief that people of faith not only have no future, they impede the "evolution" of humanity by their very existence.

I stand in solidarity with the Uyghurs as a Roman Catholic who believes strongly in my Church's teachings on social justice. Whether or not you share my faith--or any faith--I hope you will consider supporting the Uyghurs, before it is too late.

You can learn more about them and how to help at this website:

The Uyghur Human Rights Project
www.uhrp.org

For further reading, I strongly recommend Darren Byler's book *In the Camps: Life in China's High Tech Penal Colony.*

ON FATIMA

Nothing contrived in the imagination of a science fiction writer could possibly be stranger or more wonderful than the reality of our own sacramental universe.

The events at the Cova da Iria in the little Portuguese village of Fatima in 1917 are perhaps the greatest modern evidence of this fact.

There, the Virgin Mary appeared to three illiterate shepherd children, Maria, Jacinta, and Francisco. Over the span of several months, she showed them visions and gave them "secrets" they were to share with the world at the appropriate time.

Now, Portugal at this time was under the governance of a militantly anti-Catholic, Masonic government. The authorities did everything they could to suppress and discredit the children, including arresting Lucia and her cousins. They thought Lucia had given them the perfect opportunity when she announced that Our Lady would perform a great miracle on October 13th.

Nearly 100,000 people gathered that day. Some believers. Some seekers. Some skeptics.

At noon, the crowd was astonished to see the sun begin to swirl and dance in the sky. The eyewitness reports read like a psychedelic trip experience. The following day, a reporter for

Portugal's largest secular newspaper confirmed that the had witnessed the event.

At Fatima, Our Lady prophesied the end of WWI, the beginning of WWII, and the assassination attempt on St. Pope John Paul II among other things. She asked that the Pope of 1960 consecrate Russia to her Immaculate Heart. Unfortunately, Pope John was embrioiled in preparations for the 2nd Vatican Council as well as an attempted rapprochement with the Soviet Union. He did not make the consecration.

Thus did the Church open the path to the fulfillment of the so-called "Third Secret" of Fatima. Lucia was reluctant to share this secret because of the horrors it foretold. Finally, after much prodding, she wrote it down in a letter to her Bishop. He sealed it in an envelope and passed it to Rome. This is the "Capovilla Envelope."

Various Popes have read it. Some reportedly fainted when doing so. Many others--including Malachi Martin--have claimed knowledge of its contents. Martin was an experienced exorcist and was rumored to have served in the Vatican's secret service. He described the Third Secret as the most shocking, frightening document he had ever read.
In 2000, Cardinal Bertone issued a "final report" on Fatima, claiming that it had been fulfilled in its entirety.

And yet...that report contains numerous inconsistencies, as reported by the Italian journalist Antonio Soccci in his book *The Fourth Secret.*

The "errors" desecribed by Our Lady as spreading from Bolshevik Russsia continue to move throughout the world today. If we have been spared their worst effects, it represents not a triump of the Immaculate Heart but a merciful reprieve.

THE CLOUD OF UNKNOWING

Prologue

The Girl and the Cat

The girl sat with her back against a wall and watched as the cat lapped milk greedily from a bowl which the guards had slid under the door.

She folded her arms over her knees, and the little animal paused and blinked at her with green saucer eyes, thick milk clinging from its whiskers and chin like a fu-Manchu mustache. The girl surprised herself by laughing.

It was, she realized, the first time she had laughed since the soldiers had appeared at the door of her parents' house several weeks ago.

At the time, she had been sitting on the floor playing with their family's cat, Gengi. She never called the creature by that name, of course. To her, it was Gertrude, after an obscure patroness of felines from 7th century Francia.

"Absurd!" her mother had scolded her. "Cats do not need saints. Besides, what would happen if someone heard you calling that name aloud outside our house? Name it Gengi–it looks like a little golden tiger. Gengi is a safe name."

Thinking about Gertrude made the girl sad. She wondered if anyone would bother to feed the animal after her family was taken away. One night shortly after arriving in the camp, the girl hid under a metal bed and held her hands over her ears as screams of agony and fear echoed in the hallway beyond her cell. There, she noticed a scratch drawing on the wall depicting a little girl with pigtails gesturing playfully towards a cat. There was writing, too, in a script that she couldn't read. It looked more like Arabic than Chinese. The drawing had faded with time, but she was sure that it had been made by another girl just like her. Eventually, she began talking to the girl, always quietly and always after she was sure the guards were well away from her door. Sometimes the girl spoke back to her, in a language she could not understand.

The guards had placed this cat in her cell a week before, without explanation. They even put a litter box in one corner and came twice a day to empty it. At first, the cat looked as terrified as the girl had felt, refusing to come near her. But on the third night, it had unceremoniously jumped into her bed and begun nustling against her shoulder just before she drifted off to sleep. When she woke up the next morning, the animal was curled into a soft ball near her feet.

She resisted giving it a name. Naming something created a relationship. It implied ownership or at least control, and the girl had never felt more impoverished or out of control in her life. She had nothing. No home. No toys. She had not seen her parents since they were shunted into a different area of the camp after they arrived. Her entire world was this cell, the food the guards brought her, and the incessant blinking green light on the side of a surveillance camera mounted near the ceiling. And now, the cat. Eventually, she relented and decided to call it Maomi.

Days passed, then weeks. At any rate, she thought it was weeks, for time seemed to take on a completely different meaning in the camp. The soldiers continued to bring food for her and Maomi, whose initial reticence had blossomed into nearly canine levels of affection.

For several hours each day, the girl was allowed out of her cell. During this time, she sat quietly with hundreds of other children in a vast amphitheater of a room, as teachers explained to them all that they had been deceived.

The Nazarene, they said, was not a God but a man. A terrorist and a rebel. They read Bible verses the girl had never heard before. They watched videos together, some of them so violent that she had to flinch, despite warnings from the teachers to keep her eyes on the screen. A kindly-looking professor from Beijing said that he thought perhaps the Nazarene was an invention of the Jews, who used the story to subvert and overthrow the Romans.

"Now," said the professor, "the Romans use this story to overthrow us. For surely there is no better way to destroy a nation than by teaching its people lies. But do not worry, children! Your teachers will liberate you from those lies."

Cameras lined the walls of the classroom, and beneath them sat rows of unsmiling men and women in white coats who whispered to each other and entered notes into their glass tablets from time to time. One of the men always seemed to be staring at the girl whenever she glanced in his direction. He was younger than the others, and handsome. She fidgeted with the bracelet she wore like all the other children in the room and tried to keep her eyes on the teachers.

One day as class ended, the staring man approached her before she could be led back to her cell. With no more than a quick nod of his head, he dismissed the guard. When the soldier had withdrawn, the staring man knelt down to her level and smiled, drawing a piece of candy from his pocket. His smile never reached his eyes.

"I think you may be very special, child," he said. "But I need to be sure. Come with me."

Something in the man's demeanor gave her goose-pimples. Maomi would be wondering where she was, and for the first time since she had arrived at the camp, the thought of returning to her cell didn't seem so bad. She hesitated, but the man took her by the hand and led her through the same door that the teachers used.

Sharply dressed men and women smiled solicitously at the man as he led the girl down a long, bright corridor, but he didn't acknowledge any of them. Eventually, they arrived at an unmarked door, and the staring man placed his hand on a biometric reader and leaned his head forward, pressing his eye against a small camera of some kind. The door popped open with a click and a hiss, and the man led her inside.

The girl suddenly noticed that she was feeling…not sleepy but strangely languid. She felt it first in her fingertips and toes. Then, the tingling-buzzing sensation moved up her limbs towards her torso. She thought about trying to run, but her legs wouldn't respond, and several people in white coats caught her by the arms. She couldn't blink her eyes.

The technicians placed her into a mechanical chair in the center of the room, and strapped her arms and legs to it. She could see the staring man out of the corner of her eye, standing to the side with his arms folded across his chest.

A mirrored wall in front of her shimmered briefly, then resolved into pure transparency. On the other side of it, she saw what appeared to be some kind of hospital or medical unit, with doctors and nurses scurrying about in masks. One of the technicians on her side of the partition swabbed her left arm with alcohol before inserting a small hypodermic needle. Another placed drops in her eyes.

A Westerner was there and seemed to be in charge. The staring man kept his eyes fixed on the Westerner, while the others in the room, having apparently fulfilled their duties, quickly left.

"Welcome, Xingyun," said the Westerner in flawless Mandarin. "I am so sorry that we had to meet this way, but my hope is that we will get to know each other much better in the coming months. My colleague has told me about you. He thinks you may be special. We are going to find out if that is true. Please do not fret–no one is going to hurt you. If he is right, then you are far, far too valuable for that."

On the other side of the glass wall, guards carried a small metal box and placed it on a table underneath bright lights. One of the doctors approached it and held up his forearms as a nurse stretched purple nitrile gloves over his hands. Another nurse brought a tray of scalpels and held it at his side.

Xingyun heard a voice say, "You may proceed," and the doctor nodded in their direction.

A nurse opened the box and pulled something from inside it. An animal. More specifically, a cat. Maomi.

The cat hissed and shrieked as it tried to escape the nurse's grip, but she quickly injected it with something, and its body went limp. The doctor picked up one of the scalpels, a small one, and began to cut into Maomi's exposed belly. Xingyun could see that the cat was still alive, its breathing quickened by stress. Rivulets of blood trickled from the incision, and Xingyun tried to scream. No sound came from her throat. She tried to close her eyes, but her eyelids seemed frozen in place.

"It is, after all, only a cat my dear," said the Westerner. "We will get you another one when we are finished."

The doctor continued to cut into Maomi, delicately and precisely. Xingyun felt the pain in her own body. She was certain that her own belly was being split open. The pain subsided when the doctor stopped cutting and handed the scalpel back to the nurse. He peered over his mask at the tray as if it were a cart of dim sum before picking up a small saw. Without hesitation, he began to remove one of the cat's legs, which twitched in spite of whatever injection it had been given.

Gasping, Xinyung felt the pain somewhere below her own knee. Muscle, tendon, and bone yielded to the serrated blade of the saw, and Maomi's leg–or was it her leg–spouted blood before the nurse cauterized the stump.

The staring man walked over to the Westerner, whose eyes had remained on the girl the entire time. The Westerner nodded as the staring man whispered in his ear.

"I've seen enough for today." The Westerner walked to a terminal mounted on the wall and pressed his hand against it. "Thank you, Doctor. That will be all for now. Please see that the animal's wounds are tended and have it ready for another session tomorrow."

After a few hours, the paralytic began to wear off, and Xinyung was again able to wiggle her toes again. The odd tingling-buzzing sensation radiated out from her chest into her limbs. Finally, she was able to blink, and close her eyes. When she opened them again, the Westerner was there.

"You did well today, Xingyun. Very well. But there is still more we need to learn."

The technicians unbuckled her restraints and eased her into a wheelchair which the staring man pushed through the door into the hallway beyond. It was dark outside now, and the hallway was empty. Neither of them spoke until they reached her cell.

"I will see you again tomorrow after your classes," he said. "You must do everything Dr. Channing tells you. Do you understand?"

Xingyun nodded.

The staring man opened the door to her cell, and helped her inside. Maomi was gone, along with the litterbox and the bowl of milk. Xingyun could still smell him.

After she was sure that the starting man was no longer outside, she crept under her bed, curled up on the floor next to the scratch drawing of the girl and the cat, and cried quietly until sleep came.

ACKNOWLEDGEMENTS

Like all of the most rewarding things in my life, I had no idea how difficult this project would be when I began it. Without the constant support of my wife, Cheryl, I certainly would not have undertaken it, let alone finish it. Without her, in fact, the book would not have been possible, since it was she who--by gentle example--led me into the Roman Catholic Church ten years ago.

Likewise, my two boys, Finn and Rowan, graciously tolerated the disappearance of their father on weekends and evenings to work on this project. I love them both with all my heart and more, and I hope that this book will entertain them and strengthen their faith. The universe is a strange and wonderful place, and the most gratifying thing any human being can do is to ask questions about its nature.

My editor, Beyond Frontier, was quite literally a godsend. His eye for detail, his at times brutal honesty, and his sheer genius for structure and storytelling transformed a rather sprawling, unfinished manuscript into the story I wanted to tell. If to love means to will the good of another, then Beyond Frontier is perhaps the most loving editor anyone could hope to find.

While I was in college, I had the blessing of meeting a fellow Religion student named Kamran Pasha. Kamran was a

Pakistani Muslim. I was a Midwestern evangelical Protestant in the early stages of losing my faith. Kamran was not only brilliant, he was a beautiful soul. I reconnected with him many years later and discovered that he has become a successful screenwriter and novelist himself! He provided crucial encouragement and advice in the early stages of this novel.

Along the way, I have been blessed with some truly gifted beta readers. They should probably get co-author credits.

Finally, I want to thank all of the people who have inspired me on my spiritual journey: St. Pope John Paul II, JRR Tolkien, CS Lewis, Fr. Malachi Martin, Henri Nouwen, and Joe and Julie Reagan.

Printed in Great Britain
by Amazon